WALK ON THE WILD SIDE

CHRISTINE

WARREN

St. Martin's Paperbacks

This is a work of fiction. All of the characters, organizations, and events portrayed in this novel are either products of the author's imagination or are used fictitiously.

WALK ON THE WILD SIDE

Copyright © 2008 by Christine Warren.
Excerpt from *One Bite with a Stranger* copyright © 2008 by Christine Warren.

All rights reserved.

For information address St. Martin's Press, 175 Fifth Avenue, New York, NY 10010.

ISBN: 0-312-94791-7
EAN: 978-0-312-94791-0

Printed in the United States of America

St. Martin's Paperbacks edition / June 2008

St. Martin's Paperbacks are published by St. Martin's Press, 175 Fifth Avenue, New York, NY 10010.

10 9 8 7 6 5 4 3 2 1

MORE. . .

For my daddy. For teaching me to shoot a bolt-action .22 rifle. And because I think he'd be proud of me even if the only thing I could write was my own name. I love you, Daddums.

PROLOGUE

DEAR GOD, IT HURT. EVERYTHING HURT.

Kitty lay in the darkness, struggling to tear her mind from the biting pain long enough to figure out where it was coming from. Her hip, she thought, the right one, and her right leg, too, but that made no sense, because she was lying on them. Why would she lie on her hip when it hurt so bad?

The whole right side of her body felt like someone had put it in a vise and tightened it until she began to come apart. The splintering went all the way up to her head, making it hard to think, and it felt like a herd of elephants had recently danced across her chest. Just breathing made her wonder if a few of them hadn't returned for an encore. If she wanted to find out, she would have to open her eyes.

She didn't want to.

The dark was full of pain, but something told her the light would be worse. If there was any light. Frowning into the blackness, she realized she couldn't quite remember where she was, or how she had gotten there, or why everything hurt. Maybe there was no light.

Instead of opening her eyes, she listened as hard as her aching head would allow. She heard a rough, hard rasping sound first, close by and erratic. For a moment she concentrated, listening for a pattern, a clue, a source. It was when she tried to inhale and heard the sound stutter into a ragged moan that she recognized her own breathing.

She listened harder.

Crickets, tree frogs, cicadas. The nighttime chorus seemed eerily close, almost on top of her. She heard a rustling, intermittent and uneven, and realized that the wind was shaking the branches of a nearby tree. Was she outdoors? No, she couldn't smell grass or earth or the autumn night sky, and she remembered it was autumn. All she could smell was stale cigarette smoke and the pungent slap of gasoline.

Gasoline.

Car.

Driving.

Driving with Misty.

Driving with Misty the back way from Dalton.

Driving fast. Too fast. Fighting.

Headlights. Cell phone. Empty road.

Deer.

Brakes. Screaming. Skidding. Flipping. Screaming. RollingFallingScreamingThudding—

Silence.

Panic grabbed her by the neck, shaking away the last fog of unconsciousness. Eyes flying open, Kitty whipped her head around to look at the driver's seat. She saw the limp wreckage of the air bag hanging down toward her. Saw the equally limp form of her mother, Misty, dangling in the air above her, held in place by her seat belt, her pale, freckled face the color of blackboard chalk. Saw the odd drop in one shoulder.

Smelled gasoline and the thick, charred scent of the end-of-the-season wildfires that still smoldered in the foothills of the Smokies.

Kitty's heart tripped, stumbled, then righted itself and bolted toward an invisible finish line. She had to get out of here, had to get her mother out of here before a stray spark finished what the wreck had started.

The car had run off the road and down a hillside, landing on the passenger side with Kitty smashed up against the crumpled door. The driver's side pointed to the sky, the window smashed out and the door dented where it must have hit the guardrail or a tree or a boulder on the way down. The roof had partially collapsed, pressing her down against the seat. There wouldn't be much room to maneuver, and the only way out appeared to be through the driver's side window.

She didn't waste time looking for her cell phone. She remembered holding it, remembered it flying out of her hand just before the impact when she'd tried to brace herself against the seat. If it was still in the car, there was no telling where it had fallen. She'd have to get herself and Misty out, and if she managed that, she could worry about finding it afterward.

Waiting for a rescue down here would be a waste of time. Someone would come along eventually, but on the backcountry road they'd been traveling, passersby were few and far between. Even if they noticed the skid marks on the dark asphalt, she had no way of knowing how far the truck tumbled from the road. They couldn't wait.

Gritting her teeth against the pain and the surge of it that she expected moving to cause, she reached around for her seat belt and pressed the release button.

Nothing happened.

Cursing, staring at her mother's limp form, Kitty pressed again, jamming the button as hard as her trembling fingers could manage, but the belt held firm. The locking mechanism must have been damaged in the wreck. If the truck hadn't been nearly as old as she was, she might have wasted a few minutes trying to find an emergency release near where the shoulder belt connected to the frame behind the door, but it would be useless. She'd have to find another way to free herself.

With her left hand, she grasped the belt where it lay between her breasts, and pulled. The mechanism had locked in place, leaving her precious little wiggling room. She pulled as much slack as she could manage and ducked her head, unable to stop the whimper that escaped as her entire body protested the movement.

Forcing her shoulders forward and the belt up, she managed to free herself from the shoulder harness after what felt like slow, painful hours. Her fingers slipped off the hard fabric weave, and she heard the rapid-fire clicking of the belt retracting and a dull snap as it thudded against the back of the seat. She bent over her knees, fighting back simultaneous surges of nausea and dizziness. She couldn't afford to quit now.

Her lungs labored like some kind of power tool, loud and harsh and rasping in the unnatural stillness. She listened hard over the chaos in her head and finally heard Misty's breathing, uneven and much too weak.

As soon as the nausea faded, Kitty sucked in a breath, ignoring the sharp, stabbing pain in her side, and gripped the lap belt. She pulled and whimpered again when the restraint offered no give. She yanked harder, but the fabric stayed in place across her belly. God, this could not be happening.

Her brain scrambled for some alternate solution even as her hands clenched, and she poured all her strength into another pull. Misty moaned, the sound barely more than a painful exhalation, and Kitty felt the fear inside her rising. The smell of smoke and gas intensified, the air thickening, and she could have sworn she heard the faint, distant crackle of the flames.

God. If she didn't get them out of the wreck, they were going to die there, in a broken-down old truck on the side of a deserted backcountry road. It made a lousy end to her weeklong visit home, and all because of a damned stupid deer that hadn't had the sense to run at the first sign of headlights.

Kitty did not plan to go out that way.

Her heart, already racing, sped even faster, and the dizziness she'd felt before returned with a vengeance. This time, she didn't bother to put her head down and wait for it to pass. No time. She might pass out, but so long as she did it after she made it out of the truck, she could care less.

She heard Misty shift and gasp, heard the gasp turn into a cough. A series of coughs, breathless and much too quiet. Smoke was definitely blowing at them now, and if the wind was pushing the smoke toward them, the fire wouldn't be far behind.

Swearing, she pulled and yanked and tugged, but the seat belt wouldn't give. It had locked in place over her hips, blocking her escape. If she couldn't make it move, she'd have to move around it. Holding it in her left hand, she began another slithering attempt to ease herself out of her seat. The pain clawed at her, but she ignored it. It wasn't going to go away any more than the fire, and unlike the fire, the pain wouldn't kill her. In fact, it reassured that she hadn't already died.

She braced her left foot against the floorboard and tried to lever herself up in the seat. The belt slipped an inch off her belly and onto the tops of her thighs, then stopped to grip even more tightly, trapping her. Damn it, she couldn't be trapped. She had to get them out of there.

The right side of her body screamed in protest every time she moved, and she'd seen enough on television to know she might be making whatever injuries she had that much worse. She would have worried about paralysis if it hadn't hurt so damned bad. But even if she could feel every inch of her right side from tip to toenails, she couldn't move it. No more than an inch or so, and that with concentrated, sweat-inducing effort. It wasn't going to lend her any power in escaping; more likely, she'd be dragging it behind her. If she managed to escape at all.

Misty coughed again, the sound even weaker, and Kitty redoubled her efforts to escape. God had gotten His chance to kill her in the initial wreck; if He hadn't done it then, she figured she'd been meant to get out of here. She didn't intend to give Him or the devil a second chance.

Determination, though, wasn't getting the job done. No matter how she wriggled and pulled and tore and pushed, the belt and her body refused to budge. She felt her heart speed up, racing, until the pounding echoed in her ears. Her breathing became rapid, shallow pants that barely drew in enough oxygen to keep her conscious. Or maybe she wasn't getting enough. Her vision had begun to blur.

Blinking against a darkening haze, she peered at the mangled interior of the truck and made a helpless sound of protest as it started to melt and twist around her.

Her body seemed to melt and twist as well. It didn't hurt, precisely, but it frightened her, the way she had suddenly become something out of a Dalí painting. She guessed that if she looked into a mirror, she would see her own features running down the surface of her face. See her limbs twisting in ways nature had never intended them to twist. See her insides and her outsides rearranging themselves into something she instinctively guessed she would never recognize.

She heard Misty cry out, but the sound came from a great distance. Everything seemed to be more distant than it had been a moment ago, as if Kitty had been plucked out of her skin and set back down in a slightly different place than she'd occupied before. Her mind had gone quiet and blank of all thoughts but those of escape.

She reached out one more time to push the belt away from her and blinked in shock when the thick fabric shredded in front of her eyes, as if a scalpel had sliced through the tough webbing. How the hell had that happened?

Did it really matter?

Resolving not to bother asking questions, Kitty tugged her legs out from under the confining lap belt, tumbling forward into the center console when the task seemed to take a good several inches of leg less than it should have. She bumped skull first into Misty and shook her head to clear it. Actually, it had felt like she'd gone nose first, nose and mouth at the same time, which was ridiculous. Her nose was perfectly average, not big enough to precede her into a room, and no one had ever accused her of having bee-stung model lips. Her forehead must have made contact first. She was just disoriented.

Her vision still hadn't cleared. She felt almost as if she were looking through a haze of smoke at an old black-and-white television set. Her color perception seemed off, probably from the smoke, but her depth perception was all screwed up, as well. Nothing seemed quite where she thought it should be. She reached out for Misty and her hands caught nothing but air. She couldn't even seem to reach her mother, let alone grasp her under the arms like she had planned so she could haul them both to safety.

Misty cried out, an honest-to-God scream this time, and Kitty could read the terror clearly on her face. The older woman stared at her daughter as if she didn't even recognize her, and Kitty felt a stab of pain that had nothing to do with her battered right side. In fact, her right side felt a lot less battered now than it had just a couple of minutes ago. Getting free of that seat belt had been like a miracle cure. It must have been cutting into a nerve or something, preventing her from moving.

Dismissing the inconvenient curiosity, Kitty reached out again, and again missed her mother's body. Frustration welled up inside her, and she suppressed the need to roar her displeasure. The smoke was definitely thickening now. It obscured her vision and filled her lungs, and the need to get out of danger urged her on like a pair of razor-sharp spurs in her sides. She had no time left for mistakes. She had to do this *now*.

She reached for Misty one last time, completely unprepared for a small fist to come smashing down on the side of her face in an astonishingly forceful blow.

Kitty blinked, her mind reeling, her brain scrambling to make sense of an attack from the woman who had given birth to her, whom she was currently trying to save from a painful and undignified death beside a deserted country highway.

That was when something inside Kitty Jane Sugarman snapped and shifted and settled down into a place it had never been before. That was when she opened her mouth, let out a spine-chilling yowl, clamped her strong, animal jaws around the back of her mother's neck, and dragged the other woman bodily out of the ruined truck and up to the apron at the side of the asphalt roadway.

Then Kitty settled down on her furry haunches, her tail twitching behind her, and stared at her human mother through wide, green, feline eyes.

ONE

MARCUS ALEXANDER STUART HATED AIRPORTS. MOST people shared the sentiment, he supposed, but few of them probably shared his reasoning. Most of them probably despised the waiting and the lines and the inconvenience of the ever-changing rules of security screening. Marcus—Max—just hated the way they smelled.

At the area around the security checkpoint, the tang of gunpowder and the sharp bite of chemicals and electricity helped mask the worst of it, but here in the gate area, it inevitably smelled like impatience and frustration and soiled commercial carpeting. Making a mental note to have maintenance bump the carpet-cleaning schedule to twice weekly back at the office, he buried his nose in his nearly empty coffee cup and tried not to stare at the arrivals board. The information there hadn't changed in almost half an hour, which was good news for his chances of getting out of there.

What it meant for the pride, he hadn't yet decided.

The subdued chirp of his cell phone had him reaching into the inner pocket of his suit jacket. "Stuart."

"Any trouble?"

Max shrugged and stretched his long legs out in front

of him. "The flight's been delayed again. Now they're saying eleven-twenty, but that's hardly a surprise. When is a plane ever on time?"

"I meant, did you have any trouble on the drive over?"

The gruff question posed in Martin Lowe's familiar, faintly accented voice had Max frowning. "No. Should I have expected some?"

"Nick just came by to talk to me. He said you asked him to check into what Billy Shepard might have been doing spending time at Hooker's bar last weekend."

The Felix spoke calmly, but Max could hear the echo of wounded pride behind the words. Martin had never liked taking a backseat when it came to family business, and considering that the man had been leading the Leos of the Red Rock for almost thirty years, Max could hardly blame him.

"I'm glad," Max responded, honestly if a bit cautiously. "I doubt there's much to worry about, but I was hoping you and I could discuss it tomorrow. I'd like to hear your opinion."

"Oh, really? Does that mean that you think I might have something to say about some bloody upstart nomad trying to gather support to take over my pride?"

Shit.

Apparently Nick's nosing around had paid off, enough so that the *belangrik*—one of two "important men" who served as something like Max's deputies—hadn't felt like waiting for Max's return to mention it to someone. Max had been hoping there was nothing behind the rumors. He already had more than enough on his plate.

Running an agitated hand through his hair, Max struggled to soothe the Felix's temper. "Of course, I do.

And you know good and well that before taking any action on behalf of the pride, I would have discussed it with you first. I know how this works, Martin. Nick answers to me, and I answer to you. Don't send your heart monitor into conniptions. It's Billy Shepard, not a serious threat. That overgrown tabby cat couldn't get metal shavings to follow his lead if he strapped magnets to his ass."

Martin growled over the cell waves, "Just make sure you *do* remember who's Felix of this pride, Max. I'm not dead yet."

Coming from anyone else, Max would have found the reminder of his position as Martin's *baas*, or second in command and official heir, insulting and melodramatic, but Martin had a special license: first, because Max knew how on edge the older man's nerves were at the moment; and second, because the man he loved like a father really was dying.

Six months ago, Martin's doctors had informed him that his abdominal pain and weight loss were due to stage II stomach cancer and started him on an intensive course of treatment, including surgery, chemotherapy, and radiation. Just over three weeks ago, they had regraded the cancer as stage IV and transitioned to palliative care. It turned out that the amazingly efficient Other immune system that could kill a germ or heal a traumatic wound in the blink of an eye also allowed the malignant cells to proliferate at a terrifying rate. Modern medicine just couldn't keep up. There was nothing else the doctors could do.

What Max had decided *he* could do for Martin was to treat him as Felix of the pride for as long as possible and not try to baby a man who had once been able to fend off challengers to his position with one look from his vivid green eyes.

"Right," Max acknowledged, "you're alive and kicking. But Drusilla and the kids might kill you a lot quicker than the cancer if they find out about this prodigal daughter of yours before you remember to mention it to them."

Martin barked out a laugh. "My ex-wife and those kids would kill me for the fun of it if I turned my back on them long enough. Thankfully, I'm not that stupid."

"If you were so smart, you'd have told them by now."

"I'm telling them tonight, cub. Don't rush me. I know what I'm doing."

Normally, Max would have had no trouble agreeing with that. The current situation in the pride, however, was far from normal. "You know, Martin," he said, keeping his tone casual, "I'm not sure this was the best time to invite this girl to visit. Not only is your health not the best, but we've got the situation with Shepard, and Peter is already making noises about how unfair it is that you've named me as your successor instead of him—"

"Peter thinks the fact that he's only got one dick is unfair," Martin growled. "I swear, I don't know how any son of mine managed to turn out so useless. And you've already said Shepard isn't a concern. Besides, if I waited until my health improved before I invited my daughter to come and meet me, she'd be meeting my headstone instead. Forget it, Max. It's done."

Max sighed. "Fine. I didn't bring it up to upset you. I just wanted to make sure you were prepared for the possibility that throwing this extra variable into the mix could lead to a few new complications. But if you're willing to brave the wrath of that Nurse Ratchet Doc Reijznik hired for you, you go right ahead."

"She already took my laptop," Martin grumbled. "She caught me searching for a phone number for the FAA and acted like a nun who'd caught me surfing for porn."

"The Federal Aviation Administration? What, were you going to lodge a complaint?"

"The damned plane was supposed to land five hours ago!"

"And there's a line of thunderstorms stretching from Winnepeg to Monterrey. I doubt they have a form to fix that." Max shook his head. "You need to calm down, my friend. You sound like an expectant father who's been banned from the delivery room."

"Damn it, I *am* an expectant father!"

"Maybe, but harassing a government agency won't make the plane land any sooner. And at this rate, it might not even happen tonight. The thing's been rescheduled three times and moved to different gates twice. You should get some sleep and hope they land before the end of the month."

Martin made a distinctly dissatisfied sound. "Fine, but I want to hear the minute they touch down. Understand?"

"Sure, but if I'm going to be awake enough to call you, I need a cup of coffee. Let me go grab some, and I'll call you later. I have a feeling it's going to be a long night."

"A baby bird's got to leave the nest eventually, Kitty girl. You can't put it off forever."

"I'm twenty-four years old, Papaw. I'm not a baby bird. In fact, I'm afraid that if I came within ten feet of a baby bird these days, my first instinct would be to eat it."

The plane touched down with a jolt that did nothing for Kitty's already uneasy stomach. The darned thing—her stomach, not the plane—hadn't settled down in the past fifteen days, and as far as she could tell, this trip did not bode well for its future. Her grandfather had all but had to push her bodily onto the jetway.

"I know you ain't right with all these changes, Kitty Jane, but you ain't goin' to get right by ignoring 'em. Your mamaw and I didn't raise you to be a coward, and I ain't lettin' you act like one."

Lonnie Sugarman's face, coarse and tanned and wrinkled, filled Kitty's mind and made her sigh. She never had been able to disappoint him. Even after six years of living on her own and making her own way in the world, she would sooner have cut off her own arm than disappoint the only father figure she'd ever known.

"Fine, I'll go," she remembered snapping as she hauled her overnight bag out from behind the bench seat of her grandfather's pickup truck. As she recalled, she'd possessed all the finesse of a spoiled toddler, as well as the expression of one. *"But I'm only doing it because you asked me to. I'm sure as heck not doing it for him."*

"You ought to be doing it for yourself, baby girl."

"What's it got to do with me? As far as I'm concerned, the man's nothing but a stranger. The only thing I've got to say to him, I can say with a slap across the face. In fact, that's the only part of this trip I'm actually looking forward to."

"Kitty Jane, he's your father."

"He's a sperm donor," she'd said flatly, turning toward the terminal like it was the *Titanic* and she was the only one who'd seen the movie. *"You're the only father I've ever had and the only one I ever needed. You're the*

one who raised me, who taught me how to be a good person."

"*But I can't teach you how to be a good Other, can I, baby girl?*"

And that was the end of that argument.

So now Kitty Jane Sugarman, farm girl from the backwoods of southeastern Tennessee, was taxiing toward a gate at the Las Vegas International Airport on her way to meeting a father she'd never known she had and to figure out a side of herself she still went to bed praying would disappear before she woke up.

Didn't that sound like fun?

"Ladies and gentlemen," a flight attendant announced, "on behalf of your Atlanta-based flight crew, I'd like to be the first to welcome you to Las Vegas, where the current local time is eleven-twenty-seven P.M. For those of you with connecting flights, we've had a change of gates. We'll now be arriving at gate fifty-one."

It took a conscious force of will to unclench her hands from around her seat belt, but Kitty managed it, along with a slow, deep breath. She refused to get off this plane looking as terrified as she felt, even if she did have until tomorrow before she had to face her worst nightmare— meeting the biological father her mother had sworn died in a car wreck on their prom night. Of course, Misty had also sworn he'd been seventeen, red-headed, and human, so clearly an adjustment of preconceptions would be necessary.

As soon as the plane bumped to a stop and the seat belt light dinged off, the predictable mad scramble for the overhead bins commenced. Kitty stayed in her seat and told herself it didn't make any sense to dive into the chaos. She didn't have a connection or someone waiting for her long-delayed flight, so she might as well let those who did have time concerns have first crack. Really. It had nothing to do with the yellowish tinge to her belly.

"Are you here to try your luck?"

Startled, Kitty looked over at the elderly woman in the window seat beside her and blinked. "Uh, no," she said, wondering why her neighbor, who'd been silent since boarding in Atlanta, had chosen this moment to get chatty. "I'm . . . uh . . . here for a . . . a meeting."

"Oh, a convention? We get tons of those here, sugar." The woman smiled at Kitty and tugged at the string around her neck that held her eyeglasses in place. "Make sure you take a few minutes to slip away and hit one or two tables before it's time to go home. You just never know when you'll hit the jackpot."

"Right. Good idea." Kitty forced a smile and swallowed against the roiling in her stomach. For her, the only jackpot would be if she ever got to go home again at all.

"You can't spend the rest of your life afraid of your own self, baby girl. You got to face the fact that you're a shifter, and you got a lion inside you," Lonnie had told her when she first woke up after the accident. *"You got some magic most folks ain't never gonna get the chance to experience, and you can look at it as a blessin' or a curse. But I tell you what: Curses got a way of makin' life difficult. If I were you, I'd want the chance to turn it t'other way, and the only way I see to do that is to learn how it works. You got to learn to control what's inside you before it controls you. Who better to teach you that than the man who gave you that magic in the first place?"*

Sometimes it drove her crazy how right her grand-father always seemed to be, but she couldn't argue with him. She remembered too much of what had happened the night of the wreck, and since then, there had been a few experiences she'd tried hard to ignore. Like the time she'd woken up with teeth too long to fit in her mouth and eyes that could track a speck of dust in a midnight-dark room. Or the time she'd spotted a rabbit in the fal-low field behind the house and found herself crouching behind a tree stump, imagining the way it would taste. Or the way she'd snarled at her own papaw when he'd first told her the truth about her parents. For a split sec-ond she had wanted to lash out at him, but thank God, she hadn't been that far gone. Still, she'd known she could have hurt him, and that more than anything had convinced her he was right to make her take this trip. If she ever wanted to trust herself again, she needed to get herself under control.

Her family and her future weren't things she was willing to gamble with.

As soon as she saw a gap in the crowded aisle, she unclipped her belt and snatched her bag out of the bin above her seat. With a quick, murmured goodbye to her seatmate, she shouldered the bright red duffle and headed for the terminal.

Twelve hours of travel had left her muscles stiff and cramped, and it felt good to stretch her legs in the nar-row hall of the jetway. It also felt good to push her dis-turbing thoughts away by focusing on the details required by travel. Her first order of business was finding a cab, which would lead to the second order of finding the hotel she'd booked.

As her muscles slowly unclenched from their seated

positions, Kitty winced. Scratch that. Restroom first. Then cab, then hotel.

Scanning the area around her, she looked for some signage to point her toward Baggage Claim, where she assumed she'd find a taxi line. She oriented herself in that direction and dropped her gaze to a level where she'd be able to spot the stick-figure symbols of relief. That's when her eyes locked on a bank of bright, flashing slot machines planted smack-dab in the middle of the concourse walkway. Her footsteps faltered.

Holy crap, she was in *Vegas*!

Her head hadn't stopped reeling in more than two weeks, since she'd woken up from the wreck, and the carnival-like atmosphere of the slot-sprinkled airport wasn't likely to steady her. Maybe she should just resign herself to living a surreal existence. It had been that way since she woke up, and so far it didn't look likely to change.

Hitching her shoulder bag to a more secure position, Kitty found the restroom sign and began to move with the rest of the disembarking crowd away from the gate.

She felt a lot more charitable toward said crowd now that she wasn't crammed up next to a total stranger in contact so close it probably constituted a marriage in some cultures. Kitty had never been wild about crowded situations, but her distaste for them seemed to be growing. During this trip, she'd had to beat back the urge to break the elbow that dug into her ribs, although the glare she gave to its owner in the aisle seat next to her had caused its hasty removal.

Her mind skirted away from the change, which was pretty much how she'd been coping with things for two weeks now. She'd discovered pretty quickly that dwelling on her new . . . newness tended to leave her just a bit too close to a rocking, drooling mess, so her strategy for coping with all this change contained a large dose of denial. At least for now. She supposed that once she met her biological father and got to see the people she was related to, that might change. Whether she liked it or not.

The invitation to that meeting had surprised her, both because it had appeared and because it had come so quickly. She didn't know exactly what she'd expected when she'd contacted the law firm her father had listed in his letter, but the offer of a plane ticket to Nevada hadn't been it. Apparently Martin Lowe—that was his name— had anticipated the possibility that he might move once or even more than once in the years before he expected her to receive his letter. So instead of telling her how to contact him, he'd left instructions to contact the people who would always know how to reach him.

It made sense, Kitty admitted, but it also served as another layer in the barrier between them. Even now, she hadn't actually spoken directly to the man she was visiting. He had been ill, the lawyers had informed her, and his respiratory symptoms made speaking difficult. All the arrangements had been handled through intermediaries, from her first polite phone call to the number at the bottom of the letter, to the last e-mail she'd sent informing the lawyers of her flight and arrival information.

She'd never had any contact with the man who supposedly wanted to meet her, and the response to that last e-mail had almost made her start wondering if she ought to rethink the whole thing. Not that it had said anything specifically to discourage her, but there had been repeated mentions of how she should wait to be contacted by her father's representatives after she arrived in Las

Vegas. It wouldn't be a good idea for her to show up at his home unannounced, she'd been informed, in language she might have taken for ominous if she'd had a temperament more inclined toward paranoia.

Honestly, the idea of showing up on her father's doorstep unannounced had never occurred to Kitty. Why on earth would she want to just drop in on someone she'd never met? Never even seen a picture of. For heaven's sake, if she did something as simple as get the address wrong she could end up informing some innocent bystander that she was his long-lost daughter simply because she had no idea what her biological father even looked like. Every contact between them had been one person removed, including her polite refusal of his offer to purchase her plane ticket. She hadn't been able to bring herself to accept that. After all, what if things didn't work out? What if he turned out to be a jerk, or if she committed some cultural sin among Others that she had never heard of? She had been raised to hate being beholden to anyone, especially strangers. And at the moment, that's what her father was to her. A stranger.

Her stomach, which seemed since the accident to have begun training for the Olympic gymnastics team, performed another one of its slow flips. She'd just traveled more than two thousand miles to visit a man she'd never spoken to, whom she already knew to be half predator. Was she out of her mind?

Kitty slipped into the restroom and ordered herself to calm down as she locked the stall door behind her. Everything would be okay. She wasn't a complete idiot. In addition to turning down the plane ticket, she'd vetoed the invitation to stay at Martin Lowe's family home and booked herself a room in a respectable hotel on the Strip.

In fact, she'd decided to splurge and made reservations at the Savannah, which she'd heard was just spectacular. So if the meeting with her father went badly, at least she could enjoy a couple of days of vacation at one of the city's most famous hotels and casinos. She'd reserved a rental car, too, not that she expected her father to kidnap her and hold her hostage at his home, but because she liked her independence, and the idea of being trapped somewhere, even by circumstances, rubbed her the wrong way.

Shrugging did nothing to relieve the tension in her shoulders, but she did it anyway as she dropped her bag on top of her feet and stepped up to the sink. She washed her hands automatically and checked her appearance in the enormous mirror.

Considering that she'd been traveling for the last nine and a half hours, things could have been worse. The long French braid she'd woven that morning still confined most of her strawberry blonde hair, with just a few loose wisps around her face and neck. Her makeup was long gone and she looked a little pale underneath her freckles, but at least half of that probably had to do with her nerves, so there wasn't much to be done about it. Her clothes didn't worry her. Jeans and a T-shirt could stand up to almost anything, and she'd even managed not to spill any of her complimentary beverage on herself.

"Good enough for a taxi ride," she muttered to her reflection, and bent to grab her overnight bag.

She felt the air shift, heard a rustle of movement, and almost made it back to vertical before he hit her, but as her papaw liked to saw, "almost" only counted in horseshoes and hand grenades.

The body that tackled her belonged to a shortish man

of indeterminate age with dark hair, scruffy cheeks, and an unfortunate taste for cheap cologne. He reeked of it. At least, that's what Kitty's newly hyper senses told her as he pinned her to the gray tile and grabbed her head, only to slam her skull hard against the floor.

The blow wasn't enough to kill her, but the shock might have been. For heaven's sake, who expected to be attacked by a homicidal maniac in an airport restroom? A mugger, sure, but not a murderer.

Even though it seemed to Kitty that it took her hours to get her thoughts and instincts together enough to begin fighting back, in reality she had her arms around his wrists and was tearing his hands away from her head while he was still raising her up for a second slam. The only problem in that was her timing. Without the man's hands holding her head up, it fell back with a solid thunk, and she ended up giving herself a second wicked skull bumping. Apparently, the man didn't need to try to split her head open. Give her enough time and she could take care of the job all by herself.

She heard him cursing and felt his grip shifting while she was still seeing stars and little chirping bluebirds circling above her head. He scrambled and shifted and dragged her arms down, kneeling on her biceps to pin them to the floor. He managed one more blow that way and Kitty felt the itch of oozing blood beneath the tangle of hair at the back of her scalp.

Blinking against the sting of eye-watering pain, Kitty felt her surprise and fear transmute into anger with an all but audible pop. She had *not* just traveled two thousand miles so some psycho idiot could bash her brains out on the floor of a public toilet. Her mamaw had raised her better than that.

In her mind, she channeled all that anger into a sudden burst of strength that would allow her to buck off her attacker and free her long enough to run from the restroom. Then she planned to scream loud enough to bring a battalion's worth of armed security officers descending on the pathetic slimebag.

That's what she envisioned, anyway; instead, she jerked her arms in an attempt to free them from under the puss-bucket's knees and heard a startled, high-pitched scream of pain.

She blinked again and considered, but no, the sound hadn't come from her. Jerking against the man's weakening grip, she heard another scream and a muffled shout mingling with the pounding of footsteps. Or maybe that was just the pounding of her adrenaline-fueled heart inside her bruised rib cage. Either way, the sound got even louder when her attacker rolled off of her, leaving her clothing stained with his blood. Blood that was explained by the set of lethal-looking claws curving out of the golden-furred paws where Kitty's hands had been only three minutes earlier.

Oh shit.

At first, she just thought it, but when she turned her head and saw the psycho struggling to his knees with hate burning in his eyes and a wicked-looking knife gleaming in his hand, she decided the sentiment bore repeating aloud. *Very* aloud.

"OH SHIT!"

A lot of things happened in the next moment, all of them seemingly simultaneous. The cretin with the knife growled something obscene, then followed that up with a garbled warning that sounded like it could have been, *You shouldn't have come here, bitch!*—or maybe that was, *You've got this coming, bitch!*—and lunged for her.

A man's voice shouted something unintelligible. Kitty twisted, dodged the knife, and then skidded into the plumbing beneath the sinks when her center of gravity—along with her shape, skin, bone, and muscles—suddenly shifted. And finally, a complete stranger came careening around the corner at the restroom's far entrance to find the space occupied by a bleeding man armed with a pristine knife. And beneath the sinks, a 350-pound African lioness sat and stared out at him with an angrily twitching, tufted tail.

The stranger did no more than blink.

The criminal, however, looked from the frying pan to the fire and bolted out the other exit as fast as his bleeding legs would carry him. Shifting her own gaze to the newcomer, Kitty found she had a hard time blaming him.

Her would-be rescuer personified the term "intimidating." Among others. The ones that immediately leapt to Kitty's mind also included "elegant," "arresting," "gorgeous," "built," and possibly "yummy." His hair, a rich, dark brown shot through with strands of toffee, looked well-cut but tousled, and even to her country-bred eyes, his perfectly fitted suit screamed that it came with a price tag equal to the values of her first three cars. Combined. He wore it as easily as his weathered, cleanly sculpted face wore its expression of fierce displeasure under ruthless control.

She watched, fascinated, as glittering, copper eyes swept the scene and lingered on the section of tile darkened by drops and smears of blood. He hadn't even paused at the sight of a fully grown lioness in the ladies' restroom of the Las Vegas international airport. When his gaze shifted back to her, it held no surprise and no fear, just intensity and the lingering glint of fury.

"Is any of that yours?"

She found her muscles bracing against a shiver. His deep voice stroked over her like a warm, rough tongue. It held a tone of command so obviously natural to him that Kitty had her mouth open before she remembered she couldn't talk.

"I don't think so. He didn't get a chance to do much damage."

That's what she thought. What came out of her mouth was a sound somewhere between a purr and a muffled roar, with a hint of Texas chainsaw thrown in. Sitting back on her haunches—damn, she had haunches again—she shook her head impatiently and tried to will herself back into her human form.

Nothing happened.

The stranger didn't seem to notice. Some of the tension drained out of him. "Good. I'm glad you aren't hurt, but you should be careful about shifting in public places. There aren't any laws about it yet, but I figure it's only a matter of time. Humans still aren't used to it, and I'm not sure most of them want to get accustomed." He reached for her abandoned overnight bag without waiting for a reply. "I'll get this if you'll shift back. You won't get through security in that outfit."

Kitty looked down. Since her current outfit consisted of fur—the kind still attached to skin and muscle, not the kind you bought from stores with complicated security systems and sign-carrying protesters out front—she thought he might have a point.

Actually, she knew he had a point. She just wasn't sure she knew what to do about it.

Scowling, she opened her mouth and heard a low rumble emerge. She had no idea what it meant, but it stopped the stranger in his tracks. He turned back to her and frowned. "What do you mean, you can't?"

What the heck did he think she meant? That she couldn't bear to part with the handbag that went with this particular ensemble?

And how the heck could he understand what she was saying? She hadn't even realized she was *saying* anything. Did growling count as talking in this form?

Had the universe ever created a less competent were-anything?

Frustrated, tired, and sore, she just stared at him. Her tail twitched. She beat back the urge to lift a paw and begin grooming herself like an overgrown tabby. Damn it, she was still a person inside this ill-fitting cat skin. The problem was, it got harder to believe that each time she wore it.

The man stared back, still frowning. "If you can't get out of that shape, how do you explain getting into it?"

Her whiskers twitched. *Magic?*

"How long ago was your first change?"

What? Was she supposed to tap the floor once for every week since the accident? Was she Mister Ed now?

She tried another growl and thought, *Three weeks.*

"Have you been practicing?"

Oh, sure. I always practice things that scare the pa-tootie off of me and contradict everything I thought I knew about myself for the past two decades and more. It's a hobby.

His eyebrows arched. "Does the sarcasm make you feel better?"

Oh, my God. He could read minds?

"You can read minds?" she rumbled.

"I don't need to. I speak Leo, and you have the tendency to wear your thoughts on your face." He sighed, an exhalation that sounded almost as tired as she felt, and set her bag back on the floor. "Your father told me you were a late bloomer, but I didn't realize how late."

He stepped toward her, and Kitty reflexively rose to sidle away. "You know my father?"

"I work for him. He asked me to come pick you up." He took another step forward that she matched with one back. He rolled his eyes. "I'm not going to attack you. I'm going to guide your shift."

"You're going to what my what?"

His hand came down on top of her head, between her furry, rounded ears. "I'm going to help you get human again. Just be quiet and concentrate."

Kitty thought about protesting, but her head was still aching a bit and the warmth of his hand felt good. She had to work to resist the urge to tilt her head and guide his long fingers behind her ears where she should really use a good scratch. If she just focused on the fact that she was still human inside and that she was in a public restroom with a man she'd never met before, whose name she didn't know, having just survived a vicious, unprovoked attack, and attempting to transform herself from a lion back into a woman, she might almost have been able to relax.

"Close your eyes," he instructed, and she obeyed before she had time to wonder about why. "And try to stop thinking so loud."

Okay, Kitty decided she wasn't wild about this mind-reading thing, no matter what he called it. Blanking her thoughts now seemed like a really good idea.

She heard a low chuckle and then felt a soft, building warmth begin in the palm of his hand and sink slowly through skin and fur and bone until it melted over her like warm chocolate. It ran down over her head and neck, across her shoulders, her chest, all the way down to her tingling toes until it seemed impossible to repress the urge to purr long and low and rasping.

When she tried, she nearly choked on her own tongue.

Her human tongue.

Eyes flying open, Kitty looked up into the stranger's hard, handsome face and became acutely conscious of the touch of cold tile, frigidly antiseptic air, and a warm copper gaze on her freckled skin.

Her bare, nude, naked, exposed, gradually-turning-a-flattering-shade-of-blush-pink skin.

Yes, as if the day hadn't been enough for her so far, she now found herself naked, in a public toilet, on her hands and knees at the feet of the most gorgeous man she'd ever seen, with her face level with the crotch of his exquisitely tailored pinstripe pants.

"Just kill me."

Her voice managed to sound husky and pathetic both at the same time.

The stranger nudged her overnight bag closer and slowly removed his hand from the top of her head. She couldn't tell if her imagination was running away with her or if he really did stroke her hair gently as he withdrew. But since either way it did nothing to ease her humiliation, did it really matter?

"How about we skip the death part and you take your bag into a stall and put some clothes on?" he rumbled, his voice low and amused and something else that Kitty refused to speculate about. "Dare I hope that you packed an emergency outfit in there?"

As if afraid speaking would make her even *more* naked, Kitty nodded, her eyes still locked on his trousers.

"Good. Go get dressed, and then we can get out of here. I imagine that after that flight you're dying for something to eat and a comfortable place to sleep. In that order."

Kitty didn't bother to answer. That is, not unless you counted the slam of the stall door and the click of the lock sliding into place to be an answer. Leaning heavily against the door, she clutched her bag to her chest and decided that if there was any justice in the universe, she would die before she ever had to look another person in the eye for as long as she lived.

Two

WHILE MARTIN'S DAUGHTER HID IN THE BATHROOM STALL,
Max found the "Closed for Cleaning" placard in the
janitor's closet near the restroom entrance and set it out.
Then he crossed his arms over his chest and settled back
against the long bank of sinks opposite the girl's hiding
place to wait.

She wasn't what he had expected. Not even remotely.
For some reason—and he knew he had only his own prej-
udice to fault here—he'd been expecting someone older.
Oh, he knew her age—Martin had told him she was
twenty-four—but he'd still expected an older twenty-four.
Someone harder. Someone to whom a long-lost father
with an enormous fortune meant a penthouse apartment
on easy street and birthday presents as diamond-hard as
her eyes. From what he'd seen so far, there wasn't a hard
edge on this girl. She was all soft skin and round curves
and sweet, wary innocence.

And she made his mouth water.

This was an unexpected complication.

Shrugging in an attempt to distract his body from the
images in his head, Max found the attempts were made
in vain. Since those images all seemed to feature the

glow of skin like cream sprinkled with cinnamon, or the plump, round weight of a softly curving breast, it would take something along the lines of a volcanic eruption to distract his body from the memory of hers.

He tried thinking about her Leo form to see if that would help, but no dice. As a lioness, she had just as much appeal, in subtly different ways. She was one of the smaller cats he'd seen, lithe and sleek in a way their kind wasn't normally known for. Leos tended to have more muscle than grace. Cheetahs and panthers had long, slim lines and rangy, feline elegance. The expensive European race cars of the shifter world. Leos had bulk and power. Less Maserati, more Mack truck.

Except for Martin's daughter. She looked almost delicate to Max, even with her sharp white fangs and lethal, curving claws. The sight of her made all of his most primitive instincts sit up and take notice. Like his animal cousins, he wanted to cut her from the pride and keep her for himself, fighting off any other male and ensuring that the cubs she bore would be his heirs, carriers of his genes and his legacy—

Max cut himself off abruptly. Cubs? What the hell was he thinking? He'd known the girl for all of ten minutes, if that, and he still had a lot more to learn about her before he decided if she was half as innocent as she looked. Claiming her, if it happened at all, would wait a lot longer than that, and mating with her even longer still. Better not to count his cubs before they were conceived.

He cleared his throat and forced his gaze to focus on the metal stall door and not the mouthwatering treat behind it. "Are you all right in there? Do you have everything you need?"

He heard the clatter of something dropping to the tile; then a soft, slightly unsteady voice said, "Fine. I'm fine. I'll just be another minute."

Her voice was shaky and sweet and liquidly southern. He tried to remember where *Gone with the Wind* had been set and thought it had been Georgia. That's what she sounded like, Scarlett O'Hara without the whine or the self-conscious manipulation. Kitty's plane had come in from Atlanta, but he thought he remembered Martin saying she lived somewhere else.

Max smiled. "No wonder I thought you sounded strange when you were growling at me earlier. I've never heard anyone speak Leo with an accent before."

The stall door opened, and she stepped hesitantly into the fluorescent lighting of the open restroom. "I don't have an accent," she said, tugging self-consciously on the hem of her shirt.

The overnight bag had yielded a pair of casual black sandals and snug jeans with faded areas of wear along the seams and down the fronts of her thighs. The denim looked battered and comfortable and almost as soft as her skin. Her T-shirt had an equally lived-in look. The thin, blue cotton with darker sleeves and trim looked like it might have been part of a high school softball uniform, but this was the first time Max could remember lusting after an adolescent shortstop. The word "Owls" stretched across her breasts in a way guaranteed to raise his blood pressure. Especially when he realized it did so in the absence of a bra.

As soon as he pried his tongue from the back of his throat, he mustered what he hoped was a drool-free smile. "Right. Because 'fine' is really spelled with an *a-h* in the middle," he teased. This time, when he ran his gaze over her, he did so in a purely impersonal manner. Or at least he tried. "How are you feeling? Anything hurt?"

She shouldered her bag and shook her head. "I thought I'd cut the back of my head when he knocked it against the tile, but I felt around in there, and I couldn't find anything. I must have imagined it."

Max frowned. "Come here. Let me check."

She didn't exactly look comfortable with the idea, but she stepped in front of him and turned her back nonetheless. Parting her hair, he ignored the silky feel of it and searched her scalp for signs of an injury.

"I don't see anything," he said finally. "It's probably healed."

"Or I imagined it, like I said." She faced him again, her pointy little chin firmed with determination. Or maybe that was stubbornness.

Max felt his lips quirk. "You don't know much about being Leo, do you?" Her green eyes fixed on him with suspicion. "Healing is part of the package. We can heal most minor injuries just by shifting forms. Even things like broken bones, if we're in good health otherwise. If we're lucky, something life-threatening to a human, like a bullet wound, will look like a three-week-old scar after a shift. Comes in handy."

"Why? Do people shoot you often?"

He grinned. "No, but I've had more than one tell me they wanted to."

He heard her mutter something that sounded like "can't imagine why," but since she was looking away from him and inventorying the remains of the fabric and notions that lay scattered across the tile floor, he couldn't be sure.

"That was my favorite pair of tennis shoes," she said mournfully, throwing the ruined scraps of canvas and rubber into the waste bin, along with the pile of rags that had been her clothes. "I'd just gotten them broke in right." She turned back to Max. "So, I'm assuming that since you haven't attacked me like that other guy, you aren't a friend of his?"

"No. Like I said before, I work for your father. I'm Max Stuart."

He held out his hand, which she looked at warily but didn't grasp right away. "And who do you think my father is, Mr. Stuart?"

"Martin Lowe. He asked me to meet your flight and drive you to the hotel."

"And you knew who I was because he showed you the picture I sent him?"

She was a suspicious little thing, but considering the evening she'd had, he couldn't say he blamed her. "No, as far as I know, he doesn't have a picture of you. But he did give me your flight number and tell me how old you are. None of the other passengers I saw get off that plane were Leos, so it wasn't hard to work out." He paused, and his eyes roamed over her face again. "Plus, you have his eyes."

Max had thought that bit of proof might relax her, and she did look slightly less wary, but if anything, the tension in her muscles increased.

"I wouldn't know," she murmured, but she did take his hand and shake it briefly. Her palm was dry, her grip firm and pleasant. And a spark of heat leapt from her skin to his. "I'm Kitty Sugarman."

Oh, that was just too much to let pass. He cleared his throat. "Kitty?" he repeated carefully.

She made a face. "Trust me. Until a few weeks ago it was completely devoid of irony. My great-grandmother's name was Katherine, but the family called her Kitty. I always thought I was named for her."

"And now?"

"There are very few things I would put past my mother, Mr. Stuart." She adjusted the strap of her bag, her body language making clear that she was done talking about herself and her family for the moment. "If your offer is still open, I'd appreciate a ride to my hotel. I was going to pick up a rental car, but I'm not sure it's such a good idea for me to be driving around a strange city at night. Especially after what just happened."

Max accepted the change of subject, but he didn't miss the significance of those "No Trespassing" signs. He'd get the story out of her eventually. She intrigued him too much for him not to.

Placing his hand under her elbow, he guided her back out and into the terminal. "Certainly; that's what I'm here for. And I think it's a wise move to wait to rent a car. You may find you won't even need one. But if you do decide you still want a rental, a concierge at the Savannah will make the arrangements for you and have the car delivered there."

Max had deliberately shortened his strides to make it easier for her to keep up, but he found her short legs carried her through the airport with surprising efficiency. Even when she turned a confused face toward him, she didn't slow her stride.

"How did you know where I'm staying?" she asked, a hint of her quelled suspicion returning. "I'm fairly certain I never mentioned it to my father. He wanted me to stay at his house."

"I know. He mentioned that," Max said, keeping his expression open and doing his best to be reassuring. "He's still hoping you'll change your mind. But as for the reservations, Martin booked a room for you for to-night. He thought meeting him and the family at the end of such a long day might be a bit of an overwhelming way to start off your visit."

She fixed her gaze forward again and seemed to soften slightly. "That was considerate of him. And he's right. I'm not up to any more stress at the moment. I need some sleep first. And maybe a hot bath."

Shit, she had to go and say that, right? Now, instead of seeing the pale, glistening floor tiles under his feet, Max was seeing pale, glistening bubbles slowly dissolving over her spiced cream skin. This was insane. It was like someone had spiked his bottled water with Viagra.

"Talk about coincidences, though," Kitty mused beside him, mercifully derailing his train of thought. "It's kind of funny to think that my father would have booked me a room in the same hotel where I already made reservations for myself."

That got Max's attention. "You booked yourself into the Savannah? That wasn't necessary, Kitty. Your father fully intends this trip to be on him. Even if you insisted on staying at the hotel, he'd want to have your room comped. We'll arrange it with the desk when you check in."

"Comped?"

She said the word like it came from a foreign language, and Max smiled. Sometimes he forgot that not everyone lived in Vegas. "Given to you with the compliments of the house," he explained. "Free of charge."

"Oh, right. I've heard that casinos do that for people who gamble a lot," she said, sounding mildly disapproving, but more in a "don't they have better things to do" way than in a "gambling is a hobby of the devil" way. "I guess that means my father spends a lot of time at the Savannah." She shook her head. "Well, even if he wants to do that, I'm paying my own way on this trip. I don't like to be beholden to people, even if they are relations. And I don't want my father to give up his comps. He might want to use them himself some other time."

Max had led the way out of the gate area, through the security checkpoint, and onto the escalators that would take them down toward Baggage Claim. Out of habit, he placed one hand on the moving railing as they rode the stairs down. It was a good thing, too, because she'd surprised him enough that if he hadn't been holding on to something, he probably would have tumbled headfirst down the entire story between Security and the luggage carousels.

Kitty thought her father was a gambler? That he could get her room comped because he spent so much at the casino that they were willing to do him favors? Didn't she realize who her father was?

And that part about using his comps later. Did she not know how sick Martin had gotten? Had he not told her he was dying?

Max gave a mental curse. So much for his gold-digger hypothesis. It was starting to look like Kitty Sugarman was less cunning than she was clueless. Damn Martin for thinking he could let her walk into this blind.

And damn Max's own luck for being the one to find out and feeling obliged to straighten things out for her. This was the kind of job that called for diplomacy. Oh, he could manage that well enough when he had to, but he'd gotten used to relying less on charm and more on the fact that everyone who worked for him knew better than to piss him off. Maybe he should look at this as a valuable opportunity to polish his rusty skills.

Right. And maybe while he was at it, he'd look into castration as an acceptable method of birth control.

Mostly as a way to kill time, he glanced down at the bank of video monitors at the foot of the escalator. "Your bags will be coming in on Carousel Seven. That's toward the left."

On the stair above him, Kitty shook her head. "I didn't check anything. This is it." She patted the small overnighter she carried on her shoulder.

Max let his surprise show. "That's all you brought with you?"

"I'm only staying the weekend," she explained with a shrug. "And I'm not much of a clotheshorse. I usually pack light. I'm actually lucky I even brought a second pair of shoes." She gestured to the casual black sandals that had replaced her ruined tennis shoes. "I usually don't bother."

Holy Christ, Max thought. Her siblings and cousin were going to eat this girl alive. Had anyone in the history of the universe ever been less prepared for what she was about to walk into?

"Well then, we can head straight to the car," he said, praying that by the time they reached it he'd have thought of a gentler way of breaking this to her than saying, *By the way, your father is a multi-millionaire, you're staying in a high roller's suite at the hotel he owns, your half sister is a barracuda who will probably try to rip your throat out the first time you see her, and if you don't mind, I'd like to see you naked again within the next couple of days, preferably with your legs spread and your ankles on my shoulders.*

Oh, and don't forget to fasten your seat belt.

THREE

ANY TRIP THAT BEGAN WITH SOMEONE TRYING TO KILL her on the floor of a public restroom could only get better as it progressed, right?

That's what Kitty told herself as she slid into the passenger seat of Max Stuart's elegant silver Mercedes. After a beginning like that, how could things possibly get worse? Just because the last stranger she'd met had been the homicidal maniac in the bathroom didn't mean there was anything wrong with putting herself in Max's—also a complete stranger—hands on less than half an hour's acquaintance.

Lord. She just might be too stupid to live.

Kitty put a hand to the back of her head, to the place where there ought to have been a cut or a lump or some kind of evidence of what she'd been through, and sighed. For two weeks now, she'd spent every waking moment alternating between anger and denial, and here it took a good whack upside the head to demonstrate the reason for it. Apparently she'd gone through all that because being mad or pretending everything was normal were the best ways she could think of to blot out the emotion that underlay all the others.

Pure, abject terror.

Kitty was scared witless.

Oh, she'd put on a good act. She'd told herself—and anyone around her—that the knots in her stomach and the nightmares and the lack of appetite were because she was working up a good mad at the man who'd impregnated and abandoned her mother and never bothered to so much as wonder whether or not he might have left a little bit of his own flesh and blood behind. Kitty claimed that she'd accepted his invitation to visit him at his home in Nevada so that she'd finally have the opportunity to tell him just what she thought of him. But the truth was, she was terrified.

Everything scared her these days, especially the thought of what she might be capable of if the animal living inside her kept coming out without her permission. So far, she'd been lucky. Her instinct to survive had overpowered everything else, so all she'd done had been to defend herself and help her mother when they'd been in jeopardy, but what if the next time she didn't change because of some kind of threat? What if the next time she changed because someone made her angry? What if the impulse driving her wasn't fear, but anger? Did she really want to find out what she could do to someone else when she had claws like razors and teeth like kitchen knives?

No matter what Kitty told anyone, that was the real reason she'd come to Vegas. She needed to learn some control, just like her grandfather had told her. Getting an opportunity to tell off her biological father was just a bonus.

But it was starting to look like her animal side wasn't the only thing she had to fear these days. Twenty minutes in Vegas and already someone had tried to kill her. Completely out of the blue. Kitty didn't like to toot her own horn, but she thought that most people liked her. She couldn't think of anyone who didn't, or any reason why someone she'd never laid eyes on before should hate her enough to want her dead. She just plain wasn't the kind of woman who made enemies. At least, she hadn't been before.

Before, she hadn't been a lot of things.

She jumped a little when the driver's door opened, then scolded herself when Max slid behind the steering wheel and gave her a friendly smile. She pretended to look for something in the outside pocket of her bag while she waited for her heartbeat to slow down.

"It's not far to the hotel," Max said, his voice sounding even deeper and rougher in the close confines of the car. "The airport is fairly close to the Strip. We'll have you checked in before you know it."

"Thanks." She forced a smile and zipped her bag shut. No sense in looking like as big a coward as she really was.

Max paid a parking attendant and then steered the car expertly out of the airport and into traffic. Setting her bag on the floor at her feet, Kitty folded her hands in her lap and chewed on the inside of her lip. The man beside her settled back against the leather upholstery and kept his attention on the road, giving Kitty the chance to study him unobserved.

She had to admit that what she saw didn't do much to soothe her nerves. In her experience, men who looked like Max Stuart tended to be as ugly on the inside as they were beautiful on the outside. With that dark, sun-streaked hair, those vivid, copper eyes, and that bodybuilder's physique, the man probably had women throwing themselves to the floor in front of him just for the chance to play his mattress. And that was exactly the kind of thing that tended to turn a man rotten. When the universe gave men everything they wanted, they tended to think themselves entitled to even more. Normally, just the sight of a guy like that was enough to set Kitty's teeth on edge.

Tonight, though, the only thing tightening her jaw was the memory of the nut in the restroom. Even alone and technically at Max Stuart's mercy, Kitty surprised herself by realizing that she didn't feel threatened by him. Her instincts had always been good, and since the wreck, they'd proven to possess an almost eerie accuracy about people. Right now, her internal alarm system remained quiet, at least about him. Her attacker, on the other hand, had seriously upset her equilibrium.

"You know, I wasn't thinking clearly earlier," she said, her voice sounding loud in the quiet interior of the car. "I should have contacted airport security before we left and filed some kind of report. Or maybe I should have just called the police. I'm not sure how it works here."

"Normally, you would have told airport security, and they would make the decision on whether or not to involve the police," Max answered, his eyes fixed on the road.

"Should I go back and do that before we get all the way to the hotel?"

"I doubt it would be worth it. Whoever the mugger was, he's long gone by now."

Kitty mulled that over. "Still, I could fill out the report anyway and give them a description. What if he tries it again and attacks some other woman? I'd feel horrible—"

A thought occurred to her and Kitty broke off, remembering something from those frightening moments.

You shouldn't have come here, bitch!

What if that really had been what the mugger had said? What if it hadn't been a random robbery attempt and Kitty had actually been the target?

What if someone really *was* trying to kill her?

A wave of dizziness spun through her head, and she wrestled back the urge to panic. Why on earth would anyone want her dead? Sure, there were a few wacko conservatives out there who thought all Others should be put down like rabid dogs, but even if her newly discovered abilities made her a target, who in Vegas knew what she was, other than the man sitting next to her and her biological father? Since both of them were just as non-human as she was, they had no reason to target her for extermination. Maybe she was just being silly.

Kitty cast Max a sidelong glance. If she were being honest, Max had actually come to her rescue earlier. He'd been the one to scare her attacker away, and he'd been nothing but concerned and polite in the time since. He'd shown no evidence that he thought the incident had been anything but an ordinary mugging, and she didn't need to have known him long to have the impression that very few things got by this man. The chances of him overlooking attempted murder seemed more than a little remote.

Maybe Kitty's attacker had really said, "You shouldn't have come here." As in, "It was a mistake coming into this restroom, because now I'm going to steal your purse and kill you so I won't get caught." That made a lot more sense, didn't it?

"What's wrong?" the man beside her rumbled, his low, deep voice serving to remind her how large he was, how much stronger than her. "Is something bothering you? Would you feel better if we went back and you made a report?"

Forcing a smile, Kitty gave her head a quick shake. Somehow even the idea of telling him she thought she'd been a specific target of the attack made her feel like an idiot. Time to change the subject.

"Of course not," she assured, hoping she sounded more confident than she felt. "I'm sure you're right. Even if I did go back, the chances of them catching the guy are probably nil. I wouldn't want to waste your time. Especially since you went out of your way to come meet me." She faked a curious look. "How long did you say you've worked for my father?"

That brought a faint smile to his lips. "I didn't. Officially, its been about twelve years. But really it's even longer than that, now. Martin took me in when I was just a teenager. I started out earning an allowance by running errands for him, then when I was eighteen he gave me a job doing pretty much the same thing in his office, but with that job I started earning a real paycheck. I've been with him ever since."

"Wow." She laughed, shaking off the last of her uneasiness and feeling it replaced by an odd twinge of hurt. "You must know him pretty well."

"He's been like a father to me."

"Well, that makes one of us."

Max said nothing, but she felt his gaze on her and flushed. Wow, it looked like she was harboring a bit more bitterness than she'd wanted to admit, and that wasn't like her. Her grandmother would have been ashamed.

"Sorry," Kitty said, her mouth twisting. "I guess I'm even more tired than I thought. I shouldn't have said that."

She heard his jacket rustle as he shrugged. She wasn't quite ready to look at him again.

"I suppose it's the truth," he said, his tone very even.

Kitty shook her head. "Not really. At least, not all of it." She stole a glance and saw him gazing steadily out the windshield wearing that same neutral expression. "I'm not sure how much you know. About my father and me."

"Not a lot." He checked his rearview mirror, flipped the turn signal, and smoothly changed lanes. "I know this is the first time you'll be meeting him, and I know you grew up back east. I know you didn't shift for the first time until just before you contacted him."

"I didn't even know it was possible." She laughed, a dry, tired sound. "I didn't know he was Other. I thought I was human through and through."

She was silent for a long minute.

"That must have been a bit of a shock."

"You could say that."

"You seem to be doing pretty well with it." He looked at her again with a question on his face.

This time, she really laughed. "Good to know I've got you fooled. I'm holding my sanity together with duct tape and prayer." Leaning back against her seat, she took a second to enjoy the heated leather beneath her. Little, tangible things like that helped almost as much as the duct tape. "Anyway, suffice it to say, I didn't know about him, and he thought he was doing what was best for me, so I'd appreciate it if you'd forget what I said."

"I don't think you were out of line, but if that's what you want . . ."

She nodded decisively. More for herself than for him. "It is."

"I think you each have a lot to learn about the other."

Kitty continued on, anxious to lighten the mood. And change the subject. "If it's not exhaustion making me snarky, it must be that airplane food," she joked, urging him to laugh along with her. "I always heard it was no good for you."

"Not unless you're the size of a flea with the taste buds of a dung beetle." He smiled. "But I can tell you for certain that the Savannah has an excellent room service menu."

Finally, safer ground. "You've stayed there before?"

"Many, many times."

"Oh, great. You can give me a firsthand opinion, then. Is it as nice as all the guidebooks say?"

The light trickling into the car became a flood, and Kitty looked around to see that Max had turned the car into a covered area in the front of the hotel. All around them she could see other cars, taxis, limousines, and people. There were people everywhere—young women in sparkling party clothes, older women in shorts and T-shirts, men in tuxedos or faded jeans, and dozens of hotel employees in tailored khaki uniforms.

All the lights and colors and movement distracted her until Max pulled the car to a stop right in front of the hotel doors and turned in his seat to face her straight on.

"I'm afraid my opinion could be considered biased," he said when she finally looked back at him.

"Why? Just because you like it? It's fine if it's your favorite hotel. That just means you'll have lots of tips and advice for me."

He shook his head, his copper eyes bright and intense.

"It's not my favorite," he said slowly. "It's mine. I'm the president and executive manager. I run the Savannah."

Kitty shook her head. "But I thought you said you worked for my father."

His beautiful lips quirked as a valet and a doorman approached the car from either side and reached for the doors to allow them to exit.

"I do."

Abruptly, the buzzing came back.

It was the same sound she'd heard just before Misty's truck had run off the road, the same sound that had filled her head when Papaw sat her down and told her a story about her mother and a man who'd passed through town and left something important behind.

Kitty had come to think of it as the sound of the world rushing by at warp speed while she stood stock-still and dug in her heels. The trouble was, sooner or later the vacuum created by the changing world around her would generate enough power to suck her along in its wake.

Imagine that. Kitty Sugarman becoming a cosmic-scale sucker.

"What?" she whispered.

Max glanced over her shoulder and shook his head. Kitty sensed movement behind her and guessed he'd signaled to the hovering doorman to give them a minute before opening her door. If Max really ran this place, it was no wonder she failed to hear a click, she thought with just a delicate touch of hysteria.

When he looked back at her, she could see the muscle in his jaw clench and thought he looked about as pleased to deliver this news as she was confused to hear it.

"I don't know why your father didn't mention his business to you," Max said, his voice low and tense.

"That's between the two of you, though I'm guessing that once you learned his name, he assumed you'd realize for yourself."

She looked at Max in disbelief. "Why on earth would I realize? Do I look like I follow the gambling industry to you? I've never even bought a lottery ticket!"

"Have you bought a newspaper? Your father is one of the most successful self-made businessmen in the country, Kitty. His name is in the news all the time. Are you telling me you never heard Martin's name before you found out he was your father?"

"Yes, that's what I'm telling you," she insisted, her heart racing and her mind numb. What on earth was happening to her simple, peaceful, sensible life? "I'm an assistant librarian at a public university—"

"Then you're surrounded by media. You should have seen his name in the headlines at least a few—"

"I work in Special Collections. Our average text was printed in the late eighteenth century. Do you think he was heavily featured during the Revolutionary War?"

Max ran a hand through his hair, an absent, impatient gesture that left him looking like he'd just rolled out of bed, but Kitty was too shaken up to be charmed by it. She just folded her arms over her chest and glared at him. She knew he wasn't really the one she was upset with, but he was there.

"All right," he growled. "Point taken. You really had no idea who your father was. I'm sorry he didn't tell you himself. But you shouldn't let it bother you. He may be rich, but he wasn't born that way, and I can tell you for certain that in the end, he's really just a normal man."

Kitty raised an eyebrow and lowered her chin and wondered if he'd lost his mind.

A grin flashed, white and unexpectedly charming. "All right, I suppose he might not seem that way to you, since you grew up human. But for a Leo, I can assure you, he's about as normal as it gets."

Blowing out a sigh, Kitty let her eyes drift closed and shook her head. "You know, in the past month my life has been turned upside down and shaken just a few too many times, I think. And I can't say the sensation is getting any more appealing." Opening her eyes again, she glanced over at Max and managed a small smile. "Do me a favor?"

"What?"

"If you've got any more bombshells planned for me any time soon, do you think we could just go on and get them out of the way? I'm not sure my heart can handle the repeated shocks."

She saw something pass across his face, an expression she couldn't define that did nothing to calm her nerves. Not even when he nodded, slowly and deliberately.

"I can do that," he said, "but first let's get you checked in and order you some dinner. I think you're going to need to keep up your strength for this."

"Great," Kitty muttered to herself as he exited the car and crossed around to her side, waving the hovering doorman away. "That was exactly what I needed to hear."

Four

KITTY SUGARMAN KNEW HERSELF TO BE A TENNESSEE girl. Born and raised on a farm in rural Bradley County, she knew how to drive a tractor, bake a biscuit, and collect chicken eggs without getting pecked, and she could sing all three verses of "Rocky Top" in her sleep. Since leaving for college six years ago, she'd traveled a little, been to New York, San Francisco, Philadelphia, and once, memorably, even Bermuda. She was a country girl, but she wasn't a hick.

But never in her life had she seen anything remotely like the Savannah Hotel and Casino.

The lobby rose at least three stories above her, a great soaring space with sandstone tiles on the floor and a ceiling above her that had been so skillfully painted, she felt as if she were gazing up into an infinite expanse of clear, cloudless blue sky. The walls looked as if they'd been carved from the same sandstone that covered the floor, their earthy, textured surface broken occasionally by a colorful piece of textile art or by one of the trees that grew from a square of open earth and spread umbrella-like branches with sparse tufts of leaves out into space.

Exits and halls stretched out in three directions, the open space in the center filled with small groupings of wood and leather furniture arranged around low tables woven of golden and brightly dyed straw. To the right of the entrance, set just to the side of a branching hall, a curved desk of pale wood sat before two comfortable-looking leather club chairs and bore a graceful sign that spelled out "Concierge" in loops and curves of rusted wrought iron. Instead of making the sign look ugly or neglected, the reddish-orange surface patina gave it the appearance of tradition and warmth, something old, beloved, and well used.

Against the back wall, a long, solid expanse of highly polished ebony wood was manned by two men and two women in beautiful, draped garments of colorful, intricately patterned cloth. The clothes looked something like a cross between a sari and a toga, and all four of the people wearing them looked completely comfortable in them, the men as well as the women. Kitty deduced that this was the reception desk, where she would have been checking in if Fate hadn't done such a good job of using the better part of her evening to demonstrate to her that she never should have made this trip.

Feeling a little numb and incredibly tired, she began to head for the desk, but once again, Max caught her elbow and urged her in another direction.

Confused, she blinked up at him. "I thought you said I needed to check in."

"I'll take care of it," Max said, his low voice almost soothing after the noisy bustle outside. "I'm the president of the hotel, remember? You don't need to go through the front desk while you're with me."

"At the moment, you could prop me up against the wall of a supply closet and I'd sleep standing up if I had to."

"I think we can do better than that," he murmured, glancing down at her. "Are you sure you're up for more talking, though? Maybe you should sleep first. We can always hash things out in the morning."

Kitty shook her head. "No, I'll be fine. What I really need is some food. Once I get something in my stomach, I'll get a second wind. And I really will sleep better if I don't lay down still worried about what surprises y'all have in store for me."

He paused for a minute, searching her face, but whatever he found there made him nod. "Okay. This way, then."

She followed him through an archway and around a corner to a bank of elevators. Stepping toward the last car, she watched as he drew a plastic card out of his pocket and inserted it into a slot above the call button. The car dinged and the doors slid open. Max put his hand over the gap and gestured her inside.

He used the card again to access the hotel's top floors, the two rows of buttons separated from the rest by another card slot. She watched him press the button marked "20" and waited as the doors slid soundlessly closed. When they reopened, he ushered her out and into a sumptuously appointed hallway in the rich, warm earth tones she'd seen throughout the hotel. At the end of the hall, the same card he'd used in the elevator unlocked a wood and frosted-glass door to a living room that looked like a photo out of *Architectural Digest*.

Kitty wasn't sure what she'd expected, maybe more of the African safari style she'd seen downstairs, and she had to admit there were hints of it all around her. The

brightly patterned throw pillows scattered along the back
of the chocolate-colored velvet sofa, the tables and shelves
of hand-carved exotic woods, the unfamiliar species of
plants in huge, intricately decorated clay pots all whispered of Africa. The same soothing palette of sand and
earth and tall grass surrounded her, but here was an Africa of elegance and refinement. She could see it in the
clean lines of the furnishings, the sleek electronics in the
bloodwood armoire, the thick, dense pile of the area
rugs spread across the parquet flooring.

She turned to tell Max she'd be more comfortable in
something a little smaller—like that supply closet she'd
mentioned earlier—but he'd already picked up the phone
and was telling the person on the other end of the line
that Miss Sugarman would be staying in the Acacia Suite
and a bellman should bring up her bag as soon as possible. When Max turned back to her, she thought about
telling him anyway, but she never got the chance.

"What would you like for dinner?"

Kitty blinked. "I don't know. I haven't looked at the
room service menu yet." She looked around the room. "I
haven't *found* the room service menu yet."

He waved a hand. "Don't worry about that. What are
you in the mood for? French? Moroccan? Ethiopian?"

Ethiopia had its own cuisine? Why had she never thought
about that before?

Shaking off her distracted thoughts, Kitty tried to
picture what she wanted to eat. Since he hadn't mentioned fried catfish and collard greens, she figured southern comfort food wasn't an option, so she'd have to pick
something the kitchen here would be likely to have. And
something that wouldn't take too much energy to chew.

"A burger?" she hazarded.

Max nodded and she heard him order two burgers and a full cart, whatever that meant, before he hung up the phone. "I hope you won't mind if I join you, but I haven't had time for dinner myself."

"No, that's fine." Her nerves jangling, Kitty looked around the room and tried not to feel too much like a hick in a high-end china shop. "This room is . . . amazing," she said weakly.

Max smiled and gestured to her. "Come on. I can give you the nickel tour before the food gets here."

His nickel tour should have cost at least a buck-fifty. The main room may have been amazing, but the rest of the suite took her breath away. The windows at one end of the living room provided a view of the Las Vegas Strip, laid out like a Christmas display beneath them, all twinkling colored lights draped over tiny buildings, with miniature cars and trucks rolling between them. Beyond the lights, she could even see the stark nighttime beauty of the desert rolling forward toward the distant mountains. It took an effort of will to tear herself away.

When she managed it, Max led her to the other end of the room and pushed back part of what she'd thought had been a wall to reveal a small, ruthlessly modern red-clay-tiled kitchen, with full-sized appliances and golden, recessed lighting. He assured her it was fully equipped if she got tired of restaurant food, and Kitty just nodded. The living room of this place was larger than her entire apartment in Knoxville. Now that he was adding rooms to it, she felt like Goldilocks; this suite was tooooo big.

On the other side of the kitchen, he showed her a small, comfortably furnished dining area with a bar built into the wall and a painting almost as breathtaking as the view in the other room. Then he led the way back through the living room to a raised wooden platform that Kitty had taken to be a small sitting area and turned out to be the entrance to the hallway leading to the second half of the suite. Her wide eyes took in a private study full of books and high-tech business accessories, including a fax machine, printer, copier, and scanner. Everything except a computer, which, she learned, could be sent up from the A/V department if she needed one. Again, she just shook her head and tried to keep her mouth from falling open as he showed her *both* bedrooms, each with a private bath and dressing room and the biggest, plushest-looking beds she'd ever laid eyes on.

Dear Lord, when the heck was she going to feel the pinch and wake up from all this?

Max either didn't notice or had decided to ignore her overwhelmed expression. Or maybe he'd just gotten used to it. After all, she'd been wearing it a lot the last hour or so.

"Dinner should be here any minute," he said, drawing her away from the master bedroom's exquisite view, this one looking away from the Strip to the outlying suburban areas and desert beyond. "By now, your bag is probably out in the living room, too."

True to his word, the bellman had entered discreetly and left her pitiful, battered overnighter on a side table near the suite's entrance. The entire contents of the bag and the bag itself probably wouldn't have paid for the twelve-inch-square beaded wall hanging that resided just above it.

Man, was she in the wrong place.

Only the ringing of the doorbell—an actual doorbell. In a hotel room!—saved her from saying something unutterably stupid. Instead, she just stood awkwardly behind the sofa while Max answered the summons and admitted a khaki-uniformed waiter and the white-linen-covered cart he wheeled into the room. Max murmured to the young man, then let him wheel the cart toward the dining area and turned back to Kitty with a smile.

"If you'd like a few minutes to clean up before dinner, feel free," Max said. "The food will keep warm."

Kitty said nothing, but maybe he was still reading her mind and hearing her wonder to herself if he thought she'd packed an evening gown in her little bag. Did "clean up" mean wash her hands or come back looking ready to entertain the Queen of England?

He smiled and stepped closer until she felt the warmth radiating off of him like a campfire. Her breath caught in her throat, and she held as still as a doe in the path of a hunter while he raised one large, lean hand and flicked a gentle finger across the tip of her nose.

"You've got a little smudge," he said, his eyes glittering. "Right there."

No deer in the history of the natural world had ever turned tail and run as fast as Kitty Jane Sugarman. And even as she locked the master bathroom door behind her, she couldn't shake the sensation of being watched by the hungry copper eyes of a predator.

FIVE

MAX STOOD NEAR THE ENTRANCE TO THE DINING AREA and took a long drink from the dark amber beer bottle in one hand. After the last couple of hours, he could have used something stronger, but he'd decided against it. It might have helped him get through all the explanations he was about to have to give to the wide-eyed strawberry blonde from Georgia, but it wouldn't do anything to help him keep his hands off of her and to himself where they belonged.

Christ, he hadn't been this tempted by a woman in . . . ever. He certainly couldn't explain it. Kitty Sugarman was about as far from his type as it was possible to get and still be a living, breathing woman. She was soft where he'd always coveted the athletic, petite where he'd liked tall, and as innocent as a newborn baby where he'd always appreciated talent enhanced with dedicated practice. Instead of warm, tanned skin she also had a generous dusting of freckles that he itched to count with his tongue, and wide, green eyes that showed every thought that ran through her head as clearly as if she'd been projecting them onto a movie screen.

And somehow he needed to figure out a way to allow her and her father to get to know each other while keeping her other assorted relatives from eating her alive, with cocktail sauce.

It might just take a miracle.

A sensation of movement brushed his skin, and he turned to find her emerging shyly from the hallway, her hands shoved into the pockets of her jeans, her hair brushed out of its braid and pulled back into a ponytail. Her freshly scrubbed face glowed as shiny clean as a kindergartner's.

Max ignored the clenching of his gut and set aside his beer. "Feel any better?" His smile was the only easy thing about him.

She nodded and padded across the floor. She must have kicked off her shoes in the other room, because her bare feet made no sound, their neat, tiny toenails naked of the simplest coat of polish. If he'd been able to ignore the way that damned printing stretched across her bra-less chest, he might have been able to convince himself she looked all of seven years old.

"Much," she said, her lips curving. "I can almost feel that second wind already. Of course, it helps that I can smell those burgers, and they're making my mouth water."

"Well, come and find out if they taste as good."

Her murmured thanks when he held her chair did nothing to calm him down, and by the time he took his seat at her right, he was thankful to have the table between them. He'd like to say he kept quiet because he wanted to give her the chance to eat in peace after everything that had happened, but he'd never been that good of a liar. Especially not when he was lying to himself.

By the time they finished, he'd steeled himself to say what needed to be said, but there was no chance in hell he was going to like doing it.

PLACING HER FOLDED NAPKIN BACK ON THE TABLE BE-side her plate, Kitty leaned back in her chair and lifted her beer. "Okay, I'm ready. You've been more than patient, but you can go ahead now. Lay it on me."

She probably wore the same expression that some people might while saying those same words to a maniacal dentist, but she couldn't help that. Although she had needed to eat and the burger had been delicious, she could feel it sitting in the pit of her stomach in a way that wasn't entirely comfortable. Of course, these days her stomach rarely felt comfortable.

"You know, it's a good thing Martin told me how old you are," Max said with a smile as he pushed his own plate aside. "Because otherwise I'd be looking over my shoulder right now waiting to get busted for serving alcohol to a minor."

Kitty rolled her eyes. People always mistook her age, but she probably hadn't done herself any favors when she'd scrubbed off the remnants of her makeup and pulled her hair back in a ponytail. That always made her look about sixteen.

"Believe me, I get carded every time I even glance too hard at a liquor store." She looked down and picked at the label on her beer with a fingernail. She could feel her nerves roiling, and before she knew it, her mouth was moving again, completely without her say-so. "Do I look like him?"

She knew the question was sudden, but Max didn't comment on that. For several heartbeats, he didn't even speak.

"Not really," he said after a moment. "Not like people say, 'Oh, she looks just like her dad.' I'm guessing you have more of your mom's looks. She must be beautiful."

"Beautiful has always been what Misty does best," Kitty said drily. "It's one of her few talents."

"You do have his eyes, though," Max offered. "I think I mentioned that before. Same color, similar shape. And I have to say that I've seen the stubborn look you get sometimes more often than I'd care to admit."

"What stubborn look?"

"The one that obviously runs in your family. The one you're starting to get right now."

Kitty blushed and smiled reluctantly. "It's pretty weird, you know? Having people talk about my 'family.' Up until recently, I thought I knew all about them. But I suppose you learn something new every day." She took another bracing sip of her beer. "So how many of them are there?"

"I suppose that depends on how you want to count."

"What do you mean?"

He braced his forearms on the table, beer bottle cradled between his hands. His copper gaze held steady on her face, level and unreadable. "How much do you know about Leos?"

It was hard for her not to snort her answer. "How much do you know about Central American fruit bats? If it's as much as me, it's a heck of a lot more than I know about you people." The words flew out before she'd thought them through, and she winced at her own insensitivity. "I'm sorry. That was—"

"The truth, I imagine," he cut in. "Remember, I saw firsthand how new this all is to you. I imagine it's been a lot to take in, thinking of yourself one way for so many years and then having everything you thought stop being the whole truth."

She searched his expression for any hint of recrimination, but all she saw was compassion. At least, that's all she could define. She had the feeling something else lurked beneath the surface, but it didn't look like displeasure. That would have to do for now.

"It was a lot to take in when the Others staged their Unveiling, but we've all had some time to get used to that. It's been more than a year now," she said. "Finding out I was an Other myself . . . I don't think there are words for that amount of 'a lot.'"

He nodded and sat back in his chair, his mouth curving once more. "All right then. Ready for your first crash course?"

Kitty laughed and shook her head. "Not even remotely. But you go on anyway. I'll try to keep up."

"Good girl." He stood and moved to pull out her chair. "Let's go sit in the living room where we can be more comfortable. This could take a while."

When she was curled up at one end of the sofa with her bare feet tucked under her, Max settled himself at the other end with one knee drawn up on the cushions and his big body turned to face her. He'd removed his coat and tie and rolled up his sleeves before they ate, and now he looked perfectly at home. Definitely more so than she did.

"Clearly you already know the most important thing," he began, his voice patient and even. "You know that you and your father, and the rest of his family and even I, are Others. Werelions, to be specific, although we don't use that term much, if at all. We prefer to call ourselves Leos."

"Although I'm guessing you weren't all born in late July or early August."

"Were you?"

"Middle of May."

"End of October. We can compare horoscopes later." He grinned. "We have a lot in common with animal lions, but not everything. We're people, not wildlife."

Kitty nodded and kept her mouth shut.

"First off, family. There are two parts to that. The larger group you need to know about is the pride, specifically, the Red Rock Pride. Your father is its leader—we call him the Felix—and the rest of your biological paternal family are members. If you spend any length of time here, you'll be a member, too, because you're part of the family. But I'm a member of the pride, as well, and so are lots of other people who aren't your blood relations. So a pride is a family, but it's more than just a group of relatives." He paused. "Is this making any sense?"

She flipped it over in her mind and nodded slowly. "I think so. I mean, you're saying that the pride is like a big extended family, but my *actual* family members are only a part of it. There are other families and other people who I'm not related to, but who would still be like . . . like kin."

Max nodded. "That's a good way of putting it. Think of them like a big group of 'aunts, uncles, and cousins' who come to all the family reunions, but who you've never been able to verify are actually related to you."

"No problem. I've got lots of those back home."

"Good. Like I said, your father is the Felix of our pride. That means he's in charge, and everyone in the pride answers to him. Not that he runs anyone's life, but if there are disputes among pride members, he'll judge who's right or wrong, and his judgment is final. The other pride members defer to him. He also takes charge of any interactions with other prides, with human governments, or with Other governing bodies in different states. Obviously he can't do everything himself, but what he doesn't handle, he appoints other people to handle in his name."

"Sounds like some kind of feudal system. Without, you know, the part about owning peasants."

Max chuckled, a warm, rough sound that made her shiver. "It's not a completely inaccurate comparison, but we don't go on Crusades, either."

"Oh, good, because I left my sword back in Tennessee."

"You probably noticed that we don't do the Hollywood werewolf thing and only change by the light of the full moon, but then again, neither do werewolves, really. We change when we want, or in moments of extreme physical or emotional stress."

"Yeah, I definitely noticed that part."

He flashed her a smile. "You'll get better at controlling it. I promise. It just takes practice."

"Oh, goodie."

"It's not something you can dismiss, Kitty," he said, growing serious. "If you don't learn how to control it, it will start to control you. That's not something we can let happen."

"We?"

"Your family. The pride. The Other community. It's stressful enough at the moment to keep the peace with the humans. We can't afford to have rogue shifters going around with no control over their own power. It doesn't bear thinking about."

Kitty wrapped her arms more tightly around herself. "I know that. I do," she insisted, "but that doesn't mean I'm going to get all excited about it."

"No one says you have to. But you might find there are benefits."

And now it was definitely time to change the subject. "You told me about the pride, but you said before you'd tell me about my family."

"I did, didn't I?" He seemed to set his jaw and almost brace himself before he began to speak.

Kitty didn't miss the signs. "Why do I think I'm not going to like this story? Is he that bad?"

"Who?"

"My father."

"That's not—"

"I mean, I'm trying to give him the benefit of the doubt, but I have to say that knowing he knew about me for all those years and never tried to contact me?" She shrugged. "I don't know. I just think that if anyone tried to stand between me and my child, I wouldn't care about anything except getting her back."

"Your father is the least of your worries. He may be your only ally." Max's gaze caught and held hers, copper eyes intent. "I won't lie to you, and I won't pretend this isn't a big adjustment for you, but think about it from the other side for a minute. Your father has another family, one made up of people who not only share his blood but who look up to him as their leader because of his place in the pride. They have a vision of how that pride works and who fits where in the pecking order, and now you show up and throw a wrench into things. They don't know what to make of you. And your father has a son and a daughter who grew up knowing him but not knowing you. That means they've spent a lot of years believing certain things about their futures that never took you into account. Now they've got some big adjustments of their own to make."

Kitty could read between lines like those as well as anyone. She could feel herself reddening with anger. "If they think I came here to take something from them, I've got no problem clearing things up—"

Something flickered in his expression so fast, she nearly missed it. Her mouth shut fast enough for her teeth to clack together. She drew a slow, painful breath.

"That's exactly what they think," she said, searching his face. "And what's more, you think it, too."

His gaze held steady on hers. "Like I said, I won't lie to you. I admit that when Martin first told me about you, the thought crossed my mind, but it didn't stay long. Not once I'd met you for myself."

"What happened? My honesty shone like a beacon before me?"

His mouth quirked at her sarcastic tone. "Your confusion, actually."

"So I looked like I was too young and stupid to plan a swindle."

"No, you were too obviously surprised that Martin is rich."

Kitty crossed her arms over her chest and drew up her shoulders. "Right. So all I have to do is tell his kids I'm not after their inheritance and they'll welcome me with open arms, I suppose."

"I . . . wouldn't count on that."

"If they want me to sign something, I will," she offered, a mix of justified anger and inexplicable hurt fueling the defiance in her tone. "There's not a thing on this earth I want from them." Shoving away from the sofa, she paced restlessly toward the window. Looking out at the view was better than looking at Max. And anything was better than looking at the chaos inside herself. "I don't even know as I want anything from him."

"Then why are you here?"

Kitty stared out at the neon-sprinkled darkness and laughed. "Because I was too damned scared to stay at home." Her mouth twisted. "That's not much of an excuse, though, because I was just as afraid to come here. My grandfather had to all but hogtie and carry me to get me on the plane. Every night after the first time I . . . shifted . . . I went to bed praying I wouldn't do anything in my sleep. That I wouldn't wake up and find out I'd hurt someone. And every morning, I woke up wishing it had all been a bad dream, that everything was back to normal."

She never heard Max move, but when he spoke again, his voice came from right behind her, so close she flinched. Her eyes refocused on the window's reflection of the room and met his gaze in the glass.

"That sounds pretty natural to me."

"Really? Well, what would you say if I told you that I still wish that, and that I'm not here to try to get closer to Martin Lowe? Because, frankly, he has very little to do with it. I'm here to make sure I learn how not to endanger my *real* family, not so I can bond with the one that doesn't give a damn about me."

"Your father gives a damn."

"He's not my father. He's a sperm donor, and his work in this situation is obviously done."

She turned to walk away, but she never took a step. Max caught her arm gently but firmly and held on. "No matter what your reasons for coming, you owe him this meeting."

"For what? For ignoring me for twenty-four years? I don't think he had to strain himself for that."

"It's not my place to explain that, and I'm not even going to try," Max replied evenly, "but maybe he can."

"He doesn't need to bother." She tried to tug her arm free. "He didn't want me before, and his family doesn't want me now. And that's fine. I didn't come for them. All I want is a few lessons in Leo control, then I'm out of here."

He held firm. "Did you ever stop to wonder if you might find something here to make you want to stay?"

"I can't think of a single good reason to do that."

His hand slid down her arm to clasp hers, raising gooseflesh in its wake. Catching her other hand, he held them both, keeping her still and forcing her to face him.

"I can," he said softly. "Because even if you don't owe your father anything, you can't deny that he's a part of you, and you can't escape from the Leo half of yourself. Forget about Martin if you want. You're right that you owe it to yourself to learn what it means to be Leo, but you should also take a look at what this trip might make possible."

Max's warmth distracted her, made her shiver. She didn't want to be distracted by him, didn't think she could afford to be. He was one of *them*. He'd be on their side.

She struggled to find her voice and her determination, to express her need to eventually go back home where she belonged.

But did she really belong there anymore, either?

"What good could possibly come from me sticking around where I'm not wanted? Where I don't want to be?"

"This."

And his lips settled gently over hers.

He caught her completely by surprise, not just with the kiss but with the heat. He had to be generating all that fire, didn't he? She sure as heck had never felt anything like it before, and for a crazy, dizzy moment, she wondered if she could survive the burn.

The first touch of his lips felt like springtime, slow and warm and tentative, a brush and a nudge that tested the timing and woke something long dormant. It was the kind of kiss that little girls dream of and that grown women decide could only exist in fairy tales. It stirred and sensitized and savored, and it wasn't until the first kiss lifted, shifted, resettled into a second that Kitty realized it also seduced.

Her breath caught in her throat and her knees melted and her hands gripped his as if she'd been the one to take hold. His fingers stroked, eased hers apart, and slipped between them in a caress she felt all the way to her womb. When he laced their fingers together, her thighs ached to do the same with their legs, their bodies. And he'd driven her to that state without so much as an intimate touch.

The man was moonshine, and Kitty knew well enough that a smart girl stayed away from moonshine if she meant to keep her wits about her and her panties on.

She pulled away from him on a whimper, one of the hardest things she'd ever done, and blinked up at him through the haze that clouded her vision. A single, weak tug freed her hands, but she couldn't manage to step back. If she unlocked her knees, she knew she'd crumble at his feet like a stale cookie.

"Wh-what was that supposed to prove?"

Max reached out, warm fingers sliding across her cheek to tuck a stray piece of hair behind her ear. His thumb flicked over the delicate shell, then traced the curve of her jaw before falling to his side. "That maybe something even better than self-control could come out of this trip before it's done."

Her laugh trembled on her lips. "If I were smart, that would only make me run faster."

"You're smart," Max said, his voice soft and low. "But I think you're also curious. And fair. And brave."

"Boy, do you not know me well."

His lips curved, a motion Kitty could have sworn she felt against her own. "I think I know more than you'd like me to, kitten. I think meeting your father means something to you. But more than that, I think meeting the other side of yourself is what drove you here. That's your curiosity at work. And your sense of what's fair is why you're going to remember what I've said when you and Martin meet."

Kitty's knees might still be weak, but she possessed more than enough backbone to make up for the deficiency. She straightened her spine and managed a small step backward.

She didn't like people making assumptions about her, especially not ones that were so on-target. It unsettled her that this man could read her so well, so fast.

"That's curious and fair," she pointed out, "but exactly how far do you think my supposed bravery will take me? After all, you also called me smart, and it sounds like I'd have to be an idiot to stick around a bunch of strange relatives who are likely to hate me on sight."

Max's knowing smile edged into a full-fledged grin that made Kitty's pulse spike and her warning sirens wail. "But you've got one more trait that I didn't mention, kitten, and that's the one that's going to make you stay."

She kept quiet and dared him to come up with something persuasive, knowing even as she did so that she should never challenge this man. He would always come out on top.

"Your father calls it 'determination,'" Max continued. "That pig-headed, stubborn refusal to let the other side win. The rest of us call it sheer perversity when it makes you walk into a situation everyone on earth and the angels themselves warn you against, just to prove that you can. But whatever you call it, you'll stay."

He flicked a finger over the end of her nose and grabbed his discarded suit jacket, slinging it over his shoulder as he headed for the door.

He had his hand on the knob when Kitty called after him, "You seem pretty sure of yourself."

She heard the defiance in her own voice, and the frustration of knowing him to be right.

He grinned back at her and tugged the door open. "Kitten, I'd bet the house on it."

Six

MAX SAT IN THE BIG LEATHER CHAIR AT THE DESK IN his office above the casino floor with his back to his paperwork. Instead of diligently completing forms and poring over spreadsheets, he faced the bank of windows overlooking the sea of gamblers and stared through the one-way glass, seeing very little of what was right in front of him. Every bit of his attention had focused on his memories of smooth, freckled skin, wide, green eyes, and the softest, sweetest, lushest lips he'd ever tasted.

The sleep he'd gotten last night—the little of it he'd managed—had done nothing to erase the building obsession he'd developed in the twelve or so hours that he'd known Kitty Sugarman. A humbling realization for a man who'd never before applied the word "obsession" to any member of the fairer sex. But when a man spent six hours doing nothing but reliving a kiss that your average college kid would have viewed as routine, he had to face a few brutal truths. Admitting to the obsession had only gotten the ball rolling.

From there, he'd had to think about the fact that the object of his obsession bore about as much resemblance

to the women he'd become used to as she did to the calculating, money-grubbing tramp he'd originally envisioned her to be. Leo females as a rule were sophisticated,
elegant, and completely aware of their own seductive
powers. They usually exuded the sort of confidence that
bordered on arrogance and saw no benefit in underesti-
mating their own worth. They believed the word "bash-
ful" referred to nothing more than a character in *Snow
White and the Seven Dwarfs*. They didn't have dinner
with eligible men while wearing their hair in ponytails
and their faces scrubbed clean of makeup, and they certainly didn't stare at him with wide eyes full of suspicion
and innocence and tantalizing vulnerability.

No, Kitty Sugarman was like no other woman he'd
ever met. He certainly reacted to her in a way he'd never
experienced.

That intrigued him, almost as much as the woman
herself did. He'd never had any trouble responding to a
woman; he was a healthy Leo male in his prime, after
all, a future Felix of his pride. But his response to Kitty
went beyond the ordinary. He'd known her for half a day,
and he'd already decided to have her. She didn't know it
yet, but the sweet, stubborn girl with the slow southern
accent was going to be his. Soon.

Martin, he knew, would be delighted, but that meant
little more to him than the knowledge that the rest of the
pride would be horrified. Max's intentions had nothing
to do with any of them, especially since he wasn't completely sure how far beyond the initial possession those
intentions went.

Oh, he knew one fuck wasn't going to satisfy him, not
this time, but he couldn't decide how long it would take,
or if this could end up being more than sex. There was

no way of knowing this soon if the attraction between them could turn into a mating, not unless the Fates had a truly remarkable sense of timing, but wherever this took him, he intended to take Kitty along.

His mouth curved as he considered whether or not she deserved a warning. He had a feeling this might turn out to be a bumpy ride, but he also had a feeling that Ms. Sugarman was more than up to the challenge.

He was still grinning a few minutes later when he reached for his phone. He still had some work he needed to finish before he could take Kitty out to meet her father as he'd promised, and he couldn't be sure she wouldn't get restless waiting for him. Just in case she took it into her head to explore the city a little while she waited, he should arrange for someone to tag along with her. He felt pretty confident that the incident at the airport last night had been a random mugging, but with the recent tension in the pride over idiots like Billy Shepard and Peter Lowe grumbling over the line of succession, it couldn't hurt to be cautious.

Mentally, he sorted through the pride until he hit on a particular name. Ronnie Peters was about Kitty's age, had a warm, fun-loving personality, and could kick the crap out of most men twice her size. She and Kitty would probably get along like gangbusters.

Glancing at the clock, he paused. It was still early, but better to make the arrangements ahead of time. If his visitor ended up sleeping late, so be it, but if her night had been anything like his, lingering in bed alone would be the last thing in Kitty Sugarman's tempting little mind.

FOR MOST OF THE NIGHT, THE BEST SLEEP KITTY COULD manage was a light doze, and she gave up entirely when the gray sky began shifting to shades of pink, yellow, and orange. She couldn't stand to lie there for a minute longer, and she didn't think standing would do her any good, either. Not if it meant standing still. She had restless energy to burn. A walk would help. Her grandmother would have been the first to recommend it.

Kitty took a quick shower and pulled on a fresh T-shirt and the jeans she'd worn last night. The outfit was just as casual as the one she'd had on yesterday, and it did nothing to make her more comfortable in her luxurious surroundings—never in her life had she seen more complex controls for something as simple as running water!—but her first priority had just become getting *out* of those surroundings, so she didn't suppose it mattered.

When she slipped on her sandals, she spent a minute mourning the loss of her tennis shoes at the airport yesterday. But that was just another reason to get out of the hotel, she told herself. She'd find out if there was a mall or a shopping center within walking distance, pick up some new ones, and take her first look around Las Vegas while she was at it.

Remembering a certain look in Max's eyes last night, she quickly added a replacement bra to her shopping list. She could have gone without for a couple of days, but after last night, discretion seemed like the *entire* part of valor.

When she stepped out of the elevator and into the richly decorated lobby, she found it just as busy as it had been last night when she'd arrived. Instinctively, she checked her watch. Six twenty-one A.M. She hadn't mistaken that. And since a good portion of those milling about wore evening clothes, she suspected people kept different hours in this city than what she was used to.

She made her way to the concierge desk she'd noticed

last night and waited patiently for the two women in front of her to get a restaurant recommendation before she stepped forward and smiled. "Hi."

"Good morning, miss." A young man with dark hair, golden skin, and exotically tilted eyes returned her smile. "How can I assist you today?"

"Well, I'm planning on doing some sightseeing this morning, so I hoped you might point me in the right direction to stroll, but I also wondered if there was a shopping center nearby?"

The concierge blinked. "The closest place for shopping is the Savannah's Market Bazaar." He pulled out a glossy tri-fold brochure with a partial map of the hotel and used a pen to draw her a path. "You can take the casino elevators at the far end of the lobby. The floor button is clearly marked. We have more than seventy-five retailers at the Bazaar, offering everything from clothing to books and DVDs to art and home décor."

Kitty glanced to the side of the map at the list of stores. *Coach . . . Prada . . . Jimmy Choo . . . Lucky . . . Vera Wang . . . Cartier . . . Tiffany.* She fought not to choke on her tongue. She wanted to buy tennis shoes, not mortgage her first three children.

"Thanks," she managed, sounding only a little hoarse, "but what about outside the hotel? I thought it might do me good to get some fresh air while I scout for souvenirs."

The young man nodded. "Of course. The Savannah is in a great location. Las Vegas Boulevard, 'the Strip,' is right outside those doors. We're nearly surrounded by shops and restaurants, and most of the larger hotels have their own shopping centers with a variety of different retailers."

Kitty smiled. That sounded marginally cheap—er, better. "Thanks. I don't suppose you have another one of those maps back there? One that shows the hotel and the surrounding streets? Just in case I get myself all turned around."

He pulled out another piece of paper—no gloss this time—and picked up his pen. "Are you staying with us this evening?"

"Yes, why?"

"Oh, I just wanted to let you know that if you don't feel like carrying around an armload of shopping bags while you explore the city, you can tell any of the stores around here that you're our guest. Just leave them your name and they'll have the bags sent over." He handed her the map with the hotel neatly circled. "When you get back, the bags will be waiting in your room."

Kitty just nodded, smiled again, and headed for the doors. "I think I can manage a box of tennis shoes."

The day she couldn't carry her own shopping bags because she'd bought too much to manage would be the day they had a three-for-one sale on full-volume sets of the *Oxford English Dictionary*. And *that* would be a few days after she'd won the lottery.

Tucking the map into her pocket, she decided to wing it and was approaching the hotel's main entrance when a light touch to her elbow stopped her. Looking up, Kitty saw a woman a couple of years older than she was smiling at her from a pair of warm, brown eyes.

"I'm sorry, I hope this isn't rude or creepy, but you wouldn't happen to be Kitty Sugarman, would you?"

Kitty did a double take. This was her first visit to Vegas, and even back home the only people who recognized her in public were the ones who had known her since she'd been in diapers. So how was it that everyone she'd met in Nevada so far—both of them—had known who she was before she so much as looked in their direction?

"Um, excuse me?" she stalled.

"Shoot, it *is* creepy," the blonde sighed, then flashed her another friendly smile. "I swear I'm not a nut. At least, no more than the average Leo. My name is Veronica Peters, but if you have any mercy in your soul, you'll call me Ronnie." When Kitty just continued to blink at her, she extended her hand. "I'm a member of the Red Rock Pride. Max asked me to stop by the hotel this morning and see if you had everything you needed."

The Red Rock Pride. Her father's people. The ones he'd thought dangerous enough to her that he'd let her go through her entire childhood ignorant of his very existence.

It took a big dose of good southern manners for Kitty to force herself to shake the offered hand. "I'm fine, thanks."

"Good."

Ronnie's tone sounded so warm and her face looked so open and friendly that Kitty found herself struggling not to smile back.

"It looks like I just caught you on your way out," the blonde said. "You're an early riser. Did you have big plans, or were you going to play tourist for a while?"

"Tourist."

"Fab! It's a great day for it. Not too hot. How about if I tag along and show you around? Max mentioned this was your first trip to Vegas, so you don't want to be missing any of the mandatory sights."

Kitty opened her mouth to dismiss the offer but found that the words refused to come. Whether because of manners or something else entirely, she found the other woman impossible to say no to.

"I was just going to buy a new pair of tennis shoes," Kitty answered instead. "Mine got ruined yesterday."

"Oh, that's a cinch." Ronnie grinned. "There's a great little store on Harmon I can show you. Good selection and not priced for the tourists, which means it's afford-able. But it's still early, and I'm starving. Have you eaten yet? I know a place with great omelets. Come on. We can walk. That is, if you don't mind walking."

Walking was better than continuing to stand in the lobby and look like an idiot, so Kitty gave a mental shrug and followed Ronnie into the bright morning sunshine. After all, it was broad daylight and they were walking through a city crawling with people. She'd be perfectly safe. And maybe she'd stay distracted enough to keep her mind off of Max Stuart.

"I can't believe you've never been to Vegas before," Ronnie chattered, turning her head to smile at Kitty as they walked across the Savannah's entrance drive and set out along the sidewalk down Las Vegas Boulevard. "Don't tell me you're an Atlantic City girl."

Kitty shook her head. "I haven't ever been there, ei-ther. I'm not really the gambling type."

"Well, then you'll fit in like a native. Most of us have spent long enough working for the casinos that we've lost the urge to play against them. That old saying about the house always winning is right on-target."

"I'm not surprised." And she wasn't. Even if she'd been naïve enough to believe anything else, one evening in the presence of Max Stuart had been enough to demonstrate that he was not a man who would take well to losing. At anything. If he ran the Savannah's casinos, she imagined they turned a tidy profit.

She and Ronnie walked along through the crowds of tourists, who Kitty figured didn't look any more touristy than she did. She might not be wearing a Hawaiian shirt or a fanny pack, but she couldn't stop her eyes from widening at the sights around her or her head from craning to take in as much of the view as she possibly could.

She'd never seen a city as . . . electric as Las Vegas; and since it happened to be bright daylight out, that observation had very little to do with the neon lights that usually decorated every available wall of the Strip. It had the kind of pulsing energy she'd never felt before, not in Atlanta, not in New York, and certainly not in Knoxville or Chattanooga. It washed over her in a low-level hum that she didn't so much hear as she felt, ghosting along her skin.

Briskly, she rubbed her hands along her arms as if she could scrub the sensation away. She already had enough new sensory perceptions to adjust to, thank you very much.

From the corner of her eye, she saw Ronnie watching her. The other woman's laughing brown eyes seemed to be inspecting Kitty thoroughly, the tilt of her head friendly but curious. When Kitty glanced over, her companion smiled.

"So, where are you from, anyway?" Ronnie asked. "Max never bothered to tell me. From your accent, I'm guessing . . . Minneapolis?"

Kitty smiled. "St. Paul, actually, but you were close." They both laughed. "I grew up in a tiny little town you've never heard of in southeastern Tennessee. The closest place you'd likely recognize is probably Chattanooga."

Ronnie nodded. "I've never been east of Chicago, but I didn't flunk out of the sixth grade, either. That would be in the Smoky Mountains, right?"

"In the foothills, anyway. The real Smokies straddle the Tennessee–North Carolina line, and that's still a bit east of the farm."

Her escort's eyes widened. "You grew up on a farm? Like with cows and chickens and everything?"

"And the occasional horse. And pigs, too." Kitty tried to keep a straight face, but the shock and wonder on Ronnie's face was too much to resist. The other woman looked astounded that such places existed outside of re-runs of *Green Acres*. "One of my chores growing up was collecting eggs. I helped with the milking, too. Papaw didn't run a dairy herd, but he and my grandmother liked to keep a cow or two for fresh milk and butter."

"Oh, my gosh! You, like, took the eggs right from the chickens? Didn't that make them mad? Do they bite?"

"Well, they didn't love it, but I learned pretty quick how to slip in and out before they really noticed. They'll peck if you make 'em mad, but they aren't the brightest leaves on the tree."

"Wow. I can't even imagine that. I was born right here in the city. I grew up in a twelve-story apartment build-ing. The closest I've ever gotten to a farm was singing 'Old McDonald' in kindergarten."

Kitty couldn't help it. That was when she laughed. "They're not as dangerous as they sound. I promise. We only kept a few animals at home. Mostly, Papaw grew sorghum and peach trees. In fact, I learned how to drive when I was twelve. On the tractor."

Shaking her head, Ronnie slowed to a stop and reached out to push open the door of a small, quiet store. "The only wheel I got behind at twelve was on a bumper car at the amusement park. If you'd put me on a tractor, I'd likely have leveled a small city."

She grinned and motioned Kitty into the café ahead of her. They slipped into a booth and gave their orders to a prompt, cheerful waitress. While they doctored cups of strong, black coffee, Ronnie kept up her easy patter about anything and everything, drawing Kitty more and more into the conversation by asking questions about her childhood, her family back in Tennessee, and her opinion of the new trend for skinny jeans. Remarkably, Kitty found herself relaxing and laughing as if she'd known the other woman forever. They had a lot in common, including the opinion that skinny jeans looked good on absolutely no one.

By the time they dug into the omelets, which were truly spectacular, Kitty realized that talking so much really did work up an appetite. She needed a break, so maybe she should take the opportunity to ask Ronnie a question or two of her own.

"Um, do you mind if I ask you something?"

Ronnie smiled over the rim of her coffee cup. "Sure. Go ahead."

"Have you always been part of the pride? I mean, you said you grew up in the city, right?"

"Yes and yes." Ronnie slathered jam on a slice of toast. "My mother's family joined the pride right when your father formed it. She and my father had been affiliated with a small band of the others in the area, but there were a few of them in those days. Your father was the first one to pull them all together into a real pride."

"Oh, I didn't know that. I thought all Leos belonged to one pride or another."

Ronnie shook her head and chewed her bite of toast. "Most Leos do belong to a pride, partly because it's historically been more secure for us to stick to our own kind to avoid the torches and pitchforks routine, and partly because that's just how things have always been done. We call Leos not affiliated with a pride 'nomads,' but they're a lot more rare than the rest of us, and they're almost always male."

"Why's that?"

"Girls tend to live with their parents' pride longer. That's where our families and our friends are, so we don't really have any incentive to leave. The guys are different. Some make a place for them inside their family pride, but a lot of them get bent out of shape knowing they'll never get to the top of the heap unless they fight their way there."

That had Kitty blinking. "Fight?"

Ronnie nodded, her expression understanding. "Yes. We have a hierarchical system, Kitty. The Felix is the Felix because he's the strongest male in the pride. If another male wants to be his own boss and he's not the strongest in his birth pride, he has to leave. He can either find a pride with a Felix he *can* beat, or he can try to find other nomads or Leos dissatisfied with their situations and form a pride of his own."

It sounded like something out of *Mutual of Omaha's Wild Kingdom,* but Kitty didn't think her new friend would appreciate hearing it put quite that way. "That sounds very . . . uncompromising," was what she settled on instead.

Ronnie grinned. "Most of us like to stick with 'traditional,' but you're not far off the mark." She shrugged, and her smile dimmed slightly. "I suppose it must sound insane to you, but for us, it's the way things have always been. Humanity may have given up invading other humans' territories and using physical strength to gain power—in *some* parts of the world—but we aren't human. The Leo in us still has a lot in common with our animal cousins."

It wasn't like Kitty could argue with Ronnie's point. Leos, at least, weren't committing genocide, like humans in the Sudan were doing, she didn't think. And she'd never heard about Leos starting World War II. The idea that Hitler had been a Leo struck her as faintly curious. Only a human being could have possibly been so insanely evil.

She laid down her fork and reached for her coffee. "Okay, so does the fact that you're still in the pride you were born in mean that you aren't married?"

"Nope, it means I married a man in my own pride who had no desire to be in charge of everyone else's problems," Ronnie said, her eyes twinkling. "I always told my mother I'd only marry a man with a good head on his shoulders. My mate is an accountant and he says running his own life and raising a family is more than enough responsibility for any man."

Kitty looked up. "You have kids?"

"One." Ronnie's expression softened subtly and glowed with obvious pride. "A daughter. She's three and a half and grows out of a pair of shoes about every four or five hours, which is why I'm psyched you want to check out Tobin's. That's the shoe store I told you about. Are you done eating?"

Kitty nodded.

"Cool. Then let's get our check and get out of here. Before my little hellion outgrows the sneakers I haven't bought her yet!"

WHEN THEY WALKED OUT OF THE SHOE STORE AN HOUR later, Kitty was wearing a brand-new pair of white and gray tennis shoes and carrying a bag containing her old sandals and a pair of strappy black heels that Ronnie had insisted she couldn't do without.

The slim black dress Ronnie had insisted on in the last store had already been sent back to the hotel as the concierge had suggested.

"I have no idea where I'm supposed to wear these things," she said, shaking the bag and turning with her companion back toward the Savannah. "Or the cocktail dress. I'm not going to be hitting the nightclubs, for heaven's sake. The only things I brought to wear are jeans and more jeans."

"You didn't pack a single dress?"

"Why would I? I'm only going to be here for a couple of days, and it's not like I was planning on a big 'Welcome Home' celebration or anything."

Ronnie shrugged. "You can wear them to the introduction."

"What introduction?" Kitty frowned.

"The introduction to the pride. You don't *have* to get dressed up, of course, but a lot of people do."

"What on earth are you talking about? I feel like we suddenly started speaking different languages," Kitty said with a nervous half-laugh.

When Ronnie joined in with a chuckle, her amusement sounded much more genuine than Kitty's. "Sorry. I guess Max didn't mention it to you. You don't need to freak out. It's not like a huge thing, but every new member of the pride has to be officially introduced by the Felix."

Kitty just stared.

"It's kind of like an initiation, only a lot less complicated," Ronnie continued, talking faster now, as if hurrying through the explanation before Kitty, you know, passed out. "Basically, he just tells everyone he accepts you as a member of the pride and that means everyone else has to, too. It's like two minutes, but the whole pride gets together infrequently enough that a lot of people still use it as an excuse to get all dressed up." She wriggled her eyebrows to lighten the mood. "Partly because so many of them use it as an opportunity to hook up with someone new."

Kitty shook her head. With unnecessary force. "I don't think that's going to happen. I didn't come here to join the pride. Not even close. This so isn't a permanent thing. I'm only here for a few days. Maybe a couple of weeks at most. I'm not trying to become like y'all are. That's for sure."

That made Ronnie frown. "Oh, I'm sorry. I didn't realize."

"Don't worry about it. I just assumed Max explained."

They each offered the other a forced smile, then turned and continued their progress back toward the hotel. For several minutes, silence stretched between them, tense and timid.

Kitty mentally cursed herself for ruining what had seemed almost like a burgeoning friendship by slamming on the brakes as soon as the other woman mentioned joining the pride. She hadn't intended to insult

Ronnie or any of the local Leos, but she also didn't want any of them assuming she was here to stay. Especially not if that misinformation could make its way to Martin Lowe. She anticipated their meeting would be awkward enough without that kind of assumption barging its way between them.

Kind of like this meeting.

Kitty gave a mental wince. "I feel like I should explain that," she began when the silence became too heavy to bear.

"No, don't worry about it," Ronnie cut her off and offered a weak smile. "It was my mistake. No one actually said you were moving out here or anything. I just assumed. And you know what they say about assumptions and asses."

"No, really," Kitty insisted, reaching a tentative hand out to touch the other woman's arm. "I feel like a jerk. I swear I didn't mean that the way it sounded. I just meant—" She broke off, took a deep breath. "What I was saying—" Again she stopped herself. "I was only trying to let you know . . ." She closed her eyes and moaned. "Lord have mercy, I am such a jerk."

She heard Ronnie snort and peeked out from between her lashes.

"I think that's why we've gotten along so far," Ronnie said and her mouth twisted into a genuine, if wry, smile. "My brother tells me the real reason my mouth is so big is because I spend so much time with my foot in it."

Kitty laughed weakly. "I think I just choked on my kneecap." She stopped and stepped to the side of the pavement to get out of the flow of pedestrian traffic. And because the building behind her made a good support structure for her to lean against while she was weakened from her own idiocy. "I'm going to lay it out for you here, because subtlety is obviously not my strong suit, but neither is laying my problems on people I don't know all that well, so bear with me."

Ronnie nodded, her expression turning curious.

Bracing herself, Kitty started again, this time focusing not on how she sounded, but on telling the truth. It was the strategy her grandparents had always taught her to use. "I'm twenty-four years old. Until two weeks ago, I thought my father was a human kid who got drunk and died when he wrecked his car on prom night. I had no reason to think he was anything else, until I got into a wreck of my own and crawled out of it on four feet instead of two. So I'm still in something of a state of shock here."

Ronnie nodded cautiously. "That's . . . understandable."

"The thing is, I already have a family," Kitty said, "one I really love and admire, so I didn't come here trying to find that. My grandparents raised me like their own daughter, and my papaw was the best father to me any girl could ever have. No offense to Mr. Lowe, or anything, but it seems kind of late to me for either of us to pretend we're going to be like family now. It feels like a lie, and I don't like to lie." She grimaced. "Especially since I'm not real good at it."

"Well, if you didn't come here looking for your family, why are you here?"

"A question I ask myself every three and a half seconds." Kitty sighed. "I may have just found out I have a Leo for a father, but the rest of my family is human. They know even less about what I am than I do, and that's saying something. I came out here so I could learn how this shapeshifting thing works. I need to get control of it, because right now, I can't even choose when it happens. The couple of times I've changed, it's just happened, without me even thinking about it. And the last time I shifted, I got stuck. I'd still have a tail if Max hadn't been there to help me out of it."

She saw Ronnie smile and stifled a surge of pique. Maybe one day she'd be able to laugh at her own ineptitude, too.

"Basically, it comes down to fear," Kitty continued. "I'm afraid that if I don't learn how to be a Leo the right way, I could end up hurting someone, and I'd rather die than see that happen. So I'm here for a few lessons. Once I pass my finals, I'll be heading back to Tennessee where I belong. It's not because of you, though," she assured the other woman. "I just don't belong here."

"Yes, you do."

Ronnie's voice was quiet and firm and rocked Kitty back on her heels like a volcanic eruption.

"You're half-human and half-Leo," Ronnie pointed out softly, but her brown eyes fixed grave and intense on Kitty's. "To me, that means you belong with us just as much as you do with them. You just haven't given us the same chance to prove it to you."

Feeling helpless to explain herself any more clearly, Kitty's shoulder sagged. "You don't understand."

"Sure, I do. You're the one who's having trouble," Ronnie said, smiling and giving Kitty's shoulder a squeeze before linking their arms together and tugging the other woman back into the flow of traffic down the sidewalk. "You already are what you are, Kitty. Focusing on one part isn't going to make the other go away, and vice versa."

Another frustrated moan escaped Kitty's lips. "What if I try really, really hard?"

Ronnie laughed. "I can hear the violins tuning up for you, Kitty. Why are you trying to make this into such a conflict for yourself? You don't think you're the only person in the world who's ever had mixed race parents, do you?"

"This isn't black versus white, Ronnie. It's human versus animal. Those aren't races, they're species!"

"And you still aren't the only person this has ever happened to. People survive it all the time. You will, too."

"Those people probably grew up with a pretty clear idea of what they were up against. I didn't. I had two decades to get used to being human. I've had two weeks to get used to being something else. Cut me a little slack here."

"If you needed slack, I'd cut you miles of it," Ronnie said, still pulling her along toward the Savannah. "What you really need, though, is immersion therapy. I don't know what makes you think any of this will be easier if you fight it every step of the way, but I can tell you that was a dumb idea."

"Seems like I've been having a lot of those recently," Kitty muttered.

Ronnie's speech had made Kitty feel like a two-year-old throwing a temper tantrum. Not only that, but she realized that she'd been throwing it at all the wrong people. For weeks now, she'd been lashing out at anyone and everyone in her path—Papaw, Misty, Max, Ronnie. Her emotions had lumped them all together into the category of targets, and she'd been treating them accordingly, even though none of them had deserved it.

Misty hadn't been much of a mother to Kitty, but then, she'd only been sixteen when she'd gotten pregnant by an older man who left town before he even knew about the baby. What would Kitty have done in her mother's place? And some people just weren't cut out to be parents. Kitty knew that, and she'd realized a long time ago that Misty was one of them. For better or worse, Kitty's pretty, blond, spoiled mother had neither wanted nor been equipped to raise a child, but at least she'd been smart enough or lucky enough to give Kitty to Lonnie and Lily Beth Sugarman to raise. No parents could have done a better job bringing up a child that Kitty's grandparents had done with her. During her life, Kitty had been too lucky to justify her recent behavior.

A wave of shame washed over her, and for the first time since her grandmother's funeral seven years ago, Kitty felt gratitude for Lily Beth's passing. At least the woman was no longer alive to witness her granddaughter's selfish behavior.

Guilt clenched a tight fist around Kitty's stomach, and she felt overwhelmed by the need to get to a phone so she could call her papaw and apologize for the way she'd treated him just before she left. He hadn't deserved it, and she should have known better.

"Kitty?" Ronnie jiggled their linked arms a little to get Kitty's attention. "Are you okay? You just went a little pale."

"I'm fine," Kitty assured her, forcing herself to smile. "I think you just knocked a little bit of sense into me. At least enough to make me realize I owe you an apology. I'm sorry for being such a brat just now. Being a little shaken up is no excuse for bad manners."

Ronnie laughed. "Swectie, it is nothing to worry about.

I need to introduce you to my daughter. Maybe some of those southern manners of yours will rub off on her."

"I mean it. I behaved like a jerk. If I'm going to be mad, I should at least try to take it out on the right person. And you are not him."

Ronnie leveled her an assessing gaze. "Who is he, then? Your father?"

"He's the one who apparently knew about me for twenty-three years without so much as making the effort to return the favor."

They traveled another block in silence until the rich, red stone of the Savannah's exterior came into view near the horizon. It took that long before Ronnie voiced her reply.

"You know, I'm not going to say I wouldn't feel the same way in your position," she said, her tone slow and serious, "but I think you might want to meet Martin before you decide to hate him. He has a side to the story, too, and it just might be worth hearing."

Kitty shook her head. "I can't imagine how. A lifetime of neglect is a big wrong to make up for."

"It is," Ronnie agreed, fixing her gaze on the hotel ahead, "but you may find that sometimes people do the wrong thing because it's more right than the alternatives."

SEVEN

KITTY'S MIND REPLAYED THE CONVERSATION WITH Ronnie all the way across the lobby and toward the bank of elevators leading up to her room. As she rounded the corner and reached out to press the call button, she collided with an immovable object and let out a breathless grunt.

A pair of strong hands gripped her arms to steady her and a familiar voice rumbled above her head.

"Whoa, careful there," Max drawled. "Where's Ronnie?"

"She, uh, she had to get home," Kitty said, trying to push past him. She knew she owed him an apology, too, but she'd been hoping a call to her grandfather would buck her up before she had to do it.

"Kitty?" His voice deepened, filling with concern. "Honey, what's wrong? Did something happen?"

She shook her head again, again tried to pull away. His fingers didn't budge. "It's nothing. I'm fine."

"You don't look fine," Max said, shifting his grip so that his arm curved around her and pressed her inexorably to his side. "Come with me."

"I can't. I have things to do." She tried to pull away, but

it was like walking into a gale-force wind—full of effort and bereft of progress. "I have to make a phone call."

"We're going to talk first." He guided her into the elevator and used his access card to select a button. "Then you can use the phone in my office."

"There's a perfectly good phone in my room," she muttered.

"Actually, there are six of them, but my office is closer."

The elevator dinged, the doors slid open, and that arm shifted, applying the pressure necessary to herd her out of the car and into a plushly carpeted hall that looked nothing like the one leading to her room. This one was gray and masculine and pitted with open doors leading to offices and conference rooms. He guided her to the far end and through an archway, past a calm middle-aged woman in a prim suit, then through another door and into his office.

Kitty recognized the room instantly, even if this was the first time she'd seen it. The color scheme, the furnishings, the electronics, everything bore the stamp of Max's personality—strong, efficient, and quite aware of its own worth. Two walls were completely lined with windows, the farthest of them looking onto the city, the nearest overlooking the floor of the casino. In front of the closer set, a huge cherry desk stretched across a vivid Oriental carpet with two elegant leather chairs stationed before it. Max forced her gently into one, then perched on the edge of the desk in front of her and fixed her with a penetrating stare.

"Now," he rumbled, "tell me what's going on."

"Nothing."

"What's bothering you, Kitty?"

"Nothing is bothering me," she ground out.

"Kitty."

Her name was a warning. She gritted her teeth.

"Everything is fine," she insisted. "I just want to make a phone call."

"Tell me what happened. I know you went out with Ronnie this morning. Did she do something to upset you? I thought you two would get along or I would have sent someone else to check on you."

"I'm not upset," Kitty insisted. Sheesh. And she'd thought *she* was stubborn. "I just think it might be better if—"

"Kitty Jane," he cautioned, "you need to stop lying to me and start talking. What happened while you were out with Ronnie?"

Kitty glared at him. "You said I could use the phone in your office."

"I lied." He stood and reached behind him to grab a key ring he'd left near the edge of his blotter. Then he pressed a button and spoke into the air. "Cynthia, can you ask the garage to pull my car out? I'm taking Ms. Sugarman out to Martin's in a few minutes. Tenby knows, so you can forward my calls and any priority issues to him for the rest of the day."

Kitty heard a brisk female voice reply, "Yes, sir," and focused an even more intense glare on him.

"Excuse me, but did I miss part of this conversation?" she asked, pushing herself to her feet and taking two steps back. She didn't need to have him looming over her while she wrestled against his intimidating presence. "Like the part where you asked if I was ready to go see my father? Because I don't recall saying I was."

"I made an executive decision. I'm an executive." He

slid his hand beneath her elbow and turned her gently but firmly toward the door.

"But I'm not your employee." Kitty dug her heels into the carpet and scowled up at him. "Why is it that every time you don't like what I have to say to you, you think you can just resort to physical intimidation to get your way?"

He glanced down at her, looking bemused. "Is that what I do?"

"Yes, in case you hadn't noticed. You're doing it now, and you did it just a few minutes ago when I wanted to go up to my room. And last night after dinner, when you—"

The memory of what he'd done last night to convince her to stay in Vegas flooded through her, and Kitty broke off abruptly. Heat rushed into her cheeks and she cursed herself for bringing that up. The last thing this man needed was for her to acknowledge what happened to all her independence and determination when he kissed her.

Unfortunately, the spark that flared in his eyes as he halted at his office door told her that he'd figured it out all on his own. The hand on her elbow teased and stroked a slow path up to the side of her neck, left bare by her high ponytail.

"Ah, yes. Last night," he murmured, the sound rumbling out of his chest in a purr Tony the Tiger couldn't have rivaled. "As I recall, last night we came to a mutual understanding about what might come out of this visit."

"I think 'mutual' might be overstating things just a smidge."

"Do you?" His eyes sparked. "Well then, let's see if I can't refresh your memory."

The mental command telling her feet to move didn't even have time to make it to her spinal cord, let alone to her legs, before his mouth was on her.

His lips covered her, warm, insistent, and already much too familiar for Kitty's peace of mind. He tasted just as she remembered, like bitter coffee, sweet temptation, and rich, warm sin. She could get drunk on the taste of him, she thought; and when she felt her knees tremble, she knew she already had.

Her skin tightened and trembled when his arm slid behind her, curving about her waist like a living shackle from which she couldn't quite bring herself to escape. His hand gripped her about the ribs, gently but firmly, his thumb stroking through the soft material of her T-shirt just inches below her breast. The sudden awareness of it drew her nipples into tight points and sent shards of aching frustration deep into her belly.

It didn't matter how her conscious mind struggled against his touch; her body had already surrendered. She could no more have stopped her lips from parting before the surge of his tongue than she could have stopped the rain from falling. Her hands gripped his shoulders completely against her will, and it certainly wasn't her rational mind urging her hips to arch against him, to form a soft, welcoming cradle for the heavy thrust of his erection.

Dear God, what was he doing to her?

When the kiss ended, Kitty flushed at the knowledge that it had been Max who drew back, not her. Lord help her, but she didn't have that kind of strength.

"I don't know, kitten," he rumbled, the sound making her thighs clench together. "That felt pretty mutual to me."

It took much too long for Kitty to drag her jumbled thoughts into some semblance of order and even longer for her to regain control of her mouth enough to speak. "You know that isn't what I meant."

"True." He leaned forward, lips brushing the corner

of her mouth. "But isn't this so much pleasanter than arguing? Especially since you already know I'm going to get my way."

The arrogance in that statement did manage to banish a few of the cobwebs strung by his kiss, at least enough to allow her to muster a weak glare. "You jackass," she muttered. "How on earth do you manage to fit that ego through the lobby doors?"

He grinned and flicked a finger across her cheekbone. "We measured ahead of time, of course. I've got a quarter inch to spare."

The quirk of his lips invited her to laugh with him, but she wasn't ready to hand him quite that large a victory.

"Fine," she sighed. "I'll go now, but we're putting a time limit on this visit. "We need to leave early enough for me to make my call from the car on the way back."

"Deal." Max reached out and took her hand, pulling her gently toward the door. "I'll even let you use my cell. You can tell your grandfather I said hello."

Kitty just blinked. How could he possibly have gotten to know her so well in such a short period of time?

EIGHT

MAX TOLD HER THAT HER FATHER'S HOUSE SAT ABOUT twenty-five miles outside of Las Vegas, nestled in an open desert canyon that bordered the Desert National Wildlife Refuge. In his sleek, well-tuned Mercedes, the drive took approximately a hundred and forty-seven years.

Kitty sat in the passenger seat with her hands folded in her lap and her gaze fixed on the scenery passing by, wriggling her toes inside her new tennis shoes. For the first fifteen minutes or so of the trip, Max sat silently behind her, his attention focused on maneuvering through the city traffic, but once they settled into the flow of the highway, he glanced over at her.

"You and Ronnie must have been out for a while this morning," he said. "You got a little sunburned."

"Did I?" she asked, and reached up to touch the bridge of her nose. It felt slightly warm, but she didn't want to curse when she pressed on it. She shrugged. "I've had worse. I burn like nobody's business. Sometimes, I think I only have to think too hard about the beach before I'm reaching for the aloe."

"With your skin, I'm not surprised. Does it hurt much?"

She looked at him. "No, why?"

His attention remained on the road. "I just thought that might be the reason your knuckles are whiter than your new tennis shoes."

Kitty shifted her attention back to the scenery. "How do you know it's not your driving?"

"Because they've looked like that since I said we were coming out here, and that was while we were still in my office."

"Maybe I'm remembering last night."

"I know *I* am," he purred. "And this morning."

She ignored him. Her nerves had already tied themselves in enough knots over meeting her father. She didn't need Max throwing their uncontrollable attraction to each other into the mix. A girl could only take so much, after all.

"You're the one who spent last night telling me horror stories about the warm welcome I'm likely to get at my father's house," she said, ignoring his comment. "I think it's perfectly natural for me to be a little nervous."

"The only person at your father's house who needs to welcome you is your father. And trust me when I tell you, he's going to be very pleased to see you."

"Right. It's just his kids who are going to want to rip out my intestines."

He arched an eyebrow. "I think that's unnecessarily graphic. Besides, while your father and I are there, no one is going to do anything to you. You'll be under our protection, and no one in the pride would try to challenge that."

Kitty snorted. "It's good to be the king, I guess."

His grin flashed. "It beats the alternatives."

"Do you think any of the family or . . . the pride . . . Will they be there today?"

"I can't say for sure," he hedged, "but there's always a possibility. Martin has been excited about your visit, so he's been talking you up. I'm sure they're curious about you."

Max paused for a minute, then resumed with a note of caution in his voice. "I should warn you, just so you're not surprised, that you will see a couple of guards outside Martin's house. I swear they have nothing to do with you, but I don't want you to feel like you're walking into some kind of army base."

Kitty turned to look at him, genuinely surprised. "Guards? Why would he need guards?"

"He probably doesn't, but I like to be cautious." Max sighed. "There have been a few rumors circulating lately that not everyone is happy about a recent decision your father made."

"What kind of decision?"

For the first time since she'd met him, Max looked uncomfortable. "Leading a pride isn't actually like being a king. It's not a hereditary title."

"I know. Ronnie told me about it this morning. She said it's actually a position given to the strongest male in the pride."

"She's right, although 'given' isn't quite the word I'd use. Back in the bad old days, members of the pride used to fight for it. Literally. Whoever thought they had the right stuff would issue a challenge, and if he defeated the current Felix, he could assume the loser's place." He must have seen the look on her face, because he rushed to reassure her. "That doesn't happen much anymore. I promise. These days, more often than not, there's a second-in-command of the pride—we call him the *baas*—who's ready to step into the old leader's shoes when the Felix decides to retire, or in case something happens to him. That way, the transition goes more smoothly and everyone stays out of trouble."

Kitty's mouth quirked. "Let me guess. In this case, that would be you."

"Yeah. Usually, a Leo emerges as the right choice for the position in a way that everyone recognizes. He's just the right guy for the job, so everyone assumes he'll be the next Felix when the time comes. Occasionally, though, if another Leo is making noises about wanting to take over, the Felix will formalize the *baas*'s position by officially naming him heir. It's supposed to make challengers think twice."

"Does that really work?"

Max shrugged. "Sometimes, but in this case, not everyone seems to be happy with Martin's decision."

"Which would be you."

He nodded. "Since I'm younger than your father, it's possible a challenger might decide to circumvent the succession by challenging him, thinking he'll be easier to defeat. And technically, anyone who defeats the sitting Felix automatically assumes his authority."

"So that's why you have guards at my father's house," she concluded. It did make a weird, primitive sort of sense, she supposed. But it also made her think how alien the culture of the Leos seemed to her.

"It's just a precaution," Max assured her, "and I'm probably being overprotective, but I'd rather do that than risk the alternative."

"Okay. Thanks for the warning." She mustered up a smile and felt her stomach flutter again as Max began to steer the car toward an exit. "Is there anything else I should know about before we get there?"

She had expected him to give her an automatic "No," maybe laugh and tease her for being paranoid. The fact that he remained silent and frowning at the view outside the windshield turned the flutter into a full-blown knot-tying contest.

"No," he finally answered, still frowning. "I think it would be better if you just went in and let things happen naturally. There's no sense in getting yourself worked up before we even arrive."

"Oh, goodie," Kitty muttered, sinking lower into her seat. "I can hardly wait."

SHE HAD THE SAME REACTION TO MARTIN LOWE'S HOUSE that she'd had to his hotel, a bit of awe mixed with growing unease, and Max had no trouble reading her thoughts on her face. He found the trait refreshing after a lifetime of dealing with those who thought of transparent emotions as a weakness. He worried, though, that it could give others in the pride an upper hand. He'd have to watch over her carefully. Somehow, it didn't seem like a hardship.

Thankfully, the wide drive in front of the house was empty when he pulled the Mercedes to a stop. They must have arrived earlier than the others expected. He had a feeling they wouldn't be leaving without a face-off, but Max was glad it wouldn't happen until after Martin and Kitty had the chance to meet for the first time. They both deserved this moment without the inevitable warfare that would follow.

He helped Kitty out of the car and led her toward the house in silence, nodding to the two guards without stopping. He had to bite back the urge to reassure the woman beside him, but she was so wound up already, he sensed that having him tell her that everything was going to be fine would either make her distrust him or send her running in the opposite direction. Neither would do her any favors with her father or with the pride.

Using his key, he let them into the front hall and paused to listen. He could hear the hum of medical equipment and the low drone of voices on the television in Martin's room but no live voices. That was good. Max imagined the housekeeper was likely in the kitchen at the rear of the house and he knew at least two more security guards would be patrolling the grounds, but the lack of cars in the drive hadn't lied. He and Kitty were the first ones here.

He saw Kitty take a deep breath and straighten her shoulders like a warrior preparing for battle, and he felt a surge of pride. The last few weeks had turned her entire world upside down, but she just seemed to take every challenge as it came. Even when he knew her first instinct was to run, she never gave in to the urge. She faced her demons head-on and refused to back down.

Martin was going to love her.

Before he led her back to the Felix's suite, Max touched her arm to get her attention. When she looked up at him, he asked her, "Did Martin tell you anything about his health?"

"Like I said, I haven't spoken directly to him," she said, her brows drawing together, "but his lawyers mentioned that was because he'd been ill and sometimes had trouble carrying on long conversations. They said he still had some respiratory issues. Why?"

Silently, Max cursed. Damn Burkett and his almighty sense of discretion. Someone should have told her how serious things were. At least warned her. Max didn't want her walking into that room blind, but at this point, what could he say? It was a little late to prepare her to visit someone in her father's state.

"He's still ill," Max finally said. "I think he should be the one who tells you about his disease, but you should at least know that he's on oxygen and his doctors have him on electronic monitors. I don't want that to shock you."

Max watched her, searching her face while she processed the information. He saw glimpses of surprise, confusion, anger, unease, and even a trace of worry before she took another of those deep breaths and gave him a wry smile.

"I guess it's a good thing I didn't insist he come to me, then," she said. "I thought about issuing that ultimatum, you know. I figured he owed me."

"He does," Max said, taking her hand and squeezing gently. "But coming to you wouldn't have been possible." He watched her for another second, then tucked a stray piece of hair behind her ear and smiled down at her. She'd summoned up a carefully pleasant mask to hide her unease, making her look calm and strong and quietly regal. It was perfect. "Come on, then. I'll introduce you."

Raising her hand to his lips, he pressed a kiss to her chilled skin and tugged her forward.

The private nurse had left the door to Martin's room partly open, but Max knocked on the dark panels before pushing it wide. He'd called before he and Kitty left the hotel to let the older man know they were coming today, and Martin had gotten himself ready. He'd had himself dressed in an elegant pair of striped blue pajamas with neatly pressed lapels, his thinning hair neatly combed, and he'd obviously had a bath that morning. He sat upright in his bed, propped up on well-fluffed pillows like a king on his throne. He looked better than Max had seen him in weeks.

"Come in," he said, and though his voice didn't boom like it used to, it sounded strong enough to merit the tone of the command. "There's been enough waiting done around here, don't you think?"

Max grinned. Trust the Felix to cut right to the heart of the matter. "I brought you a visitor, Martin, but if you don't behave yourself, I can just take her back again."

Martin snorted. "Try it, boy, and you'll find out my bite is still worse than my roar. Where is she?"

Very aware of Kitty's position behind him, Max reached back to reclaim her hand. "Martin, I'd like you to meet Miss Kitty Sugarman. Kitty, this is Martin Lowe."

Max gave a single, gentle tug on her hand and found it unnecessary. Of her own accord, Kitty stepped around him and into the room as if she'd done this a thousand times. He noticed the square set of her shoulders and the upward tilt to her chin and felt like applauding. She took in her father's condition with a glance and never blinked.

"How do you do, sir?" she asked, her voice cautious but strictly polite.

Her father barked a laugh. "I'm still breathing, girl, and these days that's the most I ask for." He waved her toward him. "Come closer. I want to get a look at you."

Max saw the chin notch higher, but Kitty moved until she stood just out of reach of the bed.

"I suppose you can have a look, sir," she said coolly, "while I have one of my own."

The subtle reprimand had Martin grinning like a loon. "I see you inherited a mouth from somewhere."

"It came free with the ear and nose set."

The Felix laughed harder than Max remembered him doing since his diagnosis, hard enough to send Martin into a coughing fit. Max stepped forward, intending to get Martin a glass of water or thump his back, but Kitty was already moving. Gently, she grasped her father's thin forearms and raised them high over his head.

"Keep your arms up," she instructed. "It'll help your airways clear."

Sure enough, after two more rattling coughs, Martin drew in a deep, labored breath and collapsed back against his pillows. "You some kind of nurse or something?"

"No, a librarian," Kitty responded calmly, "but I come fully equipped with common sense and a certificate in first aid. Why? Are you looking to hire some help?"

"I'm looking to get rid of some," Martin grumbled, "but every time I fire them, that interfering son of a gun hires them back."

The younger man shrugged and kept his expression bland. "Well I'm sure as hell not going to be the one giving you sponge baths, old man."

To Max's surprise, Kitty shot him a scolding glance and perched her hip on the edge of her father's bed. "So," she said, folding her hands in front of her, "I hear we might be related."

"Might be?" Martin grinned. "Little girl, you've got

Lowe written all over you. I'm just tickled to death to finally be meeting you."

"You could have done that a long time ago."

Kitty's voice held no accusation, but the truth dented Martin's grin. "I know that," he sighed, "and I've already put it on the list of the things I'm ashamed of. All I can say for myself is that at the time I thought it would be for the best."

Max recognized his cue to leave. He put his hand on Kitty's shoulder and squeezed. When she looked up at him, he leaned down to her. "I'll be right outside if you need me, kitten."

She nodded, and he slipped quietly out of the room.

The temptation to hover near the door and listen almost overwhelmed his good intentions. He knew father and daughter needed privacy to become acquainted, but Max's instincts kept urging him to stay with them. He cared about them both. Martin had been like a father to Max for more than half of his life, and Kitty . . .

Max jammed his hands into his pockets and prowled toward the front of the house. In just a few short hours of acquaintance, Kitty had managed to make a place for herself inside of him that he didn't know if he could dislodge her from. He wasn't even sure he wanted to. If he hadn't known it was too soon to tell, he would already be calling her his mate.

Wandering into the living room at the front of the house, Max stood before the huge many-paned window and looked out over the front of the property without seeing a thing. The timing almost didn't matter to him at all. Something inside him already recognized Kitty as his mate and to hell with tradition.

Leos had their own way of choosing mates, a way not entirely human and not entirely leonine. Unlike their animal cousins, Leos did mate for life, or at least for long-term monogamous relationships. Like humans, they dated until they found the right person, but the recognition of someone as the "right person" didn't come from an intellectual and emotional comparison of common interests and visions of the future.

Leo mating was more basic than that. A male recognized his mate when she went into heat for the first time in his presence, and a female recognized it when her heat was triggered at the wrong time of the month by her new mate. In an animal pride, male lions seized control of a group of females and killed their cubs to force the females into estrus. Leos didn't take things that far—at least not in the modern age—but Fate had decided that the right male would still act as a trigger for his female mate to come into heat within the first two weeks of their relationship, no matter what stage of her normal cycle she might otherwise have been at.

In a way, it made things simple. Boy meets girl. Boy and girl date. After the first few dates, boy's presence stimulates girl to ovulate. Boy detects the change in her scent and does what comes naturally. Boy and girl live happily ever after. In theory.

The problem was that Max didn't think Kitty would see things in quite the same way. Even if he was right and they were destined to be mates, he had a niggling feeling she wouldn't like the idea of her body choosing the man she should settle down with. And when Max put his ego aside, he also got the feeling that he wouldn't be the kind of man she would choose for herself.

No matter how sweetly she responded to his kisses,

no matter how quickly her body melted to his touch, Max knew he made Kitty uneasy. He didn't think he frightened her; it wasn't that kind of unease, but she had trouble relaxing around him in a way that had nothing to do with their mutual attraction.

He could only speculate on the cause at this point, but he had already come up with two plausible explanations, and he thought it might just be a combination of them both. First came the fact that lots of things made Kitty uneasy right now. She'd just found out she wasn't the person—the human—she'd always believed herself to be, and she'd just found out she had a father she hadn't known existed. That would make anyone uncomfortable in their skin for a while. But the second reason had less to do with who Kitty was than with who Max was.

For some reason, Max got the impression that Kitty thought he was out of her league. It made no sense to him. He might only have known her for less than a day, but he already knew her to be beautiful, intelligent, capable, tough, spirited, and generous. He also knew the taste of her made him drool and the feel of her made his palms itch. In his mind, she had absolutely no reason for self-doubt, but he could read it on her face nonetheless.

He'd seen it the first time when he told her about her father owning the Savannah, and it had lingered on her face the entire time Max had been showing her around her suite. He'd seen it again when she'd sat down to dinner with him last night, and it had returned this morning when he drove her onto her father's property. The only thing that made sense was that she was intimidated by her father's and Max's wealth, which in his mind was completely ridiculous.

Money meant very little to Max. It made a good way of keeping score, he supposed, and he had to admit that he had gotten used to the things it could buy over the last few years, but it wasn't something that ruled him. He'd grown up in circumstances that made some of Vegas's slums look luxurious, and he could still remember what cold and hunger felt like. He preferred not to feel them again, but he didn't fear them. He'd built this life for himself, and as secure as it was, he knew that if one day it disappeared to leave him with nothing, in time he would be able to build it again. He didn't even waste time thinking about it.

He got the impression, though, that Kitty did.

How long he stood brooding in front of the window, Max wasn't sure, but when his eyes caught a flash of light at the far end of the long drive, he cursed under his breath. He hoped Kitty and Martin had made good use of the time since he'd left them alone, because it looked like the house was about to get a lot more crowded.

NINE

AFTER MAX'S WHISPERED REASSURANCE TO KITTY, HE
had slipped silently out of the room, and that was saying
something, since she and Martin had both gone so quiet,
you could have heard a pin drop over the hum of his
monitors.

The long silence, tense and awkward, stretched between them for slow-moving minutes. Kitty thought
about breaking it, wanted to break it, but now that this
moment had come, she couldn't think how. She'd grown
up fantasizing about all the things she wished she could
say to the father she'd thought was dead. She'd wanted to
tell him stories about lost teeth and schoolyard fights,
academic triumphs and girlish crushes. She'd wanted him
around to come to parent-teacher conferences and for
her to brag about to her friends, but over the years she'd
resigned herself to the fact that she wouldn't ever be able
to tell those tales to her father, and her grandfather had
been the best substitute she could ever have asked for.
She'd grown up, she'd thought.

Then, her world had turned upside down, and suddenly she had the opportunity to tell her father anything
she'd wanted, because he wasn't dead; he was alive, and

he wanted to meet her. But by now, she'd had a couple of weeks to think up thousands of insults to hurl at the head of the living man who had known about her for twenty-three years and never bothered to pick up a phone or send an e-mail or show his face to her.

She had lingered over those plans of hers, savoring them like a bittersweet delicacy. In her mind, she'd called him every foul name she'd ever heard, a couple she couldn't pronounce, and a few she'd just made up on the fly. The anger she'd generated had helped her through the days of shock and confusion, had given her something to think about beyond the pain of losing her very sense of identity and the fear of the new future that might be waiting for the person she'd just become.

But now . . .

Sitting here at the bedside of this wasted man, whose disease had added decades to a face that had obviously been handsome in its day . . . now she wasn't sure. It would have been easier for her if he'd had horns and a pitchfork, like she'd occasionally imagined, or an obvious God complex, or a disdainful sneer. Anything to help her put her back up and to fuel the resentment and anger she'd carried with her all the way from Tennessee. God, though, didn't seem inclined to answer her prayers.

Maybe it was the exhaustion of a sleepless night after a day of grueling travel, or maybe the lingering memory of the botched attempt on her life, but in that moment, facing the father she had prepared herself to hate, Kitty found that the feeling currently overwhelming her seemed more like . . . a sense of being in the right place at the right time.

Of course, that was tempered by a big ol' cloud cover of fear with the potential for occasional periods of light panic.

She forced herself to sit calmly on the edge of his bed and watch him watch her with eyes the exact color of her own. She could think of absolutely nothing to say.

Her father finally made the first move, awkward though it was. Clearing his throat, he adjusted the thin tube of plastic under his nose and shifted his stare to a point she calculated was somewhere over her left shoulder. "I, ah, hope you had a pleasant flight."

"It was fine. Very little turbulence."

"Good. Good." He smoothed a crepe-skinned hand over the bedspread. "And I understand Max put you up at the Savannah last night. I hope your room is comfortable?"

"Very. It's very comfortable. It's amazing, in fact."

Kitty felt a bead of sweat develop along her hairline. Sweet baby Jesus! The conversation during her first date hadn't been this awkward.

Come to think of it, she doubted the negotiations at the Treaty of Versailles had been this awkward. For the Germans.

"I had hoped that you would come and stay at the house for a few days," Martin ventured, now possibly looking at her shoulder itself. "It would give us more time to get to know each other."

"That sounds . . ." *As appealing as covering myself with maple syrup and lying on top of a hill of fire ants.* ". . . like a lot of trouble for you," she said, forcing a smile. "I couldn't impose."

"It's not an imposition."

"You're very kind, but I couldn't put you out tha—"

His frown deepened into a scowl, and he made it all the way to her left temple. "You're not putting anyone out. I want you to stay here."

"Really, I'd prefer to stay in town."

"And I'd prefer you to stay here!"

She gritted her teeth and felt her dander rise. "I appreciate the offer, but I'm happy with the hotel."

The scowl became a glower, one aimed square into her eyes. "Damn it, girl, you're my daughter! You should stay in my house!"

"And you should mind your own business, you old dictator!" she shouted back, her control snapping. So much for the whole peaceful thing. "If you wanted me around so much, maybe you should have done something about it two decades ago!"

Kitty ended on her feet with her hands clenched into fists, her chin thrust forward, and smoke pouring out of her ears. For a long, tense moment, neither of them said a word. They just tried to glare each other into submission like a couple of junkyard dogs. All one of them needed to do was use a leg to scratch behind the ears and the image would be complete.

Still, no matter how ridiculous the two of them looked, she refused to be the one to back down. Her temper had been riding her for weeks now. At the moment, the release of a good long shouting match sounded right up her alley.

After a few seconds, she saw Martin's jaw shift and something sparked in his bright green eyes. He pursed his lips and gave her an evaluating once-over. "I'll say one thing for you, girl: you've got guts. There aren't many Leos in this world who'd be willing to take your tone with me."

Girl? Wow, *was he a charmer.*

"I'll take any tone I like with you," she growled. "I don't take orders from men I don't know, and I am not staying in the same house with a bunch of strangers just because we happen to share a chromosome or twenty. I don't know you, so it's not like I can possibly trust you at this point."

The man had the nerve to grin. "Feel good to get that off your chest, girl?"

"My name," she gritted out, "is Kitty."

Martin snorted, still smiling. "I know, but that doesn't mean I'm going to call you that. What your mother was thinking when she named you, I cannot possibly fathom."

"Probably not, since you weren't there."

His smile cracked. "I can't go back and change the past. It's a little late to ask me to tuck you in at night, don't you think?"

"I'm not asking you for that," she said, her hands clenching into fists at her sides. The mix of anger and elation and hurt and confusion threatened to overwhelm her, but she refused to let him see it. "I didn't come here to see what you could give me, and I didn't come here to run into your warm embrace."

"So why did you come here?"

That was a good question.

Kitty clenched her teeth and took a deep breath. Part of her wanted to give him the telling-off she'd always imagined, to let him know how much it had hurt to learn he'd been out there all along and never once contacted her. But now, looking into her father's stubborn face, she started to wonder if it really mattered anymore.

Probably not, she admitted to herself. Honestly, the past was past, no matter how bad a part of her wanted to pull it into the present. And that was really the crazy part. Her past had actually been pretty great. Missing father or not, she'd had a good home, a family who loved her, and everything she needed to grow up strong and secure and independent. It was her present that was giving her nightmares.

The thought drained the tension from Kitty like pulling the stopper in the bathtub. Suddenly the urge to fight was gone and she found herself almost wanting to laugh at the absurdity of arguing with this man over something he'd done before she'd even been born. As her grandfather would have said, she hadn't walked in her daddy's shoes, so how could she know if the toes didn't pinch?

Kitty looked down at the new tennis shoes Max had immediately noticed, and grinned. When she raised her eyes back to her father's face, the smile lingered. "You know, all of a sudden, the answer I rehearsed for that question seems a little silly."

Martin sighed and waved a hand in a gesture of invitation. "Well come on, then. Let me have it. I'm sure you must have been saving up for me, and I won't deny I deserve to catch hell for some of what I've done to you, so let it out. I'm ready."

She shook her head. "Sorry to disappoint you, Mr. Lowe, but to be honest? I got nothin'. I think I've already yelled just about every fool thing I can think of to yell. How about we just agree to tell everyone we had a great big fight and leave it at that? That way we can go right on to the next stage of this thing."

Martin looked surprised, then wary. "What exactly is the next stage?"

"I'm no expert, but I'll admit I have a couple of questions I'd like to ask you."

He hesitated; then after a moment he nodded. "All right. Go ahead and ask me."

"When you left Tennessee, did you know Misty was pregnant?"

Kitty's father didn't shake his head, but he didn't nod, either. He just watched her for a moment with shrewd, green eyes.

"Yes," he finally acknowledged, his voice quiet. "And no."

She just raised her eyebrows and waited.

"Of course it was always a possibility," he said, "so we both thought about it that way, I suppose, but I didn't think it was likely. I was a randy young stud in my day, but usually I had enough sense to take precautions. 'Randy' and 'usually,' though, have gotten better men than me into messes like this, so I knew there was a chance. But I'd already made up my mind to leave town, and strangely enough, having your mother tell me she was pregnant was the thing that convinced me she couldn't possibly be." He paused. "That probably sounds like a load of bullshit to you, doesn't it?"

"Actually"—Kitty smiled wryly—"less than you might think." She searched his gaze. "She'd been trying to get you to stay, hadn't she?"

He frowned. "Mostly, she'd been trying to get me to take her with me. If she could use me to get out of Tennessee, she meant to do it. How did you know? Did she tell you?"

"Of course not. That would be admitting she failed. But I know Misty. I've known her all my life, in fact, and that's just what I'd expect she'd do."

"I thought she was lying to get me to take her with me when I left town," Martin admitted, looking even wearier than he had when Kitty had entered the room. "I assumed that if I gave in, she'd wait until we were too far from her family for me to just kick her out of a motel room and then she'd 'discover' that it was a false alarm. Or maybe she'd suddenly have a 'miscarriage.' So I ignored her, and I left."

Kitty nodded. "That sounds about right." She really could sympathize with Martin's belief that Misty would have done anything to get her way, no matter how dishonest or immoral it might have been. Not that Misty was a bad person. She was just an incredibly selfish one. She always had been, and Kitty had long ago resigned herself to the knowledge that her mother always would be.

Her other question came out before she'd even gotten a chance to think about it, which might have been for the best.

"If you knew about me from the time I was a year old, why didn't you ever contact me? Why did you let me grow up thinking I didn't have a father, and thinking the one I'd lost was somebody else?"

Martin closed his eyes and seemed to sink back into the bedding behind him. "Because I was an idiot. That's the only thing I can tell you, and I wish it weren't such a poor excuse, but there it is."

Kitty stared at him for a moment, her breath caught in her throat, her heart seemingly stalled in her chest. "That's it?" she finally said, her voice quiet against the drone of the monitors. "That's all you have to say about it?"

"I had answers rehearsed, too, you know," he answered, opening his eyes to glare at her. "I was going to tell you I thought I was doing what was best, that I thought I was protecting you. And I suppose that's what I told myself back then. I told myself over and over that because there was no guarantee that you'd ever shift, you were better off with your mother. I told myself you'd always be at risk here just because you'd be smaller and weaker than any of the other children. I told myself that I was protecting you, but the truth is I was a damned fool." He shifted his gaze to his blankets, as if he couldn't bear to continue meeting Kitty's. "I'd come west by then, and I'd decided to settle in this area. I'd already issued the challenge to my ex-wife's father, and I knew Drusilla wouldn't welcome the idea of raising another woman's daughter. It was just easier to tell myself you were better off where you were."

Kitty sat in the heavy silence and waited for the wave of anger and hurt to come rushing back, but it never did. She could hear the guilt and self-disgust echoing in her father's voice, and all she really felt was a kind of pity. He'd robbed himself of more than he'd ever taken from her, she realized. She'd grown up in a loving home, while he'd given up his own child for the sake of a relationship that still hadn't survived. Which of them had really ended up worse off?

"I was a coward," Martin blurted out, sounding as if the silence had dragged the words from his lips. "Not claiming you from the beginning is the only thing in my life that I truly regret. If I could go back and change it, I swear to you I would."

Kitty felt her mouth begin to curve and felt a weight begin to lift from her shoulders. She shook her head. "It's okay. Really. It's fine."

Martin shook his head. "Why aren't you cursing me out right now?" he demanded.

She grinned. "I did that a few minutes ago. And last night and this morning. Not to mention two weeks ago in Tennessee. Don't tell me you didn't hear me? I got noise complaints from vacationers on Lake Michigan." Her father snorted at her teasing, and Kitty grew more serious. "Honestly, I don't know why I'm not slapping your face right now. I came to town fully prepared to do it. I'm sure the beginning of our conversation made that clear."

Martin's wonder morphed into a scowl. "It's because you feel sorry for me, isn't it? You just don't want to upset the invalid."

She pretended to think about that. "No, actually, I don't think I'm all that worried about upsetting you. If I thought you deserved it, I think I'd be fully willing to kick your behind, even if you are sick. I think I might prefer it that way. It'd be easier, at least. As much as I prefer a fair fight in most cases, weak as a pup is probably the only way I could ever put you down. Besides," she teased, "I plan to use you like a Kleenex while I'm here. I've got a lot to learn about being a Leo. I figured your penance could be to teach me."

He snorted again, and Kitty sobered, shaking her head. "I don't know if it's because of that lack of sleep I mentioned and I'm too tired to get back on the road, or if maybe I just had some great spiritual awakening. Or maybe I'm just squeamish about blood. Whatever. The bottom line is that when I listen to your side of the story, all I can think about is that if I'd been in your position, I might have done the same blessed thing." She shrugged. "It gets kind of hard to hate you when I think about it that way."

The silence returned, deeper and stiller than before. Martin was the one to break it.

"I don't know what to say to that," he told her, his voice gruff with emotion. "That's not what I expected. I was prepared for you to yell and scream and curse my name, or to cry about how poorly I treated you. I think I could even have handled a cold shoulder and a 'stay the hell out of my life, you bastard!' I'd have deserved that. But this?" He shook his head. "I don't know what to do with this."

Kitty laughed out loud, a release of tension as much as humor. "Believe me, I know how you feel. But don't worry. We've only known each other for fifteen minutes, and I've only asked you two questions. The screaming and cursing might happen yet, if I don't like your answer to the next one."

Tentatively, an approach to life she sensed sat awkwardly with this man, Martin reached out and laid his hand over hers. "I think I'll look forward to that. Kitty."

His gaze locked with hers, her father's gaze, looking out at her from eyes as familiar as her own, and Kitty felt some indefinable thing click into place inside her. Slowly, she smiled back.

TEN

MAX SWORE UNDER HIS BREATH AS HE KNOCKED ON the door to Martin's suite. The last thing Max wanted to do was interrupt the father-daughter reunion taking place inside, but there was no way he was about to let the Felix's family sneak up and ambush Kitty. Not when their fangs had seen so much more use than hers.

He pushed the door open at Martin's "Come in," and found the Felix reclining against his pillows, and his daughter sitting calmly by his side. Max had heard raised voices at one point, but it looked like the two of them must have come to some kind of an understanding of the sort that didn't involve mutual hatred. He took that as a very good sign.

Martin looked up.

"You've got visitors," Max reported. "They're just pulling up the drive."

The Felix glowered. "I'll bet they are, the interfering vultures. They probably thought they'd get here before Kitty and scare her off before I got a chance to meet her."

Kitty frowned at her father's expression and looked over at Max. She rose and wiped her hands on her jeans.

"Maybe it would be better if I just slipped out the back before they get here. A big scene isn't going to help anything, and I can come back another time."

"You're not going anywhere," Martin barked. "You're a member of my family and you're here at my invitation. I might be tied to this damned bed, but I'm still the head of this family and the Felix of this pride. I'd like to see anyone try to fight me over who I can and can't invite into my own home."

"You just might get your wish," Max said grimly. He caught a glimpse of both determination and anxiety in Kitty's face and placed a hand on her shoulder. "Don't worry," he murmured, smiling encouragingly. "A few ugly things might be said, but no one is going to get the chance to lay a hand on you. Not with Martin and me in the room. It will be fine."

Kitty looked less than reassured. "Great," she muttered. "Let's just hope I don't need to go pee then."

Martin laughed hoarsely and threw her a wink. "I'll let you borrow my bedpan. That way we can still keep an eye on you."

"You're all heart, Mr. Lowe."

"Dad." He scowled.

"Mr. Lowe," she repeated, gently but firmly.

"Father, then."

"Mr. Lowe."

"Damn it, girl, you can't call me Mr. Lowe like I'm some fool off the street coming to check out a book! At least call me Martin, if you're determined to be stubborn."

Kitty opened her mouth to reply, but Max interrupted with a squeeze of his hand.

"Your father is right," Max said. "You can't call him Mr. Lowe, at least not in front of the family. It would be seen as a sign of the distance between you, and it would imply that you're not comfortable here. They'd take that as a sign of weakness."

She looked up at Max, a frown in her eyes. "I don't see how it's anyone else's business—"

"Kitty—"

She held up a hand. "But if you both think it's important, I can go with 'Martin.' I'm not trying to be stubborn, but I wouldn't be comfortable calling anyone 'Dad' who I'd only known for forty-five minutes."

Max saw the disappointment Martin tried to conceal. He didn't want to interfere in their relationship, and he doubted either one would appreciate the effort if he tried, but that didn't do anything to stifle the urge. The real reason he couldn't step in was that, for the first time in his adult life, he couldn't decide whose side he was on. Martin had earned Max's loyalty and held it for so long that supporting him felt like a reflex, but Max couldn't bring himself to side against Kitty. Not when the thing growing between them was so powerful.

In the end, Kitty made his decision unnecessary.

"I don't want to hurt your feelings, M-Martin," she said, correcting herself deliberately, "and I'm not saying or even implying that I'm unwilling to try to form some kind of relationship here. I came two thousand miles to meet you, and I'd like to get to know you while I'm here. I really would. But I can only move myself along so fast." Max saw her reach out and squeeze her father's hand. "Remember, I grew up where calling an older man 'Mr.' isn't rude; it's a sign of respect. It's a compliment that you'd like me to call you by your given name. I'll try not to let it make me overly familiar."

Her smile and teasing wink earned a smile in answer. "You watch that sass and I'm sure it'll be just fine," Martin said, his voice rough with pleasure. Max felt something inside him warm at the sight. He'd known these two would hit it off, but seeing it happen was a rare pleasure he wouldn't soon forget. Then Kitty looked up and their eyes met and the warmth turned quickly to heat.

"Good morning, Martin. I do hope we aren't intruding. Won't you introduce your guest?"

Drusilla's cold tone made it clear she didn't give a damn whether she was intruding or not, and Max bit back a curse as he turned toward the door. "Drusilla. Did we miss your call letting us know you'd be coming by?" he asked.

"Oh, Nadalie and I just thought we'd stop in on our way to the spa and make sure Martin was comfortable. We're going to have a little day of beauty."

Max took in the sour expression on the face of Drusilla's daughter, as well as the sulking figure standing behind her. "I see. And is Peter having a facial, or a cleansing seaweed body wrap?"

The young man shot Max a dirty look but didn't take the bait. He just leaned against the doorjamb with his hands in his pockets and waited, like always, for someone else to do the work for him.

His mother also chose to ignore the comment. She was too busy staring at Kitty with malice-filled yellow eyes. "Well? Who is your guest, Martin? Or did she come here with you, Max? I thought you were still seeing that circus performer."

Somehow, Max had never thought to describe Selene Latourne, a featured acrobat with Cirque du Soleil, as a "circus performer." But then, he hadn't thought of her at all since Kitty had come to town.

"No, actually Selene recently became engaged to her choreographer," Max said, keeping a short rein on his temper. "But if I see her, I'll mention you asked after her. I'm sure she'll be touched." Stepping closer to Kitty, he laid a hand on her shoulder and gave it a squeeze. "As a matter of fact, I did bring Kitty with me this morning, but she's Martin's guest. He's been looking forward to her visit for quite some time."

"Kitty?" Nadalie choked, her voice dripping with contempt. Her gaze was fixed on Max's hand where it touched Kitty. "Her name is Kitty? That's the most horrible thing I've ever heard! Does she think she's making fun of us?"

He felt the tension in Kitty's small frame and tightened his grip. She snuck him a sideways glance through narrowed eyes, but at his glare she pinched her lips together and kept silent. He didn't need her to speak to know she reserved the right to change that decision at any time.

"Kitty, allow me to introduce Martin's family to you, since they've presented themselves so unexpectedly. This is Nadalie and Peter Lowe, Martin's children, and their mother, Drusilla Van Diemen." He gestured to each of them in turn. "Peter, ladies, this is Kitty Sugarman, Martin's daughter."

IF LOOKS COULD KILL, KITTY HOPED HER GRANDFATHER would find a good use for her life insurance policy. The expressions on the faces of Martin's ex-wife and children clearly showed how much each of them would like to see her drawn and quartered, with the pieces displayed on stakes around the property to warn off other unwelcome interlopers. In fact, if she hadn't known better, she would have sworn that the one Max had introduced as Nadalie was already contemplating having hair extensions made for herself after she cut off her half sister's scalp. But judging from the way the girl was simultaneously glaring at her and eating Max up with her eyes, Kitty thought there might be more than one reason for that.

Since the phrase "I'm pleased to meet you all" would have stuck in her craw like undercooked grits, Kitty settled for nodding to the group and murmuring, "How do you do?"

Drusilla didn't even bother to acknowledge Kitty again.

"So you've finally gone and done it, Martin," the older woman spat, glaring daggers at her ex-husband. "It didn't matter to you at all how your family felt about it? You just had to take the word of the first gold digger to show up on your doorstep claiming to be your long-lost bastard! How dare you?"

Kitty blinked and took another look around her. That line sounded like something out of a really bad daytime melodrama, and now that she thought about it, the other people in the room—with the exception of her ill father—were all much too good-looking for real life. Maybe she'd accidentally wandered onto the set of some strange Nevada soap opera.

Max, she already knew, was gorgeous, but she was beginning to think that all the members of the pride must be, based on the evidence standing in front of her and currently radiating hostility like a demonic tanning bed.

The relatives—as she'd begun thinking of them—were uniformly beautiful, even the guy. She had a hard time seeing the handsome man Martin must have been before he'd gotten so sick, but even if he'd been ugly as sin, Drusilla looked more than genetically capable of making up for it.

Tall, sleek, and built like a showgirl—with the long, golden hair to match—the woman had legs a mile long and obviously considered them an asset worth showing off, if the length of her skirt gave any indication. The short, pleated garment looked like wool, but wool so fine Kitty could almost imagine it feeling like cotton. It had been paired with a knit silk tank top in a rich golden cream color with a square neckline that perfectly framed the heavy gold-link necklace around Drusilla's throat.

Kitty felt a vindictive sense of satisfaction in observing that no matter how much the older woman might work out, and no matter how much Botox or cosmetics she used on her face, her neck betrayed her true age. Though it was still slender, the golden skin had begun to wrinkle and crepe in a way that not even the best plastic surgeon could fully correct.

"I already divorced you because I couldn't stand to listen to you whine, woman," Martin growled, his pale face flushing with anger. "What I do now is none of your damned business. If you're too contrary or too stupid to realize that a blind man would recognize that Kitty's my daughter, that's your own problem, but don't you dare come into my house and presume to criticize me."

"And what about me?" Nadalie snapped, almost shaking with anger. "Have you forgotten that you already *have* a daughter? Or do you think you can replace family members like broken slot machines?"

Surprised by the girl's vehemence, not to mention her

volume, Kitty looked over at Nadalie. Her glare, like her mother's, was poisonous and aimed directly at Kitty, who could have sworn Nadalie was trying to shove her away from Max with sheer force of will.

Mother and daughter looked to have more in common than their mutual hatred of the intruder, but Kitty thought she might be able to see some of Martin in the girl as well. She had her mother's figure and fashion sense, judging by her short, elegant sundress and obviously expensive jewelry, but her face was less classically oval and more heart-shaped. More like Kitty's, as much as she hated to admit it. Nadalie's blond hair was a shade darker than her mother's, and her eyes had a touch of green, but they stared at Kitty with equal loathing.

"No one is replacing anyone, and no one is going to be replaced, Nadia," Martin dismissed. "I invited Kitty to visit because I want to get to know her like I know you and your brother. Don't be such an idiot."

While Nadalie shrieked in outrage, Peter sneered from the doorway. "Oh, I'm sure being called an idiot will make her feel lots better, Dad."

Hands still stuffed into the pockets of what even Kitty could see were jeans worth more than any ten items of her own wardrobe, the young man strolled into the room as if he were doing a bad Marlon Brando impression. When Peter reached his mother's side, he stopped and gave Kitty an insulting head-to-toe inspection.

Not that she really cared what he thought of her, but she found it interesting that all of these people were going so far out of their way to let her know exactly how much contempt they held her in. Of course, considering the impression they were making on her, it did level the playing field a little. No matter how even things were, though, Kitty didn't intend to give the Lowes any advantage. She returned her half brother's scrutiny in equal measure.

Like the rest of the family, Peter was tall, but his broad shoulders and large hands and feet suggested that if he weren't still so youthfully skinny, he'd have a much larger frame than either of his female relatives. His hair, short and stylish, was darker than theirs, too, almost a toffee color that Kitty might have admired if she'd seen it on a more pleasant person. He had his father's green eyes, but Peter's condescending manners were all Drusilla. Only less polite.

"Personally, I don't see why Nad's so worried," he continued, dismissing Kitty and turning back to his father. "If the girl's any smarter than the average pile of dog shit, she'll find out fast what an asshole her natural father is. Then we'll never have to see her again. Everyone wins."

"You little son of a bitch!" Martin snarled, and he leaned forward as if he meant to rise.

Frowning, Kitty stepped closer to the bed and laid a hand on her father's arm. "Martin," she murmured, "calm down. You've been ill. If you get all worked up, your nurse is going to come in here and throw us out for wreaking havoc on your blood pressure."

"Don't bother playing the devoted daughter," Nadalie hissed. "We all know what you're really here for, and I'll tell you right now we're not going to stand for it."

Kitty thought for a second about getting angry, but honestly, the speeches these people were coming up with sounded so ridiculous, she felt more like laughing. She turned to Max and quirked an eyebrow. "She knows why I'm here. Would you mind refreshing my memory about that? Because I can tell you, right now, I'll be darned if I can think of it."

Max smiled down at her. The gesture looked amused, conspiratorial, and almost intimate, but already Kitty could read his expressions well enough to know he was seriously pissed off at Martin's family. For the moment, though, Max seemed inclined to play along with her imperturbable act.

He pursed his lips and tilted his head to the side, looking thoughtful. "I believe you may have mentioned something earlier. About . . . conquering and pillaging?"

Kitty laughed, deliberately making the sound low and wicked. "No, silly. That's later tonight. When you take me dancing. I came to visit Martin for an entirely different reason."

She watched Max's eyes flare at her provocative suggestion, and cursed herself for wanting to use him against the others. Especially when he inched closer to her and slid his hand from her shoulder to wrap his arm around her waist.

"Ah, yes. I remember now," he purred. "You let me bring you here because—"

"Because I wanted her here," Martin snapped, his glare taking in every living thing in the room. Not even the potted plants near the window seemed to be exempt. "I'm not quite sure when it happened that the members of my pride forgot I'm their Felix as well as their relative, but they're all very much mistaken about that. No matter how much you all might be hoping to hear something different one day soon, I'm not dead yet."

Kitty saw Drusilla looking uncomfortable and frowned. She glanced up at Max, but his expression had hardened into the stony mask he'd been wearing the first time she'd seen him. The only person with a smile on his face, or at least a smirk, was Peter.

"Not yet, old man," the teenager said, sarcasm dripping, "but you can't blame us for continuing to check. We all live in hope, after all."

"That's a truly rotten thing to say," Kitty bristled, glaring at her half brother. "Especially considering your father's had a health scare so recently. You should be glad to see he's recovering. Wishing for someone's death—your own father's especially!—is not something to joke about."

Peter turned his cruelly amused gaze on her and lifted a supercilious eyebrow. "Who's joking, Scarlett? I was being perfectly serious."

Max's arm around her waist tightened, and Kitty felt a sense of uneasiness creep over her. She looked from her father to Max and back again, then frowned at Peter.

"What's the matter, *Sis*?" the young man drawled. "Didn't Father dearest tell you he's dying?"

ELEVEN

MAX SAW KITTY'S FACE GO WHITE AND SWORE. GOD damn Peter and his petty bullshit! He must have guessed Martin hadn't had time to explain things, and he'd leapt at the opportunity to make trouble, just like always. Of course, Max found himself struggling not to curse Martin out as well. What had he spent nearly an hour talking to his daughter about that had been more important than informing her of the very real danger of his being dead before the month was out?

Not that it mattered now. The damage had been done.

"God damn it, Peter!" Martin roared, struggling to push himself up off his pillows and panting at the effort it cost him. "I could kick your sorry ass for that! How dare you—"

"Oh, go ahead, Dad," Peter taunted. "Watching you try would give me the biggest laugh I've had in a long time. You're so far gone already, someone will have to play the grim reaper for you, because I doubt you even have the strength to kick the bucket, let alone my ass."

"Shut up, Peter," Max growled, his voice cutting through Martin's bellowed response. He took a step forward, instinctively tensing his muscles to appear even larger and more powerful than normal. If he'd been in lion form, his tail would have been twitching. Everyone but Peter seemed to get the message. They took a collective step back. "Even dead, your father would be more than a match for you, cub, so don't let me hear you speaking to him again with that kind of disrespect. Do you understand me?"

"I don't need anyone fighting my battles for me yet, Max, not even you," Martin said. His voice sounded harsher this time, weaker, as if even the effort it took to yell at his son had drained the older man of energy. "The day I'm no match for a scrawny weakling like my son is the day you can take me out and bury me."

Peter smirked. "I have a shovel in my car. I'll go out and grab it right now."

"You little shit," his father growled, and reached to throw back his blankets. From the corner of his eye, Max saw that it was Kitty who reached out to stop him while his ex-wife and daughter just watched for the first sign of blood, like Romans at the Colosseum.

"Martin, no, stay in bed," Kitty urged, placing her hand against his chest and using the other to tuck his covers back into place. "You shouldn't be getting up. Aside from everything else, you wouldn't get very far. You're still connected to your oxygen and your IV."

"Pull them out. I don't need them," Martin panted. "I'm going to teach that boy a lesson. If it kills me, at least I know I'll die satisfied."

"Martin, no!"

Finally, Drusilla stepped forward, but not to assist Kitty in calming her ex-husband down. "Don't be ridiculous, Martin. You're in no state to indulge in a wrestling match with Peter. And what could possess you to want to? He's your son. You can't possibly think to blame him for it if some . . . interloper happens to get herself into a snit."

Max watched as Kitty turned from her father to glare at Drusilla through narrowed eyes.

"A snit?" Kitty repeated quietly. "I don't know what you're talking about. I'm not in a snit, lady; I am righteously pissed. I was raised to respect my elders, but if you say one more thing to upset Martin, I'll show you exactly how far beyond 'snit' I've really gone."

Drusilla drew in an affronted gasp, but she never managed to let it out. The monitor recording the activity of Martin's heart began to issue an insistent beeping sound and the door to his private sitting room opened to admit a forty-something-year-old woman in smiley face–decorated white scrubs with sensible crepe-soled shoes and a frown to scare small children.

"Just what in heaven's name is going on in here?" she demanded. "What have you all done to Mr. Lowe?" With dark, capable hands, she shooed everyone impatiently away from the bed, and looked at the beeping monitor. "This is no good. Mr. Lowe, your blood pressure has gone through the roof and your sinus rhythm is tachycardic. I can't allow this type of thing in my patients." The nurse turned to glare at the rest of the room. "All of you are going to have to leave. Now."

Peter shrugged and was out the door before the woman finished talking. He didn't even bother to acknowledge his father as he left.

Nadalie and Drusilla protested loudly, but Nurse Mencina—according to her name tag—was unmoved. "No, out. Mr. Lowe is unwell. If you all need to talk to him, you can come back tomorrow and you can behave yourselves then. No more visitors today."

The women stalked outside after making a great show of promising Martin that they would return tomorrow when he was feeling better and "ready to talk sensibly." Martin scowled them all the way out of the room.

Mouth compressed into a thin line, the nurse turned her attention on Max and Kitty. "You, too," she ordered. "Out. You can come back tomorrow, if you can promise to behave like civilized people."

Max saw Kitty sizing up the nurse and prepared himself to intervene, but he didn't need to. Kitty looked from Nurse Mencina to Martin's pale, drawn face, and the combat-ready tension drained from her body.

"Okay. We'll come back tomorrow," she said, but instead of turning to go, she smoothed Martin's blankets back into place and adjusted his pillows more comfortably behind him. Then she took his hand and squeezed gently. "Let Ms. Mencina take care of you. I'm going to ask her the next time I see her if you gave her any trouble, you hear?"

Martin only nodded and closed his eyes, pressing his cannula closer with his free hand. The other, Max saw, tightened briefly around his daughter's before she stepped away from the bed.

Reaching out, Max took Kitty's hand in his own and brushed the hair back from Martin's forehead. "Get some sleep, *pa*," he murmured, using the affectionate Leo term for father. "I'll bring her back tomorrow."

Without opening his eyes, Martin nodded. With a polite nod of his own to the nurse, Max turned away and tugged Kitty out of the suite and out into the hall. Then he cursed.

Drusilla and Nadalie had stationed themselves beside the front door like guard dogs. Beside him, he felt Kitty tense, and he cursed again silently. He thought about steering her to the left, down another hallway, and back toward the rear of the house where they could exit unseen, but to be honest, the women would probably just follow. Still, he figured Kitty had had enough for one day. He opened his mouth to make the suggestion, but she beat him to the punch.

"Well, I'll say one thing for you, Max Stuart," she murmured, squaring her shoulders and raising her chin the way he'd noticed she always did right before she leapt into one fray or another. "You don't let a girl get bored around here, do you?" Turning her head, she glanced up at him with a small smile. "Shall we let them hold the door for us as we leave?"

Her eyes, steady on his, were bright green with determination and shadowed with fatigue. She might look like she could take on an army of obnoxious relatives with ease, but her eyes and the tension he could feel in her body told him she held herself together with Scotch tape and willpower.

"There's no reason you have to, kitten," he told her, squeezing her hand and watching her closely. "They've already said more than enough for anyone to handle in one day. We can go out the back and let them spit their bitterness on someone else for a while."

"Oh no." She shook her head, mouth quirking. "I've never walked away from a fight in my life. Just ask Billy Buckner."

"Who?"

But Kitty was already striding forward. Since Max refused to let go of her hand, he had no choice but to follow.

She didn't even hesitate as she moved calmly and unhurriedly toward the front door. She nodded to Drusilla and Nadalie in turn as she reached for the handle. "Ladies," she said as her hand twisted.

"My daughter and I would like a few words with you, Miss . . ."

"Sugarman," Kitty supplied evenly. "*Kitty* Sugarman."

Drusilla ignored the subtle emphasis on her first name, but Max smiled.

"Miss Sugarman," the elder woman acknowledged. "I don't see any reason for us to dissemble with each other, not now that we're away from any chance of upsetting Martin. I want to make the position of this family very clear—you are not welcome here. I don't know what you've told my husband to convince him to invite you here, but you're not wanted. You should leave immediately."

Kitty's expression remained remarkably even, and if her hand tightened a bit in his, Max was the only one to notice. "That was remarkably clear," she said, her green eyes steady on Drusilla's. "Congratulations. You have no need to wonder if I understand how you feel. Unfortunately, how you feel doesn't matter to me."

Outrage made itself plain on Drusilla's face, but Kitty didn't flinch.

"The fact is that it doesn't matter if you and your children and the entire state of Nevada don't want me here," she continued, steel in every word. "Martin is the one who invited me here, and he's the one I came to see. As far as I'm concerned, that means he's the only one with the right to tell me to leave."

"You're not one of us," Nadalie hissed. She shouldered her mother aside and got right up in Kitty's face, but she never blinked. "You don't belong here, and you have no idea how things work in our world. We can make you leave, you know. Of course, if it comes to that, you'll probably be leaving in the back of the coroner's van."

That was it. The last straw. Rumbling a very real warning, Max used his grip on Kitty to tug her back and stepped between her and the other woman. He could feel Kitty tugging on his hand, trying to free herself, but he held firm.

"You need to back off, Nadia," he growled, feeling energy crawling along his skin, urging him to shift, to assume the form in which no female of the pride would ever think to disobey him. It took a concerted effort of will to hang on to his control. "In case *you've* forgotten how things work around here, your father is still Felix of this pride, and that means he has the right to invite anyone he wants into his territory. If you don't like it . . . well, that's sad for you, now isn't it?"

Nadia backed up a couple of steps, but she didn't lower her eyes. She continued to glare at him defiantly, her lip curling in anger. "My father isn't strong enough to rule this pride anymore, and you know it. Even I could challenge him now and win. He's lost the respect of the pride. He's a burden on us now."

Max snarled and forced her back another step. "While your father lives, he rules. And if that means I have to kill anyone who tries to change that, I will." His voice was flat, his expression murderous. "Don't forget I'm *baas* here, Nadia. If you want to get to your father, you have to go through me. And I'm more than strong enough to survive your challenge."

The girl opened her stupid mouth one more time, but her mother saved her. Grabbing her daughter by the arm, Drusilla tugged her backward and reached for the door handle, keeping a wary eye on Max.

"Nadia, it's time we left," she ordered, pulling open the door and shoving her daughter through it. "Now is obviously not the time to argue about this. We've made our position clear. What the girl chooses to do now is her own business. Let her stay for a few days. When your father dies, we'll see what the rest of the pride has to say about her presence. Come along."

Max watched them go, fighting back the urge to follow and smack their stubborn ideas out of their heads. If they thought he wouldn't take the exact same position when he became Felix, they were dumber than he'd imagined. The only thing that stopped him was the feel of Kitty's hand still gripped in his. Then she squeezed and he turned to look down at her.

"Well, I had fun," she said, her expression as wry as her voice. "How about you?"

THE ATMOSPHERE OUTSIDE OF MARTIN'S HOUSE FELT so much lighter than inside that Kitty would almost have sworn that gravity disappeared altogether. She stopped in the drive to savor the fresh, insult-free air and turned her face up to the sun. Damn the freckles. Being outside almost made her feel clean again.

Max stepped up behind her and gave her a one-armed

hug. "I feel like I should apologize for them, but I doubt it would make a difference," he admitted. "They'll probably be just as unpleasant to you the next time they meet you."

Kitty just shook her head. "The part I'm most confused about is what on earth could possibly have made Martin marry that woman in the first place? After Misty, I knew he didn't have the greatest taste in women, but Drusilla takes the cake."

When Max hesitated, Kitty cast him a curious glance. "It was a . . . political alliance," he said after a moment. "In the animal world, male lions take over a pride by killing or driving off the adult males and then killing all the male cubs, which forces the females back into heat so that the new males can breed their own cubs. Leos aren't quite so uncivilized, but tradition has shown us that taking a close relative of the former Felix to mate can make for a smoother transition of power."

"So Drusilla was the last Felix's . . . what?"

"His daughter. Everyone could see it was a bad match, but for a time it served its purpose."

Kitty had a sudden thought and chuckled. "Sorry. It just occurred to me that's why Martin never remarried," she explained when Max looked the question. "After Misty and then Drusilla . . . I mean, talk about scared straight!"

Max laughed and used the arm around her waist to urge her toward the car. "Come on. I've had enough excitement for one day. Let's get back to the city and get something to eat. How do you feel about steak?"

"After that little interlude inside?" Kitty asked. "Predatory."

They had each taken about two steps toward the Mercedes when the growl of an engine had them turning to look up the drive. A heavy, dark motorcycle liberally coated with dust came belting toward them at a speed Kitty's mind subconsciously registered as insane. Before anything beyond that could register, Max had swung her around and positioned himself between her and the machine so that she had to peer around his ribcage to get a glimpse of what was happening. She could feel his muscled frame tense, but he made no move to confront the driver, who finally eased up on the throttle and brought the bike to a skidding halt just a few feet in front of Max and Kitty. Without cutting the motor, the man on the bike dropped the kickstand and yanked off his helmet in one fluid motion.

"We have trouble, *baas*," the newcomer said, ignoring Kitty in favor of focusing his intense, yellow-gold gaze squarely on Max.

Kitty felt just fine with that, considering that the stranger looked like he topped out at a hair over six feet tall and probably weighed at least two hundred fifty pounds. And if an ounce of that was fat, Kitty swore to God she'd eat her new tennis shoes.

In front of her, Max cursed. "Nick. What's going on?"

"One of the men on the perimeter spotted camp signs on the ridge above the northern border."

"Did you send someone to check it out?"

"Yeah, only by the time Lou climbed up there, the camp was gone and it looked like whoever was there made an effort to wipe the trail."

Max cursed again. Creatively. "Was he any good at it?"

"Some. He covered their trail pretty good, but he

didn't have time to wipe the places where he'd been testing the security system. And no matter how good he was with prints, no one can make two guys smell like just one."

The tension in Max's body seemed to turn him to solid stone. "Who's on their trail?" he demanded in a voice as hard as his muscles.

"David."

"Good."

"But it looks like they headed toward the dry canyon to the east of the community center."

"And?"

"Allison Avery's kindergarten class is doing a Wilderness Walk on the easy path at the base of the canyon. They were supposed to take a jeep down there early this morning and be back by one."

Reflexively, Kitty glanced at her watch. 2:42.

"Does anyone know if she took a cell phone with her?"

Nick nodded. "Jenni Jensen, the nursery school teacher, said she always has it on her, especially when she's got the kids out of the classroom, but she's not answering. Hopefully, it's just because the canyon walls are blocking the signal, but there's no way to tell for sure."

What Max said at that news was violent and comprehensive, but even before he uttered it, Kitty had grasped that the situation was not a good one. Now she wanted to know exactly what was at stake.

Stepping out from Max's shadow, she moved to where both men could see her and scowled at them collectively. "What's going on?"

Max glared down at her and reached a hand toward her shoulder. "Get back in the house," he commanded.

Kitty twisted out of reach. "After you tell me what's going on."

Copper eyes blazed for a moment, then narrowed to dangerous slits. "I don't have time. Get back in the house and stay there until I come back for you. I'm going with Nick."

"You're going to chase after a guy for camping *near* your property? Or do you automatically assume that campers are a malicious danger that can never be trusted in the same canyon as a kindergarten class?"

She couldn't help pushing, not even knowing the risk that she was taking. Max was clearly not in the mode to argue, or to slow down and answer questions, but Kitty already knew him well enough to know he wouldn't hurt her. Spank her ass, maybe, but not hurt her.

But she took another step backward, just to be safe.

Max stalked her like a predator. "We're going to find the nomad who's been trying to get through your father's security and to make sure he doesn't run into or hurt the kids who don't know he's out there. And while we do that, *you* are going to keep your pretty little ass *in. The. House.* Understand?"

Kitty would have opened her mouth to argue, but that seemed a little silly. Especially once Max unleashed his Other speed in a leap that closed the distance between them faster than she could blink. By the time she was ready to launch a protest, he'd scooped her up, thrown her over his shoulder, and carried her bodily back through the front door of her father's house. Stopping in the hall, he deposited her on the slate tile, turned away, and locked the front door behind him on the way out.

She stood for a moment, her hands at her sides, her eyes wide with disbelief. When her mind stopped spinning, she stared at the panels of solid wood in front of her and breathed, "Oh no, he *didn't*."

TWELVE

"HE DID *NOT* TRY TO LOCK ME INSIDE THE HOUSE LIKE a useless piece of fluff," Kitty muttered to herself as she eased open a door and peeked out into a corridor in the shadowed northern wing of her father's enormous, sprawling house. She barely mouthed the words, because she was trying not to make any noise. Partly because she didn't want to risk waking her father or incurring the wrath of his hovering nurse, but mostly because finding a hidden exit from a house became more difficult when people spotted you looking for it.

Oh, when she'd first recovered from the shock of Max's high-handed tactics for getting her back into the house, she'd tried to maintain some semblance of dignity by walking calmly, if furiously, out the front door. She'd decided it served the jerk right if she took his car and drove herself back to Vegas without him. Let him find his own way back to the city. After treating her like some swooning heroine in a Dickensian novel, he could walk through the whole desert for all she cared.

Unfortunately, things hadn't worked out exactly as she'd planned. She'd no sooner opened the door than two well-armed and seriously grim guards had materialized out of nowhere to inform her that the *baas* had instructed them that no one was to enter or leave the house until Max had returned. They had stood firm in the face of anger, threats, bribery, and outright whining, forcing her to close the door and indulge in some pacing to regroup.

First, she had thought that if she just explained the situation to Martin—using the appropriate epithets to describe the particular brand of contempt in which she held Max's recent behavior—he would feel bad enough at her treatment to offer her an alternative method of getting back to the city. His nurse, however, put the kibosh on Plan B, proving as determined to keep Kitty out of her father's room as the guards had been to keep her in the house.

Kitty was now deep in the implementation of Plan C.

It turned out that her father's house occupied several thousand square feet of rocky desert land near the southern edge of the Desert National Wildlife Refuge. Kitty had learned—thanks to an apple-cheeked housekeeper with long, dark braids and a fondness for gossip—that it boasted ten bedrooms, twelve baths, an indoor pool, a state-of-the-art projection screen theater, tennis courts, a library, a fitness center, a sauna, a chef's kitchen that made Mrs. Sanchez (the housekeeper) sit down and weep, and a thousand-bottle wine cellar. The architect had designed it in the shape of a letter "F," with only the lower portion and crossbar kept open since Mr. Lowe had fallen ill. Since he no longer entertained or had guests to stay, the bedrooms and most of the specialty rooms had been closed up. Only the reception rooms at the front of the house and Martin's suite at the junction of the crossbar remained open, along with the kitchens at the rear of the house. The pool and sauna at the end of the top wing hadn't been occupied in at least six months. Even the cleaners only went back there every couple of weeks these days, to dust and clean the windows. Take a right just beyond the pool, Mrs. Sanchez boasted, and you'd run into the doorway to the wine cellar her employer had ordered specially dug into the red rock below the house.

Oh, the trouble that cellar had caused! According to the housekeeper, the zoning and building inspection people had kept Mr. Lowe on edge for weeks while they sorted that one out. Because it had no windows and would be located completely underground, the contractor had been unable to complete it without adding a second exit from the stone-lined space. Just in case of emergencies.

Unlike the exits at the front, rear, and sides of the house, the exit from the wine cellar emerged not onto the well-manicured grounds immediately surrounding the house, but on the other side of the outdoor pool house. Out of sight of the main building.

As far as Kitty was concerned, making a prompt statement of independence definitely qualified as an emergency.

Straining her ears, she listened to the sounds of anyone else nearby but heard nothing beyond the faint stirring and humming of Mrs. Sanchez in the kitchen two rooms and a narrow hall behind her. The coast was clear.

Keeping her back to the wall and her steps light, Kitty glided down the hallway in almost total silence. It took some concentration, but she felt kind of proud of herself that she could manage to move with such cat-like stealth. For the first time, she could almost believe being half-Leo might confer on her some actual advantages, instead of being like some kind of chronic disease she needed to learn to manage despite her resentment. But that didn't stop her from thinking that these new sneaking skills would have come in even handier had she discovered them when she'd been fourteen instead of twenty-four.

She made it down the hall and around the corner by the pool without seeing or hearing another soul. When she smelled the odor of fresh water, copper, and ionized air, she knew the pool must be close. Turning her head, she peered halfway over her shoulder and picked out the bend in the hall that the housekeeper had described. Bingo. She'd nearly made it.

Kitty's heartbeat raced, and she struggled to keep her breathing in check as she rounded the corner and grasped the faux-antique latch on the cellar door. Pulling slowly, she gave silent thanks that her father's staff kept his house in such pristine condition that the hinges offered not even a sigh as they swung open to reveal a smooth stone stairway descending into darkness.

Stepping onto the landing, Kitty quickly pulled the door closed behind her and paused to let her eyes adjust to the darkness around her. It happened almost instantly. She swore she could nearly feel her pupils dilating, opening wide, and hungrily soaking up every small scrap of light in the narrow space. Within a couple of seconds, she could see where the plaster walls met the concrete foundation and where the foundation gave way to the rough sandstone beneath. A plain wooden handrail on the right crossed all three surfaces, pointing downward like a finger into the depths of the cellar. Unfortunately, what Kitty didn't see was a light switch.

Frowning, she lifted both hands and ran them over the face of the walls on either side of her, but she felt nothing. When she tilted her head back, she saw a small

fixture attached to the ceiling and whispered a curse.
The switch must have been outside the door. For a moment she debated stepping back to look, but she'd made
it all this way without attracting attention, and who knew
when her luck might run out? Her vision seemed keen
enough to keep her from tumbling headfirst down the
staircase, so how much more light did she really need?

Feeling a surge of confidence and more than a touch
of awe at the power of her newly discovered senses, Kitty
laid her hand lightly on the rail and stepped down.

The stairway wasn't long, but it was steep, and the
change in temperature brought the fine hairs on Kitty's
arms to attention by the time she reached the lower landing. The rail she'd been touching continued another two
feet in front of her, then took a ninety-degree turn to the
left and continued the length of two short paces before
angling downward again. Following it, Kitty stepped
down five more treads before the floor of the wine cellar
leveled out in front of her.

In the eerie quiet of the space, she could hear her
breath echoing off the low stone ceiling. Down here, almost no light penetrated, leaving the room darker than
pitch to human eyes and only slightly less inky to Kitty's
keener sight. There simply wasn't enough light for even
her Leo eyes to magnify. By straining, she was able to
make out the difference in the quality of the darkness
that indicated the presence of tall racks positioned along
the near, left-hand wall and in what looked like a free-
standing row to her right, which meant the far wall
couldn't be any closer than a few feet beyond. The only
way to tell for sure would be to look on the other side. If
she didn't find the door elsewhere, she would have to.

Stepping forward carefully, Kitty held her hands out

before her and used the bulky shape of the racks on her right to guide her deeper into the gloom. The cellar smelled of dust and wood and stone, and if she'd had a light source and a tour guide, she might have enjoyed poking around and examining labels, but at the moment, she had other things on her mind.

A few more steps brought her to a point where the wall to her left turned in, narrowing the area to a slender aisle barely wide enough for two to walk abreast. She continued on, trying to ignore the feeling that the racks on either side of her were leaning in on her, looming precariously overhead. It was just the dark playing tricks on her, she assured herself, but she hurried her pace regardless.

The cellar aisle seemed to stretch on forever. Kitty followed it, hoping like heck that the inspectors had come out to ensure that the builders had actually complied with the requirement for the second exit. Just when she was beginning to wonder if Mrs. Sanchez had known what she was talking about, Kitty reached the end of the aisle. Faced with the choice of either turning back or turning right, she glanced to the side and found another long aisle stretching off in that direction. But unless her eyes were playing tricks on her, she thought she saw a slightly lighter shade of blackness off in the distance.

Crossing her fingers, Kitty took the right-hand turn and passed the ends of two more rows before reaching the far wall of the wine cellar. While the rectangular shape of the room ended there, the aisle in front of her continued as a narrow corridor bounded on each side by walls of bare stone, and off in the distance, the blackness definitely seemed to lighten.

A surge of excitement pushed her forward and Kitty stepped eagerly. She soon discovered the hall to be even longer than she had estimated, but as she traveled down it and the increasing illumination became more apparent, she began to appreciate why it had been designed that way. Someone had thought ahead and anticipated a Leo making their way out of the cellar in darkness, because the length of the hall provided Kitty's eyes with the opportunity to adjust gradually to the increased light. By the time she reached the end of the corridor, her eyes were exposed to light equivalent to twilight shining in from a small room on the other side of the glass-and-wood door she found there.

Opening the door, Kitty found herself stepping into a small bare room with a large hexagonal opening in the ceiling and a sturdy-looking ladder stretching up toward it. Triumph had her smiling as she scrambled up the wide heavy rungs.

She slowed as she reached the top and cautioned herself not to charge out into the open like an escaping prisoner. Just because Mrs. Sanchez had told her the tunnel came out away from the main house didn't mean someone like Max would leave it unguarded, especially since a secret exit from any building provided an equally discreet means of entrance. Holding tight to the rungs, Kitty peered over the top of the aperture and swept a look around her.

The tunnel, she quickly realized, emerged in a large gazebo several yards beyond the outdoor pool house, just as Mrs. Sanchez had described. The hexagonal opening had been concealed by a set of benches built all around it and facing outward as if to take advantage of the property's wonderful views. Unfortunately, from what Kitty could see, the main views from the structure consisted of the back side of the pool house to the south, a sheer rock face to the east, and rocky desert stretched out toward the infinity of the west. To the north, the landscape sloped upward in the increasingly rocky terrain of the foothills of the nearby mountains.

Having grown up in a place where mountains grew thick with foliage, and green battled for supremacy with a thousand other shades of life, Kitty couldn't imagine the gazebo as a place where visitors would be eager to stop and take in the beauty of nature. It looked too harsh and forbidding for comfortable contemplation. Which was probably why someone had felt it would be a good place for the tunnel exit.

And, apparently, a good place for a man to stand guard, armed with what looked like nothing but a pair of binoculars and an impressively complicated-looking walkie-talkie.

The guard actually stood about thirty feet to Kitty's right, facing the sparse, rocky landscape to the north. He had his hands crossed over his chest, and his hip leaned against the side of a boulder as he scanned the horizon for any potential threats. She couldn't see his face, but she caught a whiff of dust and denim and sweat and realized the slight breeze she felt against her skin was coming from the direction he faced. He was upwind of her and she must have been fairly quiet, because he didn't even twitch as she eased herself over the top of the south-facing bench and crouched down behind its solid shelter to come up with a plan for her next move.

With her back exposed to the pool area and the house beyond, Kitty didn't want to waste time. She needed to move quickly in order to minimize her chances of being seen, but her confidence in her new-found sneaking skill didn't extend to walking across the gravel landscaping that surrounded the gazebo. It seemed likely that someone had laid it down deliberately to keep skulkers like her from taking the house and the guards by surprise. Maybe if she could gather up a few pebbles, though, she could throw them and create a distraction long enough to bolt around the side of the house and up toward the drive. It wasn't much of a plan, but at the moment, it was the best Kitty could come up with.

Crossing the fingers of her left hand, she mouthed a prayer as she plucked up four large pebbles in her right and all the while strained to keep a weather eye on the guard. He wasn't moving.

Just as she was looking for the best target for her first throw, Kitty heard the unmistakable cracking pop of a rifle firing somewhere in the hills to the north. Her head shot up, her concern for secrecy forgotten as she scanned the horizon for a sign of the shooter. In other circumstances, she might have dismissed it as a hunter, but the time of day, and the fact that she knew Max had perceived a threat in the stranger Nick had reported in the area, made her wary. It didn't help that the sound of the guard's sharp curse reached her just before he thrust his radio back in its loop at his belt and sprinted into the rocks at top speed.

This was her chance. Crouching low, Kitty sprang from the raised floor of the gazebo and over most of the surrounding gravel. She swore as her right heel came down with a crunch, but she didn't have time to check to see if the guard had heard. Hopefully he'd rate the shot more important than a possible footstep near the house. She'd taken two running strides westward, intending to round the house and head for the road beyond the drive, when a thin, high sound snapped her to a teetering halt.

Lord almighty, that had sounded like a child.

Heart pounding with a combination of adrenaline and nerves, Kitty strained her ears and prayed that her mind had been playing tricks on her, but no. A few seconds later, the sound came again, muffled as if the youngster were trying to be quiet, but it definitely sounded like a child's sob, and this time it was accompanied by the sound of something scraping against rock.

Kitty didn't hesitate. Faced with the choice between freedom and the safety of a child who was probably lost and was definitely frightened and in danger from whoever was shooting, she spun on her heels and raced toward the sound.

The rocks soon forced her to slow down, but she still climbed over and around them faster than was likely wise. She knew her hands were taking a beating from scraping against rough stone as she braced herself over a couple of uneven patches, but she didn't stop to think of it. She just kept concentrating on the occasional quiet sounds of fear that drifted toward her from the hidden child.

In the distance, she could hear the sound of pounding footsteps as the guard obviously chose speed over stealth in his pursuit of the shooter, and it took a great deal of concentration to block out the distraction. She needed to tune in to the smaller, closer sounds the child was making if she wanted to find it unhurt. She hoped the guard was on the right track in chasing the shooter away from her and the child, but she didn't plan to take chances. The quicker she found the child, the quicker she could hustle them both back to the house and safety.

Kitty wanted desperately to call out, but she feared the child would be too scared to respond and might even run away from the sound of her voice. Cursing the speed it cost, she made an effort to quiet her own movements in hopes of preventing such a startled reaction. She knew she was too late, though, when a tiny gasp was followed by a long stretch of quiet. She'd already scared the child, and now he or she had stopped moving and done something to stifle the sobs Kitty had been following.

Clenching her teeth in frustration, Kitty froze and listened hard. Nothing. She had to give the kid credit, whoever he was, he'd obviously be a champion hide-and-seek player. Without the clues of sound, it had become almost impossible to track him down. The ground around here was too rocky for footstep impressions, and searching every nook and cranny where a child might be hidden defined the term "futile." The time had come for a change in tactics.

Lifting her face to the bright clear sky, Kitty blanked her mind, closed her eyes, and inhaled deeply.

At first, all she could smell was her own scent, along with dirt and rock and a hint of old wood and musty vegetation, but on the third sniff it came to her. The barest, faintest, sweetest whiff of peanut butter she'd ever detected.

She turned her head back and forth, trying to decide where the scent was strongest before she opened her eyes and followed her nose.

She moved quietly this time, carefully checking for loose rocks or twigs before each footfall, her eyes alternately scanning the ground in front of her and the rocks around her. She thought for a minute that she might have been deluding herself in imagining that familiar scent, but when a draft of milk accompanied it on the next breeze, Kitty all but felt her ears perk up. Turning to the right, she walked into the wind a few more feet before a flash of color caught her eye. Tucked into a crevice between two large boulders, she saw a scrap of bright yellow cotton and sent up a silent prayer of thanks. Less than five seconds later, she lowered herself to her knees in front of the tiny alcove and smiled at the small figure within.

"Hi," she whispered, trying to convey calm and reassurance even as her instincts reminded her of the urgency of returning to the house. "My name is Kitty. What's yours?"

A girl of about five stared up at her from a pair of greenish-gray eyes set in a smooth round face and framed by a pair of straggling braids bound with yellow elastics. She didn't answer, just pulled back into herself and clutched a battered and stained pink backpack in front of her.

"I was here visiting Mr. Lowe down at the big house when my friend had to leave to do something important," Kitty continued, speaking softly and quietly. "Did your friends leave you, too?"

The little girl stared at her silently for a long minute before her head moved in a tentative shake.

"Did you get lost?" Kitty asked. "I remember when I got lost in a department store, once. I got real, real scared."

"I losted my teacher," the little girl whispered.

Kitty's mind raced. Before Max's high-handed stunt, Nick had mentioned something about a kindergarten class being out on a nature walk in the area where the intruder's camp had been spotted. She'd thought the area was farther away, but either Kitty had guessed wrong, or this little girl had wandered for quite a ways looking for her classmates after she'd gotten separated from the group.

"That must have made you pretty afraid," Kitty offered. She had to fight against the instinct to scoop the girl up and run back toward the safety of the house, but she'd rather the child wasn't calling attention to them by screaming when they made their escape. "I remember that I was real afraid before my mamaw came and found me."

The girl chewed on her lip and inched forward a touch. "What's a mamaw?"

Kitty smiled and prayed this was a good sign. "That's what I called my grandmother. Mamaw. And I call my grandfather 'Papaw.'"

"I call them Gramma and Grampa," the girl whispered, her little hands twisting around the straps of her bag.

"And what do they call you, honey?"

"Sometimes they call me 'baby,' but mostly they just call me Maisie. Unless I been bad. Then they call me Mary Elizabeth."

"Is that your name? Mary Elizabeth?"

"Uh-huh. But I only get called that when somebody's mad at me." Her lower lip quivered and her gray-green eyes filled with tears. "Mommy and Daddy are gonna be real mad at me now."

Kitty felt her heart melt in her chest. "Aw, Maisie, I don't think they'll be mad. I think that when they see you, they're going to be so happy, they won't even think about calling you Mary Elizabeth."

"I wanna see them now!" The little girl broke down,

her little face scrunching up as the tears began to stream down her reddening cheeks. "I wanna go home!"

"Oh, I know you do, baby girl." Reflexively, Kitty reached out to the sobbing girl and felt a surge of relief when two little arms crept around her neck and clamped down like a vise. Maisie's fists clutched Kitty's T-shirt in a death grip, smashing the backpack between them until whatever hard, pointy object was inside threatened to impale Kitty through the navel. At the moment, Kitty couldn't have cared less.

"I want my mommy!" Maisie bawled, her words barely understandable through the gasping, whimpering, and hiccupping that accompanied her tears. Not to mention the fact that since she had buried her face against the side of Kitty's neck, the little girl's voice sounded slightly muffled.

"Sh, I know, sweetheart," Kitty soothed. "I know you do. Why don't you hang on tight now, you hear? We'll go straight back to Mr. Lowe's house and call your mama on the phone to come get you. You'll see her in just a little bit, I promise."

Maisie continued to sob, soaking Kitty's top, but she nodded her little face against the fabric at the same time.

"Okay, here we go," Kitty said, tucking the girl closer against her and rising into a crouch. "Wrap your legs around me and hold on tight, okay, baby girl?"

Another watery nod provided an answer.

Carefully, Kitty stretched to scan the area around them, but saw nothing. She could hear movement in the distance, but she hoped it was the sound of the guard pursuing the shooter. Either way, she didn't have time to check. She needed to get herself and the child back into the house just in case she was wrong and the shooter had doubled back toward them.

She tried to keep low and use the terrain for cover, but the soft, crying weight in Kitty's arms made that difficult. The best she could do was to keep one eye on the landscape and the other on the ground in front of her, trying to strike a balance between awareness of the danger from the shooter and the danger from tumbling down the rocky hill with a five-year-old in her arms.

When she came around a large boulder and saw the bottom of the hill and the more level ground ahead, Kitty gave a wordless prayer of thanks. Picking up the pace, she began to jog toward the side of the house. She didn't think she could manage the vertical ladder down to the cellar with the girl in her arms, and she didn't want to take the chance of finding the back doors of the house locked. At least if she went around to the front, she could keep the building between herself and the shooter and alert the guards out front about what had happened.

The only problem was the stretch of level, open ground between them and the nearest corner of the house. It looked to be no more than a couple hundred feet, but that was a lot of ground to cover when someone with a rifle was in the rocks behind you. Still, it was Kitty's only choice.

Taking a deep breath, Kitty tucked her shoulders, tightened her grip on Maisie, and broke for the house at a dead run. A noise behind her made Kitty look over her shoulder in time to see a flash of movement and feel a wave of answering fear. Instinctively, she dove for the ground, twisting her body to spare the child from the impact just as the crack of a gunshot echoed in the clear desert air. It was a good thing she had shifted, because Kitty landed hard enough for the wind to exit her body in a hard rush, leaving her dazed and gasping on the ground, still clutching a very frightened little girl to her chest.

Blinking against the shock and pain of muscle and bone meeting rock and more rock, Kitty thought she heard a roar come from nearer the house. She shook her head to clear it and felt a rush of air as several large objects rushed through the air above her head even as a second shot sounded. Panicking, she tried to scramble to her feet while her lungs fought for air. Hard hands closed over her shoulders and pressed her back to the earth.

"Shit. Can you stay where I tell you for one damned minute, you little idiot?"

The sound of that familiar growl opened Kitty's airway like a breathing tube, allowing rich oxygen to rush back into her chest.

"Someone . . . out there," she gasped. "Shot . . . before . . . guard . . . chased . . ."

"Shut up," Max ordered, but his hands were gentle as they ran over her arms and legs and those of the girl in her arms, checking for injuries. "It's being taken care of. Some of the security team tracked him here from the campsite, and Nick, David, and I doubled back around via the road when we guessed where he might be headed."

When he'd satisfied himself that neither of them was seriously hurt, he leaned down until his nose nearly bumped hers and spoke in a voice so low and menacing it actually sent a shiver coursing along Kitty's spine. "I want you to listen to me and listen good, Kitty Jane

Sugarman," he said, his copper eyes glowing with an unsettling light. "The next time I put you in a safe place and tell you to stay there, you're going to do it or so help me God, I will paddle your ass so hard, you'll cry every time you look at a chair, do you understand me?"

She opened her mouth to protest his dictatorial tone—not to mention the words themselves—but he pressed a finger against her lips to shush her.

"Nope," he said in that same ominous tone, "no arguments. It's either that or I put an armed guard on you every time you get farther than arm's length away from me. Which is the lesser of two evils?"

He turned away before she could catch her breath, but now she wasn't so sure that the impact of her fall was what made the process so difficult.

"And as for you, young lady," he said, his growl softer though still stern as he scooped Maisie out of Kitty's arms and propped the little girl up against his chest. "You've had an awful lot of people out looking for you, and they were very sad about not being able to find you. Ms. Avery especially. Didn't she tell you to keep with your classmates?"

Kitty tilted her head so she could watch as Maisie ducked her head and stuck two fingers into her mouth before nodding reluctantly.

"Then why did you wander off by yourself?"

When the little girl just shrugged and hunched her shoulders up around her ears, Max drew his brows down into a frown. "Mary Elizabeth," he warned.

"Ahfwnnddufeedaunneewnnt."

Max turned his scowl on Kitty. "Did you catch any of that?"

Kitty nodded and pressed her hand to her chest. She

continued to breathe hard, but it no longer felt like an elephant was sitting on her ribcage. "She wanted to see . . . a bunny rabbit."

"That's no reason to leave your class, Miss Mary, and you ought to know better."

Kitty opened her mouth to plead the child's case, but once again a loud noise startled her and drew her attention toward the rocks.

Actually, this one was a series of loud noises, beginning with a shout, followed by a woman's scream, a gunshot, and several men bellowing in rapid succession. Pushing herself into a sitting position, she reached out and caught Maisie when Max thrust the child against her chest and took off without a word to her for the second time that day. As he sprinted toward the uneven, rock-strewn slope, Kitty heard one bellow rise above the others.

"Max," a man was shouting, "It's Liv! She's hit!"

KITTY CLUTCHED A PAPER CUP FULL OF WEAK, COOLING tea against her chest and tried not to fall asleep in the waiting room chair Max had shoved her into as soon as they'd reached the hospital. Even if she hadn't been too tired to argue with him by that point, she'd decided she would still have let the arrogant action slide. After all, Max had been forced to explain to the man he loved like a father that Martin's niece had been shot while struggling with the assassin who had meant to break into the Lowe house and kill the Felix of the Red Rock Pride.

Under the circumstances, Kitty could cut Max a little slack.

Liv, Kitty had discovered, was named Olivia Anderssen and she was the daughter of Martin's sister, who had died when Liv was a teenager, leaving her in the care of Martin and Drusilla just before they divorced. When the couple split, they had decided Olivia needed a mother's influence, and Dru had taken custody, raising Olivia alongside Nadia, who was younger by about four years.

Whether Olivia shared her female relatives' feelings about the sudden appearance of Martin's long-lost daughter, Kitty didn't know, because while Drusilla and the kids were trying to nail Kitty to a tree, Olivia had been volunteering at the community center. Apparently, she worked as a lawyer for the firm that represented Martin, and she donated time to help low-income pride members with routine legal matters. She'd still been at the center when the news of the intruder came in, and when the pride had learned about the missing kindergarteners, Olivia had been among the first to volunteer to join the search party.

She had been following Maisie's trail when she ran into the armed man everyone had been searching for and nearly been shot herself. She had tackled the stranger, and in the struggle for the gun, both she and the shooter had taken bullets. Olivia's injury turned out to be a relatively superficial graze through the muscle at the top of her arm, while the man had died almost instantly when the shot pierced his skull and destroyed half his brain.

Superficial, though, hadn't meant anyone took Olivia's injury lightly. Kitty had barely caught a glimpse of the woman's pale, striking face before they had her hustled into the house and then into a car for the trip to the hospital in Vegas.

The sound of footsteps made Kitty raise her head. Max strode toward her, looking intolerably masculine in his dirty, torn clothing with his dark hair mussed and the day's growth of stubble shadowing his chin.

"She looks good," he rumbled, halting in front of Kitty's chair to scowl down at her. "So now it's your turn."

Kitty shook her head. "I've already gotten my door prize." She pulled aside the collar of her T-shirt to show off the edge of a gauze square held in place with white adhesive tape. "A nurse checked me out while you were talking to the doctor. A couple of bruises and a few scrapes. No breaks, bends, or bullets. I got some antibacterial cream and a bandage, and was told to leave the emergency room to the people who really need it."

Max's scowl didn't lighten, but he didn't force the issue. Kitty could tell it was a struggle for him and hurried to change the subject.

"So how come Olivia came to the hospital?" she asked. "Why didn't she just shift? I thought that could heal almost any wound faster than stitches."

"It can, but the pain injection Martin's doctor gave her at the house numbed the arm enough that she couldn't tell him where it hurt and he wanted to make sure the bone was properly aligned before she shifted," Max explained. "It's her right arm, and Liv is right-handed. If she shifted while the bone was out of alignment, she could have ended up with a permanent misalignment that would give her trouble in the future."

Kitty made a face. "I guess the Lord really does look after idiots, then, 'cause heaven only knows how many broken bones I had when I shifted that first time. I'm lucky I don't look like the hunchback of Notre Dame."

Max's scowl deepened.

"What about Maisie?" she rushed to ask before he could scold her for something that had happened weeks ago. Ever since he'd rescued her and the little girl behind Martin's house, Max seemed to have made scolding her his new mission in life.

"Her pediatrician already sent her home with her parents. She didn't even really need the examination. That was mostly to make John and Heidi feel better." Max reached out a hand and plucked the tea from Kitty's hand, setting the paper cup on the table beside her chair. "Come on. It's nearly seven, and you've had a long day. Let's go back to the Savannah and have that steak we talked about earlier."

"Sounds good to me," Kitty said, rising. "But I have to tell you, steak was enough when I'd only had to deal with a few insults. After being shot at, bruised, and scared half to death, I think I definitely qualify for chocolate."

SETTING HER FORK DOWN WITH A WEAK CLINK, KITTY slumped a little in her chair and placed a hand over her chocolate-stuffed belly.

"Now that has what I call medicinal value," she sighed, grinning at Max across the china-littered table. "Nothing can improve the attitude or soften the memory like good dark chocolate."

He chuckled at her over the rim of his wineglass. "I'm glad you enjoyed it, kitten. I'll have to remember to give your compliments to the pastry chief."

"Compliments, schmompliments," she muttered and reached for her cappuccino. "If he makes that for me every night, I'll head back to the kitchen and kiss him smack on the lips."

"Her."

Kitty froze, her eyebrows shooting toward her hairline. A second later she pursed her lips and shrugged. "Then I'll let her make the call. But if she wants tongue, she has to throw in raspberry napoleons on the weekends."

Max laughed at her cheeky grin and drained the last of his very nice cabernet. God, he couldn't remember the last time he'd smiled this much, and considering the day they'd had, that was saying something. He didn't think he'd ever forget the way his heart had leapt into his throat when he'd rounded the corner of Martin's house and seen her fall to the ground just as the gunshot sounded.

She'd lain so still at first that he'd feared the worst until she'd opened those brilliant green eyes of hers and tried to struggle to her feet with little Maisie Theron clutched to her chest like the crown jewels. Relief had driven him to his knees and he'd wanted to hug her to him and keep her safe for the rest of her life. Then he'd wanted to turn her over his knee and beat her ass cherry-red for scaring him that way.

As it turned out, he hadn't gotten time for either reaction. The sound of another gunshot and the news that Olivia had been injured and the assassin killed had yanked him back to his duty to the pride. Cleaning up the mess that the late Billy Shepard had caused for the Red Rock had taken several hours to accomplish, but now it felt like a weight had been lifted from his shoulders. From what Nick and David, the pride's other *belangrik,* had been able to uncover, so far it looked like Shepard had been working alone. Max would have them do some more checking, but he had no reason not to think the threat to the pride had finally passed. The threat to Kitty, on the other hand, still had him concerned.

All evening he'd been unable to quite put a finger on the reason why the hair at the back of his neck continued to prickle even after the Shepard matter was settled. It wasn't until he'd been driving Kitty back into the city that he'd begun to count up the times she'd been in danger recently. Taken separately, each incident, from the car accident in Tennessee that had prompted her first change, to the airport mugging and the shooting this afternoon, appeared unrelated. In each of them, Kitty just seemed to have been in the wrong place when fate and bad luck converged into disaster. If there hadn't been three separate close calls within the space of three weeks, Max himself would have dismissed each of them as nothing more than an accident. But no one, his instincts growled at him, was *this* accident-prone.

When they had reached the hotel, Max had escorted Kitty to her suite to change for dinner and taken advantage of the time it took her to head up to his own apartment on the hotel's top floor and make a couple of calls while he cleaned himself up. One call had been to David to request that the *belangrik* poke around into Kitty's car accident, and the second had been to Nick to order protection for Kitty anytime he couldn't be with her himself. He intended those times to be few and far between, but he wasn't a man to leave things to chance. Just because he ran a casino didn't mean he liked to gamble.

Everything had been arranged before he reappeared at the door to Kitty's suite in time to escort her downstairs to the Savannah's acclaimed French-African restaurant for dinner. He trusted Nick and David completely and knew that each one would carry out his orders to the letter, which meant that until one of them gave him renewed reason to worry, he could turn his attention to more interesting matters. Many of which, coincidentally, prominently featured Miss Kitty Sugarman's very luscious backside.

"Are you finished?" he asked, setting aside his glass and pushing away from the table. "You saw the Strip in the daytime, but now is when it really comes alive. I thought we could take a stroll."

"That sounds great. I need to walk off at least three of those courses."

She didn't protest when he took her hand and tucked it into the crook of his elbow. In fact, she seemed to lean against him as they stepped out into the cool night air.

"Tired?" he asked.

She smiled. "A little. But mostly, I'm just trying to figure out how to walk in these shoes without killing myself."

He glanced down at the sexy, black heels and noticed they seemed to have almost more strap than sole. While he appreciated the view it gave him of her slender, delicately arched feet and delectable little toes, he understood her dilemma. "I see what you mean. Would you rather I hailed a cab and took us straight back to the hotel?"

"No. I'll be fine. Just keep to a nice, level sidewalk and I should be able to avoid serious injury. It's been a while since I've worn party shoes is all."

"And why is that?"

He watched her watching the city around them, her eyes wide and glittering. The neon lights of the signs and billboards all around them seemed to glint off her bright red-gold hair like a crown of fairy lights as she turned back and forth in an attempt to take in everything.

"Probably because it's been a while since I've been to a party." She laughed. "Librarians don't tend to be the first ones on most people's guest lists."

"I don't see what your job has to do with it. Unless you spend so much time hiding between the stacks that people don't get a chance to meet you anywhere else."

"I go out, but my idea of a good time isn't what gets most folks excited. I like bookstores. And old movies. And hikes and museums and tours through historic sites and buildings. Most people look at an afternoon doing any of those as one step above working on a chain gang. But I've always been good at entertaining myself, ever since I was little, so I don't usually mind."

Max heard the assurance in her voice, as well as the wistful note behind it. "Since you were little? Didn't your mother or your grandparents like to do things with you?"

"Mamaw always tried to do things with me," she said, sounding a little wistful, "but there was always so much to do on the farm. We had to sneak in time when we could. My grandmother is the reason why I fell in love with books almost before I could read, because she was always reading to me. And whenever Papaw had any time, he'd take me out walking with him and tell me stories about our ancestors who settled the land, and the people who'd been there before them, or we'd go fishing down at the creek. I had a great childhood."

"And your mother? What about her?"

Kitty shrugged. "Misty had her own priorities, and entertaining a kid wasn't one of them. By the time I was in school, I'd figured out it was better when she wasn't around too much, anyway. When she was, she was always picking fights with Mamaw and Papaw and alternately cooing over or whining about her latest boy-friend."

"She had a lot of those?"

"Misty goes through men like I go through sticky notes," Kitty snorted. "If I'm not losing whole stacks of them in the clutter on my desk, I'm sticking one to something every time I have a new thought."

She sounded amused, but Max had a hard time imagining that kind of woman as a mother. "You approve of her social habits?"

"Of course not. They make her miserable and don't seem to do much for anyone else, either. Misty is a grass watcher. She's always looking over the next fence to see if it looks a little greener. The trouble is, she doesn't seem to realize that in the end, grass is just grass. To make it green, you have to water it. But that's way too much work for her. She'd rather take over someone else's lawn, and move on again when it starts to go brown on her."

Max fought back a smile. "That's a heck of a metaphor, kitten."

She chuckled. "I suppose it is. But you know what I mean. I'm sure you've met people like her. They always want what they don't have, but when they get it, they're not interested in doing what it takes to keep it. Sometimes I think she'd be better off if she just stopped wanting things so bad."

Keeping his gaze on the path in front of them, Max digested that little tidbit. No wonder Kitty seemed to dote on her grandparents and hadn't seemed all that enthusiastic about meeting Martin; she'd seen her grandparents as her real parents and hadn't felt like she needed any others.

Beside him, Kitty tottered a little, and his arm went around her automatically. He pressed her against his side to steady her. "You all right?"

"I'm fine," she said, "just clumsy. You should be glad you didn't decide to take me dancing."

The image of holding Kitty in his arms, pressing her small, sweetly curved body to his as they swayed to a seductive rhythm, filled his head, and Max gritted his teeth against a surge of arousal. The idea sounded lovely to him.

"I think you're about as clumsy as your namesake, kitten," he murmured, unable to stop his fingers from stroking the soft curve where her waist flared into an inviting hip. "I'd like to dance with you one of these days. I have a feeling we'd fit well together."

He heard the swift hiss of her indrawn breath and felt the subtle tension of awareness stiffen her body. Breathing deeply, he caught the sweet, spicy smell of her, and his nostrils flared as he detected the change in her scent. It deepened suddenly, growing rich and dark and compelling.

He caught himself just as his other hand began to reach across his body to grip her more securely and tug her feminine form against him. The beast inside him wanted her to feel his arousal, to know that neither of them was fooling the other. Desire sparked between them like an electric current, making Max curse himself for suggesting their evening stroll. He'd have given anything in that moment to have had her alone in the privacy of her hotel room, where he could show her exactly what it did to him to know she couldn't stop herself from responding to him.

Kitty straightened, attempting to put distance between

them, a move that had his beast snarling. He had to physically bite his tongue to keep from echoing the sound.

"Look, I can see the Savannah up ahead," she said, her voice sounding suddenly quiet and nervous. "I want to thank you for a wonderful evening. I really enjoyed myself, especially after everything that happened today. I mean, I am sorry that man died, but I'm glad that threat to the pride is gone—

She never got a chance to finish. He didn't give her one. His beast didn't give her one.

It sprang free with a muffled growl, turning on her and herding her backward into the shadows of an alley at the side of the building. It saw the way her eyes widened, saw the mingling of surprise and want in their depths, but it didn't care. It pressed her out of the crowd, out of the lights, and pinned her against the cool, rough stone of the wall behind her. It made a prison of its arms, a barricade of its body, and with a rumble of hunger and domination, it dropped its head to feed.

Her lips tasted like paradise and felt like home. Max groaned against them, wanting to savor them, and battling against the compulsion to plunder. He lost.

His teeth nipped at the plump, sweet flesh and felt it tremble. Her mouth opened on a gasp, and he stole the sound, burying it in a growl of satisfaction. She yielded to him slowly, trembling and moaning in thin, high tones. Her hands clutched his shoulders, wrinkling the fine wool of his suit jacket, digging into the muscles beneath. The pressure made him imagine how it would feel with no fabric between them, just skin against silky skin, so that her nails would bite into him and urge him on.

As if he needed urging.

He took her mouth like a marauder, leaving no corner untouched, no recess unexplored. Lips, teeth, tongue, body, he used every part of himself to get closer to her. The way she sank into him was driving him crazy. The way she responded to every touch as if she'd been made for him. It threatened to shatter his tenuous hold on reality, to shatter his control like so much glass. He had to get ahold of himself.

Instead, he took ahold of her. One hand gripped the back of her head, angling her for a deeper kiss, holding her in place. The other slid down the sleek curve of her side, her waist, her hip, curling around the soft weight of her thigh and hooking it over his hip. The adjustment seated him firmly against her center, and he groaned into her mouth at the incredible, agonizing way their bodies fit together.

Her hips cradled him as if he'd been made to rest there. Nothing in his life had ever felt so perfect, but he knew that being inside her would be even better. If only she weren't wearing so many clothes.

Sliding his hand up the back of her thigh, he paused briefly to knead her plump ass before reaching for the zipper at the back of her dress and giving a tug.

She tore her mouth from his with a muffled shriek. "Stop!"

Max shook his head, trying to clear the fog of lust that filled it. "What?"

"Sweet baby Jesus and lawsa mercy!" She pressed both palms against Max's shoulders and shoved, hard. He forced his hands to release her and stumbled backward. "We're in an alley, for heaven's sake! Oh, my God, I can't believe I almost forgot where we were! I almost let you . . ." She shuddered and repeated, "Sweet baby Jesus."

Max struggled to catch his breath. His mind still felt like it was operating at the speed of winter molasses, but even in that state, he understood what Kitty was saying. He'd been about five seconds away from shoving her panties down to her ankles, raising a skirt, and fucking her up against the side of a building where the two of them being arrested for lewd conduct and indecent exposure would have been the least of their problems.

Holy shit. What the hell was the matter with him?

"I'm sorry," he bit out, shoving a hand through his hair and wondering if maybe she should have just slapped him. Maybe that would have cleared his head a little faster. "I shouldn't have done that."

"Agreed."

"I got carried away."

"I noticed."

"We should probably go inside—"

"I should think so."

"—and talk about this."

"Alone?"

"Of course alone."

"Um, I'm not sure that's a good idea." She sidled away from the wall until she stood in the open alley and could fix her eyes on an escape route. "I think I should just . . . not."

"Kitty," he began, but she just shook her head and began to edge back toward the hotel entrance. "I just want to talk. I promise."

"No, I think it would be better if we didn't." She smiled a little wryly. "I've already got enough to think about. Like you said before, it's been a long day."

Grimacing, Max admitted she might have a point. One that his libido certainly didn't want to hear. With a sigh and a half smile of his own, he shoved one hand in his pocket in an attempt to keep it off her and used the other to wave Kitty before him.

He escorted her to her door and left her with a quiet goodbye, turning away before she could close the door in his face. A man's pride could only take so much, after all. Instead of taking the elevator back downstairs or up to his own apartment, Max headed toward the stairwell at the end of the hall and the bottle of bourbon in the bottom of his desk. It wouldn't change what had just happened, but if he was really, really lucky, it might make him drunk enough to render the topic a moot point. After all, with enough alcohol in him, he wouldn't be able to make love to Kitty even if he remembered how.

At the moment, he really wanted to forget.

THIRTEEN

KITTY EXAMINED THE MAP AS SHE WALKED, TRYING TO get her bearings and plot her route at the same time. She didn't want to stay out too long, since at some point today, Max would take her back to see her father, but she needed a distraction. Bad. If she sat around in her room all morning, she would have nothing to do except brood about kissing Max Stuart. And wrapping her leg around Max Stuart. And nearly letting Max Stuart have sex with her in an alley like she was some kind of cheap hooker.

Feeling the heat of embarrassment stain her cheeks yet again, Kitty forced the memories aside and focused resolutely on her sightseeing plans. None of those other options boded well for her sanity.

Smiling at the attendant who held the hotel door open for her, Kitty stepped outside and glanced up from her map. She didn't plan on getting lost, and her sense of direction wasn't bad, but even if she had gotten confused, she didn't imagine it would be difficult to find the Savannah again.

The hotel's rich, earthy stone facade stood out among the whites and grays and reflective glass surfaces of the other buildings, and its landscaping made an even more striking contrast to the other hotels. She hadn't noticed so much yesterday, but then she'd been with Ronnie, and that had made her a little nervous. Today, she could really appreciate the resort's unique beauty.

Provided she kept her mind off Max Stuart's masculine beauty.

Instead of featuring lush landscaping and the seemingly obligatory fountain in the forecourt, her father's hotel looked as if it belonged in this desert-and-scrubbrush environment, as if it had grown in this place and could survive and thrive even if the earth around rose up and reclaimed the rest of the city. Its plantings consisted of thorn trees and acacia, tall exotic grasses, and stunted shrubs suited to a place where water was scarce and the sun unrelenting.

Kitty breathed in the warm, dry air, as foreign to her as the gnarled branches of the huge, unfamiliar tree at the center of the hotel's semi-circular drive. To her, heat was heavy, wet, lush. It wrapped around you like a coat everyone resigned themselves to wearing outside between Arbor Day and Halloween. This heat felt light and clear and fiery, like whiskey, and sharp, like clear blue flames. Despite herself, she was fascinated and seduced. She felt energized and aware and uncomfortably at ease. Almost as if she belonged here, or in some other place remarkably like this, half-remembered from a long-ago dream.

Considering the last day and a half, that kind of thinking could prove to be dangerous.

"Did you need a taxi, miss?"

The doorman's question startled her, dragging Kitty back to reality.

"Oh no," she said, her smile sheepish. "Thank you, but I'm fine. My mind was just wandering, so I think I should follow my mamaw's advice and let my feet follow."

Glancing left and right, Kitty made sure the path was clear, then stepped off the curb to cross the drive and let her gaze drop back to the map.

Where to first?

"Oh, my God!"

"Look out!"

"Someone get her out of there!"

"Lady, *move!*"

The panicked voices jerked Kitty's nose out of her map and her attention back to reality. Her head snapped to the left and her eyes widened, locking on the startlingly clear image of a huge, black SUV careening toward her down the hotel's curving driveway. In the space of a split second, her mind drew three rapid conclusions: one, that the driver was going much too fast for an enclosed space inclined toward meandering pedestrians; two, that the dark-haired man behind the wheel wore huge, black sunglasses and a grim, angry expression that made the back of her neck itch and tickled the front of her brain; and three, that there was a very good chance that she was about to die.

She could still hear screams and instructions, but they seemed to have faded in the distance. All she could do was stand in the middle of the pavement and stare at the vehicle barreling down on her and think about how much she was beginning to hate motor vehicles in general.

Fortunately, while her mind had all but frozen, her instincts had not. With no input from her dazed consciousness, she felt her thighs tense and bunch, felt her center of gravity shift, and felt her muscles propel her off the ground and through the air with a momentum she hadn't known she was capable of producing. How far it would have taken her she couldn't be sure, because her leap halted abruptly when the right side of her body made brain-rattling contact with the trunk of the hotel's massive and rough-barked baobab tree.

The impact forced the air from her lungs in a wheezing grunt and halted her forward trajectory so rapidly that her head whipped forward and back as if her car had just been rear-ended. For one ridiculous microsecond, she pictured herself in a neck brace, answering the inevitable question *Were you in a car accident?* with, *No, a tree accident.*

But you said you weren't in a car accident.

I wasn't. I was on foot.

But that's about as far as she got in that little scenario before gravity caught up with her and sent her sliding toward the ground with the slow-motion, squeaky scraping noise she'd always thought only happened in cartoons. The next thing she knew, she'd probably have little stars and bluebirds circling around her head like an animated halo.

As she slumped, dazed, to the rocky ground at the base of the tree, all she could think about was the fact that it was starting to look like the mugger in the airport bathroom really had wanted her dead, and he'd just tried to finish the job.

WHEN THE HELL HAD FOCUSING ON SOMETHING AS SIMPLE as a profit-and-loss statement become so damned difficult? Max wondered as he reread the same paragraph for the third time.

About the same time that you first set lips on Ms. Kitty Jane Sugarman, his subconscious answered with the kind of smug satisfaction that could make a man growl into his coffee.

Max sighed and tossed the papers back onto his desk. It wasn't the first lip-lock with Miss Kitty that was giving him fits, he admitted. It was the one from last night. The one where more than their lips had locked and it still hadn't been enough.

Being an intelligent man, Max had never tried to claim that he understood women or that relationships made a whole lot of sense to him. He recognized the limits of his intellect in that regard, but in the past he'd been content to let the friendships he'd formed with women happen naturally and to mosey along without a whole lot of intense examination. After all, the attraction between a man and a woman was natural and healthy and the simplest thing in the world, right?

Bullshit.

For the first time in his life, he'd come to realize that nothing in heaven or on earth could possibly be more complicated than what he felt for Kitty Jane Sugarman, and if he managed to hold on to his sanity for another five minutes, it would be a bloody miracle.

It certainly made no kind of sense he could think of for him to have gotten this twisted up by a woman he'd known for less than thirty-six hours. She'd hit him like the first hit of an addictive drug, hard, unexpected, and completely exhilarating. From the moment he'd set eyes on her, he'd wanted her, and the more time he spent with her, the more intense the wanting grew. If things stayed like this, he'd become a feature in a urological textbook—a fascinating case of unrelenting priapism.

Viagra had nothing on Miss Kitty; he could swear to that. In his life, no other woman had affected him like this. The only consolation he could think of was that he seemed to have a similar effect on her.

She'd been with him every step of the way until he'd tried to strip her naked, and thank God at least one of them had retained a little sense. It sure as hell hadn't been him, but in his own defense, the hunger had blindsided him. He hadn't thought need like that existed. He certainly hadn't expected to find it in anyone but his mate, and there was no way Kitty Jane Sugarman could be his mate after less than two days' acquaintance. Things like that didn't happen any more than love at first sight.

Lust at first sight, though . . . well, he could certainly vouch for that with complete honesty.

Behind him, the phone on his desk trilled. Turning his chair back to face the interior of the office, he forced his mind off Kitty and pressed the speaker button. He was supposed to be working, after all. He'd made the conscious decision to come to the office instead of seeking her out because he thought a little time apart would do them good.

And because he'd been afraid she would run away as soon as she saw him.

"Stuart," he barked.

"Mr. Stuart. I'm glad I reached you."

He heard the tension in the voice of his door supervisor and forced his mind back onto business. "Tommy. What's the matter?"

"I called the front desk and they put me through to your suite first. They said you left instructions that you should be notified if a certain guest left the hotel."

"I wasn't expecting her to be out so early this morning." He frowned. "Did she ask you to call her a cab?"

"No, sir. I offered, but she said she wanted to walk. I'm sorry, but she didn't mention her name. I only found out you knew her when we pulled her ID and called up front."

His heart stuttered. "Pulled her ID? Why? What happened?"

The urgency in his voice had Tommy stuttering. "Sh-she's fine, sir. I swear. She's sitting up and talking, but she nearly got hit out front. An SUV came this close to crashing straight into her. Somehow she managed to—"

Whatever Tommy had to say next, Max never heard it. He was out the door and tearing toward the lobby before the phone clattered back into its cradle.

FOURTEEN

KITTY WAVED AWAY A THIRD OFFER TO CALL A DOCTOR and pressed an ice pack against the knot slowing forming on the side of her forehead. "I'm fine, really. Just a little bruised."

"Ms. Sugarman, please. For the staff's peace of mind."

"There's no need. I mean it. It's just a bump on the head and some bright colors along my side." She attempted a smile and winced when even that movement made the throbbing in her skull worse. It felt like an entire team of Appalachian clog dancers had decided to use her head for the site of their rehearsals.

The faces hovering over her looked unconvinced, so she forced her way through the pain and tried to lighten the mood. "The color will do me good. I always said I was too pale."

"Ms. Sugarman, we saw the impact. You could have a cracked rib, or internal injuries." The front supervisor leaned over her with what looked like genuine concern in his faded blue eyes.

"No, don't be silly. It's not that serious, I swear. All I

need is a couple more ice packs and a tube of Bengay. I'll be fine."

The hotel manager's eyes were cocoa dark, also concerned, and more than a little determined. "Ms. Sugarman, our insurance requires that you have an examination and let a doctor make the determination on whether or not you require further care. While we're naturally concerned for your well-being, we also have liability issues to consider."

For heaven's sake, Kitty hadn't had this much fuss made over her since she'd had her tonsils removed in the third grade. She wished these people would just offer her a bowl of ice cream and be done with it.

Darn it, she still needed to get away from this place for a while. She'd already been having enough trouble thinking, which was obvious from her thinking the driver had been the same man from the mugging. With the knock she'd just taken to the head, making her brain work anywhere within five square blocks of Max Stuart had as much chance of happening as immediate global world peace.

"I'll sign a release form if you want," she offered. "I promise not to hold the hotel responsible, but really, I'm *fine.*"

That time her voice held a definite edge, but none of them seemed to notice. They continued to huddle in little groups around the base of the tree trunk she'd leaned herself up against and speak in hushed murmurs. She got the distinct feeling they were trying to stall her for some reason, and the idea made her nervous. Or maybe "paranoid" was the right word.

In the next instant, she discovered exactly why.

"I want to know what the hell happened here, and I want to know NOW."

Kitty had never heard a voice so low, so tight, or so lethal in her entire life. And she didn't even have to look to know exactly who it belonged to.

"Mr. Stuart." The assistant manager snapped to attention like a marine and turned to face Max with an expression of disciplined unease. "I'm afraid we had an incident in the unloading area. Ms. Sugarman was attempting to cross the drive to the street and didn't see an SUV exiting. She was nearly hit, but managed to get out of the way just in time. Unfortunately, she hit the tree instead and managed to knock her side and her head fairly hard against the trunk."

"Where's the driver?"

"He didn't stop," the assistant manager reported, and from the expression on her face, it had taken an act of will akin to an act of God for her to force those words out. "Dorian got his license plate number, but the police said that since the driver didn't actually make contact with Ms. Sugarman, no crime has been committed. They said there's nothing they can do."

Max didn't make a sound, but then again, he didn't have to. The energy radiating off of him made his displeasure clear. All the way to the international space station.

"Call the police again. Ask for Lieutenant Del Anno, and tell him I'd like to speak with him as soon as possible," Max ordered, still not raising his voice. Kitty really wished he would.

He also hadn't yet said a solitary word to her, but his blazing copper gaze had been fixed on her face since the moment he'd barged out of the front doors. His face could have been carved from stone and shown more expression.

She couldn't read a thing there, but she could see the tension in him, the tightness of his muscles that made him look as if he were puffed out like an exotic animal bristling against a challenge.

After last night, she'd expected their next meeting to be a little awkward and had hoped against hope that he'd adopt her own chosen strategy and pretend nothing had happened. She certainly hadn't expected to see him under circumstances like these, where he looked more fierce than an invading army of Visigoths.

This . . . could be worrisome.

"Where's the doctor?" Max continued, and his eyes finally shifted. Not to someone else, but to scrape over her from head to toe, cataloging every scrape, bruise, dent, and smudge along the way. With every one, his expression tightened, until she worried the muscles might snap.

"Ms. Sugarman has refused medical care," the assistant manager said neutrally.

Kitty scowled at the woman. She couldn't remember the other woman's name, but from now on, Kitty planned to call her Benedict.

"I refused medical care because I don't *need* medical care," Kitty said, wishing she could just tape-record the statement and press replay. "I'm fine. I'm bruised and sore, and if someone can go to the gift shop and get me some ibuprofen, I would be willing to name my first-born child after him, but I am *fine*."

Max twitched. "Call Dr. Reijznik. Tell him what happened and ask if he would rather meet us at the hospital or in Ms. Sugarman's suite."

By that point, Kitty had had enough. Her eyes narrowed and she removed the ice pack so as to glare at the man more directly. "Are you hard of hearing, or just plain stupid?" she asked, her own jaw clenching. "I said I don't need a doctor, and as long as I'm conscious and coherent, you can't force me to see one. Which means you can take your dictatorial tendencies, drop trou, and shove them all the way—"

Her suggestion ended in a shriek as Max lunged forward, hooked an arm under her knees, wrapped the other carefully around her back, and lifted her up against his chest.

"Tell one of the valets to bring my car around," he said, ignoring her astonished expression and the smoke pouring from her ears. "The doctor can meet us at the hospital. We'll be in the emergency room."

"Over. My. Dead. Body."

Max dipped his head until his nose nearly pressed against hers. "No, but if it has to be over your hog-tied and gagged body, that's fine with me, kitten. So think very carefully before you answer this question. Do you want to ride in the front seat of my car or in the trunk?"

Kitty opened her mouth ready to breathe fire on him, but either her common sense finally kicked in, or the strange expression she could see shifting behind his eyes managed to stop her. Either way, she closed her mouth and watched for a few more seconds before she turned her head and let her body relax into his arms.

"If you're going to insist that I see a doctor, I'd rather he came here," she sniffed, staring over Max's shoulder. "I don't like hospitals, and it would be silly to clog up the emergency room just so someone can verify what I've already told you. That there's nothing wrong with me."

"And as soon as Dr. Reijznik tells me that, I'll let you do whatever you want with the rest of your day."

"Your generosity is heartwarming."

He let that slide and carried her silently into the hotel, through the lobby, and into the elevator before speaking. "Do you have your key?"

"In my pocket."

"Can you reach it? I have my hands full at the moment."

Kitty saw his mouth curve and managed another glare, despite the throbbing in her head. Without answering, she arched her body and shoved her hand into the pocket of her jeans to pull out the plastic card. She slid it into the slot, punched the button for her floor, and went back to ignoring Max. It required all her concentration.

She used the key again to let them into her suite and tossed it on the table by the door rather than wriggle it back into her pocket. When Max set her gently on the huge, cushy sofa, she scrambled back into the corner, kicked off her sandals, and folded her arms across her chest. "I don't like being treated like a child."

"What a coincidence," he said, heading for the kitchen. "I don't like when you act like a child."

"When I *what*?"

She heard the refrigerator door open and close; then Max reemerged with a small towel and a bottle of cold water. His expression as he made his way back to her side was still tight, but he walked without quite as much of a stalk as he had when he'd first appeared outside.

"Can you think of a better description?" he asked, handing her the water and pressing the towel—apparently filled with ice—against the bump on her head. Her old, melted pack he threw on the table. "Who usually throws a tantrum at the suggestion that they need to follow the rules and do what's best for them even when they don't want to?"

"I haven't thrown a tantrum since I got out of diapers," she gritted out, "but if you keep acting like some kind of bloody emperor, I'll see what I can work up for you." She took the pack from him, wincing as she shifted it into more direct contact with her lump.

"Look, I'm touched that y'all are so concerned with my well-being," she said, striving for a tone of calm and reason, "but like I told the rest of the staff, I'm not seriously hurt. The SUV never touched me, not for lack of trying, and the only thing wrong with me is this knock on my head and some nasty bruises, all of which I gave to myself. I am not a child. I'm twenty-four, not four, and I've been taking care of myself for a long time now. I can tell when I'm hurt and when I'm not, and I resent the hell out of someone else making decisions for me that I'm perfectly capable of making myself."

Max sank onto the cushion beside her knees and braced one arm on the back of the sofa. "If you were perfectly capable of making this decision, you wouldn't have objected to the doctor. You have a head injury. Again. An examination by a professional is the only way to be sure that it's nothing serious."

She was prepared to work herself up into an impressive rage—after all, she did have some energy to burn from last night—but she saw the shadow of worry in Max's expression and felt herself softening. Just a little, mind you.

Kitty rolled her eyes. "For heaven's sake, Max, it's a bump. My skull isn't cracked, my brain isn't bruised, and I don't have any internal bleeding."

"Been to medical school in the last couple of hours, have you?"

She pressed her mouth into a thin line. "Why on earth hasn't some woman killed you by now?"

"I'm quick on my feet."

"You'd have to be."

Closing her eyes, Kitty sank deeper into the sofa and let her head settle back against the soft pillows piled up against the arm behind her. Now that her muscles were beginning to relax, it felt like every single one of them had been whacked with a stout stick. Which, actually, was pretty much what had happened. She ached from head to toe, but the worst by far was her head. The clog dancers had invited friends over, and a construction team had started using jackhammers to repair the rehearsal space. She'd have sold her left kidney for a painkiller. Or even another blow to the head, one hard enough to knock her out this time.

She closed her eyes and groaned. "Does this doctor you called carry morphine?"

She heard Max chuckle and felt his weight shift. A gentle finger touched her temple, skimming over her skin and tucking a strand of hair behind her ear. "I thought you weren't hurt?"

"I said I'm *not* hurt. That doesn't mean that I *don't* hurt."

"Right. Silly me."

She slitted her eyes open and found him leaning over her, his lean, handsome face just inches from hers. He still had one hand braced on the back of the sofa, but the other stroked softly over her face, the backs of his fingers tracing the line of her cheekbone in a gesture that had her stomach clenching and her heart melting.

He was so much bigger than she was that he blocked out the rest of the room completely, his shoulders as wide as her horizon, his chest hard and broad. Last night when he'd kissed her, she'd been so busy worrying about keeping her legs from melting—and then about keeping her clothes on—that his size hadn't really sunk in. She'd known he was tall and heavily muscular, but he moved with such grace and wore his clothes with such elegance that it became easy to overlook. But now every time he got close to her, she suddenly found herself feeling small and vulnerable and intensely feminine. She felt like someone who *needed* to be taken care of, and that feeling made her more nervous than anything else.

Max Stuart was a dangerous man. At least as far as her heart was concerned.

She moistened her suddenly dry lips. "At least you admit it."

His mouth curved, slow and sensual. "I have a number of things to admit to right now, kitten. Want to hear some more?"

Lord, the man could make her shiver without so much as a touch. There might be more than her heart at stake here.

She swallowed. "I suppose that depends."

"On what?"

Her heart fluttered, and she decided that her plan to ignore last night had a lot of merit. After all, nothing terrible had really happened. She'd stopped things before they got completely out of control.

And that just made her wonder what it would feel like if that control slipped again.

She placed her free hand tentatively on his shoulder, fighting with the urge to knead the hard muscle. Just because she recognized the danger in the situation didn't mean she was smart enough to turn back. "On how you plan to break it to me."

"Gently," he whispered, bending closer until his lips just barely brushed hers, tracing licks of fire over her sensitive skin. "Very . . . very . . . gently."

Gently enough, she decided as she strained closer, to qualify as torture. She stretched up, ignoring the pulling in her ribs, craving the fuller taste of him. Lips brushed again, parted, and she made a sound of frustration.

He returned, his lips curving against hers, then sliding away to tickle the corners of her mouth.

Kitty contemplated homicide.

"Gentle," she hissed, opening her eyes to glare up at him, "can be highly overrated. I've had plenty of opportunities to break this weekend, and it hasn't happened yet. So don't strain yourself, okay?"

Max chuckled and nipped softly, leaving her lips plump and tingling, and parted around her quickening breath. "Don't worry. I'm strong. I can take it."

"So can I."

Her hand shifted, cupped the back of his neck, and dragged him down to feast on.

MAX SANK INTO HER MOUTH THE WAY HE WANTED TO sink into her body, slow and deep and dominant, claiming everything she offered and making it his. He heard her moan in satisfaction and stifled the urge to growl his response. She tasted just as sweet as he remembered, sweet and hot, a taste he thought he might already have become addicted to. At this rate, by the time their relationship hit the forty-eight-hour mark, he'd probably be dragging her by the hair into an all-night wedding chapel.

Strangely enough, the unaccustomed thought of becoming someone's husband didn't even make him pause. He only sank deeper into the kiss, his hand coming off the back of the sofa to curve around her back and press her closer to him. Beneath the relaxed fabric of her T-shirt, her body felt warm and soft and resilient. He wanted to sink his fingers into her and knead the giving flesh.

He wanted to sink his body into hers.

The urge was familiar; he'd certainly felt it last night, but this time there was less frenzy, less haste. This time he didn't want to frighten her, and he didn't want to repeat his mistakes. He wanted to make up for his impetuosity, wanted not to rush things. He wanted to savor her.

His hand stroked around her side and underneath the hem of her shirt until his fingers whispered over the undersides of her breasts. Her soft, luscious, naked breasts. Again, she was missing a bra and he was too grateful for her oversight to spend much time wondering if she ever wore one. He felt certain he'd come back to that later.

Shifting his hand, he cupped it beneath her soft weight, lifting and plumping the inviting mound. His thumb brushed over her nipple, bringing the skin to tight attention. She moaned softly against his mouth. He could smell her arousal, lush and tempting, and when she pressed her nipple into his hand, he felt his eyes cross. He burned with the need to bare that little bud, to know its color, its shape, its taste.

Maybe being impetuous wasn't always such a bad thing.

Carefully he slid his hand beneath the hem of her cotton top, brushing his fingers teasingly over the tender flesh. He felt it quiver, felt her breath hitch against his lips, but she made no move to pull away. Thank God.

More confident now, his fingers traced the gentle bow of her rib cage, moving slowly and cautiously until the fabric of her shirt was bunched over his wrist and the backs of his fingers brushed the soft underside of her breast.

She jumped a little, a sharp whimper quivering into his mouth, then melted, softening and trembling in his hands.

His fingers cupped her, tested her weight, savored the way the plump curve nestled against his palm as if it had been made to rest there. He rubbed his thumb over the firm tip, felt the crinkled skin of her areola, and swallowed as his mouth began to water.

He couldn't wait any longer.

Shoving her shirt up out of the way, he fixed his gaze on the rose-tipped cream of her skin for a long, fraught moment. Then he dipped his head and took her within him.

Kitty moaned, the sound low and ragged, and her hands clutched at his head, tangled in his hair, and cradled him to her. He drew strongly, teeth rasping, tongue soothing the sensitive peak until he felt her arch beneath him and knew he was once again in danger of losing his mind over this woman.

Reflexively, he drew his other hand down to pull her to him, his fingers tightening around her rib cage, and she pulled away on a gasp of pain. Max cursed and drew back. "I'm sorry. I wasn't thinking."

Her skin had gone a little pale under a soft flush of arousal, but when he spoke, she blew out her breath in a slow exhalation. Her lips curved. "Neither was I."

Max leaned his forehead very carefully against hers. "I don't want to hurt you."

She tried to tug him back to her. "You won't."

"I'll believe that as soon as the doctor tells me so."

Max saw her green eyes narrow; then she released him with a groan and let her head fall back against the cushions.

"I swear to God, you are the stubbornest man I have ever met."

He grinned and tugged her shirt back into place. "And that's why we're so perfect together, kitten. You're stubborn enough to try to go your own way, and I'm stubborn enough to keep you in line."

The pillow she threw at him missed, but only because the doorbell rang at that moment and he rose to answer it. But her grumbling followed him all the way to the door.

SHE HADN'T THOUGHT THOSE BIG, BLACK DOCTOR'S bags existed outside of reruns of *Little House on the Prairie,* but Walter Reijznik carried one and put it to irritatingly thorough use. By the time he'd poked, prodded, questioned, and examined her to his and Max's satisfaction, Kitty figured Dr. Reijznik probably knew more about her than her grandfather, mother, and childhood sweetheart combined. And he managed it all while wearing a natty plaid bow tie and matching suspenders with his pale, gray suit.

"Well, I'm afraid you're going to be sore for a few more hours, Miss Sugarman," he finally concluded, removing his stethoscope and tucking it safely back into the voluminous bag. "But other than that, everything looks just fine. No permanent damage done and no sign of concussion."

Kitty could hardly be expected to resist an opening

like that. "Right, exactly like I've been telling everyone I've seen for the past two hours," she said, sitting up and casting Max a pointed stare. "So there's no need to coddle me or treat me like an invalid, because there's no damage done."

Max simply quirked an eyebrow and stared down at her from his position behind the sofa where he'd been hovering during the entire examination.

"I wouldn't go quite that far," the doctor cautioned her, his expression turning stern. "From the bruising on your rib cage, I suspect you probably gave yourself a couple of hairline fractures, but your Leo metabolism has already begun to knit them back together. That doesn't mean you're not going to experience some serious lingering soreness, as well as some fatigue while your system recovers from the demands placed on it. Unless you're planning a shift, that is."

That had Kitty scowling and Max smiling smugly because the louse knew very well she couldn't force herself to shift on command yet, and he'd probably told Reijznik that, as well. Between Max and the doctor, she couldn't decide who to glare at.

"And given the fact that your last set of extensive injuries was sustained within the past month, I think it would behoove you to take it easy for a few days." The doctor stopped her before she could protest. "I'm not suggesting you should stay in bed, but you don't need to be afraid to sleep. You need to take better care of yourself, young lady. Just stay out of the gym and don't start any wrestling matches and you should be back to normal in another day or two. Do you think you can handle that?"

"She can," Max answered for her. "I'll see to it."

"Because I, of course, have a sign on my forehead that reads 'Incapable of taking care of myself.' You guys are just so perceptive."

They both ignored her.

"Have you been to see Martin today?" Max asked Dr. Reijznik.

"I was with him when I got the call from your manager. He did ask me to give you a message."

Max snorted. "Don't bother. I'm sure I can guess the contents."

"I'm sure you can."

Kitty pushed herself up off the sofa and gave a silent prayer of thanks when her head didn't throb at the movement. The painkiller the doc had given her—not morphine—was apparently working. At least, well enough to keep her skull from splitting open. "I think I'm going to go change my clothes. No, no. Please. I don't want to interrupt your ignoring me. You two carry on."

"You might want to brush your hair, too," Max called after her, his deep voice sounding amused. "Since Dr. Reijznik has said you're good to go, I thought we might as well take a drive out to your father's house. He'd like to see you again."

Kitty paused for a fraction of a second, but she didn't look back. "Great," she called. "That sounds like fun."

Because, really, why let those nice painkillers go to waste?

FIFTEEN

"DID YOU EVER SEE THE MOVIE *GROUNDHOG DAY*?" SHE whispered, leaning toward Max but keeping her eyes on the rest of the room.

"The one where the guy relives the same day over and over?"

"Yeah. For the first time in my life, I think I completely understand what he was going through."

Before driving her out to the house, Max had called to see if Drusilla and the kids were there. Martin had assured him they weren't and urged Max to hurry out. But like some kind of mutant psychic homing pigeons, Drusilla and Nadia had arrived less than twenty minutes after Max and Kitty and wasted no time in launching a renewed attack against the interloper.

And to make matters worse, the painkillers were starting to wear off.

"Martin, when I stopped by to check on her, Olivia said the partners are beginning to worry about you," Drusilla was saying, her face wearing a faint look of worry. It made quite a contrast to yesterday, so either the woman had the emotions of a sea anemone, or she'd gone overboard on the Botox injections during spa day. "I came out here this afternoon so we could discuss it privately." She shot a glance in Kitty's direction. Her expression, of course, didn't change, but the look in her eyes dripped with venom. "I agreed to bring Nadalie because she's family, but I don't think we should be discussing this in front of anyone else."

Martin scowled. "We're all family here, Dru," he said. "Kitty is my daughter, and Max might as well be my son. There's nothing you can tell me that I'd worry about them hearing."

"But that's the problem," Nadia snapped. "They're not family, Father. Max, at least, is a member of the pride, but the girl is nothing to us!"

Kitty sighed and rolled her eyes. She was too tired to have this conversation again after she'd made herself perfectly clear yesterday. She didn't give a bat's butt how Nadia or anyone else in the family felt about her; she was here for her own reasons and she'd leave when her visit with Martin was over, and that was that.

Of course, it would be nice if her skull didn't split in two before then.

"We talked about this yesterday, Nadia," Martin said, his weak voice firming. "It won't do any good to go over the same ground again. Kitty is as much my daughter as you are, and I'm not going to listen to any arguments to the contrary."

"How can you be so sure?" the blonde demanded, her voice shrill enough to have Kitty wincing. "From what I hear, her mother was such a slut she could be anyone's bastard. She doesn't have to be yours."

Okay, that was enough. Eyes narrowing, Kitty stood, shaking off the restraining hand Max laid on her shoulder. Misty might not have been the best mother a girl could ask for, but by God *no one* was going to talk about her like that. Not in front of Kitty.

"Since your mother is a stone-cold bitch, Nad, I wouldn't be the first one to cast stones if I were you," Kitty bit out, taking a step forward. "Of course, since you don't seem to have a shred more morals than she does, maybe you should speak freely. There's that 'takes one to know one' principle, after all."

Faster than thought—and a hell of a lot faster than Kitty expected—Nadia sprang across the five feet that separated them and slapped her hard across the face. Hard enough that Kitty's head snapped to the side, and when she turned back to her half sister she knew her eyes would be blazing a sharp, cutting emerald.

Even before the loud crack had faded to an echo, Martin's bellow had Nadia stepping back and adopting an expression of the wounded party.

"Did you hear what she said about me, Martin?" Drusilla demanded while her daughter sniffed back crocodile tears. "How can you let her talk to me like that? About your own daughter! How can you even stand the sight of her?"

"I can stand it a lot better than I can stand you at the moment," he bit out. His eyes were narrowed slits the same color as Kitty's and he struggled to breathe through the fury that poured off of him in palpable waves. "Apologize to Kitty right now, Nadalie, or so help me, I will get out of this bed and show you what it means to respect your pride mates. I don't care if it kills me to do it."

The girl didn't even have time to obey. A shrill beeping had her gaze snapping to Martin's cardiac monitor.

All thoughts of Nadia faded from Kitty's mind.

"Martin, lie back down," she urged, moving toward his bedside. "You can't let yourself get all worked up like this. You should be resting. Why, if Ms. Mencina sees us getting you het up this way, she'll skin us alive."

Drusilla had been closer and she was urging her ex-husband back against the mattress before Kitty took more than a couple of steps forward. "Martin, calm down. You'll make yourself even sicker this way. There's nothing to get so upset about. I'm sure Nadia didn't mean to hurt . . . her. Just—"

"I warned you what would happen if you set those monitors off one more time," a very unhappy voice snapped just before a very unhappy nurse emerged from the next room. Ms. Mencina descended on them like a fury, her hands making shooing motions to clear the visitors away from her patient's bed. "This is the second time I've had to throw you people out. If it happens again, I'm going to stop letting you in! Now get! All of you!"

Kitty felt Max's hand on her shoulder and took a step backward. She noticed that despite her pout, Nadia did the same.

"The partners are worried," Drusilla said, backing away from the bed when Ms. Mencina turned a narrow glare in her direction. "They may be calling on you to see for themselves what—"

"I said *scat!*" Ms. Mencina hissed, as if she were talking to a stray tabby with a bad attitude. "All of you, get out. Mr. Lowe needed rest before you got here, and now he needs a heck of a lot more. I hope you're all proud of what you've done."

Kitty knew better than to fight back. Instead, she

smiled at her father and gave him a wave as she turned toward the door. "Feel better, Martin. I'll see you soon," she promised.

Then she fled with Max right behind her before she could be crushed like the bug the nurse clearly thought she was.

As soon as she stepped into the hallway, the headache she'd forgotten in her anger came rushing back like a locomotive, nearly dropping her to her knees. She heard Max swear and felt his arm come around her to steady her. Gratitude flooded her until she wanted to weep with relief. God, it felt like her skull was being split in two, and she couldn't remember ever being this tired. Not even in college when she'd stayed up all night cramming for finals.

Leaning against his reassuring strength, she barely even noticed when Nadia pushed by them and marched toward the front door, her nose so high in the air, she'd have drowned if it started to rain. But Kitty wasn't too tired to notice the look of pure, malevolent hatred Drusilla shot her way as she followed her daughter out to the drive.

If Kitty had been capable of it, that look might actually have made her shudder.

"Come on," Max rumbled, urging her forward. "I can tell your headache is back. I brought your pain pills with us. You can take one as soon as we get to the car. There's a bottle of water in there, too."

Kitty didn't even bother to nod. She stopped trying to fight the exhaustion and let her eyes drift closed. The room seemed to be swaying around her and she'd hoped that closing her eyes would make the disconcerting sensation go away, but instead it just got worse. Maybe it was her swaying, not the room. Her eyes cracked open to confirm this.

Immediately, Max's angry expression vanished, crowded out by one of concern. "Come on, kitten. It's been a hell of a weekend for you, hasn't it?" He shifted his arm around her waist and tugged her to him, cradling her against his side. "I think we need to get you somewhere quiet where you can lay down for a while. You could use a nap."

He looked even more concerned when she didn't put up so much as a token protest. She just let him half-guide and half-carry her out to the car and buckle her carefully into the passenger seat before he hurried around the hood and slid behind the wheel.

"I'm going to fall asleep," she mumbled, her head lolling back against the leather headrest, her words slightly slurred. "Wake me when we get to the hotel. Don't want you carrying me through the lobby again. People stare."

The engine turned over smoothly, the powerful car purring around them. "Don't worry, kitten," he soothed, shifting into gear. "We aren't going back to the hotel. I know somewhere closer where you won't be disturbed."

Kitty didn't answer. She was too busy falling asleep.

DEAR GOD, WHAT EXACTLY HAD SHE HAD TO DRINK last night?

Waking up with a pounding headache worse than the only hangover she'd ever had, Kitty lifted a hand to her temple and moaned. Someone should just kill her. It would be more merciful.

Disturbingly, it was the thought of being killed that jogged her memory. Her hand flopped back onto her pillow, and she rolled over to bury her face alongside it.

How on earth had she gotten into this situation? For twenty-four years, Kitty had managed to live a peaceful life in which no one ever wanted to kill her. Now, in less than two days, she could think of at least three people who probably wanted to, one who'd threatened it, and at least two—depending on whether or not she'd been right about the guy in the SUV being the same one from the airport—who had actually attempted it.

"Dear Lord," she muttered into the fluffy down and silky soft cotton, "I swear on Your holy name that I will never again wish for more excitement in my life."

"Amen."

Lifting her head up, she looked back over her shoulder to see Max standing in the door of the bedroom. He had one shoulder propped up against the rough timber of the door frame, and he smiled as he watched her. The sleeves of his shirt had been unbuttoned and rolled up his forearms, and the tails had been untucked and left to hang loose over a pair of disreputable faded blue jeans she could have sworn he hadn't been wearing when they left the hotel this morning.

Of course, now that she took a look around, Kitty realized the bed she was in wasn't one she remembered from the hotel, either.

Bunching the pillow under her chest, she looked around her and frowned. She'd lay money on the fact that this room did not exist inside the Savannah Hotel and Casino. First off, it was way too small, almost a normal size by Kitty's standards. The king-sized bed she currently occupied took up most of the space, leaving just enough room around the perimeter for a walnut-colored dresser that owed its rich patina more to age than the designer staining, two small, equally aged nightstands, and enough room to make the bed without personal injury.

The bed itself was covered with luxurious cotton sheets softened by many washings and a hand-stitched quilt in a mariner's compass in warm, dark shades of burgundy and blue. The headboard had been pieced together from narrow slats of walnut fitted into a top molding that looked as if it had been carved by hand.

The whole room looked lovingly assembled and decorated, from the tight-fitting logs that made up the walls to the furniture and even the small piece of braided rag rug she could see on the polished wooden floor. It was a room Kitty actually could imagine feeling comfortable in, at home in, and she frowned as she tried to remember how she'd gotten there.

"I thought we were going back to the hotel?" she said, puzzled.

Max shook his head. "I thought it might be a good idea for us to stick closer to your father's house for a little bit. Besides, you made me promise not to carry you into the hotel, so I carried you in here instead." His grin flashed through the dimness.

"Where's here?" she demanded. Then the dim light registered. The bedroom was nearly dark, the only light spilling in soft and golden from the other side of the open door. "What time is it?"

"It's after seven," he said easily. "You slept a good five hours, but I'm guessing you needed it. You nearly passed out before I got you into the car back at the house.

And here is my cabin. It's on your father's land about ten or fifteen minutes' drive from the house."

"What are we doing here?"

"Like I said, it's closer to Martin in case there's any more trouble or in case you want to see him again, and it's a lot more private than the hotel. More comfortable, too, I think. I figured that after this morning and that run-in with Dru and the kids, you'd be happier staying where things are less . . . crowded."

"And complicated," she muttered.

"Exactly." Grinning, he strolled to the end of the bed and twitched the blankets over her feet. "Tonight, we're keeping it simple. Just the basic biological necessities satisfied. You slept; now we'll eat. Hungry?"

Right on cue, her stomach rumbled. Kitty blushed.

Max grinned. "I'll take that as a yes. Come on. Get out of bed and come join me for dinner."

She sat up and pushed her hair back, then threw back the covers with a grimace. "I'll be right behind you. Speaking of biological necessities, there's something else I need to take care of before we eat. Which way is the bathroom?"

He chuckled and pointed her in the right direction, then headed back toward the other room. "Don't take too long," he warned. "Food's getting cold."

Kitty hurried to the toilet, then washed her hands, taking an extra second to splash water over her face. Maybe it would wash away the last of the sleep fog. Patting her face dry with a fluffy white hand towel, she stared into the mirror above the sink. She didn't look so different from a month ago, but no matter how hard she tried to deny it, already Kitty could feel something inside her shifting. She might wish otherwise, but she was no longer the same woman she'd been before that car accident, before the letter. Before this trip.

Before Max.

Making a face, Kitty turned away from the mirror and tucked the towel back onto the rack. She had enough to deal with at the moment without letting her mind wander back to those kisses. Besides, he'd promised her dinner and, quite frankly, she was starving. Time enough to worry about her new surrealistic world later. After she'd eaten.

The cabin was cozy, not a hint of a draft creeping in from between the logs, but Kitty still found herself shivering and wrapped her arms around herself as she made her way through the bedroom and followed Max's trail out into the cabin.

She needn't have worried about getting lost.

It looked like Max hadn't been speaking in understatement when he'd called the building a cabin. Aside from the bedroom with its attached bath, it looked as if the main room was the only other room in the dwelling. On her left, she saw a small, efficient kitchen area with a tiny dining table perfect for two and maybe big enough for four, providing that everyone seated there was good friends. The outside door was straight ahead opposite the bedroom, and the living area stretched out to the right, just big enough for an oversized sofa, a battered armchair, an old wooden rocker, and a scarred coffee table. A fire roared in the fieldstone hearth, and Kitty moved toward it instinctively, drawn by the warmth.

"Cold?" Max asked, coming up behind her and closing his hands over the skin of her arms, bare beneath her

T-shirt's short sleeves. "You're shivering. Stay right there."

Since she had no inclination to move away from the fire, Kitty obeyed, staring into the flames while Max went back into the bedroom. She heard drawers opening and closing; then he reemerged holding a huge flannel shirt so well-worn, the stripes in the plaid seemed to run together in a solid wash of blues and grays.

He returned to his place behind her, shaking out the garment and holding it open while she slipped her arms into the sleeves. The thing was ridiculously big on her, the tails dangling to her knees and the shoulder seams hanging near her elbows, but the fabric felt soft and worn and blessedly insulating, enveloping her in a fuzzy cotton shield against the cold.

"Thanks." She smiled, busying herself with pulling up the cuffs and rolling them up until the tips of her fingers finally emerged from the cloth. "I was kind of chilly. That always seems to happen when I nap."

Max said nothing, just took her by the shoulders and gently turned her to face him. He tugged on the collar and tucked flaps into place, then slid his hands under her hair and pulled the long strands out from under the shirt to let them fall behind her back in a shining mantle.

Her fingers fumbled on the cuffs and she looked up, her eyes wide, taking in the sight of him, burnished in the firelight, his expression warm and almost tender as he smoothed her hair and tucked the sides carefully behind her ears.

"I think it looks better on you than it ever did on me," he murmured, letting his hands slide over her shoulders and down her arms in a caress that made

Kitty's shivers return with a vengeance. Only this time, they had nothing to do with cold.

His tone told Kitty that whatever he was imagining, she didn't want to hear about it. Not if she wanted to retain the power of speech. And thought. And probably motion as well.

Nervously, she cleared her throat and blushed again when her stomach punctuated the quiet with another demanding rumble.

Max laughed. "Come on. I can hear where your priorities lie at the moment. Let me feed you before you fall over."

He held her chair for her and settled her at the table, then opened the door to the oven and pulled out two heavy stoneware plates piled with food.

Kitty felt her eyes go wide as he set one in front of her and took his own seat across the table. He'd prepared what looked like a perfectly grilled steak, so obviously juicy it made her mouth water just to look at it. Accompanying that, she found a buttery baked potato and bright, crisp green beans. Her fork was in her hand before she got over the first whiff of the tantalizing aromas. "Wow. You must stay here a lot to have the place so well supplied. I'm impressed."

Max shrugged and sliced a bite of steak. "Not as much as I'd like to, actually. This stuff is all basics. The steak and vegetables keep for a long time in the freezer, and things like potatoes and onions do pretty well in the root cellar." He grinned at her a touch wickedly. "If you find this impressive, I can't wait until you taste my omelets."

Kitty's gaze dropped to her plate. Having him make her breakfast was not something she felt comfortable contemplating right then. Instead, she sipped from the glass of red wine at the top of her plate and raised an eyebrow. "And I suppose this keeps for years in the wine cellar?"

"Actually, it's really just the root cellar, but yeah, it does okay."

He looked so smug and so pleased with himself that all Kitty could do was shake her head and apply herself to the delicious meal. When she pushed back from the table half an hour later, her stomach was pleasantly full of food and her head pleasantly fuzzed with wine. She wasn't drunk—she'd only had a little more than a glass—but she definitely felt a lot more relaxed than she had for at least twenty-four hours.

"That was delicious," she said, smiling at Max over the rim of her wineglass. "Thank you so much."

"It was my pleasure."

When he reached across the table to take her plate, Kitty smacked his hand. "Uh-uh. No touching."

"Kitten, it's empty," he pointed out, clearly amused. "If you're still hungry, I'll have to see what else I can find for you, but you won't be eating it off this plate. Let me have it."

She scowled at him playfully. "I'm stuffed, if you must know, but you are not going to clean up after me. House rules: He who cooks doesn't do dishes. I'll take care of it."

"I think you're forgetting something, kitten."

"What?"

He stood and leaned over until his breath tickled her skin when he spoke. "This is my house," he murmured, his eyes glinting. "I get to make the rules."

Then he brushed a kiss over her parted lips and whisked her plate away while she was still trying to get her head to stop spinning.

Oh, Lord, she was in such serious trouble. Her reaction to him only got worse and worse every time he came within three feet of her. At this rate, she'd be tripping him and beating him to the floor before another day went by.

"I'm sorry, did you say something?" Max looked up from where he stacked dishes in the sink and smiled at her. Wickedly.

Kitty narrowed her eyes. "Not a thing. You must have been mistaken."

"Hmm. I guess." But he winked at her as he filled the sink with water and dish soap.

Whose brilliant idea had it been to unleash that man on an unsuspecting female populace? Kitty wondered, pushing back her chair and neatening the table just to give herself something to do. Other than stare at Max's very appealing behind as he industriously soaped and rinsed.

When the crumbs had been deposited in the trash and the salt and pepper shakers were lined up like little ceramic soldiers—which took all of about twenty seconds— Kitty gave up and joined him at the sink, picking up the clean dish towel she spotted sitting folded on top of the microwave. She plucked a handful of silverware out of the drying rack and set to work.

Max glanced at her and shook his head. "You don't have to do that. There isn't much here. I grilled the steaks outside, and the potatoes baked in the oven right in their skins. This will only take me a few minutes. Why don't you take your wine into the living room and relax for a bit?"

"If I get any more relaxed, I'm going to fall asleep again."

"Good. I find the sound of your snoring very soothing." He plucked the utensils out of her hand and snapped the end of the dish towel against her bottom. "Now, scat."

"I do not snore," Kitty grumbled, but she took her wine and did as she was told.

She quickly discovered that the sofa was just as comfortable as it looked. The overstuffed arms and the soft, plush fabric of the cushions beckoned invitingly and she stretched out on her side with her sock-clad feet pointed toward the fire. A few minutes of staring into the flames and she found herself beginning to drift into a contented doze just as she'd predicted.

Dishes clinked and silverware clattered softly in the background as Max finished cleaning up after their meal. The sound provided a homely accompaniment to the crackle of the logs in the hearth, emphasizing the impression she'd had in the bedroom that this cabin was a place she could really feel at ease in. Unlike the luxurious hotel room and her father's sprawling designer mansion, she could imagine this little cabin tucked up in the foothills of the Smoky Mountains back home. She could imagine herself being content in a place like this, a cozy, simple little cabin perfect for sharing with a lover.

The wine, the sofa, and the fire conspired to send her into a peaceful trancelike state where nothing could possibly disturb her. She wasn't asleep. She could still hear Max moving around, the fire spitting, and the wind moving around the outside of the windows, but her eyes had drifted shut and she couldn't think of a single good reason to open them.

When the cushion behind her dipped and she felt Max settle onto the sofa beside her, she also couldn't think of a good reason to protest. He gathered her up in his arms and lifted her, stretching out where she'd been lying and depositing her in his lap. She found herself oddly disinclined to protest and simply let her head rest against his chest as he cuddled her close with one arm and sipped his wine from the other hand.

"I guess you weren't kidding when you said you were going to fall back to sleep," he teased a minute later, his breath ruffling her hair.

"Told you so." She forced her eyes open and looked into the fire, her mind still just a little too hazy for her to remember why she ought to be protesting this closeness. "I had an exhausting day, if you'll recall."

"I do." He pressed a kiss to the top of her head, and Kitty felt like it was the most natural thing in the world. "I wore myself out just watching. I don't know many girls who can get hit by a car in the morning and then hold their own against a pride of nasty she-cats in the afternoon."

Kitty shrugged and smiled, letting her hand rest beside her cheek on his broad chest. "I got some game."

Max chuckled. "I'll say you do, kitten." His arm tightened around her. "I'm sorry you had to deal with that, though. I was hoping Drusilla and the kids would give you some time before they showed up, even if I couldn't quite make myself believe they'd be content to give you the cold shoulder instead of attacking you outright."

"It's okay. Number one because it's not your fault, and number two because I walked away with all my limbs and no new scar tissue. From where I see it, it could have been a lot worse."

"That still doesn't make it okay," he rumbled, the sound welling from his chest and vibrating in Kitty's ear. He paused for a moment, and she could feel his eyes on her, watching her watch the fire. "I'm also sorry for what Peter did. You shouldn't have had to find out about your father that way. I'd hoped he would tell you while I was in the other room, but I guess he never got around to it, huh?"

"No."

For a long time she said nothing else, just stared into the flames and absorbed the peaceful feeling of being in this moment, in this place, with this man. Somewhere in the back of her mind, a tiny remnant of her sanity was screaming about how she ought to know better than to let herself be alone with this man, know better than to let him touch her, to let him comfort her, when clearly the only way things could end between them would be with her heart breaking into a thousand tiny pieces.

After all, in the end, she'd be going back to Tennessee, back to the life she'd known before—mostly—and he'd be here in Vegas surrounded by beautiful women and living a life she knew nothing about. He'd be using words like "Felix" and "pride," "*baas*" and "challenge." She'd be in the library using words like, "I'm sorry, but you can't take that document out of the Special Collections area. It's too fragile."

Not exactly a storybook romance.

But at the moment, that part of her mind was locked up in a dusty old closet somewhere in the back of her subconscious and other, more reckless parts were pointing out how pleasant she found him to be around, how she loved his wit and the way he always seemed to be there when she needed to lean on him, both literally and figuratively. How she felt stronger when she was with him and had already come to rely on him. How he made her breath catch and her stomach clench and her nipples harden.

Which, she figured, might qualify as a romance of an entirely different kind.

She felt the muscles in his chest shift as he drained his wineglass and set it on the coffee table beside hers. Then his arm came up to wrap around her, completing his hold on her, capturing her securely in his embrace. She couldn't think of another place she wanted to be.

Her breath sighed out slowly, and she snuggled deeper into his chest. If she had to talk about this, she was probably in the best possible position for it. At least she was warm, comfortable, safe, and just tipsy enough to dull any potential pain.

"What's wrong with him?"

Max rested his chin on top of her head. "Cancer. It started in his stomach, but no one recognized the symptoms at first. He kept dismissing it as something he ate that didn't agree with him, or as heartburn. By the time he finally saw a doctor, it had already spread to his lungs, his colon, and his lymphatic system. That was the last time he agreed to any testing. When anyone brings it up, he just says that by now he's got more tumors than tissues. And he's probably right."

"Is he getting treatment?"

"He has an oncologist who monitors his case, but there's nothing they can do to cure him. They can help manage his pain and keep him comfortable for as long as possible, but beyond that . . ."

Max trailed off, one hand stroking slowly over her hair and down her back. Kitty tilted her head until she could see his face. "Why did he let it go so long before he saw a doctor?"

Max shook his head. "He just didn't know. Gastric cancer isn't the most deadly form of the disease, but it's one of the forms that tend to be fairly far advanced before they're detected. People think stomach problems are just part of life. They ate some bad clams, or their food was too spicy, or they've picked up a bug. And, of course, it didn't help that he's Leo."

"What do you mean?"

Max's hand came up and he rubbed his thumb gently over the knot in her head that she'd gotten that morning. Already the bump had gone down until you could barely find it even if you knew where to look. And Kitty had noticed that her headache had disappeared hours ago.

"You know firsthand how quickly we can heal ourselves," he said. "That's because our metabolisms are significantly faster than a human's. Once you start shifting on a regular basis, you'll find you have to eat a lot more than you used to just to keep your energy up. It's one of the things that give us extra strength and speed as well. But every silver lining has a cloud, right?"

He smoothed her hair back and stroked the backs of his fingers over her cheek. "Our fast metabolism means that our cells divide more quickly and make new cells faster. That's how we heal, which is great. But cancer is when cells mutate and become diseased and then begin to reproduce out of control. The same gift that makes our healthy cells divide faster also makes the cancer cells divide faster. In Leos, and in most of the other shifters, cancer spreads through us like a forest fire. Before we even see the flame, half the forest has been destroyed."

Kitty replaced her head on his chest and frowned into the fire. "Well, that kind of sucks for us, doesn't it?"

"Pretty much. Fortunately, our immune systems are stronger than the average human's, as well, so our bodies are more likely to find the diseased cells and get rid of them before they have a chance to go crazy. Cancer's rarer for us than for humans. It's just more deadly when it does manage to take hold."

"It's still so weird to hear that."

"Hear what?"

"Hear the words 'us' and 'humans' and not have them mean the same thing."

Max's arms tightened around her. "I can imagine it is. You've had a lot to adjust to in the last few weeks, haven't you, kitten?"

"You have no idea."

"No, I know I don't. I've always known what I was, even when I didn't know where I belonged. I never had to wonder about that."

She looked up at him, her brow furrowed in a frown. "What do you mean, that you didn't know where you belonged?"

His lips curved. "I'm kind of like you, that way. I wasn't born into the Red Rock Pride, either. I wasn't even born in Nevada, actually. I just sort of ended up here when I was about fifteen or so."

"Where were you born, then?"

"Los Angeles. My mother was a wannabe actress who paid the rent—most of the time—by waiting tables. My father took off when I was two or three. They weren't part of a pride, so they had no support system to fall back on when things got tough."

"I'm sorry," she said.

"Don't be." He smiled down at her. "It wasn't the best childhood, but no one abused me and I never really went hungry. But I also didn't stick around long once I got old enough to try going somewhere else. Without a pride, I had no reason to. I worked and hitchhiked my way out to Vegas without getting into too much trouble when I was about fifteen. Of course, it helped that I'd just had my first shift and felt like the king of the universe." He chuckled at the memory. "I figured someone would have to be stupid to try and hurt me, king of the beasts that I was."

"How did you meet my father?"

"I'd gotten to Vegas by the time I turned sixteen and gotten a job running for a bookie. It was good money, and like I said, I thought no one could touch me. Then a couple of years on I ran into some other nomads, Leos who weren't members of any pride, and they kicked my ass hard enough to leave boot prints. They stole my bookie's money and dropped me off in the middle of the desert to rot. Lucky for me, their idea of the middle of the desert was smack-dab in the center of Martin's property. He found me, got me to a doctor, and offered me the two things that saved my life: a job, and a place in the pride."

Explanation finished, Max lapsed into silence and Kitty let his story sink in.

"I guess it's no wonder you're my father's right-hand man," she finally said. "I guess you two have gotten pretty close over the years."

"He's my real father," Max offered simply. "The man who got my mom pregnant was nothing more than a sperm donor."

Kitty snorted quietly. "That's the same term I've been using to describe my father since I found out about him." She sighed. "I've sort of had to rethink that."

"Just because I have a high opinion of your father doesn't mean that I expect you to fall all over yourself with joy before you really get to know him. I know he had his reasons for leaving you with your mother's family, and I know that because he told me a little about them, but that doesn't mean I agree with him. He left you alone for a long time. He needs to find a way to make up for that. Or at least make peace with it."

"Right. I don't know if that's the kind of thing you can make up for." Her mouth curved wryly and she glanced up at him from under her eyelashes. "Though I have to say that meeting Drusilla and Nadia gave me a much fuller understanding of what he meant when he said he was doing it to protect me."

Max's chuckle vibrated through her like a massaging chair. "It does lend something to the saying about seeing and believing, doesn't it?"

Kitty rolled her eyes. "Dear Lord. How y'all put up with those women is beyond me. And excuse me for saying it, but Peter doesn't seem to be any better."

Max winced. "They may have become a little spoiled."

"You think?"

That had them both chuckling. When his chest finally stopped shaking, Kitty wriggled a bit to correct her position and found herself rubbing her face against him as she settled back, just like the kitten he'd taken to calling her.

"Comfortable?" he asked, his voice ripe with amusement. But Kitty noticed that his hands didn't pause in their long, sweeping strokes of her back.

She smiled into his shirtfront. "You'll do."

Without lifting her head, Kitty could sense his smile.

She also sensed the change in his muscles. Not tension so much as alertness, as if a wave of new awareness flowed through him from his head all the way down to his toes, invading every strong inch in between.

It spread to Kitty's muscles, too. She didn't shift an inch, didn't change the rhythm of her breath, didn't say a single word, but slowly she became aware of the shifting energy between them. Her lazy peace melted away, replaced by something no less pleasant but infinitely more complicated.

She knew the instant he felt it. Or maybe it was the instant he noticed that she felt it, too. His body hardened beneath hers. His touch on her back firmed, slowed, its range widening. One hand slid down to grasp her hip, and the other burrowed under her hair to cup the sensitive nape of her neck.

Helplessly, she shivered.

"Cold, kitten?"

Not even remotely.

She shook her head but kept her eyes on the flames. Her attention, however, had focused entirely on him.

His thumb rubbed tiny circles in the hollow at the base of her skull, his hand on her neck firming, urging her to look up at him. She resisted for a moment, not knowing who she fought, his touch or her own rioting senses, then surrendered and tilted her head back until she saw the hard planes of his face gilded in the light of the fire.

In the flicker of light and shadow, his mouth looked hard, almost cruel, but she could remember with vivid detail how soft and seductive it had felt moving against hers. His eyelids had drifted down, half-veiling his expression, but she could see hints of the bright copper color shifting and glinting like molten metal beneath thick, dark lashes.

Kitty shivered again, and the hand on her hip moved lower, sliding over worn denim and warm woman until it cuddled half of her bottom in its broad palm. Together with the hand at her nape, it lifted her, urged her forward until her mouth was on a level with his. The sweet, spiced wine of their breath met and mingled between them until they drew each other in on each inhalation, offered themselves to each other on each soft sigh.

His eyes met hers for an instant, and Kitty had about that long to realize he posed a greater danger to her like this, in this state of seeming lazy comfort, than he had that morning. Even when he'd stood in the crowd in front of his hotel barking questions and orders with cold rage pouring off of him like vapors off dry ice, she'd felt safer than she did right now. None of his anger had been directed at her, but she knew that the melting heat she saw in his eyes now had no other target.

Fascinated and helpless, she watched as his gaze drifted closely down, caressing her brows, her cheeks, the soft sides of her nose, before it settled, bright and intent, on her mouth. Her tongue darted out, completely against her will, to moisten her suddenly dry lips.

He made a sound like a purr just before he shifted, his hands drawing her down to him until her lips settled over his by *his* decree, not hers. She might lie sprawled over his powerful body, but he was in control, moving her like a rag doll at his whim.

It was hard to care, though, when his taste went to her head like moonshine, and the heat of his kiss warmed her faster than a flame. She sank into him as if he belonged there, and he welcomed her as if he'd always known she was missing. His hands on her anchored her while his mouth on hers sent her senses reeling. It seemed impossible that she could have forgotten that he kissed like a god—it had only been since that morning, after all—but the power of it seemed impossible to comprehend even while it dragged her under like a riptide.

His mouth ate at hers, devouring, consuming, and at the same time she felt as if his taste, his touch, filled her up, gave her something she'd been lacking without being aware of it. His tongue stroked, teeth scraped, fingers tightened, stealing her breath and her will so that when their lips parted, it was because he pulled back. She didn't have the strength.

Her eyes drifted open and she looked down at him, dazed and shaking, while his fingers traced erotic patterns on the back of her neck. She felt as if she'd been hypnotized. His touch was light, his hands caressing rather than holding, but she knew trying to escape would have been futile. He'd bound her to him with something stronger than rope, something she couldn't see and didn't understand.

"You look tired," he said, his voice rasping like rough cloth against her skin. But his lips were velvet smooth as he dragged them across her cheekbones and nibbled delicately at the shell of her ear. "Ready for bed?"

Kitty blinked, struggling to think, struggling to breathe, as the question hung in the air between them like a living thing.

Finally, she cleared her throat and brought a trembling hand to his face. "That depends," she whispered, her voice soft but surprisingly clear. "Where will I be sleeping?"

The fire in his eyes flickered. "Where do you want to sleep?"

She pressed her palm to his jaw, felt the prickle of evening stubble and the strong, clean lines of muscle and bone. He pressed his skin against her like a cat begging to be stroked and she smiled as she leaned down and brushed her lips to the soft, smooth patch of skin just at the crest of his cheekbone.

"Under you," she whispered, and laughed with excitement as his body instantly hardened in response.

Max swept her into his arms and stood in one smooth motion, holding her cradled against his chest like something small and precious. When he held her, that's exactly what she felt like.

"Your wish is my command," he growled, and headed for the door to the bedroom.

"Oh, goodie," she whispered, burying her face in the curve of his neck and inhaling the warm, intoxicating scent of him. Her tongue darted out to taste and she heard his rumbling groan. Her mouth curved into a satisfied grin.

"In that case, I really wish you'd hurry."

Sixteen

MAX HAD NO INTENTION OF LYING. WHEN HE'D DE-
cided to bring Kitty to his cabin in the hills surrounding
her father's home, Max had hoped things would end up
just like this, but that didn't stop his heart from leaping
at the sound of her whispering that tonight she wanted to
sleep beneath him.

It also didn't stop his body from tightening to a painful level of arousal when he felt the playful touch of her
tongue against his skin and heard her husky voice urging
him to hurry. The way he felt at the moment, she should
be begging him to slow down. He had to fight hard to
keep from giving in to the urge to toss her onto his rum-
pled bed, where her scent still clung to the sheets, and
drive into her slick little body before he'd gotten them
properly stripped.

He felt like a barbarian, but he'd have cut his own
hands off before he caused this woman an instant of
pain.

When she wriggled a hand out from between their
bodies and slid it down his stomach toward the button on
his jeans, he growled a warning. "If you don't want to
roll over in sixty seconds and wonder what the hell just

happened, I suggest you keep those clever little fingers of yours to yourself."

He felt her smile against his skin and heard her husky laugh.

"Am I not allowed to touch you?"

"Of course you can touch me," he said, depositing her in the center of his big bed and crawling up after her. When she slid her hands over his chest, he grabbed her delicate wrists and stretched them above her head, pinning them in place. "You can touch me next time."

Kitty's mouth turned down in a pout, displaying a teasing, provocative side of her he hadn't seen before now. It made his hands burn with the need to touch her, to drive her so crazy, she wouldn't be able to think of ways to torture him. When she accompanied it with a full-body shimmy that had her hips and belly rubbing against the painful length of his arousal, more than his hands caught fire.

Grunting, Max pressed a knee between her legs and urged them apart. "Don't worry," he growled, gripping both her wrists in one of his big hands and sliding the other down to the button on her jeans. "At the rate we're going, next time is going to be about four and a half minutes from now."

She giggled and reached up to nip his chin. "What's the rush, sweetheart? I'm not going anywhere. Take your time."

"I'd rather take you."

He suited words to action, popping open her button and dragging her zipper down until he could slide his hand into the warm valley between her legs. He heard her gasp, felt her arch beneath him, and grunted in satisfaction. He'd barely touched her, and already she'd caught fire for him. He couldn't wait to see her burn.

Light, teasing strokes along her inner thighs made her tremble and spread her legs wider. He smiled grimly and prayed his control would hold long enough for him to accomplish what he'd been craving since the first time he'd laid eyes on her.

His fingers feathered up the inside of her thigh, feeling the tightly corded tendon flex and shiver as she arched to bring him closer. She had thrown her head back and closed her eyes, and as Max watched, she parted her lips and moaned at the feel of his long fingers parting her delicate folds to reveal her sweetest secrets.

He pressed forward lightly, his movement hampered by the confining folds of her clothing, but he didn't care. He could feel her flesh swelling and opening beneath his touch, could feel the rush of liquid heat as her body wept for him, and he knew he couldn't have waited for another second to discover exactly how much she wanted him.

Kitty moaned softly and pressed against his hand, her hips shifting in a futile attempt to guide his caress. He soothed her with soft, meaningless sounds and watched her face intently as he scissored his fingers around her swollen clit and drove forward toward her tender opening.

"Max . . ."

The sound of her name on his lips was like music, sweet and soft and stirring. Her lips trembled around the single syllable, and he fought against the urge to taste them, needing to see her face for just a few more minutes.

"Max . . ."

His fingers traced the sensitive rim of her entrance, taunting with the promise of pleasure, until her breath broke on a gasp and his self-control broke along with it. He pressed forward, sliding a finger past the tight ring of muscle and deep into her welcoming core. Her body tightened, clinging to him, and he swore in anticipation of feeling those sweet, intense contractions milking the length of his cock.

Her breathless cry, broken and urgent, drove him on like a lash. He'd spent last night wanting her, had woken up this morning with her taste on his lips. If he didn't get inside her soon, he was going to lose his mind.

Dragging his hand from between her legs, he felt her shudder beneath him and gritted his teeth. Without releasing her wrists, he used one hand to strip off her jeans and toss them to the floor. Her socks followed, but when he reached for her shirt, his eyes caught on the cinnamon-flecked cream of her freckled skin and he froze.

She painted such an erotic picture, lying half-nude and supplicant in the casual disarray of his tangled sheets. The shirt he'd helped her into earlier lay spread open and puddled at her sides, and her short, snug T-shirt ended just at her belly button, exposing that tempting hollow in teasing little flashes. Just below it, her belly curved gently in the faint, soft rounding of a healthy, fertile female. The urge to sink his teeth into that soft, fragrant skin nearly overwhelmed him.

His breath caught in his throat at the length of her pale, round thighs and the neat triangle of curls at their junction. They really were the color of cinnamon, a rich reddish brown many shades darker than her hair, and already dewed with her arousal. His mouth watered at the sight.

"Max . . ."

Again, that breathless whisper, a note of urgency creeping into the background. She might as well have taken spurs to him.

He reached for the hem of her shirt, intent on dispensing with the last remaining barriers between them, but his dilemma became immediately clear. In order to pull the T-shirt up over her head, he'd have to take the button-down off her first, and to do that, he'd have to release her hands. But she looked so delicious, stretched helpless and needy beneath him. He felt like a conqueror, a warrior, a king, and it would take a stronger man than he to give that up.

Decision made, he leaned down and brushed her mouth with his. Whispering an apology against her parted lips, he fisted his hand in the collar of her T-shirt and ripped, at the same moment that he seized her lips and thrust between in a shameless act of claiming. Instead of protesting, Kitty moaned and arched against him, her little hands clenching until her knuckles whitened, her hips and belly rubbing against him beseechingly.

He growled against her lips and discarded the shredded remains of cotton so he could glide his free hand over the creamy skin of her stomach, up her smooth side to curve possessively around the warm weight of her breast. His growl of satisfaction mingled with her soft gasp and drew another strangled cry from him when his fingers firmed and gently kneaded. His thumb brushed over the rosy crest of her nipple and felt it crinkle and harden at his touch. It drew up into a firm little point that begged for the touch of his fingers, the warmth of his mouth.

Deliberately, he withdrew from her mouth until his lips just brushed hers with a teasing, feathering pressure. He heard her whimper, felt her strain closer, but his grip on her wrists held her pinned. He couldn't quite give up the hot, sweet taste of her, but he wanted her focused on his hand, not his mouth. He wanted her to feel every stroke, every pinch, every teasing flick of his fingers on her breast.

The new tension crept over her slowly, tightening her already-trembling muscles, creating a maddening little hitch in her breath. When he saw her eyelashes flutter and caught a glimpse of dazed, glittering green, he let his lips curve and his fingers tighten around her nipple with excruciating slowness.

Max savored every moment of her reaction, following her body's and her expressions' clues like a treasure map. He saw her eyes widen, felt her lips part, and heard the rush of air as she drew in a quivering breath. A little more and she pulled back from his kiss, her mouth rounding into an *o,* her head falling back to the pillow to expose the slim length of her throat. With a growl, he buried his head in the seductive curve where neck slid into shoulder and sank his teeth lightly into her skin at the same time that his fingers closed tighter.

Kitty cried out, a low shudder of sound, and pressed her breast farther into his hand. Her breath roughened, soughing in and out of her lungs in harsh pants. He felt her thighs quiver against his legs and knew he couldn't go another second without tasting her.

Abruptly, his fingers released her nipple, making

her moan as blood rushed back into the aroused tissue. Changing the moan into a scream as he dipped his head and drew the red little bud deep into his mouth.

She jerked, her knees drawing up, her elbows down, as if she would curl herself around him and trap him against her, but Max held firm and pushed her wrists insistently back against the mattress. He sucked hard at her nipple, even as his fingers stroked the curve of her neglected breast and closed with teasing hesitation around her other nipple.

"Oh, God," she whispered, and her body drew up like a bow against his. Humming around the tasty morsel in his mouth, he forced his knee between her tightly clenched thighs and brought his denim-clad leg hard up against her.

He could feel her moisture soaking through the thick fabric, feel the power in her legs as she gripped his thigh and rubbed herself frantically against him. Chuckling wickedly, Max drew his lower body away from her, making soothing noises when she cried out a desperate protest.

"Sh," he murmured. "I'll take care of you, kitten. Trust me."

"Hurry," she gasped, nearly choking on her own voice. "Please, hurry."

"Ah-ah. It no fun to rush." He reached up and parted her wrists, grasping one firmly in each hand and drawing them down to her sides and pinning them against her hips. "You are definitely something I want to savor."

Kitty whimpered, but he doubted she had the strength or the will to fight his decree. Smiling against her skin, he dragged his mouth down the center of her body, tasting her from her collarbone to her belly. When his lips hovered just above her curls, he raised his head.

"Bend your knees, kitten."

Breathlessly, she obeyed, spreading her thighs and opening herself to him.

"Good girl," he murmured. "Wider now. Bring them up against your sides."

She whimpered but complied, drawing her knees up until she lay before him completely exposed, totally vulnerable.

Max stared down at her, entranced by the sight of her dusky folds all soft and swollen, pearls of moisture trembling on the tempting flesh. He wanted to eat her up like candy, and seeing that he was the one in control here, he saw no reason not to give in to the urge.

"So pretty." Unable to resist, he lowered his head and blew a stream of air against her, knowing the breeze would feel icy against her overheated body. She cried out and Max grinned, lifting her wrists and guiding her hands into a new position.

"Right here." He curled her hands around the backs of her thighs just above her knees so that she held legs up for him, held herself open for him. Offered herself to him without reservation. He'd never seen a more beautiful sight in his life. "Now hold on, kitten. Whatever you do, don't let go."

Her whimper echoed in his ears, but he just smiled and slowly released her hands. When she remained motionless but for the uncontrollable shivers wracking through her, Max slipped his own fingers between her thighs and used them to part her slick fold, exposing her fully to his devouring gaze.

"So pretty," he repeated. Then he bent his head and set his tongue to her flesh.

Kitty screamed. The high, frantic cry filled the room, filled his head, but he didn't care. He'd never tasted anything as delicious as this woman. She ran like honey against his tongue, thick and melting, and like honey she was sweeter than sugar. He lapped at her hungrily, consuming her, using lips and teeth and tongue to explore every inch of the body he was claiming as his. When he drew his tongue slowly up the length of her slit, she shuddered, and when his tongue flicked hard against the tight little knot of her clit, she let go of her legs, clutched handfuls of his hair, and released a high, keening wail that reverberated through him like a symphony.

A warning rumbled in his chest as he lifted his head and pulled her hands from him. "I said to hold on," he reminded her sternly.

She blinked at him, her bright green eyes wide and unfocused as if she couldn't understand him. Max felt a surge of masculine satisfaction and smiled as he took her hands and positioned them back where he wanted them.

"Now don't move," he warned, keeping his hands over hers as he bent his head to taste her again.

Kitty might not have moved her hands, but her hips arched into his tormenting mouth, trying to force his tongue back to her clit. She whimpered and moaned and begged, but she tasted too amazing for Max to hurry through his snack. He explored every fold, delved into every crevice, savored every drop, while her voice grew higher and thinner every second.

He could feel her quivering on the edge of climax and debated for a moment whether to shove her over before him or to give in to both their desires and plunge into her right now. His tongue teased her entrance while he considered his options, but in the end, he couldn't withstand her pleas any longer.

Whispering soothing words of praise and pleasure, he released one hand, skimming the palm down the inside of her thigh to tease the damp skin where leg curved into buttock. When she drew in a frantic gulp of air, he bent his head and closed his lips around her clit, at the same time plunging two fingers deep inside her clenching warmth.

Her explosion shook him. Every inch of her body seemed to burst into flames. Her clit throbbed against his tongue; her pussy clenched around her fingers; her scream of pleasure pulsed in the air around them, as loud and wild as a lioness in heat.

His lioness.

In that moment, feeling this woman come apart in his arms, he knew he didn't need to wait for her heat to know she belonged to him. It didn't matter. She had to be his mate. No other woman could ever taste, ever smell, ever *feel* this good. No other woman could ever make his dick so hard or his heart so soft. No other woman could give his cubs those green eyes and that incredible resilience. In that moment, Kitty became his, and Max knew he would never let her go.

Panting, he raised his head and tore at the fastening of his jeans, yanking them open and freeing his swollen length. He wanted to feel her bare skin against his own, but he knew that if he paused long enough to strip, he'd go completely insane. He had to get inside her now.

He rose to his knees and settled himself between her thighs, guiding her hands to pull them wider, stretching the tight tendon on the inner face of each leg until it quivered with the strain. She still breathed raggedly, sucking great gulps of air into her starved lungs, but her eyes had drifted shut and her pale cheeks were stained pink with the remnant of her climax. She looked like a goddess and as he fitted himself to her entrance, she made Max feel like a god.

His forearms braced against the backs of her legs, keeping her in position as he slowly, deliberately, pressed forward into her tight sheath. His breath caught in his throat at the exquisite feel of her body spreading before him, then closing like a fist around the sensitive crown of his cock. He forced just the head inside her and paused, struggling for restraint. His head bowed and his muscles trembled as he fought to control himself. To keep from plunging into her with the delicacy of a battering ram. To stop himself from hurting her, from abusing the tender body he treasured.

If he thought he would go mad from waiting to have her, Max realized then that he might lose it anyway. She felt too good. Too wet, too hot, too tight.

Much too tight.

Gritting his teeth, he opened his eyes and glared at her, his gaze boring into hers the way his body ached to do.

"You're too tight," he growled, fighting for the power of speech.

This was important, but he had to search for every word and yank it from the deepest reaches of his mind where the civilized part of him had retreated while his primitive self held sway. Her eyes, dazed and sleepy with satisfaction, blinked up at him in confusion.

"Virgin?" he demanded, not knowing what the hell he would do if she said yes. He needed her too badly to wait, much too badly to be gentle, yet the thought of hurting her made him furious.

For a moment, she seemed not to understand his question; then her blush deepened and she shook her head hesitantly. "No," she whispered. "But only once before. Years ago."

Christ, that was almost as bad.

Max clenched his teeth, threw back his head, and swore a stream of words so foul he doubted Kitty even recognized half of them. If he'd known that before, he would never have let her come. Her climax had left her passage swollen and tight, making it even harder to enter her than it should have been. She was such a tiny little thing compared to him, and even for his build, Max was not a small man. If he entered her now, he could hurt her.

If he didn't enter her now, he would die.

He felt her gaze on him and lowered his head until their eyes met. He knelt poised on the edge of insanity, unwilling to rush forward but unable to pull back. Her gaze moved over him like a caress, searching his expression, and he could only hope that what she read there wouldn't send her bolting in the other direction. If it did, he knew he would have no choice but to follow, to chase her down and claim her despite her fear of him.

Fear, though, wasn't the emotion he saw on her face. To his amazement, her green eyes held only tenderness and acceptance. Her lips curved as he watched, and his heart stopped when he felt her hips shift under his, her pelvis tilting up, ass pressing into the mattress, positioning herself to take him. The movement caused her passage to tighten around his cock and sent a shudder wracking him from head to toe.

"Please," she whispered, and his heart clenched. "Please, Max. I want you inside me. Now."

With a word that was both a curse and a prayer, Max let his head drop until his forehead touched hers. "I don't want to hurt you, kitten. I never want to hurt you."

She smiled and nuzzled against him, her lips clinging for a moment to his. "Sometimes the thing that hurts is the thing that gives the most pleasure." Her whisper touched him like a caress. "It's okay, Max. I want this. I need it. And I trust you."

"God, honey, you're killing me," he groaned.

"I don't mean to. I only want to give you pleasure."

"I want the same."

"Then come inside me," she urged. "I need to feel it. I need to feel you."

Max closed his eyes, unable to face watching the shadow of pain darken her eyes. "I'm so sorry, kitten," he whispered, kissing her as sweetly as he could manage. "I promise I'll make it up to you. I swear it."

"You won't need to."

He hoped she was right.

Dragging in the deepest breath he could manage, Max kissed her again, telling her with his mouth how much he cared for her even as he flexed his hips and slowly, carefully, deepened his invasion.

He'd never felt anything like it. She quivered beneath him, around him, like something small and soft and delicious trapped in the hand of a predator. He didn't smell fear on her skin, though. All he smelled was desire and affection and the rich, sweet scent of Kitty.

Her body closed around him like a fist as he forced himself deeper, forced her to accept him. Two inches. Three. He broke out in a sweat, every muscle in his body trembling with the strain of going slowly. Beneath him, he heard her gasp, felt her pussy tighten almost unbearably, then felt the whisper of air against his cheek as she blew out a long, slow breath and slowly forced her body to relax.

"It's okay," she whispered, her voice unsteady but sincere. "I'm okay." Her brow furrowed and she licked her lips. "More."

She was going to kill him. Even if Kitty could survive this, Max knew he couldn't.

His cock, though, didn't care. All it cared about was the snug, wet haven slowly enveloping it, drawing it reluctantly deeper.

With another curse, he pushed forward. Four inches. Five. Six. Every time he sank deeper, her passage seemed to narrow. He began to wonder if this was even possible. He knew women were built to stretch, and surely Fate wouldn't be so cruel as to send him a mate he couldn't fully claim?

Kitty cried out and dug her heels into his flanks. "Wait," she gasped. "Please. Wait. Just a second. I just need a second."

His aroused body screamed a protest, but Max ignored it. He didn't care if his heart gave out from the strain. If she needed him to wait or to slow down or to stop, that was exactly what he'd do. Never mind the roar in his head that told him slowing down was impossible and stopping unimaginable. He didn't care if it killed him so long as he never had to face seeing this woman look at him with disgust.

Another long, slow breath teased his cheek; another slow, deliberate wave of relaxation moved through her body until her passage unclenched enough to allow him to move.

"Okay," she whispered. "It's okay. I'm okay." Then the idiot woman shifted her hips to urge him even deeper. Again, she prompted, "More."

He tried to resume his slow pace. He intended to do the right thing, to ease inside her one bare inch at a time, to give her body time to stretch for him, to adjust to his presence within her. He wanted to treat her like the delicate treasure she was, but when he began to ease forward one more time, his cock nudged hard against her inner walls and she went wild in his arms. She cried out, breathless and hungry, and her hips jerked hard up against his, forcing him deeper inside her. That was all it took for his hard-fought control to snap like a worn-out rubber band.

With a roar, Max threw back his head and thrust deep within her, burying himself to the hilt in her tight, clenching passage. Kitty screamed, a frantic combination of pleasure and pain, and her hands flew to his shoulders, her nails digging unknowingly into his flesh.

He didn't even notice. How could he feel such an inconsequential pain when his body was being flooded with the most intense pleasure of his life? He could feel the head of his cock nudging the entrance of her womb, feel every ripple of her muscles as they clenched and released along his thick length. Even when they relaxed, she gripped him tighter than anything he'd ever known, and he wanted to stay inside her until he died.

Displaying a mind-boggling flexibility that Max vowed to remember the next time she let him touch her, Kitty pulled her legs higher and hooked her knees over his shoulders. The movement drove him hard against her inner limits, and the two of them shuddered in unison.

"Never," Kitty mewled, her breathing quick and ragged, "never . . . thought . . . you'd fit."

Max swore and slid his hands beneath her to cup her ass and hold her steady against him. "Little idiot," he growled, slowly circling his hips and savoring her broken cries of pleasure. "I could have . . . hurt you. . . . You taunted me . . . one . . . too many times."

She lifted one hand from his shoulder and tangled her fingers in his sweat-dampened hair. Pulling insistently, she urged his mouth down to hers and kissed him with a heat that threatened to melt his bones.

"You did," she whimpered. "It did hurt." When he swore and attempted to draw back, she yanked his hair and kissed him again. "And it was worth every minute."

He read the truth in her eyes and snarled with satisfaction. She had just given herself to him, completely and irrevocably, whether she knew it or not.

Digging his fingers into the soft flesh of her backside, Max lifted her into his thrusts and set about establishing a pounding rhythm guaranteed to drive them over the edge. It started slow, out of necessity. Her passage was too tight to allow him any greater speed, but gradually her body began to grow accustomed to him and he began to pick up speed. By the time she was throwing her hips up against him, he knew he had only seconds before he exploded.

With a shrug of his shoulders, he freed one hand and eased it carefully between their bodies, searching for the point of their joining. He found it with two gentle fingers and pressed lightly, hearing her breath break and her moans accelerate into desperate whimpers. His own breathing felt like sandpaper in his chest, and he could feel his balls tightening, the base of his spine tingling. Grunting, he thrust even faster and spread his fingers until his thumb flicked lightly, just once, over her engorged clit.

She flew apart in his arms and came screaming his name. It was the sweetest sound Max had ever heard.

Finally unclenching the fierce claws of his self-control, he threw back his head, lunged forward to bury himself as deep as he could go, and let himself flood her depths with hot spurts of semen.

In the back of his mind, beneath the incredible, mind-numbing pleasure, he detected the insidious thought that it was too bad she hadn't come into heat yet. He wanted her body to welcome his seed, to embrace it and nurture it, to let it divide and grow until her belly swelled and her breasts ripened and her pelvis broadened for his cub.

For the first time in his life, Max understood the drive to reproduce, to see his child be born and grow, knowing a part of him lived on in a new generation.

Kitty dissolved beneath him, her arms and legs slipping from around him to tumble limp and useless to the mattress. He heard her struggling to breathe and sent up a prayer his shaking arms would hold out for a few more minutes until the last spasms, or his orgasm had passed, because there was no way he could keep from crushing her until the last drop of seed had left his body.

When it did, he groaned and let himself collapse, but as he did, he gathered his mate's limp body in his arms and rolled so that she landed on top of him instead of the other way around.

Her head fitted perfectly beneath his chin, and her arms and legs hung limply over his sides as if she were a rag doll spread across his chest. No doll, though, had ever felt this warm and alive in his arms, and no one else's body had ever clung so sweetly to his cock, as if it couldn't bear to let him go.

Max closed his eyes and let himself relax, Kitty cuddled safe and motionless in his arms. By the time he finally caught his breath, her lack of motion almost had him worried, and he cracked an eye open to look down at her.

"You okay, kitten?" he asked, his voice gruff and low.

Still, she didn't stir. But her lips parted on a sigh. "Well, I'm going to be in a wheelchair for the rest of my life, but other than that? Sure." Then she frowned. "On second thought, scratch that. I'll just be bed-ridden. There's no way in hell I'm going to be sitting anywhere for the foreseeable future."

Max winced even as he felt his ego swell. "Poor baby. I'm sorry I hurt you." He stroked his hands gently down the length of her spine until they closed around her hips. Pressing a kiss to her forehead, he gritted his teeth and swore to himself. This was not going to be pleasant for her. "Take a deep breath, kitten. Ready? One, two, three."

On the count of three, he lifted her and pulled his cock from her battered body. She let out a long, shuddering moan and bit her lip against the pain. When he slipped free, she swore softly.

"Damn." She drew in an unsteady breath and slowly forced her muscles to relax until she lay limp atop him once more. "I have to tell you, that was my least favorite part."

Max brushed her tangled hair away from her face and

kissed her softly. "I'm sorry, kitten. I promise it won't be so bad next time."

Her eyes slitted open and she glared up at him. "I don't know about that, mister," she warned him. "The way I feel right now, I doubt you're getting that thing near me again for a good solid year. Maybe two."

Gently, he cupped her face in his hands and lowered his mouth to hers. "I'm sorry I hurt you," he repeated, "but I'm not sorry I took you. It was the most amazing thing I've ever felt in my life. If I have to wait ten years to have you again, I'll do it happily." He saw her eyes mist and her mouth soften into a tender smile and couldn't resist a little devilment. Sliding a hand to her bottom, he kneaded gently and brushed his mouth over hers. "Of course, that doesn't mean I won't spend all ten years trying to change your mind."

Laughing, Kitty grabbed his hand and wrapped it back around her waist. "Go ahead and try, sweetheart. At this point, even if you did manage to change my mind, my body would still be exercising its veto power. I feel like I have a bad case of internal rug burn."

Max sighed, not because he couldn't have her again right then—though he wouldn't have fought her off if she'd tried to force him—but because the knowledge that he'd hurt her ate at him. He wanted to fix it, to make everything all better.

"How about a warm bath?" he suggested, stroking her back soothingly.

Kitty shook her head. "Maybe later," she mumbled, her voice muffled against his chest. "Sleep first."

He smiled and cuddled her closer. "Whatever you want, kitten."

He pressed a kiss to the top of her head and felt her go even more boneless as she slipped off to sleep.

"Stay here," she breathed just before her dreams claimed her. "All night."

"You couldn't make me go anywhere else," he murmured, then pressed his cheek to her shining red-gold hair and followed her into sleep.

Seventeen

KITTY GUESSED THAT SHE'D CAUGHT HIM BY SURPRISE the next morning when she followed him outside after breakfast and faced him in the bright morning sunshine. "I want you to teach me how to shift."

"Why now?"

Kitty leaned her hip against the railing of the cabin's small porch and shrugged, her mouth quirking. "Because time is fleeting."

When Max remained silent, she sighed. "Because learning how to shift, how to control what I can do, is the real reason I came here. As cold as it makes me sound, it wasn't so I could meet my father, and it wasn't so I could get to know the pride. I just wanted to learn how to tie a leash on the lion inside me so that I wouldn't have to be afraid of losing control and hurting my friends or my family one day."

"But now?" Max prompted.

"But now things look different," she admitted, gazing out at the landscape to avoid having to meet his eyes. "Nothing is what I expected here, well, except maybe Drusilla and her awful offspring. But everything else is different. Martin. Ronnie. You. The pride. Yesterday really brought that home to me."

"How?"

Kitty searched for a way to answer that wouldn't make her sound like a small-minded bigot, but she couldn't find one. Maybe that was a sign that she had been, and now she should take her lumps for it and move on.

"I was horrified when I realized I wasn't human," she admitted, wincing as she admitted out loud something she hadn't even admitted to herself before. "I was afraid that being a Leo meant that I wouldn't think the same way or feel the same way or *be* the same way. And when I thought about the pride, I thought it would be this primitive thing, that somehow a bunch of Leos together were even less human than one alone."

"A lot of people think that," he said, and the lack of judgment in his voice made her feel even worse somehow.

"But it's not true, and now I've seen that with my own eyes. I saw the way everyone pulled together to save those kids when you thought they were in danger, and I saw the pride itself endangered." She struggled to find the right words. "Now that I know you all, I hate myself for thinking that my father's blood was some kind of curse. And I don't—"

She broke off and Max caught her chin in his fingers and forced her to look up at him. "What?"

Kitty searched for strength, felt her breath catch when she found it in his eyes. "I don't want my father to die still thinking I'm not part of his family."

"The only one who thinks that is you, kitten."

She shook her head. "No, I know I don't belong here, and that's the problem. That's why I need to learn to shift. Maybe after I do, I'll decide that I'm not meant to be a real member of the pride, but I want it to be my decision. I need to know that wherever I end up when this is over, it's because that's where I wanted to be, not because I wasn't strong enough to make a place for myself anywhere else."

"Why now?"

Kitty shrugged, her mouth quirking. "You're the one who told me we heal faster when we shift. Maybe I don't want to wait a year or two after all."

"Nice try." He caught her chin in his fingers and forced her to look up at him. "While I'm flattered to think you can't get enough of my expert sexual technique"—his sarcasm was obvious—"I'm not buying that story. Why now?"

His expression was calm and serious and patient, just like he was. When he looked at her, she couldn't help but tell him the truth.

"Because I don't belong here, and I know I don't belong here," she told him. "And maybe after I learn to shift and learn how to be a Leo, maybe I still won't belong here. I don't know. But if that's what happens, I want it to be my decision. I want to leave here knowing it's because this isn't what I wanted, not because I wasn't strong enough to handle it."

Max was quiet for a long time, his face set in that unreadable mask she hated.

"You know, you don't always have to be the strong one," he finally said, his tone just as even as his expression. "Sometimes you're better off letting someone else take care of things for you."

"I'm not arguing with that. I'm a modern kind of feminist. I think it's all right for a woman to let someone else take care of her, but only when that's what she wants. The only way I could ever let someone else fight my battles would be if I already knew I could still win them on my own."

Kitty wasn't sure why she'd told him that, especially not why she'd phrased it that way, but Max didn't even blink. He just studied her for another long minute, then nodded and drained his coffee.

"All right. Let's do it, then."

Suddenly, Kitty shifted uncertainly. "Should I change?" She tugged at the hem of the blue man's dress shirt she wore. "I don't want to ruin your clothes."

"Don't worry. You won't be wearing them long."

THE MAN WAS TRUE TO HIS WORD.

Forty-five minutes later, Kitty crouched naked in the sandy hills behind the cabin and swore. Half the words she used didn't even make sense to her—not surprising, since she'd never heard them before Max had used them last night—but that didn't seem to matter. Her own vocabulary had already proven woefully inadequate to express the frustration that had been building since they'd begun this ridiculous exercise.

"Come on. Try it again."

Kitty glared up at her tormentor, who sat cool, clothed, and unruffled on a boulder about ten feet in front of her. When he had started her lesson by ordering her to strip, she'd looked at him like he was crazy, an expression that didn't alter when he explained that if she wanted to have undamaged clothes to put on for the return trip to the cabin later, she had better not try shifting while fully dressed.

She had taken them off reluctantly, blushing every time she released a button or pulled off a garment. To his credit, Max had behaved with admirable restraint, not touching, not so much as leering, as she bared herself to the warm sun and his hot gaze. If it hadn't been for that heat, she might even have been insulted by his apparent uninterest in her body. But the glint in his copper eyes told her he wasn't uninterested at all; he was just biding his time.

Now, she barely even noticed her own nudity. The heavy layer of dust that coated her from head to foot almost felt thick enough to qualify as cloth, and her temper had been worn so ragged she didn't have time to feel self-conscious.

Or energy. Max had sapped every shred of that from her with his endless exercises.

"I've already shifted three times," she snapped at him. "Why are we still doing this? I just wanted to know how to shift on demand. Clearly, I've accomplished that."

"The first time took you fifteen minutes," he said bluntly. "If you're in a situation where shifting instantaneously means life or death, are you going to ask everyone else to hold on and give you a quarter hour or so to prepare yourself?"

She hated when he had a point. "The last time wasn't nearly that long."

"Five minutes and forty-seven seconds."

"What? Are you carrying a stopwatch?"

He just stared at her, wearing his superior expression.

Kitty swore again. "You know, I've never used language like this in my life," she said with a pointed glare. "Not before I met you, anyway."

He grinned. "I'd apologize for corrupting you, but since I have every intention of doing it again as soon as you're able, it would feel a tad disingenuous." He glanced at his watch. "Ready?"

"At some point, I am going to make you pay for this."

"Just let me know when you're ready to start, kitten."

Grumping and grousing under her breath, Kitty took several deep, cleansing breaths, then closed her eyes and nodded.

Just like he'd taught her, she pictured herself standing just as she was, then began to visualize the transformation taking place. She saw herself bending over, her spine stretching, her hands and feet broadening, fingers shortening. She saw her face pull outward, her ears sliding up toward her scalp, a tail emerging from the tip of her tailbone. She saw fur growing from her skin, the same strawberry blond as her hair, saw the joints in her knees reverse themselves, and felt the warm earth of the desert against her haunches as she crouched in the dust.

Felt!?

Her eyes flew open and she gasped, a sound that came out as something closer to a sneeze. Glancing down, she lifted one huge claw-tipped paw, and her gaze flew back to Max. He was grinning from ear to ear.

"By George, I think she's got it."

Kitty felt the thrill of success, and for the first time experienced the comfort of feeling at ease in her own skin. Or at least, this version of it. For the first time, she wasn't wondering what had happened or how she was going to get out of it. She was just feeling the pleasure of the novel arrangement of muscle and sinew, and wondering what incredible things she might be able to accomplish with all this power and strength at her disposal.

I feel as if I could take on the world, she thought, licking her chops and surveying the desert around her with her eyes. *I could climb a tree. Jump a river. Catch a rabbit. I could hunt a gazelle, if there were any around here and I didn't get squeamish at the idea of killing my own dinner.*

She felt Max chuckle. Or maybe she heard it. It seemed like she heard it, only she heard it with her mind and not her ears.

Slow down, Miss Queen of the Forest, he said, voice rich with amusement. *How about we start off slow? Like a nice game of chase.*

Kitty looked back at Max, but he had disappeared. In his place lay the most magnificent African lion she had ever seen. His fur was the color of honey, rich and darkly golden, his body thick and heavy with muscle. He was enormous, almost twice her size it seemed, or maybe it was the thick ruff of his mane that made it look that way.

Just like his hair, his mane was the color of coffee, almost black, until the light hit it and uncovered hidden tones of gold and red; and like his hair, the dark strands were interspersed with streaks of rich, golden toffee. Having never been this close to an adult male lion—not even during the few times she'd been an adult female lion—she hadn't realized that the mane would cover more than his head and neck. In reality, it covered the whole front of his chest and formed a thick pelt all along his belly until it gradually thinned and then disappeared on the undersides of his back legs. It made her want to sink her hands into it and feel all that dense fur and the powerful male underneath.

Since she currently didn't have hands, Kitty let her instincts guide her and walked slowly toward him, her head down and her tail twitching restlessly behind her.

I can't remember the last time I played, she admitted, her thought accompanied by a sound almost like a purr. She remembered reading somewhere once that lions didn't purr the same way cats did—vibrating their throats on both the in- and exhalation—but that they did make a similar sound, one that paused and resumed every time they drew breath. She guessed she'd just proven the truth of that.

When she reached his side, she tilted her head flirtatiously and rubbed her cheek against his, the purr sound growing louder as she ducked and rubbed the top of her head on the underside of his chin.

You might have to remind me of the rules, she thought, and when she pulled back, she saw a light in his dark-rimmed copper eyes that she remembered very vividly from the previous night.

The rules are very simple, he told her, mouth opening until she could see his fangs under the feline grin. *You run; I chase. And if I catch you . . .*

She shivered and backed away skittishly. *Yes?*

When I catch you, he corrected himself, *I get to do anything I want.*

That hardly sounds fair, she protested.

Maybe not, he acknowledged as he pushed lazily to his feet, *but I guarantee it's a hell of a lot of fun.*

She took one look at his fierce, predatory expression, spun on her haunches, and launched herself into a full-out run.

He let out a fierce, joyful roar and sprang after her.

She was too smart to look back to see how far behind her he was. He was so much larger, he'd clearly have a big advantage in the length of his stride, so she couldn't afford to lose even a fraction of a second.

It didn't take her long to get the rhythm of running all out on all fours, and she savored the feel of her muscles bunching and stretching as she propelled herself over rocks and through scrubby desert vegetation. Unfortunately, it also didn't take her long to realize there was a big difference between being a werelion and being a werecheetah. Her big, heavily muscled form had been designed to overpower the prey she hunted, not to outrun it. In other words, she was a born wrestler, not a sprinter, but with Max breathing hard on her heels, she figured it was time to broaden her horizons.

Not that she would mind so much if he caught her. In fact, she found the idea positively intriguing. The handful of shifts she had managed really had seemed to speed her healing, and the painfully bruised feeling between her legs had faded to the kind of delicious soreness that only made her want to experience again the cause of that poignant physical reminder. Judging by how large he'd been last night, though, she wasn't sure she wanted to find out firsthand if the increased bulk of his lion form translated to every last inch of him. She wasn't sure she could take it.

Digging her claws in for traction, Kitty twisted her body and veered to the left, headed for a concealing rock formation a few dozen yards away. Maybe she could hide herself under an overhang or behind a boulder and let him tear past before she backtracked toward the cabin.

She laid on a last, desperate burst of speed and skidded behind the first boulder just as a hard, heavy body slammed into hers, knocking her off balance and sending her tumbling several more feet until she landed on her back, belly-up, paws stretched toward the sky.

She lay there dazed, blinking up at the bright blue sky until a shadow blocked out the sun. She twisted her head to the side to see Max standing above her, his mouth open and his sides heaving as he struggled to catch his breath. Far from looking upset with her, though, his eyes glowed with excitement and mischief, and she could feel his arousal as clearly as if he'd slid a hand across her bare skin.

I win, he purred, lowering his head and nudging her belly with his blunt, dark nose. *And I see I have a few things to teach you about your body language in this particular form.*

Kitty thought about that for a moment, searching her instincts and her mind and her heart for an answer, and the one she found surprised her. *Actually,* she responded slowly as she rolled onto her belly, *I don't really think you do.*

She saw surprise and desire flare in his eyes and pushed to her feet just as he would have moved to cover her. Her heart pounded in her chest, and she walked several paces forward, her tail twitching until she could almost picture the little tuft on the end tickling his nose, taunting him as she moved away.

Something about this form made her feel so incredibly feminine, as strange as that sounded. She felt powerful like this, sensual, as if she were the world's sexiest temptress. She wanted to flirt and tease and drive Max completely out of his mind. She wanted to hear him roar his desire for her and demonstrate to her powerfully and primitively that she belonged to him.

This time, she didn't run but strolled slowly away from him for the pure pleasure of knowing he had no choice but to follow. Desire drove both of them, and she felt as if the sway of her hips held him hypnotized, completely under her seductive control. She heard the noises he made, low, rough rumbles of hunger, and when she looked back over her shoulder, she saw his gaze fixed with obvious intent on her prowling, teasing strides.

Her breath caught and a shiver rolled through her. She saw the flare of heat in his gaze just before he lunged forward and raked his teeth gently along her flank, turning the shiver into a full-bodied shudder. Instinctively, she halted and sank to her belly, stretching herself out for him like an offering, exposing herself to her mate. To the man she needed like air and light and water.

He made a growling sound of approval, and when he moved to stretch over her, to press his chest against her back, her head fell forward to expose the back of her neck. She purred when his hot breath stroked the sensitive spot, and whimpered when she felt his teeth close around her nape. He bit down gently, holding her still, dominating her with power and pleasure as he began to ease himself inside her.

Kitty wanted to sob with relief. She hadn't realized how empty she'd been until he'd filled her, hadn't realized how much she needed until he gave. Arching her back, she lifted her hips to take him deeper and shuddered when his rumble of satisfaction vibrated through her like a full-length caress.

He still felt huge within her, nearly overwhelming as he thrust high and hard inside her sensitive passage, but it felt so incredibly right that she doubted she would have noticed more pain even if he had caused it. His possession felt so wild, so primitive, so absolutely perfect, that her heart threatened to burst inside her chest. He had her pinned beneath him, his mouth holding her in place with teeth that could easily have injured her, and she felt dominated, helpless, and so incredibly treasured that she felt tears gather at the corners of her eyes.

Nothing in her life had ever felt more perfect.

And nothing in her life would ever be the same.

It overwhelmed her in a flash of understanding just as he pressed deep and threw her over the edge into climax. She had changed. This man, this place, this experience, had changed her. For the first time in her life she felt complete, and for the first time since her mother's truck had run off the road, she felt . . . perfect.

She pressed her cheek to the ground and let the tears fall as Max shuddered and roared at the power of his own orgasm. When he finally lay still and heavy above her, she pictured how the two of them would look, twined together in the bright desert sun, pale freckled curves pressed against wide planes of golden muscle, his face relaxed in the aftermath of passion, hers streaked with tears.

Slowly, she opened her eyes and saw exactly that. She didn't know when they had shifted back, at what point their lion forms had melted back into human, but it didn't really matter. She understood now that a body was just a body and that each of them was the same person no matter what skin they happened to be wearing.

Max wrapped his arms around her and rolled to his side, cuddling her against his chest.

"Hey, what's this?" he asked, lifting a finger to wipe a stray tear from her skin. "Kitten, what's wrong?"

Shaking her head, Kitty pressed her lips together and buried her face against his shoulder. "Nothing," she whispered. "Everything is just perfect."

And it would be, she promised herself, if she could just figure out how to fall back out of love with him.

EIGHTEEN

SHE WAS QUIET ON THE WAY BACK TO THE CABIN, BUT that didn't worry Max. He didn't talk much, either. Of course, he knew that his speechlessness was a direct result of the most erotic experience of his life. The trouble was, he couldn't be entirely sure Kitty's had the same cause.

He wouldn't have worried so much if it hadn't been for the tears. She had dismissed them easily enough when he'd asked, laughing that he knew women got overly emotional at times, and that was true, as far as it went. Hell, when he'd come back to his senses after that orgasm, he'd almost teared up himself. He'd never felt anything as intense as that primitive outdoor mating with her, not even the night before when he'd taken her for the first time and realized he'd do whatever it took to make sure she never left him. Not even when he'd pictured her heavy with pregnancy and glowingly, obviously, his. Something special had happened in the desert, a true mating, and he could only hope she felt the same.

As they crested the last hill behind the cabin and the small structure rose up ahead of them, he laid his hand on the back of her neck, on the place where his teeth had marked her, and squeezed gently.

"Are you okay, kitten?" he asked quietly.

The smile she gave him was quick and bright and patently false. "Of course. Why wouldn't I be?"

He frowned and shook his head. "I'm not sure. That's why I'm asking. You just seem like something is bothering you."

"Don't be silly. I'm fine." Then she looked down at herself and grimaced. "Well, I will be as soon as I take a shower," she corrected herself, pinching the fabric of her—his—shirt away from her skin. "I feel like I just climbed out of a mud bath and forgot to rinse off before I got dressed."

He had to admit, she did look a little darker than usual, her freckles blending together in places due to the fine coating of red desert soil on her fair skin. Personally, he thought she looked adorable, especially with little pieces of sagebrush tangled in her hair, but he figured she wouldn't appreciate him pointing those out.

"Well, if you're sure . . . ," he said, leaving the question between them.

"I'm positive," she insisted. So he let it drop. At least for the moment.

He did not, however, lift his hand from the back of her neck. As far as he was concerned, she needed every signal he could think of, no matter how subtle, to remind her of whom she belonged to. And even if she didn't, he did.

With his hand on her warm skin, he guided her across the rough ground and around the side of the cabin. When he'd built it several years ago, he hadn't bothered to add a back door. Technically, there was a second exit through the root cellar, but with only one story and wide, tall windows on every side, he'd never worried about escape routes in the unlikely event of a fire. And what else could hurt him out here? The building site was surrounded on all four sides by Red Rock land, and if someone threatened him, he could shift into a five-hundred-pound African lion with anger management issues. Somehow, he wasn't worried about burglars.

He hurried her over the last stretch of open ground, wanting to get her inside. Maybe once she stripped off her clothes and washed off the dirt of their impromptu encounter, she'd feel more comfortable about confiding in him what was bothering her. He knew there was something, and to be blunt, sitting on his hands while his mate brooded and fretted about something without telling him how he could help did not sit well with him. He was fundamentally Leo; his first instinct was to claim his mate, but his second and third were to protect her against all danger and to help her over any obstacle.

It would make things a whole lot easier, he reflected grumpily, if she would just accept that as the way things were and let him help without a fight.

They were rounding the corner of the cabin when the first shot rang out. He didn't recognize it right away—few Leos carried guns after all . . . what would be the point?—but Kitty froze the instant she heard it and looked around, her expression intent and alert and slightly worried.

"Does Martin allow hunting on his property?" she asked.

Misunderstanding, Max chuckled. "Of course. It's one of our favorite pastimes. I'll take you one day, if you

want. I'll even promise not to make you bring down the
prey yourself."

Scowling, she smacked him lightly on the shoulder.
"That's not what I meant. I'm talking about hunting. You
know . . . 'duck season, rabbit season' . . . men in pickup
trucks carrying Thermoses and wearing bright orange
vests?"

The light dawned and Max's smile faded just as the
second shot cracked through the air and a stone about
three feet to his left exploded in a cloud of dust and de-
bris.

"Holy fucking shit!"

Without stopping to think, he grabbed Kitty's hand
and sprinted for the cabin door, kicking it open and
shoving her inside as bullet number three embedded itself in the wood of the porch post just inches from where
their heads had just been. He heard someone cursing, it
sounded like a man, then the sound of a motor revving
and the bump and scrape of tires peeling out on the
gravel and dusty soil of the surrounding landscape.

"What the fuck was that?" Max yelled, flinging open
the door just in time to see a dark shape on a dirt bike
disappearing over the top of a hill about a hundred yards
to the east.

"Lucky for us, just a twenty-two," Kitty said from just
behind Max.

He whirled to face her, his heart pounding in his chest
as if it would burst through his ribs, while she looked
as cool and collected as a spring breeze.

"A what?" he growled, fisting his hands to keep from
grabbing her and shaking a decent sense of fear into her
pretty head.

"A twenty-two," she repeated, watching the cloud of dust behind the motorcycle settle back to the earth before she turned to meet his gaze. "Twenty-two-caliber long rifle. Back home, they mostly use them for hunting squirrels. Around here I don't imagine they'd be suited to much beyond the occasional jackrabbit."

Her voice didn't even quaver. He'd nearly had a heart attack thinking she could have died, and she barely blinked. He doubted her blood pressure had even gone up. And to top it all off, she'd had the unmitigated gall to refer to someplace else as "home." If she survived the next sixty seconds without winding up end over ears across his knee, her guardian angel deserved a brand-new harp of gold.

"What about a person?" Max ground out, quietly shutting the door and forcing her back into the coolness of the cabin. "Would they be at all suited to hunting a person, do you think? Could they put a bloody little hole in someone? Stop her heart? Tear through a vital organ and make her bleed to death?"

She actually pursed her lips and considered the question. "At that range? Maybe. He about picked the limit for accuracy. They say a twenty-two can kill a man a mile away, but I'm pretty sure that would take a miracle. Not to mention a good tailwind."

He just stared at her.

She'd struck him speechless. Completely and utterly speechless. All he could picture was her body lying still and pale and bloody in the dirt, and she was cracking jokes.

Lord give him strength.

"You goddamned little fool," he hissed, and, finally,

something he said seemed to get through to her. Her head jerked up and her eyes widened as they traveled over his grim expression. "You could have been killed. You almost were killed! He could have shot you and there was no way in hell I could have gotten to him in time, no matter how fast I might be. He could have shot you and then driven away and I wouldn't have known so much as who he was. Do you have any idea how that made me feel?"

Hesitantly, she shook her head.

He barked out a laugh, even though he'd never felt less amused in his entire life. "Well, let me tell you, honey. It scared me shitless. But what I want to know is why it didn't scare you. Huh? How can you be so calm?"

He stalked toward her, his steps slow and deliberate, noting with satisfaction that at least she'd developed the good sense to be nervous.

"I-I don't know," she stammered, stumbling and nearly falling when her heel caught on the edge of the braided rug. "I guess when you have a close call for the fifth time in less than three weeks, the shock starts to wear off."

Max muttered a vile curse and grabbed her by the arms, yanking her soft body against him and crushing her mouth beneath his. It was either kiss her or kill her, and he knew this was the one choice he wouldn't live to regret.

Kitty uttered a startled squeak, but he'd already trained her body too well to accept him. Her lips flowered automatically beneath his, her teeth parting, her tongue welcoming his with softly encouraging strokes. He growled low in his throat and released his grip on her arms, only to wrap his around her and press her full-length against him.

In the back of his mind, he worried that he might be giving too much away, might be frightening her with the intensity of his feelings, but it didn't matter. He couldn't have let her go if he'd tried. He couldn't have kissed her more gently. His fear rode him too hard. He'd come too close to losing her, and having her remind him that it wasn't the first time only made his need to reassure himself of her well-being all the stronger.

He didn't ease the pressure on her mouth until she melted against him and returned the kiss with equal fervor.

Swearing silently, Max tore his mouth from hers and glared down at her. "You've been attacked four times in the two and a half days since you've been in Vegas, Kitty. You need to take this seriously. You're the daughter of a Felix someone already wants dead and now you're being linked with his successor. That gives someone twice as much incentive to kill you."

"Whoever it is doesn't seem to need much incentive," she grumbled, pushing away from him and crossing her arms over her chest. "I don't get what anyone gets out of killing me, though. It's not like I'm heir to the throne. Why aren't they trying to kill you?"

"Because he wants to take the easy way into becoming Felix. Like I told you before, if Martin dies before the title passes to me, it would be a lot easier to divide the pride and convince at least some of them to follow him. But once you came into the picture, things got complicated."

"Complicated how? I'm no threat to the next Felix."

"You are if I take you as my mate."

Kitty's jaw dropped, and she stared at Max as if he'd just spoken to her in Esperanto. "If you what?" she whispered.

"It's how Martin cemented his control over the pride when he became Felix," Max reminded her, wishing he could tell if the expression on her face represented shock or horror at the idea. He already knew she was his mate, but he hadn't yet figured out how to convince her of that.

"I'm not saying I'd force you into something," he tried to reassure her while not appearing to be lying through his teeth. He didn't want to force Kitty into anything, but he had no intention of ever letting her go. "I know you wouldn't want that, and I wouldn't want it either, but there is a history of it among our people, and some people might assume—"

The door behind him swung open.

"Forgive me for interrupting, *baas,* but I have a message for you."

The tall redheaded man framed in Max's cabin doorway looked about as comfortable as a virgin at a swingers' party. If Max hadn't been standing between them and threatening to beat her, she could have kissed the man for barging in like this.

"Unless an atomic bomb is about to explode over our heads, David, I don't want to hear it," Max growled without turning his head. "Don't let the door hit you in the ass."

Max should have turned around, she reflected. That way she would have had the opportunity to signal to this David guy like a convenience store clerk with a robber's gun trained on her when an off-duty cop came in for a cup of coffee and a Slim Jim. But Max never even glanced the other way.

Of course, neither did David obey Max's order and leave them alone. That struck Kitty as slightly odd.

"Max," David insisted, his tone low and serious. "This is important."

Cursing, Max swung around and glared at his pride mate. "What's the matter?" he barked.

"It's Martin. He's taken a bad turn," the redhead said quietly. "Dr. Reijznik said you should come up to the house. Right away."

Nineteen

THE HOUSE SEEMED ODDLY QUIET, EVEN WITH THE crowd of vehicles out front and the crowd of bodies inside. David had warned Max that Nick had gone to spread the word to the rest of the pride while David went searching for Max and Kitty. Apparently, Nick had a real gift for efficiency.

Bodies parted in front of Max like the Red Sea before Moses, and Kitty followed along at his side, clinging to his hand as if it were the only stable thing in her universe, because, frankly, that's what it felt like. They made their way slowly down the hall toward Martin's suite. No one tried to stop them, but occasionally someone would murmur something to Max in a low voice and earn a nod or a pat on the shoulder as they passed. None of those people tried to speak to Kitty, but more than one stared at her with blatant curiosity. She did her best to block them out, but it wasn't easy. Her mind was constantly searching for something to distract her from the knowledge that her father lay in the bed where she'd visited him the day before, quietly and inexorably slipping away from all of them.

When they finally reached the bedroom door, which was guarded by a huge man with long blond hair and a bushy red beard, Max pulled her to a stop and gently tipped her chin up until her gaze met his.

"Are you okay?" he asked softly.

Kitty nodded, then swallowed and shook her head. "I guess. I don't know." She looked up at him and wished fervently that he would just take her back to the cabin, take her back to bed, and make her forget about all of this. "Max, I . . . I don't know what to do. I don't know how to act. When Mamaw died, it was terrible, but I knew I had to be strong. I knew she wouldn't want to see me making myself sick crying or anything like that. But she raised me. She took care of me all my life. I just met my father."

Max reached up to tuck her hair behind her ears, and she realized it must still be tangled and tousled from their encounter outside. And she never had gotten a chance to shower. She was filthy. She closed her eyes in embarrassment. How on earth could she stand at someone's deathbed looking like this? Mamaw would have whupped her good if she could have seen it.

"Are you worried because you don't know Martin well enough to know how he'd want you to act?" Max asked quietly. "Kitten, it's okay. You don't have to stress yourself out about it. Just be yourself. That's all he'd expect from you."

"That's not what I meant," she confessed, shaking her head and feeling like she would burst into tears at any minute. If she didn't throw up first. Her stomach was lurching again, just like old times. "I don't know him, Max. He's my father, but he's still a stranger to me. I'm sorry he's dying, but I can't mourn him like he deserves to be mourned. Like a father. Maybe you should go in alone."

Smiling, Max used the pad of his thumb to wipe a tear from her cheek. "Just be yourself, kitten," he repeated. "That will be more than enough for Martin. I promise."

She didn't get time to launch another protest. Max wrapped his arm around her waist, nodded to the guard at the door, and then guided her through when it opened to admit them.

The room looked so different than she remembered. Though it was still light outside—she had noted with amazement as they drove over that it was only a little after 3:00 P.M.—the curtains had been drawn in this room, creating a dim, cavelike atmosphere well suited to death. Unlike the rest of the house, this room was nearly empty. She recognized the nurse she'd seen yesterday, the one who'd kicked them out of the house, and Dr. Reijznik, but other than the two of them, and her and Max, the only other figure in the room lay still and quiet in the room's only bed.

Kitty forced her gaze in that direction and saw that all but one of Martin's monitors had been turned off. Only the cardiac machine still functioned, and its sound had been turned all the way down to silence the electronic beeps that accompanied every beat of its patient's weary heart.

Martin looked even smaller than he had yesterday, thinner and paler. His body barely formed a mound under his thick blankets, and the head of his bed had been lowered so that he lay flat on his back like the effigy on the top of a stone sarcophagus.

Kitty shuddered at her own thoughts and swallowed against the roiling in her stomach. She didn't want to think of him that way, didn't want to think of death at all, but in this room it seemed impossible to avoid it. She felt like she stood enveloped in a giant funereal shroud, and the coldness of that image seemed to penetrate clear to her bones. Instinctively, she moved closer to Max's reassuring warmth.

He murmured something reassuring and the sound caught the doctor's attention. He looked up from his place at Martin's bedside and nodded to them, gesturing them closer. If he noticed that Max had to use the pressure of his arm around her to urge her forward, he pretended not to notice.

He rose from his chair as they approached and met them a couple of feet from the foot of the bed. "I'm glad you're both here," he said quietly, but his attention had focused on Max. "He's been insisting on seeing you, and he's asked several times after his daughter."

Max nodded and rubbed his hand over the gooseflesh covering Kitty's arm. She found his touch reassuring, gave thanks for it, but she didn't think anything could warm her just then. She felt frozen through to the core.

"How—" Her voice broke, and she had to clear her throat before she continued. "How much longer . . . ?"

She trailed off, unable to finish, and pressed a hand to her belly.

Dr. Reijznik glanced over at her and opened his mouth to reply but seemed to catch himself. His sharp gaze swept quickly over her, then darted to Max before he collected himself and shook his head. "I can't say for sure, but I'm guessing no more than a few hours. Probably before nightfall. Definitely by morning. He's growing weaker almost by the minute."

She nodded and leaned heavily into Max's side. It

wasn't fair of her, she knew. She should be the strong one, the one supporting him. After all, he felt closer to her father than she ever would. Max would suffer the greater loss, not her. But he felt so strong and solid beside her that she couldn't resist. She felt so lost, and he glowed beside her like her own personal North Star.

"Is he in pain?" Max demanded, keeping his own voice low. Trust him to get straight to what was important.

The doctor hesitated. "I'm not sure. I increased his morphine as much as he would let me, but he refused to allow himself to fall unconscious until he'd spoken to you."

Max nodded once and tightened his arm around Kitty. "Then let's go talk to him."

He guided her across the thick carpet to the foot of the bed. He stopped there, his gaze on the man he'd said he thought of as his father, and stood still and silent for a long moment. Kitty tilted her head to look up at Max and saw that he had his blank mask firmly in place again.

In that instant, she understood what that mask was all about. The only times she had seen him use it had been when he was dealing with someone he didn't trust, or when his strong emotions threatened to overwhelm him. It was his defense mechanism, protecting him from the pain of open vulnerability.

Her heart contracted in her chest, and she felt a rush of strength infuse her. She released her arms from their defensive position across her chest and slipped one of them around the waist of the man beside her, the man she loved. From the first moment she had met him, he had never hesitated to run to her rescue. She'd come to rely on him utterly without really realizing it, but now he needed her almost as much as she needed him. There was no way she could ever allow herself to let him down.

When her arm squeezed, Max tore his gaze from Martin's still form and glanced down at her. She managed a smile and a whisper as she urged, "Go on. I'll wait here. You deserve the chance to talk to him alone."

Max didn't protest, just searched her expression with warm copper eyes before he nodded. Bending to her, he pressed a lingering kiss against her forehead, hugged her close for a second, then released her and moved the last few steps to his foster father's side.

THOSE WERE THE HARDEST STEPS MAX HAD EVER TAKEN, he realized as he sank down on the edge of Martin's bed and took the older man's cold, thin hand between his own. Harder than the ones that had taken him away from his birth family, harder than all the ones that had helped him cross the 270-odd miles from Los Angeles to Las Vegas, harder than the ones that had forced him to choose between fear and the new home he hadn't realized he'd needed until it had been offered to him.

They were even harder—infinitely harder—than the ones that had taken him over the cliff and landed him heart-deep in love with a half-human wildcat with a face like an angel, a body like a goddess, and an accent like Scarlett O'Hara.

Because these steps brought him face-to-face with the greatest loss he'd ever had to endure.

He forced himself to concentrate on his breathing—slowly, evenly, in and out—and to ignore the sharp pricking at the corners of his eyes. He wasn't ashamed to cry, but he didn't want that to be Martin's last sight of him.

Like Kitty, Max wanted to be strong for the person who had always been strong for him.

The warmth of Max's hands began to penetrate the cold of Martin's, to take away the worst of the chill. The old man must have noticed, because even as Max thought it, Martin's eyelids flickered and lifted and he peered up at his visitor with green eyes still as bright and vivid as springtime. But the sparkle in them was gone, and when Max saw that, he knew the doctor had been right to send for him. It was nearly time.

He didn't waste time on platitudes, didn't bother to ask how Martin was feeling. He didn't need to. Instead, he gently pressed the frail hand between his own and spoke softly. "I hear you wanted to talk to me, *pa*."

Martin nodded, his head barely shifting on the pillow. "Kitty?"

Max tipped his chin toward the end of the bed. "She's standing right there. She came here with me, but she said you and I should have time to talk alone."

The thin, bluish lips curved as Martin sighed in satisfaction. "Knew it," he whispered. His voice was thin and weak, nothing like it had sounded yesterday when he'd threatened his natural son. "Knew she'd . . . turn out right. In spite of her mother . . . knew I was right to . . . leave her . . . with her grandparents."

"They did a good job," Max confirmed, even though he knew he was biased. "She's strong, smart, courageous, honest." *Sexier than Aphrodite herself.* "Everything a man could ask for."

Martin's gaze sharpened for a moment. "Everything . . . you could . . . ask for?"

The question took him by surprise. He hadn't bothered to hide his attraction to Kitty, even when he'd brought her to meet her father yesterday, but Max hadn't thought he'd been that obvious. Martin had never given any indication that he'd seen—or even looked—beneath the surface. But now he waited for Max's answer with intense concentration, as if something very important depended on what he said.

Gradually, the light dawned. "You devious old coot," Max said slowly, shaking his head in disbelief. "How in God's name did you know it would work?"

The older man smiled, truly smiled, his happiness obvious. "Didn't," he whispered. "Hoped . . . took a chance . . . *am* a gambler . . . after all."

"Well, you hit a royal flush this time, *pa*." Even Max found a smile over that. "I can't believe you set me up."

"Good reason." Martin curled his fingers around Max's, and even though his grip was disturbingly weak, his intensity came through clearly. "Needed someone . . . to look after her. Some-someone . . . I could trust. Family . . . won't like it . . . when they find out."

Max nodded. He already knew that. Martin had mentioned his new will earlier, the one leaving the bulk of his fortune to Kitty, and it didn't take a genius to realize that certain members of the pride wouldn't take it very well when Max claimed Kitty openly as his mate. The list of things the family wouldn't like was getting longer by the second.

"Knew you'd . . . handle the pride," Martin continued, struggling to draw enough oxygen into his diseased and failing lungs. "Never worried . . . about that. And . . . maybe Kitty . . . won't want to . . . stay. But . . . want her . . . to have the choice. Family . . . won't give her that."

"She'll stay," Max whispered, leaning forward and pressing Martin's hand. "I promise she'll stay. She's going to be my mate, *pa*. Just as soon as I get around to mentioning it to her."

He saw the flash of joy in Martin's eyes, whether at the thought of Max and Kitty forming a mate bond, or at Max's affectionate and automatic use of the Leo word for "father," he wasn't sure. It didn't matter. He felt tears sting his own. "I wish you could stick around for a while. She's going to give me beautiful cubs, *pa*."

The older man pulled his hand free and lifted it until he pressed the trembling palm against Max's cheek. "Always wished . . . I'd been your father," he whispered.

"You are."

Martin smiled and patted the son-of-his-heart on the cheek. Then the frail man turned his head and looked toward Kitty, standing silent at the foot of his bed. "Tell her to join us."

Max nodded and held out his hand. Immediately, Kitty moved toward them, taking his hand in hers and letting him pull her to his side. She stood awkwardly for a moment, but Max had other ideas. Wrapping his arm around her waist, he tugged again until she tumbled into his lap. He kept her there with a firm grip, but she must have been too concerned for her father to risk struggling.

"I wanted . . . to apologize," Martin began, but Kitty shook her head firmly.

"You did that yesterday. It was enough. I'm not angry with you anymore," she reassured him.

Her father smiled. "Not for . . . that," he whispered. "For . . . leaving so soon. I . . . I had hoped . . . we'd get more of a chance . . . to get to know each other."

"Me, too."

She reached forward and took the hand Max had warmed with his own. Lifting it gently, she bent her head and pressed a kiss against the back. Touched and proud, Max reached for her father's other hand, forming a circle among the three of them.

Martin gazed up at the daughter he barely knew and the son he'd never had, and Max could see the light of true happiness in his eyes.

"This," the Felix mouthed, the words barely audible. "This . . . is the best ending . . . any man could want."

Then his eyes drifted closed.

Max heard Kitty's soft gasp and hugged her reassuringly. "It's okay," he whispered. "He's just unconscious."

She leaned back against Max and shivered. "I suppose it's silly of me. I mean, we all know it's just a matter of time."

"It's not silly. It's who you are."

They sat silently for a few minutes, each holding a thin, cool hand, before Kitty stirred.

Max looked down at her, his expression questioning.

"I know you want to stay with him," she said softly, "but I don't know if I should. I'm sure his family is on their way, and they won't like me being here."

"You are his family," Max argued, his jaw tightening.

"You know what I mean, Max. They'll make a scene, just like they did yesterday. He shouldn't have to listen to poison. Not now."

Max let his forehead rest against hers and sighed. He wanted to keep her with him, wanted her warmth, her softness, her open, tender heart, where he could touch them. He needed the comfort she gave him just by being close, by being herself, but he knew she was right. Martin deserved peace in his final hours, not spite and malice.

"There's a sitting room through there." Max nodded to the door just a few feet away in the bedroom's far wall. "There's a comfortable sofa and an afghan blanket he liked to use in the winter. There's only the one door, so I'll be able to keep an eye on you. Why don't you stretch out in there and see if you can take a nap? I don't know how long this will take."

She nodded and slid to her feet. "I'll keep the lights off and leave the door cracked. That way no one will know I'm here, but if you need me, you can just call."

She bent to press a kiss to his lips, and Max pulled her close for another minute, reluctant to let her go.

"You shouldn't have to hide," he muttered, burying his face for a moment against her breasts. "He's your father. You have as much right to be here as the rest of them."

Briefly, Kitty cradled Max's head to her; then she released him and stepped back. "This isn't about my rights. It's about what's right for Martin."

"I know," Max growled. But he didn't have to like it. He jerked his chin toward the door. "Go on. Try to get some sleep."

She nodded and slipped silently through the door, leaving Max to his lonely vigil.

TWENTY

DESPITE WHAT MAX SUGGESTED, KITTY HAD NEVER IN-tended to sleep. She hadn't imagined she'd be able to. She'd only stretched out on the sofa because pretending that she intended to nap seemed to make more sense than sitting alone and silent, staring into the darkness. So when she jerked away with a low gasp, she surprised herself as much as anyone.

It took a moment for her to remember where she was, but the uneasy feeling in her stomach provided a decent clue. Her father's house. Her father's deathbed. Hiding from her father's family. No wonder she felt vaguely sick.

Pressing a hand to her queasy belly, Kitty sat up and pushed back the light covering she'd spread over herself when she lay down. The dim room had gone completely dark while she slept, but she remembered seeing a DVD player on the shelves built into one of the walls while it had still been light enough to see. A glance in that direction proved her memory to be sound, and the glowing blue numbers told her the time. 7:46. She'd been asleep about three and a half hours.

Kitty sighed softly and rose to her feet, pausing to

stretch muscles stiff with tension and sleep. As she let her arms fall back to her sides, she heard the quiet murmur of voices coming from the bedroom.

Careful not to make a sound, she turned and padded softly toward the slightly open door. Of course she had slipped off her shoes before pulling her legs up onto the sofa, and now her stocking feet moved silently across the floor. Sticking to the shadows, she peered into the other room and saw several figures gathered around Martin's bed.

Max sat where she'd left him, her father's hand still clasped in his. He hadn't moved the entire time she'd been sleeping. Kitty didn't know what else she had expected. She might only have known the man for a couple of days, but since that had been long enough for her to fall in love with him, it had also been long enough for her to understand what kind of person he was—strong, decent, kind, protective, and absolutely, unswervingly loyal. It would never occur to him that he should be anywhere else right now but at the side of the man he called his father.

Dr. Reijznik had joined Max, pulling a chair close to the bed near Martin's shoulder where he could watch the cardiac monitor and occasionally check the IV that delivered merciful analgesia to his failing patient. Kitty just hoped that after Martin had spoken to her and Max, he had allowed the doctor to increase his dose of morphine until the last of the pain washed away in a tide of drug-induced numbness.

When she looked to the rest of the people surrounding the bed, Kitty had to work to stifle the thought that she could use a dose or two of the hard stuff herself.

Drusilla and Nadalie had positioned themselves on the side of the bed opposite Max. The older woman dressed in an elegant black dress that looked as if she planned to head straight from her ex-husband's side to a swanky little cocktail party. Her daughter, meanwhile, sobbed loudly and falsely into a white handkerchief, and every minute or so, Dru would reach over and pat her consolingly on the leg. At even shorter intervals, Nadia would check to see if anyone was watching her, her eyes lingering on Max before she buried her face once more in her suspiciously dry cloth and resumed her weeping.

Behind the women, Olivia stood still and expressionless with her back against the wall and her gaze fixed on the black and green readout of her uncle's cardiac monitor.

A final figure slouched casually at the foot of the bed. In his black jacket and expensively faded jeans, Peter looked like nothing so much as a particularly skinny vulture perched on a fence post while it waited for its next meal to stop with that annoying breathing. Unlike his mother and sister, he didn't even have the decency to fake grief, instead staring blank-eyed and bored at his father's dying body.

Kitty's nausea increased, and she forced her gaze back to Max as her hand pressed more firmly against her stomach. He sat like an island of honest sadness in an ocean of pretentious greed. More than anything, she wanted to go to him, wanting to climb back into his lap, wrap her arms around him, and hold him, to offer him comfort and companionship during this hideous experience.

She knew how he felt. She could read it in his posture, in spite of that blank mask he showed to the world. He looked the same way she had as she'd sat with Lonnie at her grandmother's side, watching the woman they both adored slip irretrievably away from them. The memory of her own face staring back at her from the bathroom mirror would never leave her, the blank expression, the dazed, red-rimmed eyes, the heavy baggage of grief. No matter how skillful Max might be at concealing the signs, Kitty could still read them. Because while everyone else looked at Max with their eyes, she saw him with her heart.

She didn't know what had happened. It seemed impossible that a heart could grow so much love for one person in so short a time. Somehow, in just forty-eight hours, he had come to mean more to her than anything else in the world. She breathed him in like oxygen, swallowed him like nourishment, absorbed him like water.

How in God's name was she ever supposed to walk away from him?

Her stomach lurched again, and Kitty pushed the distressing thought away, burying it in the back of her mind. She had plenty of other things to think about and more worries than she could shake a stick at. Right now, she needed to focus on Max and what he was going through.

She felt a twinge of guilt that she wouldn't be the one to mourn her father most deeply. It seemed like something a daughter should do, but when it came right down to it, Martin wasn't really her father. Maybe if he hadn't been ill, if she had gotten a chance to know him, to talk to him and spend time with him, maybe then something more would have grown between them, but she would never really know. In her heart, her father was and always would be Lonnie Sugarman.

Papaw might be a generation removed from biological fatherhood, but he had been the one who'd walked her at night when she was sick, who'd taught her to ride a bicycle and bait a fishhook. He'd waited up for her when she had her first date, and held her when she cried over her first teenage crush. No father could ever have loved her better.

Still, Kitty could never regret coming here and meeting Martin Lowe, and a part of her had genuinely come to love him while she was here. Not because he was the man who had given her life, but because he was the man who had given Max a second chance at life. Even if she could never feel for Martin what he may have wanted, what *she* may have wanted, she would always love him for helping to shape the man who had stolen her heart. When Martin passed, she would regret his loss and would be sorry for the chance of a greater connection dying with him, but her tears would be for Max and for the pain she knew he would suffer. Somehow, she didn't think Martin would mind that if he knew.

As she watched from the shadows, she saw Dr. Reijznik frown and lean forward over Martin's still form. She saw the doctor glance at the monitor and then press two fingers to the inside of his patient's wrist. She saw Max tense and then watched as the green blips on the black screen gradually moved farther and farther apart until they stopped altogether and a thin straight line scrolled off the edge of the monitor.

In the bedroom, Max bowed his head for a moment, then pressed a final kiss to the back of his father's hand and gently tucked it back beneath the smooth covers. Kitty saw him speak briefly to the doctor, but Max's voice was so low that she couldn't make out the words.

The older man responded with a nod, then turned and quietly flipped the switch on the monitor, turning the small screen still and black.

Kitty winced as Dru and Nadia seemed to take that as their cue to moan and wail like a couple of well-dressed banshees. They collapsed into each other's arms with true dramatic flair and clung together for several long minutes while they waited for someone else—Max, for instance—to notice their distress and hurry along to comfort them. Instead, Max looked at them from the other side of the bed and spoke softly.

Kitty saw both women shake their heads and step away from Martin's still form.

"No," she heard Dru say in a quavering voice with just the right touch of regal forbearance. "I'd rather remember him the way he looks in my memories, tall and strong and healthy. The body is just a shell. I'm sure you'll make all the appropriate arrangements."

"I can't! I just can't! How can I bear to look at him this way, let alone touch him!" This from Nadia, loud and shrill and predictably subtle. "It's too horrible. I can't even stand to be in the same room with it. I have to leave!"

Kitty saw Nadia spin around and head for the door and noted acidly that Peter already had his hand on the knob even though no one else had moved.

"Maybe it's better if you all leave," Max said, his voice rising enough for Kitty to hear him but still low and calm and even. "Dr. Reijznik will have some paperwork to fill out, some formalities to take care of, and I'd like a last minute with Martin."

Dru frowned at Max. "You should come outside. The pride needs continuity."

Max had his back to Kitty, but she didn't need to see his expression to understand the anger in the set of his wide shoulders. "And they'll get continuity. In just a few more minutes."

"But—"

Drusilla looked like she wanted to say something else, but the expression on Max's face must have told her better. Lifting her chin, she took one of two small purses off the night table and turned to face her daughter. "Come along, Nadalie. We can wait outside and inform the rest of the pack of your father's death while Max has his chance to sit shiva."

One by one, the rest of the family filed out of the room. Olivia left last and pulled the door closed behind her.

As soon as the latch clicked, Max turned toward the sitting room door and held out his arms. "Come here, kitten."

Kitty didn't wait another heartbeat. Pulling open the door, she raced back into the room and into Max's embrace. This was where she had needed to be all along, and when his arms pulled her tight against him and rocked her slowly from side to side, she knew he'd needed her there, too.

Bending down, Max buried his face in the curve of her neck and let out a shuddering breath. "God," he sighed, burying one hand in her hair and clenching her fingers in the long strands. "I hated not having you with me. I hated watching them sit there and pretend to be upset when I knew they would rather have been shopping, or drinking, or playing golf."

She heard him swallow hard, felt tears dampen her skin, and tightened her arms around him.

"He deserved better than them," Max whispered, his voice cracking with emotion. "He deserved so much better."

Gently, Kitty pulled Max's head up from her shoulder and cupped his face in her hands. Dragging her lips across his cheeks, she kissed his tears away, then pressed her mouth softly against his.

"He *had* better, Max. Remember? He had you."

Max shuddered again and yanked her back against him, seeming unable to let her go. Kitty didn't mind. He could hold her like this forever if he wanted, and she didn't think she would ever complain. Who could complain about being needed so badly?

She wasn't sure how long they stood there, but it hardly mattered. Occasionally, she heard the sound of the doctor or the nurse bustling discreetly around, but neither of them disturbed the couple. In fact, Dr. Reijznik and Ms. Mencina seemed very concerned with giving them their privacy, so much so that Kitty felt herself smile in spite of the somberness of the occasion.

When she heard the click of a door latch, it didn't really register as anything important. She just assumed it was Ms. Mencina or Dr. Reijznik entering or leaving the room, so Kitty didn't even bother to look up. Not until she heard the cry of outrage and felt Max jerk his head from her neck. Dread knotting in her stomach, she turned with him and saw Nadalie silhouetted in the doorway with her mouth gaping open and a look of poisonous fury marring her pretty face.

"What the fuck is that bitch doing here?!"

TWENTY-ONE

MAX HEARD NADIA SHRIEK AND MUTTERED SOME-
thing foul under his breath. If only Martin had learned
to keep his pants zipped after his affair with Kitty's
mother, all of their lives would have turned out to be a
lot easier. As would Martin's death.

Lifting his head, Max turned toward the door, automatically nudging Kitty behind him and out of the line
of fire. "Nadia, go back outside and wait with your
mother. I already told you I'd be out in a minute."

"You told us you wanted a minute alone with the
body," the Leo female hissed, outrage and jealousy feeding on each other to contort her usually pretty, if arrogant, face into an ugly mask. "You didn't mention that
you planned to spend it groping a human whore! And
my father hasn't even gone cold, you bastard!"

Rage left Max with a dull roaring in his ears. Only
the touch of Kitty's soft hand on his back reminded
him of where he was and why he had to keep his temper. It was bad enough for Nadia to come bursting in
here and making a scene in front of her father's corpse.
Max had too much respect for Martin and too much
respect for the dead to add to the unpleasantness. He

drew in a deep breath and hauled hard at the ties of his self-control.

"However much you chose to demonstrate your disrespect for the man who raised you, Nadia, I am not going to let you make a scene. Not here."

Nadalie opened her mouth, but Max cut her off with a low snarl.

"Wait outside. If you don't go now, I'm happy to throw you out the door bodily, but either way, I will *not* have this conversation in here. If you have a problem with me or with my behavior, we can talk about it *outside*."

For a moment, the woman just stood there, glaring at him. Or rather, through him, since she looked as if she wanted to tear out Kitty's heart and eat it. Max would have no compunction about killing Nadalie before she laid one fucking finger on his mate.

"Fine," she hissed. "I'll wait outside. But don't think we're not going to have this out, Marcus Stuart, and don't think we're going to just sit back and let you bring that mongrel slut into this pride. I know that personally, I'll see her dead first."

Nadalie slammed the door so hard behind her that the heavy wood rattled in its frame.

Max stared after her, half-tempted to follow so he could wring her neck and be done with it. He knew exactly what she was doing now. On the other side of that door, she was painting a graphic and venomous picture of Kitty, styling herself and her family as victims to her father's failing mental stability and a hardened gold digger's grasping machinations. By the time Max came out to set things straight, Nadalie would have them so tangled in the minds of the pride that some members would never look at Kitty without suspicion.

For one tempting moment, he considered saying to hell with them. Let them find another Felix. Let them run their own pride. He would take Kitty and disappear. He'd find his own land somewhere else, start fresh with a new home, a new business, and a new mate. He'd found his own pride, starting with the cubs Kitty would give him, and his legacy would leave the Red Rock in the shadows.

But then the rage began to subside from a boil to a simmer and he knew he couldn't do it. As much as he wanted to walk away, he owed too much to these people. They were his family, the only real family he'd ever known, and even if he hadn't owed them, he owed it to Martin to stay. The older man had expected Max to take up the reins and guide his pride into the future. It had been one of the last things Martin had mentioned to Max, and it had been obvious that the knowledge of it had given him comfort in the end. Max wouldn't be able to live with himself if he let down the only father he'd ever know.

Sighing, he bowed his head and fought for control, for strength, for wisdom.

A small hand stroked over his, eased his fingers open, and slipped inside, fitting palm against palm and curling protectively around him. Opening his eyes, Max looked down and found everything he was looking for in his mate's bright green eyes. As soon as she touched him, he knew everything would be fine.

Oh, she didn't make the difficulties go away. There was still the pride to face, Nadalie and the other family members to deal with, responsibilities for him to shoulder. He knew that. But he also knew that with Kitty by his side, he could do all that and more. It touched him to know that she would protect him if she could. Hell, she'd probably try to do it, no matter that he had twice her size and three times her strength. That was just who Kitty was, strong and fierce and undyingly loyal.

How the hell had he gotten lucky enough to find her?

She looked up at him with those beautiful wide eyes, and he saw them start to twinkle.

She tugged his hand. "Marcus, huh?"

"Marcus Alexander," he replied, his voice gruff with unspoken emotion. "And not even my mother ever called me that."

"Hmm. And why didn't I know that before now?"

His lips twitched. "Probably because I didn't tell you."

"Hmm."

God, he loved this woman. This had gone beyond recognizing his mate. When he looked at Kitty, he recognized his heart.

"I'll make you a deal," he said, pulling her into his arms one more time and cuddling her briefly against him. "After I get everything settled here, I'll take you back to the cabin and we can play twenty questions. When was the last time you played a good game of that?"

He watched her blush at the reminder of the other game they'd played that afternoon and grinned.

"It's been a while," she admitted, stroking her hands over his back. "You may have to remind me of the rules."

Max bent his head and brushed his lips over hers, relishing the way she instinctively stretched up to meet him, the way her lips parted at his slightest touch. "The rules are very simple."

He kissed her.

"In fact, you only need to remember one."

He kissed her again.

"Oh?" she whispered, and this time she kissed him. "And what rule is that?"

Max pressed his mouth to her for a long, deep kiss, and when he pulled back, he was smiling. "Now that I've caught you, I get to do whatever I want."

IT TOOK A SERIOUS ACT OF WILLPOWER FOR KITTY NOT to give in to her newly acquired nervous habit and press her hand to her stomach as she gripped Max's hand and followed him out of her father's bedroom. She knew a large portion of the pride would be waiting in the other part of the house, and worse than that, she knew her ex-stepmother and half siblings would be there as well, just waiting for the chance to tear out her throat. She trusted that Max wouldn't let them, of course, but that didn't erase the nausea-inducing knowledge that they wanted to.

Before she and Max left the bedroom, he had spoken softly and urgently for a few minutes, letting her know what was going to happen. Most important, he'd told her, let him do the talking. In the best of circumstances, he would present himself in front of the pride, give them the official news of the death of the Felix, and lay ceremonial claim to the title himself, after which everyone in the pride would greet him as the new Felix and they would all live happily ever after.

In reality, after he proclaimed himself Felix, the other male members of the pride would be given the opportunity to challenge his right to the title. "Challenge" being a euphemism for trying to kill Max and seize the title for themselves. Max could not honorably refuse any of these challenges and would be forced to fight all comers in order to prove himself worthy of leading the pride. He hoped the number of challenges would be small, if any were offered. He'd been Martin's heir presumptive for a long time, and most of the pride liked and respected him, but he wanted her to be aware of the possibilities.

After the challenges, or maybe before or during, depending on what Nadalie had in mind, any member of the pride who did not wish to accept Max as Felix would be given the opportunity to leave peacefully. Then the remaining members would be acknowledged as belonging to the pride, Kitty included if she wanted to be, and, again, they would all live happily ever after.

God, Kitty had never wished for anything so hard in her entire life as she wished for the first possibility. But as she'd acknowledged before, she'd never had that kind of luck.

As they passed through the hallway, Max paused to speak to the large man who had been guarding Martin's door when they arrived.

"How many are here, Steve?" Kitty heard him ask.

"'Bout fifty or sixty inside. Maybe four hundred out."

"Four hundred and fifty Leos," Kitty repeated to herself, swallowing hard. And if Nadalie had gotten her way, they all probably hated Kitty's guts by now.

But Max didn't seem fazed. He just nodded his thanks and continued to guide Kitty toward the front door. As they approached it, the chatter she could hear coming from the living room abruptly died and Drusilla stormed out to meet them.

"Nadalie tells me she saw—"

Max cut Drusilla off with an impatient gesture. "Not now, Dru," he said. "I have no desire to repeat any of the same information a hundred times tonight. If you want to talk to me, listen to me, or discuss something with me, you can do it outside."

He didn't wait to see how she took his decree, just yanked open the front door and ushered Kitty out before him with a hand in the small of her back.

Kitty saw the response, though. She saw the look of pure, hateful contempt on the older woman's face and felt her stomach clench. Again. If she'd known that particular organ would be back to its old tricks tonight, she'd have put some Pepto in her purse. She'd been drinking a lot of pink since the car wreck.

People began to follow her and Max outside, filing out of the house to join those who already milled about in the desert landscape. Kitty saw the doctor in the crowd, as well as the man who'd come to the cabin to alert Max to her father's failing condition. Most of the rest of the crowd were strangers.

She let Max guide her through the throng, feeling vaguely surreal as the Leos began to follow them through the darkness. She took hold of Max's hand again and gripped it tightly.

"Where are we going?"

"Not far." He squeezed her hand but kept his eyes on the path ahead. "There's a *vergaderplek* nearby. A meeting place. Your father had it laid out years ago. It's where the pride holds important ceremonies."

Kitty nodded and lapsed into silence. That made sense, but it didn't make her any more comfortable with having almost five hundred adult Leos at her back.

When they reached the site, she stood beside Max and watched as several men began moving around and lighting tiki-torch-style lamps around the perimeter of an area about the size of a baseball field. At one end near where they stood, she saw a large flat rock, roughly rectangular in shape and elevated about three feet off the ground on a pile of other rocks. As people began to gather and position themselves at the meeting place, they all faced that rock. Faced her.

Kitty held on to Max's hand and worked to keep her expression calm and confident.

When most of the crowd had gathered, Max squeezed her hand and drew her to stand by the narrower end of the large stone. Then he released her and leapt easily onto the top of it. When he held up his hands, the chatter of the crowd died down and every face turned to watch him.

"Most of you already know that this is a sad night for the Red Rock Pride," he announced, projecting his deep voice so that it boomed out across the meeting place. "Martin Lowe, who has been Felix to our people for many years, has left us now for his eternal hunt, and we will all mourn his passing. He led us well, with a strong heart and a thick mane, and he will be sorely missed."

A murmur swept through the pride but quickly subsided when Max resumed speaking.

"I was with the Felix when he died, and he spoke to me of his wishes. It is my duty as his pride mate, to honor them. As his *baas,* I seize this opportunity as mine to claim the title of new Felix of the Red Rock Pride. In this way, I vow I will honor the wishes and the memory of Martin Lowe."

Kitty heard the strength, the pride, and the grief in Max's voice and swallowed against the knot in her throat. She wished more than anything that they could have spent the night like normal people, comforting each other on their loss, alone and quiet with grief and each other. But she understood the power of tradition, of responsibility. She would never stand between this man and what he felt to be right.

"I claim the title of Felix, and I claim for my own the Red Rock Pride," Max bellowed again, looking huge and proud and fierce. "Does any Leo present wish to challenge my claim?"

The breath caught and held in Kitty's throat as she heard the words she had dreaded. Her eyes scanned restlessly over the crowd, searching for movement, waiting to see men striding forward with anger on their faces and envy in their hearts. But no one moved. Her heart began to pound as, slowly and cautiously, she began to wonder if her luck might be changing.

Then she heard a murmur in the crowd and her stomach clenched. She saw a ripple near the front of the crowd, saw someone pushing forward, and then Nadalie, Olivia, and Drusilla emerged from the crowd and lined themselves up in the clear area at the base of the stone, their eyes trained on Max.

Kitty frowned, unsure of what was happening. Max had told her that only men were allowed to challenge for the position of Felix. Sexist it might be, he admitted, but it was the duty of the Felix to defend the pride from attacks by outsiders and by coalitions of nomadic males who sought to seize control. Because male Leos were so much bigger and stronger than females, the Felix had to be male in order to succeed in that defense. At the time, she had muttered something about sexism, but honestly, she had to admit it made sense. Having experienced the difference between her size and Max's, she thought he had a valid point.

So why were three women the only one to respond to Max's call for challenges?

"No one disputes your claim to the title of Felix," Drusilla called out, her voice loud and sharp in the night air. "The pride accepts you gladly. But we do not accept the newcomer in our territory. As pride females, my niece, my daughter, and I wish to exert our right to challenge the new female for acceptance. Either she can accept our challenges and defeat us for the right to remain in the pride, or she can show herself a coward, leave now, and never return to Red Rock territory!"

Well, Kitty thought, her mind spinning crazily. *When she put it that way . . .*

TWENTY-TWO

KITTY GUESSED FROM HIS LOUD AND VIOLENT ROAR that Max wasn't particularly fond of the idea of her fighting any of her female relatives to the death. Frankly, she could think of more pleasant things to do herself, but as she looked out over the curious faces lining the meeting place and straining to get a look at her, she really wasn't sure what other choices she might have.

Well, there was one. She could leave. She could pick Drusilla's door number two, turn around and walk away from her father's family. Just return to Tennessee the way she'd intended to all along. If they wanted to think her a coward for that, so be it. She'd know the truth, after all, and she'd know that her retreat was all about her original plan, not about running away from anything.

Except that's not what it would feel like.

Turning her head, Kitty looked up at Max as he stood atop the large chunk of sandstone that had given his pride its name. Every muscle in his body had tensed, every fiber of his being proclaiming his outrage. His expression was no longer blank; it was taut with fury, etched in lines of blazing anger. For her.

Her heart turned over in her chest and Kitty forced

herself to accept the truth. If she left now, if she left at all without telling Max how she felt about him, she really would be running away. She'd be running scared.

It was true that she had never intended to stay here, just like she had never intended to become a Leo, to learn to shift her shape, or to embrace the wildest part of her soul, the part she'd tried to deny while she'd been human. The part that overwhelmed her when she was something else. She'd never intended to form attachments, or even to forgive her father, really. She'd intended to meet him and to show him that she didn't need him any more than he needed her. She hadn't intended to sit by his bed as he lay dying, or to comfort those he'd left behind. She certainly hadn't intended to learn to play chase.

Or to fall in love.

But somehow, while she wasn't looking, Kitty had done all those things. She had become a woman who could be at peace with the animal living inside her, who could grow to love it and embrace it, and in doing so, she had become more herself than she had ever been before. This time, she finally *had* grown up.

Once she realized that, her decision became easy. She had no idea what the future would hold for her and Max, whether they would stay together or drift apart, but she knew that she would never, could never, let anyone take her choices away from her. If she had to fight and to die for the right to make the love she felt last forever, that was exactly what she'd do.

Well, hopefully not the dying part.

Calmly, her head up and her expression serene, Kitty climbed up onto the rock beside Max and looked down at the three Leo women.

"Fine," she said, her voice strong and carrying. "I accept."

OVER HIS DEAD BODY.

Max had felt his heart contract from fear when Drusilla had issued her challenge, but that was nothing compared to the blinding rush of terror that swept over him when Kitty appeared beside him and calmly spoke her acceptance. He had no idea what the hell she might be thinking, but he knew that as soon as he got her alone again, he'd be happy to bend her over his knees and beat the sense back into her, ass first.

She couldn't possibly know what she was doing. He had explained the general concept of a challenge to her before, but that had been when he'd thought she might have to witness him fighting one, not so she could accept one herself. There were pertinent points he had left out at the time to keep her from worrying, and those were the very points that worried *him*.

Grabbing Kitty by the arm, he pulled her aside to glare down at her. "What the *fuck* do you think you're doing?"

"Don't you use that kind of language with me, Max Stuart," she said, glaring right back. "What does it look like I'm doing? I've been issued a challenge, and I've accepted it. I thought that was pretty clear."

"You can't do this."

She narrowed her eyes at him. "I beg your pardon. I know I may not be the most experienced lioness on the block, but I don't think that gives you the right to tell me what I can and can't do. I'm an adult. I can make decisions for myself. If I want to accept a challenge, that's what I'll do."

Over his head and *rotting* body.

"I forbid it," he growled, crossing his arms over his chest so he wouldn't be tempted to wrap his hands around her throat.

Kitty sucked in a hissing breath and turned a rigidly cold expression on him. "You do *what* now?" she demanded softly.

Okay, he realized. *Better try another tactic.* "I can't let you do this, kitten. It's too dangerous. Dru and the others don't just dislike you; they want to hurt you. Maybe even kill you. I can't let you put yourself in that kind of danger."

"I don't believe I've asked you to *let* me do anything. This is my decision, and I've decided to fight."

He grabbed her by the shoulders and shook her. "Do you have any idea what you're saying? Kitty, Drusilla is the top female in the pride. She's won more challenges than I care to think about, and her lion form outweighs you by at least seventy-five pounds! And Nadia and Liv are almost as big. You only learned to control your shift *six hours ago*! There is no way in hell I am going to take the chance of you getting hurt."

She set her jaw mulishly. "Then it's a good thing that it's not your chance to take."

Max shut his eyes. "If that's the way you feel, then you've given me no choice." When he opened them again, he knew they had to be glowing with anger. "I want you to remember that I intended to do this differently. But you know what they say about intentions."

Releasing her abruptly, Max stepped toward the front of the rock and glowered down at the three female challengers.

"I, Max Stuart, Felix of the Red Rock Pride, hereby claim Kitty Sugarman as my mate!" he roared, not caring if they heard him in Utah. "As is my right, I also declare that any challenges to her status must now and forever go first through me!"

EARS RINGING, KITTY STARED AT MAX IN SHOCK. HE did *what*? Called her his *what*? Declared *what* would go through him? For *how* long?

Apparently, Kitty wasn't the only one he'd surprised. Nadalie screeched in fury, and Drusilla used a few phrases that Kitty had never before heard issuing from the mouth of a woman. Olivia just stared at the two figures on top of the rock with a gaze of pure malice.

"The challenge has already been issued," Drusilla shouted. "It was given to the interloper before she became your mate. Therefore, it stands as it was meant to!"

In one smooth movement, Max sprang off the stone and landed with easy grace toe-to-toe with the woman. "Are you issuing a challenge to me, female?" he purred, his voice soft and lethal.

Kitty saw fear flare in Drusilla's eyes and felt a moment of pity. No matter how much bigger and stronger than Kitty the other woman might be, she would be no match for a male Leo in his prime.

Drusilla dropped her eyes to the ground, her face flushed with anger. "No, Felix," she said, but Kitty could see her fists clenching at her sides. Drusilla might be too smart to go up against Max directly, but she was furious about the turn of events.

"*Bitch!*" Nadalie screeched, her roar eerie and inhuman in the cool night air. "You stupid, fucking *BITCH!* This is all your fault, you little slut!"

Before Kitty had even managed to turn toward the sound, the younger woman had launched herself into the air and into a shift, claws extended and fangs bared, clearly aiming for Kitty's throat.

Instinctively, Kitty ducked and rolled, trying to get out of the way. She heard a crack at the same time that she reached the edge of the red rock and went over, slamming into the ground below. The fall wasn't far, certainly not enough to seriously injure her, but she hadn't been expecting it, so she hadn't had time to brace for it. Once again, her skull made impact with an unforgiving surface—that must explain the loud cracking sound, she thought fuzzily—and came out the distinct loser. Reaching up, she touched the back of her scalp, remarkably near where her attacker at the airport had managed to slice it open, and her finger came away dark with blood.

Kitty moaned, but she could barely hear herself over the commotion of the crowd. The cracking sound had been another shot, she realized, and it had driven the crowd into panic. Dozens of people were shouting, and at least one woman was screaming. Kitty could hear Max alternately shouting her name and orders as he arranged for a few of his men to join him in tracking the source of the shot. She registered his shout that she stay where she was, heard him order David to find her, and she tried to push herself up to reassure him she was all right, but as soon as she moved her head, the rest of the world moved, too. Unfortunately, it moved by spinning in crazy circles like a drunken clown on a unicycle.

She let herself slip back to her prone position and closed her eyes. *A few more minutes,* she told herself. Just a few more minutes down here and then she would try again. Honest.

While her head might not have been working right, Kitty's instincts still functioned perfectly, a fact that saved her life when something told her she needed to move to the right *RIGHT THEN*.

Without thinking, she threw herself into a spin, ending up half-buried beneath the overhanging edge of the red rock while a set of lethal fangs snapped together exactly where her face had been a split second before.

Scrambling into a crouch, Kitty watched a red-gold lioness shake her head in frustration, then turn to face Kitty with a threatening growl, and murder in her muddy green eyes.

Olivia.

Instantly, Kitty recognized her, the color of her fur and eyes providing the identification. What it didn't provide was the reason why her half cousin would want to see her dead.

Nadalie's attack had seemed almost inevitable. Not only had the young woman resented the attention her father had given Kitty, but Nadalie had also been wildly jealous of Max. Kitty had known the first instant they met that Nadalie was obsessed with the *baas*, now the Felix, and had hated the little signs of attraction between him and the woman she saw as the interloper. Kitty hadn't been surprised by that attack. But Olivia? It didn't make sense.

But there was no time to puzzle it out now. Olivia slinked toward Kitty's hiding place, her intentions more than obvious in her lowered head, her twitching tail, and the ears she had pinned back against her head. Plus, the sounds she was making, something between a roar and a growl, didn't exactly inspire comfort or security in the listener. At least, they didn't in Kitty.

What they did inspire in her was a split-second decision and the uttering of a quick prayer that the lessons Max had taught her that morning had taken with a vengeance. Briefly closing her eyes, Kitty imagined her feline form materializing in an instant, and she opened her eyes just that quickly. When she saw the night landscape around her lit up like the view through a night-vision camera, she offered up another prayer, this one of thanks. Then she gathered her legs beneath her and sprang from beneath the rock, snarling.

She deliberately overshot her target, clipping Olivia's shoulder as she dove past, hoping to knock the other female off balance. Kitty's real goal had not been to take her attacker down, just to get out into the open where she couldn't be cornered. While the crevice beneath the rock might have saved her life initially, it would be a very bad thing to be trapped there when Olivia launched a renewed attack.

Kitty's strategy almost worked. She saw Olivia stumble a little as she flew past, but it didn't take the larger lioness very long to right herself, or to turn on Kitty with even greater fury. But this time, she was ready.

As Olivia sprang, Kitty rose up, bracing herself on her hind legs and intercepting the other female. They came together like wrestlers, grappling and straining, each trying to overpower the other and shove her down into the dust. They snapped and snarled at each other, making sounds like heavy grunts as they struggled. Kitty trembled with the effort of holding back the heavier, more powerful lioness. Pouring her strength into one urgent shove, she managed to throw Olivia back a couple of steps, but not to knock her over.

Already panting, Kitty dropped back to all fours, pinning back her ears and crouching low as she and Olivia circled each other warily, each one searching for an opening in the other's defenses.

In the back of her mind, Kitty realized vaguely that this was not a position she'd ever expected to find herself in. Her last physical fight had been that one with Billy Ray Buckner, when she'd punched his tooth out. When she'd been six. She'd never had a girl fight, and even if she had, she didn't think it would have prepared her for this. But it didn't matter. Instinct had taken over. She might not know much about form or tactics, but she had already developed a basic strategy with which she felt comfortable. Put simply, it said, "Don't get killed."

Words Kitty intended to live by.

The crowd in the meeting place seemed to have dissolved into chaos when Nadalie had attacked. Certainly they had given Kitty and Olivia a wide-open area to settle their differences. Kitty was aware there were other people and other lions present, but she couldn't focus on them. She had to keep her attention fixed on the one currently trying to kill her. She couldn't even look around to see where Max had gone. She couldn't give Olivia that opening, so Kitty stared intently at the other female and hoped he was okay.

"You were supposed to die, bitch," Olivia grunted.

Literally.

Kitty heard the sounds Olivia made, and if they hadn't come straight from her lion's mouth, they could have been mistaken for the sounds of a pig at the trough. However she made the sounds, though, didn't seem to matter. Kitty's brain took them in and immediately translated them into words.

"The bullet wasn't supposed to miss," Olivia continued. "You were supposed to die and I wasn't going to get the pleasure of killing you myself. It wasn't my first choice, of course, but I had to admit it was cleaner, so I agreed anyway. Against my better judgment. But then Nadia got in the way and Fate handed me a second chance. I couldn't be happier."

Kitty tried not to let her surprise show but wasn't sure how to accomplish that on a feline face. She should have realized that cracking noise had been too loud to be her head. It had been a shot, from something more powerful than a .22, and something a lot closer. Whoever had fired on her this time hadn't intended to miss. Wouldn't have missed, if Nadia hadn't chosen that exact moment to go ballistic and try to rip Kitty's throat out.

Circling warily, Kitty stared into Olivia's poisonous green eyes. "But why, Olivia?" she asked, guessing she sounded no better than a pig herself. "I understood Nadia hating me, but I can't figure out why you should. I wasn't taking anything away from you. Martin wasn't your father, and you never gave any indication you were in love with Max. What would you get from killing me?"

"God, you're stupid!" Olivia roared. "Do you have any idea how rich Uncle Martin was? A hundred and fifty million dollars, Scarlett. Cash money. That doesn't even include the value of the casino and the resorts. Those are owned by Pride Enterprises and are all tied up in stocks, so it doesn't matter that he left the controlling interest to Max. The money was going to come to us. Can your little hayseed mind even comprehend how much money that is?"

Actually, Kitty wasn't really sure it could. Even after she had been staying in the hotel and had seen the house and talked to Max, it hadn't really sunk in when he'd told her Martin was wealthy. After all, none of that money was hers. She'd never even stopped to wonder what it would be like if it were. She didn't need that kind of money. She didn't want it.

"Oh, is the light dawning over marble head?" Olivia sneered. "That was fifty million each, in case you're doing the math. He was going to split it three ways, between Nadia and Peter and me, because I've always been like a daughter to him, you know. But then you came along, and you fucking ruined everything!"

Screaming in fury, Olivia attacked again. She swiped one huge paw at Kitty's face, missing her target but catching the top of her head as she went by.

Kitty yelled in pain and shook her head. Why the hell did everyone have to aim for her goddamned head? She was getting sick of it.

"What did I ruin?" Kitty screamed, hurt and furious. "I never asked Martin for anything. I certainly never asked him for money, so don't blame me if he realized you were too much of a psycho bitch to deserve his money and decided to write you out of his will."

Olivia dove at her, her teeth nearly catching Kitty in the side, but she spun away just in time.

"He didn't change anything until you came along." Head lowered, Olivia stalked and circled like the predator she was. "I saw his will. All I had to do was pull his file at the office and read it. And it always looked the same. Until he got the call about you. Then do you know what happened? He decided to leave a hundred and forty-seven million to you and left the three of us with a paltry fucking million each!"

"Still not my fault," Kitty grunted, dodging a paw to the head. "I didn't change the will and I didn't ask for the will to be changed. Whatever Martin changed, it was his own decision."

"One he never would have made if it hadn't been for you!"

She batted a second paw away, baring her teeth and snarling. Olivia lunged, but Kitty parried, dropping her head and ducking beneath the other female's chin to snap at her chest. Kitty felt her teeth sink into fur and skin and tasted blood in her mouth, but the adrenaline rode her too hard for her to pause and really think about that.

Olivia tore herself away, screaming, a jagged line of red opening up between her front legs, staining her paler chest fur crimson.

Kitty shook her head, sending drops of blood flying from the cut between her ears. Now each of them had drawn blood, and Kitty began to wonder if it would end before one of them couldn't bleed anymore.

"I've been planning to kill you for weeks," Olivia panted, glaring at Kitty. "Ever since your father mentioned you. But now I'm going to enjoy it a hell of a lot more."

"You don't need to kill me," Kitty panted, feeling herself begin to tire. She wasn't used to this form, let alone this form of exertion. If this went on too much longer, she might not be able to hold Olivia off. "I told you, I don't want the money. I'll refuse it. I'll sign it over. Whatever. I don't want it."

"It's too fucking late for that." Her head low to the ground, Olivia dropped her belly and lifted her shoulder blades and began to stalk closer to Kitty. "The will is binding, unless you die before it can be executed. If that happens, everything goes back to the way it was before. With the added bonus of you being dead."

Kitty's mind worked frantically. "But why settle for fifty million?" she asked. "Why split it with the others? If I inherit, I'd sign it over to you. You could have it all. Wouldn't that be better?"

"Ah-ah. Be careful how you answer that, Cuz," a masculine voice said, and the blood in Kitty's veins froze solid.

TWENTY-THREE

KITTY TURNED AND SAW A MALE LION APPROACHING. HE was smaller than Max and less filled out, but he was still bigger than Olivia, and much bigger than Kitty, with a medium golden pelt and a light toffee mane. And he had Martin's green eyes.

"It wouldn't be very sporting of you to try and cut a deal with my father's bastard," Peter continued, speaking to Olivia. "Especially not after I helped you find someone willing to shoot an innocent woman, for a reasonable fee."

Olivia snarled at her cousin. "If the shooter you'd found had been any good, she'd have been dead before your father, so don't rely too much on that to provoke my sense of honor, Peter."

Kitty looked from one murderous family member to the other and shook her head. She was starting to think she liked Drusilla the best of any of these people. At least she had the decency to issue an almost fair challenge, rather than hire an assassin to do the dirty work with a rifle.

Suddenly, a thought occurred to Kitty.

"I suppose I ought to be happy you sent someone to bash my head in at the airport and didn't just take out my whole plane, innocent bystanders and all," she said, watching Peter's face carefully.

The reaction he gave her looked almost like irritation. "That was my first choice, but he wouldn't do it. He said it was too hard to get the right materials past security. The restroom was supposed to be a sure thing."

"As was the hit-and-run, I'm guessing." She shook her head. "Maybe next time you ought to check a hit man's references before you hire him, Pete. From what I can tell, the one you used sucks."

Her half brother roared and lunged at her, but Kitty danced out of his way. She knew she had no chance in a wrestling match with him. She'd barely held her own against Olivia. The best thing Kitty could do was try and stay out of his way. The only advantage her smaller size offered was agility. She'd have to make the most of it.

Then he spoke again, and she felt her stomach sink.

"Circle around behind her, Liv," he growled. "She can't fight in two directions at the same time."

Kitty roared, a sound of outrage and frustration mingled with fear. Damn it, she wasn't supposed to go out this way, either! She hadn't clawed her way out of that car wreck and dragged her mother to safety just to be taken down by a couple of psychotic half relatives who had never learned to share their toys!

Kitty had lived through the wreck, a mugging, a hit-and-run, and two attempted shootings, for God's sake. Now she wanted her happily ever after, and she didn't care who she needed to take down to get it!

With a wary eye on each of her attackers, Kitty began to inch backward, broadening her field of sight. She had no idea how she was going to get out of this mess, but if there was a way, she'd find it. And then she'd find Max and smack him senseless for not rushing in to save her the one time she actually would have been grateful for his help!

"Don't bother looking for a white knight, sis," Peter sneered. "No one's coming to the rescue. The shot was timed to keep Max busy looking for the gunman, and I'm afraid David might have run into a small spot of difficulty. Or maybe I should say, six spots of difficulty, since that's how many men I put on the task. The *belangrik* is a hell of a fighter, and I didn't want to take chances."

Olivia and Peter stalked toward Kitty in unison, shoulder to shoulder. Then they began to drift apart, each one trying to find an angle of approach that would force Kitty to divide her attention between them. It sucked, but she knew it was going to work.

When she felt her right flank hit something solid, Kitty froze. The bastards hadn't just been stalking her; they'd been herding her, forcing her back toward the red rock in an attempt to box her in. Fortunately, their aim had been off. They'd guided her in at an angle, and out of the corner of her eye she could see most of the rock stretched out to her right. Praying frantically, Kitty hitched her hips to the left and backed up again. She took two free steps and rejoiced to have skirted the end of the monument, but froze again when she sensed something behind her.

Please, God, don't let it be Nadalie, Kitty prayed. *I'm already outnumbered. Throwing her into the mix wouldn't be fair.*

"Nadalie is dead," a grim voice answered. "She took the bullet meant for you square in the back of the head. It was the first decent thing she ever did. But don't think that will keep me from beating you for putting yourself in danger, just as soon as I get you alone."

Max!

She would have recognized his voice anywhere, especially when he was lecturing her about something, and she'd never been so happy to be yelled at in her entire life.

She didn't turn around, couldn't afford to with Olivia and Peter still crouched in front of her, preparing to pounce. So instead she flicked her tail in his direction and purred, "It's about time you showed up, mister. I was beginning to think you'd forgotten me."

He didn't bother to respond to that, just stepped out from behind the red rock and padded around to sit on her left side, his hard, copper stare fixed on Peter and Olivia.

The cousins jerked back, surprise and unease creeping over their expressions. When it had been two against one, them against Kitty, their malevolent arrogance had been palpable, but neither of them was a match for Max, and they both knew it. In fact, Kitty could see them mentally calculating the odds of the two of them against Max.

"I wouldn't try it if I were you," Max snarled, baring his razor-sharp fangs. "Not only are both of you together not enough to take me on, but you'd be signing your own death warrants. Take a look around you. We're surrounded by witnesses. Witnesses who know when a legitimate challenge hasn't been offered or accepted. Even if you were, by some miracle, able to take me down, you'd never make it out of the territory alive. Are you really stupid enough to take the chance?"

Blinking, Kitty turned her head and peered into the torch-lit shadows. She'd been focused so intently on the lions trying to kill her that she hadn't had a chance to see what had happened to the crowd that had originally gathered for Max's announcement. She knew they had scattered when Nadalie had attacked her and the shot had been fired, but it looked as if most of them had reassembled at the meeting place. There were Leos everywhere, the majority of them in their furry forms at the moment, though Kitty thought she saw a few two-legged shapes in the distance.

Every single one of them, no matter what shape they wore, had their eyes fixed on the little scenario playing itself out beside the red rock.

Olivia had noticed the same thing. Immediately, she dropped to the ground and rolled to her back, exposing her belly to the sky in a sign of her submission. Apparently, she wasn't crazy enough to make a last try for Kitty's throat. At least, not in front of four hundred witnesses.

Beside her, Kitty heard Max's snarl of displeasure.

"I would like nothing more than to rip your belly open for what you've done," he said, his eyes glowing with fury, "but unfortunately, the days of meting out that kind of justice are gone. Now we have to deal with humans asking questions when the bodies turn up. So instead, I have no choice but to simply banish you from the pride. You will leave my territory and never show your face here again. If you do, we'll find a way to hide your body so that the humans never find it. Do you understand me?"

Olivia whimpered a reply. Slowly, she rolled back onto her feet and belly-crawled off into the night.

When she disappeared beyond the crowd, Max turned to Peter. "You," he snarled. "I'm not even sure I have the words for you. Not only did you attempt to kill my mate, but you succeeded in killing your sister. Can you think of a single reason why I shouldn't damn the interference of the humans and tear your throat out where you stand?"

"Because I am begging you for mercy," Drusilla answered, stepping out from the crowd with her head held high but her eyes down. "I know that what Peter has done is truly unforgivable, but he's all that I have left. I've already lost one child tonight. Please do not ask me to stand by and watch while I lose another."

Kitty heard the pain in the older woman's voice and felt a surge of pity. It didn't matter that Drusilla had tried to drive her from the pride a short time ago. She could almost understand why Drusilla had done it. After all, she had been trying to protect her children even then. Maybe they hadn't been in danger of being killed, but in Drusilla's mind they must have looked like they were in danger of being supplanted in their father's affections.

It all seemed so silly to Kitty. If any of them had bothered to stop and ask her, instead of going on the attack from the very beginning, she could have told them that they had no reason to worry.

"You had nothing to fear from me," she said, stepping forward and ignoring Max's rumbling protest.

Kitty could see she had nothing to fear from Drusilla, and she wanted to try to make the older woman understand. It wouldn't change what had happened, but maybe it would help her to understand that whatever feelings

Martin had held for his legitimate children had not been diminished by his meeting with Kitty.

"I had no intention of coming between your children and their father," she said, her gaze locked with Drusilla's as if it would somehow convince the woman of her sincerity. "Martin was their father, not mine. I wanted to meet him because I needed to know about this side of my heritage, but I never intended to come between him and his family. I didn't ask for an inheritance, and I don't intend to accept one. I don't want his money. All I wanted was to be able to look him in the eyes and ask him why he left my mother and me in the first place. And I got that. That was enough for me."

"My God, you're pathetic," Peter sneered. "I wish our father were here now so he could listen to this sentimental bullshit. That would have made him change the will right back. He always admired drive and ambition. Listening to you go all 'very special episode' on him would have made him sick."

Kitty turned and bared her fangs at her half brother. "You know what's pathetic, Peter? You are. If you had the kind of drive you think Martin admired, you wouldn't be content with flunking out of college and waiting around to inherit a fortune you didn't earn. You'd be building a name and a fortune of your own." Sneering, she turned her back on him dismissively. "I guess that's why he made Max his *baas* and the president of his company instead of you."

When she'd first met him, Peter hadn't impressed her with his keen intelligence, but never had she thought he would be so stupid as to attack her with Max sitting just a few feet away.

She'd misjudged Peter.

He hit her with all the enthusiasm of an amateur blackjack dealer, catching her by surprise and sinking his fangs into her shoulder before she had time to react. She screamed in pain, bucking like a rodeo horse, trying to get him off of her, but his superior mass crushed her protests as if she'd limited herself to a polite, *Please stop.*

Distantly, she heard a noise like the fury of hell, but the pain had gripped her too tightly for her to wonder at the source. Desperately trying to shake Peter, she turned her head and snapped at his flank, but it was no longer there. She saw a blur of coffee and caramel and felt her half brother's weight lift off her. Sinking weakly to her uninjured side, she saw a quick, fierce battle raging between Max and the young Leo he obviously meant to kill.

Kitty screamed.

"Max!"

She doubted he heard her. With a powerful lunge, he knocked Peter off his feet and slammed a heavy paw onto his neck, pinning him to his side in the dirt. She saw Max rear back and bare his fangs, and knew that in another minute she would see those fangs sink into the vulnerable flesh of Peter's belly.

"*Max!* Damn you, stop it!"

He froze, his mouth just inches from the other lion's underbelly. Pushing painfully to her feet, Kitty limped over to his side and butted her head against his.

"I swear to you right now, Marcus Alexander Stuart, if you spill so much as one drop of this boy's blood, I will never forgive you."

Max kept his heavy paw planted on Peter's neck to prevent his escape and stared at her in abject confusion.

"But he paid someone to try to kill you. He attacked you. He *hurt* you. You're bleeding!"

"Yes, I had noticed that. I'm rather observant that way," she snapped. "That's not the point."

"Of course it is!" Max roared. "He doesn't get to hurt you! No one gets to hurt you! Damn it, woman, you're my mate!"

"I'll be gone if you kill that boy." She met Max's stare levelly, hoping like hell he wouldn't call her bluff. "You stopped him, Max. You defended me. I love you for that. But if you kill Peter now, it's not about defending me. It's about revenge. And 'revenge' is just another word for cold-blooded murder. I won't live with a murderer, Marcus. Do you hear me? I'll take the first plane back to Tennessee before I will. Just see if I don't!"

He stared at her for a long moment until something different began to shift behind the blind rage in his eyes. Something softer and finer and filled with wonder.

"Does that mean you'd consider staying here? Staying with me?" he asked.

"Not if you kill that boy, I won't."

Max didn't even hesitate. He just lifted his paw from Peter's neck and brought it back down on the side of his head with brutal force. The young man's eyes closed on a grunt of pain.

"Marcus Alexander!" Kitty roared.

"What? I didn't kill him. I just knocked him unconscious. You never said I couldn't hit him."

She stared at Max, her whiskers twitching. "Did anyone ever tell you that you're a very bad man, Max Stuart?"

"Of course," he answered, leaning down to gently swipe his rough tongue over the wound on her shoulder. "But I've heard that what every bad man needs is a good woman to reform him. Know anyone who might be able to help me out?"

"I do," she answered promptly, rubbing her head against his, savoring the way his thick mane tickled her sensitive ears. "But I'm afraid that if any of them tried to take you away from me, I'd have to kill them."

"Well then," he purred, eyeing her with a great deal of satisfaction. "It looks like I'm stuck with you, doesn't it?"

"For the rest of your life," she assured him, and leaned gratefully against his strength.

IN THE COOL QUIET OF THE DARKENED GUEST ROOM, Kitty snuggled close to her mate's side and ran her hand over the warm muscles of his chest. His human chest.

They had shifted back after reaching the house, because she hadn't been able to bring herself to shift in front of the other four hundred pride members who had still been watching from the perimeter of the meeting site. None of them, she had informed him tartly, needed to see her naked, no matter how quickly it might heal the gouges on her shoulder. Instead, she'd made Max help her back to the house on all fours and get her a spare sheet to wrap around herself before she changed back and let the doctor examine her.

Dr. Reijznik had peered at and poked the bright pink scars on her back that had been the only sign of her injury by that point, and proclaimed her physically fit, if slightly mentally unbalanced for having provoked her mate that way in front of so many witnesses. Then the doctor had jabbed a needleful of antibiotics into her arm—just in case—packed up his bag, handed her his business card, and left the newly official mates alone to discuss their future.

Which they might actually get around to doing, now that they lay warm and sated in each other's arms.

"I wasn't joking about beating you," Max rumbled, hugging her tight against his side. "If I ever catch you doing something as stupid as accepting a challenge again, I promise you won't sit right for a week, no matter how many times you shift."

Kitty tilted her head to look at him and lifted an eyebrow. "Oh, but I suppose it's perfectly fine for you to put yourself in danger, hm?"

"I'm a man," he said, as if that explained everything.

As if that explained *anything*.

"So?"

"So, I'm bigger and stronger than you are. If there's any danger, I'll be able to handle it."

"You are so full of it," she snorted. "How exactly would you 'handle it' if someone decided to take a shot at you? Or run you over with a car? Or double-team you?"

He glared down at her. "I have lived all of my thirty-three years without any of those things happening to me, and I don't expect them to happen to me any time soon. In fact, since the only person any of those things have ever happened to, at least one of them twice, is you—and all of them in the space of one long weekend!—I believe my logic holds."

Kitty thought long and hard about her answer to that, then stuck her tongue out at him.

"Oh, very mature," he said, rolling his eyes. "Now I see what I've gotten myself into."

"A life of eternal bliss?" She batted her eyelashes at him.

"Something like that." His tone was dry, but he hugged her again as he said it, so she just chuckled and settled her head back down on its favorite spot on his shoulder.

They lay quietly for a moment, each enjoying the comfort of the other's presence, but something was still bothering Kitty.

"What do you think Dru and Peter will do now?" she asked.

After tonight's events, the entire pride had been behind Max's decision to banish Peter as well as Olivia. Drusilla had been offered the right to stay, but she had chosen to leave with her son. As she had said, he was the only thing she had left.

Max sighed. "Dru has family in the Midwest, I think. If their pride will agree to take her in, she'd be best off staying there. And if Peter is smart, he'll stay with her, at least until he grows up a little. If he's not smart, he'll probably go nomad until he can take over an existing pride or establish one of his own."

"I feel bad for Dru," Kitty murmured. "It must be horrible to lose a child, but to know that your other child is responsible . . . I can't even imagine that. I'm glad Nadalie will be buried on Red Rock land, though. Despite her failings, she should end up next to her father."

"She will. The funerals will be on Thursday, as soon as all the arrangements are finalized."

"The day after tomorrow," she noted idly.

"Tomorrow, actually. It's almost three in the morning."

Kitty groaned. "Lovely. Just what I needed. Another night without sleep."

"You, you had a nap this afternoon," he protested. "That's more sleep than I've had."

"Yes, but like you said, you're so much bigger and stronger than me," she teased, making her voice high and breathy. "I'm sure you could just go days and days without sleep if you had to."

"Smart-ass," he grumbled, swatting said body part with an open hand and making her yelp. "God save me from sassy women."

Kitty smirked. "You love it."

Max only grunted, but Kitty could see his smile in the darkness and felt her lips curve in response. She was about to close her eyes and settle down to sleep when a glimpse of white on the night table caught her eye. Dr. Reijznik's card.

"I wonder why he left me that," Kitty murmured, frowning. "I certainly hope he doesn't anticipate seeing me quite so often in the future."

Max's eyes were already closed, but he answered her anyway. "He's the pride doctor. He probably thought you should have it in case of emergency."

She snorted. "The only emergency I see in my future is getting to the bathroom in time if my stomach doesn't settle down. I'm hoping that with all the excitement behind us, it will finally get back to normal."

Max's eyes cracked open. "You've been sick to your stomach?"

"Just a little. It hasn't been that bad. I mean, I haven't barfed or anything, but ever since we got the news about Martin, it's been like I'm living on a sailboat."

"So it started this morning."

"You just said it was yesterday."

"After we played chase."

She gave him a look. "I might not be as big and strong as you, studly, but I'm not such a delicate flower that what we did upset my poor little system. I'm sure it's just stress."

"Are you . . ."

That didn't sound like a question, so Kitty didn't bother to answer. But she did blink in surprise when Max sat up in bed and reached over to flip on the bedside lamp.

"What's wrong?" she asked.

He had a very odd look on his face, one she'd never seen before. One she couldn't quite define. She was trying to figure out what it reminded her of when he pulled back the sheets, buried his face in her stomach, and inhaled deeply.

"You insane man!" she squeaked, thumping him on the shoulders. "What in heaven's name has gotten into you?"

When Max raised his head, he wore what could only be described—forgive her language—as a shit-eating grin.

"I think the more appropriate question," he purred, bracing his hands on either side of her shoulders and leaning down until his lips hovered just inches from hers, "is what's gotten into you? And I already know the answer."

"Care to enlighten me?" she drawled.

"Oh, I'd be glad to. The answer to the question of what's gotten into you . . ." He paused to lean down and brush his lips against hers. ". . . is me."

"Well, that's hardly news." Kitty rolled her eyes. "After the way you announced to the entire world that you were claiming me as your mate, I doubt that was a burning question in very many minds."

Max laughed softly and shook his head. "I don't think you're fully appreciating what I'm telling you, sweetheart."

"Then what are you telling me?"

"Did I ever explain to you how Leos take mates?"

"Of course not. You were too busy taking me."

He grinned. "Right. But that was just the public formality. Think of it like the wedding ceremony. The actual mating is where two people realize they're the right mates for each other. It's more like the proposal, if you will."

"Oh." Kitty frowned, wondering where this was all leading. "So when was our mating?"

"Apparently, it was during our game of chase. The excitement afterward distracted me so much, I didn't have time to think about it until now."

"What do you mean? You just said the mating is when you realize a particular person is right for you. How can you not realize when you've realized that?"

"Because the kind of realization I'm talking about isn't a conscious choice," he explained, his copper gaze blazing with intensity. "The realization I'm talking about is a physical one."

Kitty growled in frustration. Maybe her new mate hadn't "realized" it, but he'd clearly lost his mind. "I'm sorry, are you speaking English?"

"Did you know that lions are induced ovulators?"

She threw up her hands. "Did you know that you're making absolutely no sense?"

Max chuckled, taking one of her hands in his and raising it to his lips. "Stay with me, kitten. We're almost there. Lions are induced ovulators," he repeated. "That means that the sexual act is what signals the female's ovaries to release an egg, unlike humans, where the egg is released whether or not a woman is sexually active. Leos, though, aren't quite like lions, but they aren't quite like humans, either. And that's where mating comes in."

"You're losing me."

"Once a Leo female is part of a mated pair, she ovulates on a regular cycle like a human woman. But the first time she finds her mate, she experiences an induced ovulation. Meaning that even if she just ovulated a couple of days ago, when her body realizes that it has met its mate, it will ovulate again in response to his presence, especially if the couple has begun having sex."

Kitty's jaw dropped open with a thunk. She might still be in the dark about a lot of this Leo stuff, but she wasn't stupid.

"Are you trying to tell me . . . ?" Her voice trailed off weakly.

Max nodded and looked incredibly, immensely smug. "Like I said, kitten, I'm what got into you. Me and my cub."

The room spun crazily around her and Kitty closed her eyes as her stomach rebelled, seemingly on cue. "Oh, my God."

"The average Leo pregnancy is about six months. You should be due around the beginning of April."

"Oh, my God."

"Dr. Reijznik will be able to recommend a good obstetrician. I'm sure that's why he gave you his card tonight. He's a sharp one. Nothing gets past him."

"Oh, my God."

Kitty felt Max's big, warm hand settle over her belly

and cracked her eyes open to see him watching her, an anxious frown on his face.

"Are you upset about it?" he asked quietly. "I know it's fast, and I know you weren't expecting it, but—"

She pressed her fingers to his lips and shook her head. "Being flabbergasted is not the same as being upset," she assured him, and as the numbness of shock began to wear off, she felt the first flutters of excitement in her chest. She was going to be a mommy.

Her hand came down on top of Max's and she twined their fingers together, pressing both into the softness of her stomach. She felt the prickle of tears in her eyes and realized she couldn't hold back the words for one more second.

"I love you."

Max blinked, his copper gaze losing focus for just a second before it shot up to her face.

"What did you say?" he demanded, his voice gone harsh and low.

"I love you," she repeated, and laughed at his look of astonishment, because she was sure she could feel it radiating off of her like starlight. "What? Did you think I agreed to stay out here with you for the healthful climate?"

He shook his head, obviously dazed. "No. No, I didn't know. I mean—I . . . I hoped, but I didn't *know*, you know?"

Kitty laughed again, because it was either laugh or feel her heart burst from a surfeit of joy. How strange, how magnificently perfect, to see this powerful man at such a loss for words. "Oddly enough, I think I do know."

"I love you," he whispered, and kissed her tenderly, reverently. "I love you. God, I can't believe how much I love you. I can't explain it. I don't know how it happened. I didn't realize . . ."

His voice trailed off, and he buried his face in her neck with a muffled choking sound. Kitty hushed him, pressing a kiss to his cheek, using her free hand to stroke his hair, his back, every inch of him she could reach.

But her right hand . . .

Her right hand remained entwined with his, resting lightly over the child growing in her womb. She wasn't sure if that hand would ever move, because it felt too perfect just where it was.

"You don't have to explain it," she whispered, pressing their hands softly so that they could include the baby in their embrace. "You didn't have to realize. Our bodies realized for us. And look what an amazing job they did."

"Thank God for that," he muttered against her throat. "Thank God."

Epilogue

KITTY CALLED HER PAPAW FIRST THING ON WEDNESDAY morning—which ended up being Wednesday afternoon in the Eastern time zone—to tell him she was happy, she was safe, and she was getting married. Both of them cried.

She promised she would come to visit as soon as she could and would bring her new husband to meet him, but in the end it was two more weeks before Max pulled their rental car to a stop behind the rambling old farmhouse in which she'd grown up.

"You know, it's not too late to book that flight to Tahiti," he murmured, eyeing the kitchen door with deep suspicion.

"Don't be silly. Papaw is going to love you," she told him, and she thought there was a chance she might actually be right.

When she'd told Papaw her news, he had immediately demanded to speak to the "no-account cardsharp" who had stolen away his little girl. Though she had only really heard Max's end of the conversation, that had been enough for her to understand that her grandfather might have given her mate a wee bit of a hard time. But really,

she was convinced that once they met and Papaw realized how happy Max had made her, the two men would
get along famously.

Maybe.

Sighing, Max unfastened his seat belt, climbed out of
the car, and walked around to help Kitty to her feet. "All
right, but I hope this makes you realize what a favor I've
done you by not having any family of my own," he
grumbled, bending down to kiss her, lingering over it for
just a moment. "And if he shoots me, remember that I
always loved you."

"That's not funny," she said, smacking him on the
shoulder and then taking his hand to drag him up the
porch steps. "Papaw!" she called out, reaching for the back
screen door. "We're here!"

"I've got eyes in my head, girl. I can see that for myself." Lonnie Sugarman emerged from the shadows at
the end of the porch with a scowl on his face and his old
shotgun in his hand.

"Papaw!" Kitty gasped, staring at the shotgun. "What
in heaven's name do you think you're doing?"

"That's a question I'd like to ask you, baby girl," he
answered, but his gaze was fixed on Max. "I'd also like
to know who raised you to go running off to Vegas and
to marry a man you hardly know, because it surely wasn't
me and your mamaw."

Kitty opened her mouth to protest, but Max took her
by the arm and gently tugged her backward, positioning
her behind him. It was the man's favorite place for her.

"Mr. Sugarman, I'll say I'm pleased to meet you because I know how much Kitty loves you," Max said
evenly, "but I think you should know that she's my wife
now, and I won't permit you to speak to her that way. Kitty

is one of the sweetest, kindest, most loving, and most decent women it's ever been my pleasure to meet. I'd say that you and her grandmother did a fine job raising her, because she's also strong, capable, and intelligent. And what's more, she's an adult fully capable of taking care of herself and making her own decisions. I think she deserves to have you respect that."

Jaw dropping, Kitty stared wide-eyed at Max's back and wondered who the heck that man was who looked like her husband but said things she never in a million years thought she'd hear her husband say. Reaching down, Kitty grabbed a piece of skin and pinched herself, just to make sure she wasn't dreaming.

For a long moment, the porch was silent but for the wind whispering through the trees and the soft lowing of the milk cow out behind the barn. Then her grandfather carefully leaned the barrel of his shotgun up against the wall of the house and held out his right hand.

"In that case," Lonnie said, a smile breaking out over his weathered features, "I'd like to be the first one to welcome you to the family."

Kitty stared at her grandfather, then turned her head and looked at her husband, who was shaking the other man's hand and grinning like a loon, so she stared at him for a minute, too. Then she stared at each of them again for good measure, planted her hands on her hips, and scowled at the two of them together.

"I will never—not if I live to be older than Methuselah—" she proclaimed, "understand men."

Her grandfather laughed and slapped her husband on the back.

"Oh, we're simple creatures, kitten," Max said, wearing the smug expression she'd seen more often than she liked since he'd realized she was pregnant. "Just give us food, family, and affection and you'll have us eating out of the palm of your hand."

"Sure," she snorted. "Because that's clearly how I keep you in line."

He grinned wickedly. "Maybe not, but the methods you use with me work even better."

Lonnie shook his head and waved the two of them into the house. "Well, come on inside so we can sit a spell and talk. I want to hear some more about what y'all got up to out there in Las Vegas."

Kitty shook her head adamantly. "Not until someone tells me what just went on out here."

"But it was so simple." Max tried for an innocent expression and failed miserably. "Your grandfather wanted to let me know how he would respond if he found out I wasn't treating you well. So I assured him that I hadn't manipulated you into an unhealthy relationship or entered into a marriage I didn't intend to work at for the rest of my life. I also let him know how much I love you and respect you, and he gave us his blessing. And that was that."

" 'And that was that,' " Kitty repeated. "The two of you got all of that out of a scold and a couple of compliments."

Both men nodded, looking rather pleased with themselves.

Kitty sighed and placed both palms flat against her belly. "I swear to you right now, Max Stuart, if this baby turns out to be a boy, I am going to demand a refund."

Lonnie burst out laughing so hard he nearly popped clean out of his overalls, but Max just smiled and leaned down to kiss her sweetly and thoroughly on the lips.

"No refunds," he murmured as he pulled back, his eyes gleaming. "But I'd be glad to offer you a do-over."

It was the way he wriggled his eyebrows that finally got to her. Chuckling herself, Kitty wrapped her arms around her husband's neck and kissed him back in full view of her approving grandfather. "I'm sure you would. And I'll be glad to let you practice until you finally get it right."

It only took him two more tries.

Read on for a sneak peek at the first novel of The Others

ONE BITE WITH A STRANGER

by
Christine Warren

Coming October 2008 from St. Martin's Paperbacks

Just because the gods had abandoned her to a cruel fate didn't stop Reggie from praying they'd keep her from breaking her ankle.

She took as deep a breath as the black satin corset her friends had laced her into would allow, and concentrated very hard on balancing on her four-inch heels while she descended the steps into the darkened club.

Seven solid days of frantic pleading, threats, and attempted bribery had failed to sway Ava or any of the other three women from their determination to "Fix" Reggie. They insisted on making the scheduled trip to the Mausoleum, an unrepentantly Gothic nightclub in the heart of the East Village. None of them had even shown any sympathy for Reggie's pleas, except for Missy.

Even then, as softhearted as she was, Missy refused to side with Reggie against the others. Instead she'd tried to offer reassurance.

"It's not like Ava is really going to pawn you off on a loser, Reg," Missy had said over the phone earlier. "She was just trying to get your goat for giving us such a hard time. You know what she's like. She'd kill me if she knew I told you this, but she knows a guy she's been planning to hook you up with forever, and she's having him meet us at the club. I've met him, and he's great. Now will you relax?"

The answer to that, a resounding no of a headache, currently throbbed behind her temples in time to the industrial-techno music that boomed through the loud-speakers. She tried her best to ignore it and stuck like glue to her friends. If she lost them, she'd never find them again in the gyrating throng of identically black-clad bodies.

Of course, that went both ways. If she could slip away unnoticed—

A hand clamped over her wrist.

"Stay close!" Ava leaned into their little huddle, but she still had to shout to make herself heard any farther than six inches away. "Let's head over to the bar and get a drink before we plan our attack."

Ava always had been perceptive, and she refused to let go of Reggie while she squeezed and shimmied her way through the crowd toward the black-lit bar at one end of the cavernous room. Reggie figured Ava had guessed she'd been planning to bolt.

The women squirmed their way across the dance floor like an amoeba with five pseudopodia. Getting up to the bar required the judicious use of a few elbows and immunity to insults. As the first to reach an empty inch of space, Danice yelled their drink orders, and the others closed ranks around Reggie, who promptly rolled her eyes.

"Come on, guys," she protested when they hurried to snag a tall bar table that had just been vacated. "Don't you think you're being just a little paranoid? I'm here. I came. I answered my door when you picked me up instead of refusing to buzz you in. I put on these excuses for clothes you told me to wear. I even let you plant a bag full of sex toys in my closet! I've surrendered. I'm not likely to go anywhere now."

"But we know you well enough not to trust you," Corinne pointed out, accepting a dark brown beer bottle and taking a moment to survey the crowd. "Ava was the one who thought the corset would be enough to keep you from running. But I brought a leash along just in case."

"Bite me."

"Oh, you'd like that, wouldn't you?"

"Children, please. We have more important things to do than squabble like three-year-olds. Regina looks fantastic in her corset, and I'm sure a leash won't be necessary, unless her fantasy wants her to wear one." Ava glanced discreetly at her watch. "We have exactly four hours and fifteen minutes before the party ends and Regina turns back into a pumpkin. Battle stations."

Reggie's four friends faced the four corners of the bar and started scanning for potential partners. Frowning, Reggie leaned close to Missy's ear and spoke in a low murmur, "I thought you said Ava already had someone picked out."

"She does, but she wants you to squirm a little," Missy hissed back, her eyes on the masses of men and women passing before her. "Could you at least look a little nervous? If she knows I warned you, she'll kill me."

Looking nervous would not be a problem. Reggie felt more than a little out of place surrounded by so many strangers, all of whom seemed to have a genuine fear of sunlight and rather theatrical wardrobes. She hadn't known you could see so many white faces outside of a mime convention.

With a sigh, Reggie scanned the crowd and hoped Ava's friend turned out to be significantly different from any of the men she'd noticed so far.

The crowd really wasn't her type. Most of them were too young for her, and even the ones who were her age or older, somehow managed to look like children playing dress-up. How could she feel attracted to someone who put so much time and effort into pretending to be a fictional character? She had always preferred her men to have a tighter grip on reality, not that you'd know it from her track record.

After finishing her drink on an empty stomach—she'd been too nervous to eat dinner earlier—Reggie could almost see how Ava might have a point. Maybe she just needed to relax and let herself go with the flow.

Reggie pushed away from the table, taking a minute to brace herself against the alcohol racing to her head, just as the DJ spun into a new tune. The song had a deep, hypnotic beat and a dark, haunting melody. Signaling for another drink, she consigned her instinctive reticence to the wind and let her hips pick up the rhythm of the music. The black leather pants she'd thought would be too confining turned out to move quite well with her shimmying hips. She ignored the looks her ass attracted from a few guys at the bar.

When the waitress set a fresh glass in front of her, Reggie raised it to her lips and turned to face the bar. She wondered if she'd be able to pick Ava's friend out of the crowd.

Not the one right in front, she decided, watching a pretty, pale boy gesture grandly to the bevy of emaciated young women who surrounded him. Ava knew Reggie well enough to realize she'd never go for an overly theatrical kid. How in the world would she take someone like that seriously? He'd pull out a pair of handcuffs, and she'd have to ask if his daddy knew where he'd gotten them. She similarly dismissed a handful of brooding punks and a couple of leather-clad biker types. Ava's taste ran to something significantly more sophisticated.

Stubbornly ignoring her headache, she started to think Ava's friend might have stood them up when her gaze hit the end of the bar and skidded to a halt.

The most perfect man she'd ever seen sat there in the shadows with a hand wrapped around a glass of amber liquid and his eyes locked directly on her face.

Dmitri Vidâme nursed his single glass of Scotch and wondered if there might be enough liquid in the glass to drown himself. Literally. Because he was about four minutes away from burying his face in it and breathing deep. Perhaps the fumes would counteract the odor of sweaty, chemically enhanced humans with sex in their minds and cobwebs in their heads.

If it hadn't been for Graham's insistence that this "Vampire Ball" made a perfect place for a young rogue to hide in plain sight, Dmitri would never have let himself be caught within ten city blocks of the place. Such a gothic circus as this club hardly fit his normal thinking as to what constituted a good time, and frankly, the attendees who filled the Mausoleum's vast basement dance floor had begun to annoy him.

Look at them, he marveled, struggling to keep the sneer from his face. *If any of these children ever came face to face with a genuine vampire, they'd soil themselves and go running home to Mommy.* Barely cut loose from apron strings, and the little humans thought themselves misunderstood and tormented. They thought they felt more comfortable in the dark than in the sunlight, thought they knew what it meant to be isolated and tormented.

Dmitri wanted nothing so much as to slap some sense into them.

Actually, that wasn't precisely true. Even more than a

little judicious violence, he wanted to go home. A quiet evening in front of his fireplace sounded infinitely more appealing to him than another five minutes surrounded by pretentious children in "gothic" garb. Even one of the endless, politically charged meetings of the Council of Others, which he currently headed, sounded more appealing, considering that body had been founded to govern the uneasy alliance of the vampires, werewolves, changelings, and other non-human inhabitants of New York City.

He swore under his breath and tossed back half of his drink in one swallow. He had let Graham, his good friend and fellow Council member, talk him into coming to this torture session. Rumors had recently reached the Council about a few young vampires who had taken to frequenting these Goth events and feeding off the eager attendees. The fledglings risked exposure with their behavior, and the Council had decided they needed a stern warning.

It hardly counted as a crisis of epic proportions, and Dmitri would have been happy to let a few of Graham's packmates do the Council's dirty work, but the Lupine leader had volunteered Dmitri and himself for the job instead. Dmitri was tempted to "volunteer" Graham for the French Foreign Legion.

Neither man had spotted any of the suspected rogues during their two interminable hours at this event, and Dmitri was more than ready to go home. As soon as Graham stopped sniffing around that blowsy little blonde he was currently "questioning," Dmitri would say his goodbyes and head out. Maybe he'd stop for a bite on the way home, just to wash the taste of this place out of his mouth.

He had so many better things he could be doing, he reflected, trying to pick Graham out of the shifting crowd.

Where had he and that blonde disappeared to? The Council had been busy lately, but even diplomatic problems hadn't kept his mind occupied. He felt boredom creeping up on him and wondered if it were time for him to step down from his Council seat in favor of new pursuits.

Restless, he waited at the bar, tapping his fingers on the scarred wooden surface, sorely tempted to just forget his goodbyes and leave Graham to his fate and his bimbo. He reached for his glass to drain the last drops of fiery whisky, and that was when he saw her.

Temptation.

She stepped up to the bar, swept along in the wake of four other women, but Dmitri could not have described a single one of them. He saw only her, with her face like a vision and her body like a gift from the gods.

The woman looked impatient and a little nervous and sadly out of place among the ridiculous throngs that surrounded her. For one thing, she had the look of a woman, rather than a child. He could see she was young, probably in her late twenties, but she wore her age comfortably, as a mature woman should. Her skin, milk-white and dusted with freckles the color of honey, looked smooth and unlined. Dmitri saw a great deal of it, from her hairline to the generous swell of her breasts that were cuddled and lifted by the black satin of her corset, from the graceful curve of her shoulder to the tips of her slender fingers. Her snug, black leather pants and tall, black boots covered everything else, hugging her curves with loving care and making his body tighten.

Lord, she was stunning.

He certainly felt stunned. He hadn't reacted to the mere sight of a woman in longer than he could remember, but he reacted to this one. Already he could feel his cock hardening beneath his trousers, filling with blood and heat, while his sense of boredom died a sharp death.

She stood out in stark contrast, relieved against the sea of sameness that surrounded her. She, too, had dressed all in black, but she shared nothing else with the other women in the room. Her skin had the pearlescent glow of natural fairness, and her hair had not been dyed a flat and light-absorbing black. It rippled over her shoulders and down her back in waves of burnished mahogany. When she turned her head, the light caught it and sparked dancing flames across the shiny surface. Dmitri imagined burying his hands in it, using his grip to hold her still while he drove into her body.

He wanted that body, he acknowledged, wanted to feel those pale, white curves against him, under him. Her body flowed beneath clinging, black cloth and stiff metal boning in a reflection of Venus's glory. Smooth, graceful shoulders curved down to generous breasts, and the corset accentuated the way her waist nipped in waspishly beneath their enticing fullness. Her hips flared from that narrow span, round and lush and firm, and her legs, gloved by the smooth leather pants, looked round and soft and perfect for clasping around his hips, or throwing over his shoulders, or tangling firmly with his.

He sat there at the bar, staring and fantasizing and wanting her, and while he did so, he gave in to his instincts and slipped lightly inside her mind.

She didn't notice him, as wrapped up in her thoughts as she was, but he'd have been astounded if she had. Most people didn't notice his mental presence even when he didn't keep quiet, like he did now. Very few people out there had any sort of psychic talent, and even fewer knew how to use it. He didn't probe deeply enough into the woman's mind to see if she did; he just wanted to get a sense of her, to decide if more than her beautiful body intrigued him.

More than intrigued, he found himself entranced and unexpectedly entertained. This woman possessed a lively mind and a sharp-edged humor.

Look at that. He heard her voice in his head, husky and feminine and arousing. *Lord Velveteen thinks he's just the shit sitting there with those silly little stick figures fawning all over his poet shirt. Does he have any idea how ridiculous it is for a grown man to have a visible ribcage and lacy shirt cuffs?*

Oh, wait. That's right. He's a long way from a grown man.

He watched her raise a glass to her slick, painted mouth, and his eyes narrowed. He wanted those lips to part around his cock, and the violence of his lust surprised him. This woman had an unsettling effect on him.

And that one, he heard her scoff. *How ridiculous does he look? He's got more mascara on than I do, and he didn't even check for clumps. Is he* crooking. His. Finger. *at me? Get real, Sonny. I'm not about to answer that insulting little summons with a makeup tip, let alone with what you're after.*

Dmitri's head whipped around, and his gaze locked on the mascaraed Romeo. A quick mental push sent the kid reeling back against the bar and put the fear of God into him—or, at least, the fear of Dmitri.

Where is this guy Ava invited? If I have to wait around this circus much longer, he can kiss his chances for some nookie goodbye. I don't care how badly they think I need this. I refuse to consider sleeping with someone who can't even manage to show up on time for it.

Rage turned his vision black for a split second, and he actually felt his fangs lengthen in anticipation of the wounds he would inflict on any man who dared to touch her. He would show these pretenders a real vampire's fury if a single one of them thought to lay a hand on what Dmitri intended to claim for his own. His woman would not be touched by any man but him.

His woman.

Dmitri registered the possessive term with surprise and tested the phrase in his mind. In all his considerable lifetime, he'd never felt such an instant proprietary interest in any woman. He'd never been tempted to conquer and claim so quickly. But in this case, he wanted to mark the woman so the entire world would know to keep its distance.

When he saw the woman turn her gaze to him, he ruthlessly tamped down his emotions and moved his touch to the edge of her mind. He didn't think she had noticed his presence within her, but he felt it prudent to be cautious. Already, he detected a stubborn and independent streak in her. He didn't want her to struggle against him. Not yet.

He felt her gaze on him, and he met her stare with a bold one of his own. Heat arced between them, slicing through the crowd as if to remove all barriers separating them. He wanted no barriers, wanted her bared to him, body and mind, so he could sate himself with her flesh, her thoughts and her blood.

She was perfect, and she would be his.